ADVANCE ACCLAIM FOR *STRESS TEST*

"Packed with thrills, *Stress Test* is a lightning-paced read that you'll read in one breath."

— TESS GERRITSEN
New York Times best-selling
author of *Last to Die*

"Original and profound. I found the Christian message engaging and fascinating, and the story a thrill-a-minute."

— MICHAEL PALMER
New York Times best-selling
author of *Oath of Office*

"Sirens, scalpels, and the business end of a revolver—*Stress Test* offers Code 3 action and a prescription for hope."

— CANDACE CALVERT
best-selling author of *Code Triage* and *Trauma Plan*

"*Stress Test* comes with a warning: Prepare to stop life until you finish the last page."

— DIANN MILLS
author of *The Chase*
and *The Survivor*

"Recurring legal, medical and romantic thrills. Diagnosis: Pure entertainment."

— JAMES SCOTT BELL
award-winning suspense author

STRESS TEST

STRESS TEST

Richard L. Mabry, MD

THOMAS NELSON
Since 1798

NASHVILLE   DALLAS   MEXICO CITY   RIO DE JANEIRO

Published in Nashville, Tennessee, by Thomas Nelson. Thomas Nelson is a registered trademark of Thomas Nelson, Inc.

Thomas Nelson, Inc., titles may be purchased in bulk for educational, business, fund-raising, or sales promotional use. For information, please e-mail SpecialMarkets@ ThomasNelson.com.

Scripture quotations are taken from NEW AMERICAN STANDARD BIBLE®, © The Lockman Foundation 1960, 1962, 1963, 1968, 1971, 1972, 1973, 1975, 1977, 1995. Used by permission.

Published in association with the literary agency of WordServe Literary Group, Ltd., 10152 S. Knoll Circle, Highlands Ranch, CO 80130. www.wordserveliterary.com.

Publisher's Note: This novel is a work of fiction. Names, characters, places, and incidents are either products of the author's imagination or used fictitiously. All characters are fictional, and any similarity to people living or dead is purely coincidental.

Page design: Walter Petrie

Library of Congress Control Number: 2013931020

ISBN 978-1-4016-8708-3

Printed in the United States of America

13 14 15 16 17 18 RRD 6 5 4 3 2 1

For all the writers who light up a dark world.

ONE

Dr. Matt Newman knew all about the high. He'd experienced it many times. The high was intoxicating, even when the low inevitably followed. Of course, sometimes there was no high at all, no pleasure, only the sadness, the melancholy. How many times had Matt asked himself if it was worth it?

It began tonight, as it frequently did, with a phone call that rolled Matt out of bed after less than an hour's sleep and sent him speeding to the hospital. A teenager lay bleeding to death from internal injuries, the victim of a car crash that killed the girl riding with him.

Tonight Matt's efforts were rewarded with a high unmatched by anything from a glass, a bottle, a syringe. Tonight there would be no heartbreak of telling a grieving family your best hadn't been enough to save their loved one. Tonight Matt could savor the high—at least for a little while. This case was a good way to go out, to leave private practice behind.

But already Matt's exhilaration was giving way to fatigue. His eyes burned. His shoulders ached. His mouth was foul with the acid taste of coffee left too long on the hot plate. He was running on fumes.

The pneumatic doors closed behind him with a hiss like an auditory exclamation point. As Matt moved from the brilliance of Metropolitan Hospital's emergency room into the mottled semi-darkness of the parking garage, he imagined the weight of responsibility slipping from his shoulders. Tomorrow Tom Wilson would take over his patients and his practice. Tomorrow Matt would assume his new position as assistant professor of surgery at Southwestern Medical Center here in Dallas. He'd teach medical students at Southwestern and instruct residents at Parkland Hospital, always emphasizing not only the science but the art of medicine. Matt knew he had a lot to give. He could hardly wait.

One of the benefits of the new job was supposed to be a more structured life: less on-call time, responsibilities shared with other faculty members, assistance from residents in patient care. Matt was looking forward to the change, not just for himself, but for the way it might benefit his relationship with Jennifer.

Matt couldn't give up medicine entirely—he'd invested too much of his life in it, and it remained a passion with him—but he also felt a passion for Jennifer, perhaps even loved her. She was beautiful, witty, and fun to be around. She might be "the one."

It wasn't hard for Matt to spot his silver Chevy Impala in the darkest corner of the deserted garage. There weren't many cars still there at two a.m., and soon there would be one fewer. He fished his keys from the pocket of his white lab coat and thumbed the unlock button on his remote. His hand was on the door handle when something yanked him backward and cut off his air in mid-breath. Matt dropped the keys and reached up with both hands to pry at the arm that encircled his neck.

In an instant Matt was slammed facedown to the cement floor. He heard a crack and felt the knife-like agony of breaking ribs. The searing pain in his chest made each labored breath more difficult. A weight pinned him to the ground like a butterfly on a specimen board.

Matt struggled, but his assailant held him fast. Fire shot through his shoulders as his arms were yanked together. There was a quick rip of tape, and in seconds his wrists were bound tightly behind him. Rough hands encircled his ankles with more tape, leaving him helpless and immobile. At the same time, someone else grabbed his hair and lifted his head. Matt gave a shrill cry before three quick turns of tape muffled his voice and turned the world black.

He tried to lift his head, but stopped abruptly when something hard and cold pressed against the back of his neck. Matt lowered his face onto the garage floor and went limp. He felt hope escape like air from a punctured tire.

There were murmurs above him, questions in a high-pitched singsong, answers from a harsh rasp like grinding gears. At first the words were indistinguishable. Then they became louder as the exchange heated.

"Why not here?" Was there a faint Hispanic accent to the whining tenor?

"The boss said not at the hospital." The growling bass flung out the words, and spittle dotted the back of Matt's neck. "I know just the place to get rid of him. Let's get him into the trunk of his car."

In the darkness that now enveloped him, Matt struggled in vain to move, to speak. He strained to hear what was said. He could only make out a few words, but they were enough to drive his heart into his shoes. "Get rid of him."

He angled his head to catch the sounds around him: a jingle of keys, the sharp click of the trunk lock. Hinges squeaked. Matt had a momentary sensation of floating as he was lifted, carried, dropped. His head struck something hard. Splashes of red flashed behind his closed eyelids, then vanished into nothingness.

Matt floated back to consciousness like a swimmer emerging from the depths. How long had he been out? Hours? Minutes? A few seconds? At first he had no idea where he was or what was happening. Little by little, his senses cleared. He tried to open his eyes but there was no light. He tried to speak, but his lips were sealed. He cried out, but the result was only a strained grunt. Finally he heard the faint sound of voices from inside the car, a menacing rumble and a high-pitched whine. The voices brought it all back to him.

He was on the way to his death. And the trunk of his car would be his coffin.

TWO

Sandra Murray watched the red numerals on her bedside clock roll from 2:32 to 2:33. Usually when she crawled into bed, sleep was never far behind, but not tonight. Her analytical legal mind scrolled through the possible reasons why she lay wide-eyed rather than sleeping peacefully.

Was it her profession? No, she'd long since come to grips with the dichotomy between being a criminal defense attorney and a practicing Christian. Despite the fact that her days were spent defending criminals, some of whom undoubtedly belonged in prison, she believed that everyone—even someone charged with rape or murder—deserved the best possible defense. Jesus ate with sinners; why couldn't Sandra give them the protection and defense the law promised?

Was it because she had no family to speak of? The distance between her and her divorced parents was more than physical. True, her mother was in Costa Rica trying to "find herself," and her father was in Alaska with his new wife. But even if they lived across the street from her Dallas home, Sandra's contact with them would be limited. That's the way it had always been, and she'd come to accept it. She had no siblings, few close friends, and no—

There it was again—the same problem that kept cropping up in her mind to keep her from sleeping. She had no mate, no significant other with whom to share. She knew somewhere God had a husband for her, and when she met him and moved forward, she trusted that her life would finally be full.

Unfortunately, that longed-for fiancé apparently wasn't Dr. Ken Gordon. She'd gone out with the handsome neurosurgeon for almost a year, and although The Question hadn't been popped and her ring finger remained bare, they seemed to have reached a tacit understanding that marriage was around the corner. But that changed last night when the problem about Ken, the one that kept bouncing around in the back of her mind, resurfaced. So, during a beautiful dinner that neither of them tasted, with a view of the skyline of Dallas that neither of them saw, they finally admitted they weren't meant for each other.

As Sandra stared into the dark, she wondered if she'd done the right thing, breaking it off with Ken. Well, it was done, and all she could do was wait for God to fill the void in her life. She squeezed her eyes shut and felt the tears forming. *God, if there's a husband out there for me, please show me.*

Satisfied with this final effort at a bedtime prayer, she dabbed at the corners of her eyes with the covers, then pulled them to her chin and once more tried to sleep.

"Let's get out of here."

Lou slammed the trunk closed, clambered behind the wheel, and started the engine. He had the car in motion by the time his companion scrambled in. Lou reversed out of the parking slot, stopping with a screech of brakes. Then he slammed the gearshift into drive, stomped on the gas, and the car screamed down the ramp. His rearview mirror gave a glimpse of parallel stripes of black rubber on the cement.

Beads of sweat stung Lou's eyes. He blinked them away and peered into the night. He slowed the car to navigate the narrow streets behind the hospital, but his mind was working full-speed.

Edgar's voice interrupted Lou's thoughts. "Where are we going now?"

Lou steered the car through a stop sign with only the slightest tap on the brakes. "A quiet place where we can put a bullet into this guy."

Beside him Edgar fidgeted but kept silent. Edgar didn't look like much, but he was good with a gun and knife. Lou knew Edgar was anxious to do his thing, but Lou planned to do the honors himself on the man in the trunk. He'd let Edgar take care of the next one. This one was too important.

Lou clutched the wheel and leaned forward to follow the headlight beams through the warren of dark streets. The lights of downtown Dallas rose up ahead of them, bright in the inky sky. Lou took a sharp left, away from that glare.

The neighborhood's few functioning streetlights only accentuated the gloom that lay beyond their dim glow. Lou drove by bars, strip clubs, and hole-in-the-wall stores peddling XXX-rated videos, all of them silent at this hour, and most secured by burglar bars or steel shutters. Nobody in his right mind would be here at this hour of the morning—at least, not without a weapon of some sort.

Lou saw the pothole too late to steer around it. The car bounced crazily before settling down on protesting springs.

"Hey, watch it."

Lou heard a click as Edgar fastened his seat belt. His reply was a growled, "Sorry." Lou slowed and scanned ahead for more holes in the pavement.

"You sure you know where we're going?"

"Yeah, but whoever laid out these streets must have been drunk. Let me concentrate." Lou squinted to read the street signs in the faint light. Finally he found the one he wanted and steered the car in a sharp turn. It lurched as one wheel bumped the curb.

"Did you hear something back there?" Edgar asked.

"Relax. He's not going anywhere." No, for the guy in the trunk, this would be his last ride ever.

Matt lay curled in a fetal position. Not even the faintest glimmer of light penetrated the tape over his eyes. All feeling was gone from his bound hands, and his feet tingled with a thousand needles. He tumbled about as the car swerved, slowed, accelerated, stopped, started. At times, what must have been huge potholes sent him bouncing against the trunk lid. The muscles in his back cried out with every bump and jolt. His injured ribs made each breath torture. Although he knew there was enough air in the trunk, he felt as though he was suffocating.

Matt summoned all his strength and strained at his bonds. He figured he'd been immobilized with duct tape, the modern equivalent of baling wire. For all the good his struggles did him, his restraints could have been welded steel bands. There was no way he could part them with brute force.

Sometime in the distant past Matt had read about Houdini's escapes from handcuffs. Now he tried to recall the tricks the master illusionist used. *First, get the hands in front.* If Matt could do that, maybe he could use his teeth to tear through the tape.

He bent his back, trying to ignore the pain it caused. He tucked his legs up behind him and strained every muscle, but without success. He took a deep breath and paid the price for it as pain coursed through his chest. He tried rolling over onto his stomach, but that was worse. He returned to his side.

He struggled and strained to no avail. Despite regular exercise and an athletic body, Matt was unable to duplicate Houdini's maneuver. Apparently what worked with handcuffs didn't translate so well when your wrists were bound together with tape that left no slack for movement.

Matt's mind churned. Was there something in the trunk he could use to free himself? Maybe he could saw through the tape with the slotted end of the jack handle. No, the jack was stowed, along with the spare tire, under a cover screwed down with a wing nut, forming the floor of the trunk.

As he kicked about in his efforts to escape, Matt's feet hit a blanket stuffed into the corner of the trunk. He heard a dull *clunk* and remembered the sack of emergency tools. He'd bought them after one of Jennifer's faultfinding comments, this one about him being unprepared for a road emergency. He pictured the contents in his mind's eye. A pair of jumper cables, a fire extinguisher, a can of Fix-a-Flat, a roll of duct tape, and two road flares. Not much to work with and not a sharp edge in the bunch. *Except* . . . The only flares he'd found in the store were a version favored by police and highway patrol, flares with a spike on one end to be stuck into asphalt. If he could get one of those flares out, he might scratch through the tape on his wrists.

Matt squirmed and turned his body with agonizing slowness until his bound hands reached the bundle. His shoulders ached, his back muscles cried out, and every breath brought fresh pain in his ribs. He strained against his bonds, cutting off the last bit of circulation to hands already numb. When the car hit a bump, he was thrown back and had to start the process again. As he reached the point of total exhaustion, Matt got one hand inside the folds of the blanket. He flexed his fingers in a vain effort to restore feeling, then explored the contents of the sack.

Jumper cables. Duct tape—like he needed more duct tape. Where were the flares? *There! There's one!* His hand closed down on a spike, puncturing his palm in the process. He felt blood coursing down his fingertips. His slippery fingers lost their grip twice before he could grasp the sharp end of the flare.

Matt sawed at the tape on his wrists. Time after time, the point of the spike went beyond the tape and gashed his wrists, adding more blood to the flow from his palm. Soon the work became mindless repetition, leaving Matt to ponder whether he might eventually free himself, only to bleed to death from his self-inflicted slashes.

As he labored, Matt wondered if praying would help. He was a little out of practice. A *lot* out of practice, if he was honest about it. But he figured if there was ever a good time to pray, it was now. *They say there are no atheists in foxholes.* He was pretty sure the same thing went for persons bound hand and foot, locked in a car trunk, on their way to death. There was nothing to lose. *God, I don't know how to ask this, so I'll just say it. Please help me.* Was there something else he was supposed to say? Oh yes. *Amen.*

Matt's aching shoulders cried out. Nothing was working. He was about to give up when he felt the tape's grip on his wrists loosen. Had one strand separated? He worked furiously now, sawing through more layers, until at last he felt his hands come free.

Matt pulled the remaining tape from his wrists. Sharp stabs of pain signaled the resumption of blood flow into hands too long and too tightly restrained. He struggled to move his fingers, but at that moment they might as well have belonged to someone else. He flexed them and bit his lip in pain as restored circulation brought fire to his fingertips.

Now Matt fumbled with the tape that encircled his head. He took a deep breath, winced at the pain it caused, and steeled himself against what he knew was next. He ripped away the tape with a continuous unwinding motion that felt as though it took not only his day-old beard but also a layer of skin and a good portion of his hair. Tears coursed down his cheeks. His face felt like a pound of hamburger. But this was no time to stop and feel sorry for himself.

He reached down to free his ankles and felt more of the painful, electric tingle as blood flowed to his feet again. He'd done it. He was free. But how was he going to get away?

The car moved slowly now, probably taking side streets. Matt was certain that once his captors stopped, his chances of escape were somewhere between slim and none. He had to do something and do it quickly.

He could think of only two options. He could arm himself with something like the spike end of a flare or the fire extinguisher and fight his two assailants, counting on the element of surprise to help him overpower both of them. The second option was to try to escape before his captors reached their destination. As far as Matt was concerned, the choice was obvious.

But how was he to escape his steel prison? He remembered that, when he bought the car, the salesman reached into the trunk and pointed out the emergency release. Matt hadn't thought much about it then, just recognized that it could be a lifesaver for a child accidentally locked in a trunk. Well, he wasn't in this trunk by accident and he wasn't a child, but that release just might save his life . . .

He groped above him in the darkness until he could wedge the numb, blood-soaked fingers of one hand into a crevice in the under-surface of the trunk lid. With the other hand, Matt searched until he found a T-shaped lever. He pulled, but his bloody fingers slipped off the slick plastic. He wiped his hand on his pants and tried again. This time he was rewarded with a satisfying *click* as the latch released.

Matt eased the trunk open just far enough to glimpse his surroundings. The car was moving along a paved street, slowing and occasionally swerving to miss a pothole, then speeding up again. There were no other cars in sight.

Matt figured they were somewhere in the Trinity Industrial District. The occasional dim light from deep inside the buildings around did nothing to keep the darkness at bay. The few streetlights that hadn't been shot out or succumbed to target practice with rocks provided little illumination.

The car slowed again. It was now or never. Matt released his hold on the trunk lid and rolled over the sill and out. When he hit the pavement, there were new waves of pain, and he clenched his teeth to keep from crying out. He thought he heard another crack from his injured ribs. He forced himself to roll to the side of the road, then scrambled to his feet and made for the nearest buildings. He glanced back in time to see the car move ahead for perhaps fifty yards before the brake lights came on and two forms piled out.

Matt didn't wait to see what they would do next. He already knew what he was going to do.

Run for his life.

THREE

Lou glanced up at the rearview mirror and looked away. His eyes snapped back as his mind processed what he'd seen. The trunk lid was open, bouncing with each rough spot in the road. He brought his foot off the accelerator and hit the brake pedal hard enough to make the chest strap of the seat belt cut into him. He jammed the gear lever into park and was out the door while the car still rocked on its springs.

Behind Lou, Edgar's door slammed. "What happened?"

"He got out," Lou rasped. "But he can't go far."

The headlights lit an empty street ahead. Lou pivoted to look behind him. The industrial district was deserted. Buildings were dark. The only illumination came from a distant streetlamp and an occasional security light shining dimly through dirty windows. Alleys, black as the inside of a coal mine, divided each building from its neighbor. Lou completed a full turn but saw nothing except Edgar, motionless beside him, his eyes darting left and right. He cocked his head to listen.

There were no cars around; no sign of life anywhere. Their captive couldn't have gone far. They'd find him—they had to.

Lou heard a faint metallic scrape to his left. He swung around and cupped his hand over his ear, the way he'd seen his almost-deaf aunt do. There it was again, coming from that alley. Lou pointed first to Edgar, then to the source of the sound, and jerked his head. The little man nodded once and together they edged slowly forward.

Lou's snakeskin Gucci loafers, although elegant and guaranteed to impress the ladies, were not designed for this kind of activity. The leather heels clicked with every step; the leather soles slipped and slid over oily patches in the road. At that moment, he would have traded his five-hundred-dollar shoes for a pair of Converse high-tops. He forced himself to slow his pace and tread carefully, like a hunter moving through the jungle.

At the entrance to the alley, Lou stopped and looked back at Edgar, who stood five yards behind him, his head on a swivel. Lou pointed first to himself, then into the alley. He indicated Edgar and gestured for him to stay put. His cohort pulled a revolver from his waistband and nodded his understanding.

Lou opened his coat and drew his own gun from its shoulder holster. He cursed himself for not taking the time to search the car for a flashlight. Maybe the lighter in his coat pocket would do. If he lit it after he was in the alley, it might spook the fugitive into running. Lou would fire as soon as he saw the man. If he missed, Edgar was ready at the mouth of the alley. Either way, they had him dead to rights. Lou chuckled silently at the pun.

He thumbed the safety of his Beretta to the firing position and cocked the hammer. He had ten rounds in the semiautomatic. The fugitive had nothing. Nothing fair about this fight, but then again, Lou gave up any pretensions of fighting fair long ago. He held the pistol firmly in his left hand, finger inside the trigger guard. He stretched his right arm in front of him, stuck out his foot, and, like someone walking through a minefield, took a careful step forward. *Ready or not, here I come.*

———

Matt paused before moving deeper into the alley. He took a few deep breaths, and each one brought a new wave of pain that threatened to immobilize him. He clutched his white coat around him against the early morning chill and, for a few moments, felt marginally warmer. Then he looked down and realized the coat was like a white beacon in the dim light. *Be warm or be a target for men trying to kill me? Not much of a choice.*

With a sigh, he rolled the coat into a tight ball and shoved it behind one of the dozens of trash cans lining the alley. Now the wind that swirled around him seemed to go right through the thin material of his surgical scrub suit. His teeth chattered, from both cold and fright. He shivered, and each muscle twitch caused more pain.

He was in a narrow passageway between two industrial buildings. Ahead in the dark was a veritable obstacle course. He didn't know if there was escape at the end of the alley. All Matt knew was that he had to keep moving.

Matt stretched his hands in front of him like a blind man entering a strange room. He moved close to the right-hand wall and worked his way into the darkness. As his eyes adjusted he could make out dim shapes. He circumnavigated garbage cans, empty crates, and piles of debris, following an irregular course along the wall, moving steadily deeper into the alley. He encountered metal doors at irregular intervals. He checked every one. Locked.

He mentally kicked himself—he could call for help. Matt felt at his waist for the cell phone usually clipped there. Gone, knocked loose at some point. Perversely, his pager was still at his waist on the other side. He thumbed it to the off position and dropped it behind a pile of debris.

Matt's heart sank as his dark-adjusted eyes showed him a wall a few feet ahead. This was a blind alley. He was trapped.

He heard a series of faint shuffling noises behind him. *They're here.* Matt stopped dead still and quickly compressed his six-foot frame into a doorway. He held his breath. He tensed his aching muscles, ready to run, then realized he had no place to go.

The sounds stopped. Matt peeped out of his hiding place and caught the faint outlines of two men, the smaller silhouetted against the entrance to the alley, the larger moving slowly toward him, one careful step at a time. He heard the rasp of a lighter, saw a brief flicker, then the flame died. Despite repeated sounds of flint on metal, with an overlay of profanity, the darkness remained unbroken. Good. Darkness was Matt's friend right now.

Matt's mind's eye replayed the images from that momentary flash of light. Something had glinted in the big man's hand—a gun. Probably the same one Matt had felt pressed against the base of his skull. Did the smaller man have one as well? No matter. A single bullet from one weapon would be enough to kill him.

Matt groped around him for a weapon of some kind, any kind. Nothing. He had nowhere to go, nothing with which he could fight. His only hope was to hide. But where? How?

When he was about to give up, his fingers touched rough wood. He squinted against the darkness and used both hands to explore further. Near the brick wall that blocked the end of the alley, a stack of wooden pallets had been shoved against the wall. Matt stretched as high as possible and was barely able to touch the top. Would the stack hold him? If it came tumbling down, the noise would certainly bring his captors. He held his breath and wedged his toe into an opening in the stack. With infinite care, he scaled the rickety pile, wincing over every sound, praying the big man was still too far away to hear it. At the top he pulled himself up and stretched prone. He wiggled around to peer back over the edge, his legs hanging off either side of the improvised platform.

There was the sound of a step, a long pause, another step, another pause. Then, from the mouth of the alley, a metallic cacophony was followed by a spate of curse words erupting into the night. Apparently one of his pursuers had found the garbage cans Matt had so carefully avoided.

"Lou, I need help." The loud whisper's high pitch told Matt this was pursuer number two. "I cut my leg on this—"

"Shut up! A cut won't kill you." There was a guttural laugh. "But if I can find the doc, I'm going to kill *him*."

Matt willed himself to be perfectly still. As the shuffling moved toward him, Matt peeped over the edge and could faintly see the dark bulk of the larger kidnapper creeping closer. The man's hand traversed left, right, left, right in concert with the motion of his head. If he looked up, Matt was dead.

The kidnapper continued along the alley, trying doors along the way, moving on when he found them locked. He stopped at the wall that blocked the end of the passageway, turned, and retraced his steps along the opposite side of the alley. Matt hardly dared hope he would escape, but there was a chance . . .

Finally the man reached the entrance to the alley. Matt could see him, silhouetted by the faint light of the street, as he shook his head and dropped the pistol into his coat pocket. He ducked his head and whispered to his partner, who was bent at the waist, holding his right shin. In a moment, they disappeared from Matt's view, the injured man limping and hopping, struggling to keep up.

After what seemed like an hour, Matt heard two car doors slam. There was quiet for a few seconds, then an engine revved and accelerated away. Matt couldn't believe his good fortune. They'd missed him. They were gone. Or were they? Had one of them crept back to keep watch? He couldn't take the chance.

Matt's back muscles were in spasm. He forced his nails into the palms of his hands to keep from crying out as he kept his body pressed against the rough wood.

He decided to count to five hundred before he moved. By the time he reached a hundred and fifty, he thought he'd never be able to lie on his perch for another second. He swallowed hard, gritted his teeth, and continued his count.

At last Matt drew a deep breath and willed his muscles to relax. Like an old man getting out of a chair in which he'd sat too long, Matt hunched himself slowly into a crouch. He turned his back to the alley, intending to descend backward from his hiding place. Matt groped with his foot for purchase in the stack of pallets, but found only air. He teetered as he struggled to keep his balance, then threw his arms wide in a futile attempt to hold on to something, anything. Instead, gravity grabbed him and pulled him head-down into black oblivion.

FOUR

Dr. Hank Truong placed the last careful stitch in the face of the teen-age boy. "I've closed the wound the knife made. There'll be a scar," Hank said, "but only a small one. Now try to stay out of trouble. I don't want to see you back here again."

Odds were the teenager would be back—maybe even brought in DOA—but there was always hope. That was what made this duty in the Parkland Hospital Emergency Room tolerable for Hank: hope that what he did for some of his patients might help.

A nurse stuck her head into the room. "Patient in trauma room 2," the nurse said. "Unidentified white male, early to mid-thirties, brought in unconscious. EMTs say the call came from a guy who owns a pawnshop down on Riverfront Boulevard. He went into the alley to throw some boxes into the Dumpster and found the man lying there. No ID."

"Be right there," Hank said.

As he strode past patients on gurneys, many with family members hovering around them, Hank's mind clicked along as though powered by a microchip as he sorted out the possibilities for the diagnosis and treatment of an unresponsive patient.

Someone found in an alley in that neighborhood was a likely candidate for head trauma—probably a mugging. But Hank had to consider alcohol, drugs, diabetic coma, epilepsy, stroke, and many other possibilities. He wasn't worried. He was confident he'd come up with the right diagnosis. He generally did.

Hank tapped on the door of the trauma room and eased it open. The man on the treatment table was naked from the waist up, his skin as pale as the sheet over the lower half of his body. Dried blood covered his scalp and obscured his facial features like a Mardi Gras mask.

A surgical scrub shirt and pants, the stenciled name on them partially obscured by black splotches of dried blood, were crumpled on the shelf beneath the gurney. Hank wondered what a psychiatrist would make of the fact that the blots reminded him of a Rorschach test showing a hand holding a gun. *I've been in the ER too long*, he thought.

Was the scrub suit significant? If they washed out the blood, they could probably read the name of the hospital. But would that help? This could be a patient who'd grabbed the clothes to slip away without waiting for his discharge . . . or his bill. Or he might be a hospital worker—dietary, janitorial, laboratory, whatever. Lots of them wore scrub suits they "borrowed" from the hospital. But most likely this was just a bum who either found or stole the clothing. No, there wasn't going to be any help there.

"What have you got?" Hank asked.

A nurse whose name Hank couldn't remember stood at the patient's side, scribbling on a clipboard. "Here's what we have so far." She passed the clipboard over, and when she did, Hank saw her name tag.

"Thanks, Allison." Hank scanned the ER intake record. White male, estimated to be in his thirties. Unconscious, bleeding from a scalp wound. No odor of alcohol. No Medic-Alert bracelet. Nothing that would help.

"Vital signs?" Hank asked.

Allison looked at the ballpoint scribbling on her palm. "Haven't had time to chart them. One-ninety over sixty, fifty-four, ten."

The information clicked into Hank's brain as though he'd hit Enter on his well-worn laptop. Systolic blood pressure up, diastolic down, slow pulse. Cushing's triad—evidence of increased pressure on the brain. "Could be developing a subdural hematoma, if he doesn't already have one," he said. "We need a stat CT of his head. I'll go with him in case he goes south while he's in radiology. And get a neurosurgeon down here."

"Do you want to clean up that scalp laceration?"

Hank whirled and noticed the nursing student who stood in the corner. He swallowed the answer he had planned for the ER nurse—she'd know better, but this girl might not. "No, it's barely oozing now. We don't want to mess with it until we know there's not a fracture. We'll wrap some gauze around his head and get the CT first."

For the next forty minutes, Hank functioned on automatic pilot. His actions were dictated by lessons initially learned through countless hours of textbook study and hammered home by involvement in the care of case after case of head trauma. Stabilize the airway, get an IV going, give Mannitol to decrease the pressure in the brain, administer Dilantin to ward off convulsions, confirm the diagnosis through CAT scans, keep a careful eye on the patient's neurological status.

"What have you got?" The staff neurosurgeon, Ken Gordon, strode through the door and stopped next to Hank.

"John Doe with a head injury," Hank said. "Thought it was an acute subdural, but it's actually an epidural hemorrhage."

Gordon had been a standout basketball player at SMU, a crackerjack medical student and resident at Southwestern Medical Center, where he was now associate professor of neurosurgery. Gordon was the typical tall, dark, and handsome man—six-two, wavy brown hair—and all the nurses tended to follow him with their eyes when he walked by. Hank didn't care about that. What he cared about was that Gordon, the best neurosurgeon at the medical center, was on call today for Parkland Hospital.

"Think he's going to need burr holes?" Hank asked.

Gordon held up one finger in a "just a minute" gesture. He finished scanning the chart that Hank handed him, then began a rapid but thorough neurological exam of the still-unconscious man. Finally he stepped to the viewbox on the wall and spent a moment studying the CT scan of the patient's head. "Yep," Gordon finally said. "Acute epidural hematoma." He pointed. "There's the fracture line. Non-displaced, though. That's good."

"Glad you agree," Hank said as he basked in the undeclared glory of having made a good pickup.

Gordon yawned and stretched. "Want me to let you know how he does?"

"Please," Hank said. He didn't ordinarily have time to keep up with the hundreds of patients who passed through his hands each month, but for some reason, he felt a special interest in this John Doe. He wondered why.

Jennifer Ball slammed the phone into its cradle. She'd forced herself to tolerate, even expect, calls from Matt to cancel plans at the last minute. But to simply stand her up? And then not return her calls, her texts, her emails? This was too much.

She belatedly looked around to make sure no one in the office had noticed her display of anger. No, the work of the district attorney's office was proceeding uninterrupted. Phones rang, computer keyboards clicked, printers spat out documents full of legal terms.

Jennifer opened her center desk drawer and extracted a small compact. Not a blond hair was out of place. No tear tracks marred the makeup on her fair skin. There was nothing to tell the world how upset she was. She picked up a folder and held it in front of her face to hide the flush she felt spreading across her cheeks.

Everything had seemed so right, but now it was all going wrong. Jennifer and Matt had been an item for a while. Matt was handsome, funny, and made a good living as a general surgeon in private practice, although she didn't know exactly how well he did. A few weeks ago Matt shared with her his plans to leave his practice and take a position at the medical center, and the news had thrilled her. Being the wife of a medical school professor sounded even better than the wife of a surgeon. Jennifer didn't intend to be a secretary all her life. On the contrary, she had her life with Matt carefully planned: their two children would attend a private school while she lunched at the club with her circle of friends and frequented the better stores in Dallas.

Of course, if she and Matt were to become man and wife, he needed to know there were things she wouldn't tolerate, even with his new position. No more dinners that cooled as she waited for a husband delayed at the hospital, or movies interrupted by the silent buzz of Matt's pager and his whispered words, "We've got to go. Emergency." A serious talk was in order. But before anything like that could happen, she had to get in touch with him. And that appeared to be impossible.

———

No matter how Lou Hecht squirmed and twisted, the arms of the unpadded wooden chair in the waiting room prevented him from achieving any degree of comfort. Finally he perched on the front edge of the seat, moving first one haunch and then the other into the confined space, barely managing to avoid sliding forward onto the floor. He nervously tapped first one foot, then the other on the carpet.

Lou looked around the small outer office. Nothing much had changed in the two years he'd been coming here. Gold leaf letters spelled out "Grande Limited" on the frosted glass upper panel of the hall door. Plain, industrial-grade gray carpet covered the floor. Three visitor's chairs, one of them currently torturing Lou's anatomy, were arranged along the left side of the room. Two framed reproduction prints of generic landscapes hung above them, the only concession to decor. Locked filing cabinets occupied most of the space against the right wall. Two closed doors provided the only break in the rear wall. The one on the left led into the boss's office. Lou had seen the other door opened only once, just long enough to glimpse corrugated file boxes stacked along the back wall of the room.

An attractive young Latino woman sat behind the reception desk guarding the entrance to the inner office. Before her were a computer monitor and a multi-line phone that rang frequently. She answered each call the same way: "Grande Limited." She continued the conversation in English or Spanish, depending on the language of the caller, he guessed. The calls were always brief, and after each one she typed a few notes directly into the computer.

Lou had seen a stranger enter this outer office only three or four times. Each time, the scenario was the same. A few words, in English or Spanish, and the visitor left in a hurry. From what Lou gathered, the receptionist conveyed with an economy of words that Grande Limited was a private business, didn't have any dealings with people who walked in without an appointment, and that situation wasn't likely to change anytime soon.

In marked contrast to Lou's discomfort, Edgar's slim frame fit easily into the chair next to him. The small man sat quietly, apparently lost in his own thoughts, listening to sounds no one else could hear.

"How much longer?" Lou growled under his breath.

The receptionist surveyed him coolly. "He's busy. Besides, you've been coming here long enough to know that he'll see you when he's ready. Not before." She hit a key on the computer and winced. She checked her blood-red nails, apparently found no damage, and returned to her work.

After what seemed to Lou like hours, the phone on the receptionist's desk buzzed softly, a different signal from the muted ring that signaled an incoming call. She picked up the receiver, listened a moment, and hung up without comment. She looked up at Lou, ignoring Edgar as though he were a piece of furniture. "Go in," she said dismissively.

Lou pushed out of the chair, cocked his head to signal Edgar it was time to move, and started toward the unmarked door on the left, his size 14 shoes thudding on the poorly padded carpet.

He knew people took one look at him and decided such a big ox had to be dumb. That was okay. The more they thought he wasn't too swift in the brains department, the more advantage he had when the chips were down.

Lou never felt fully at ease in the boss's office. Lou was a big man who carried a gun and wasn't hesitant to use it. To anyone who encountered him he was an obvious danger. But the man behind the desk was not only bigger than Lou, he was much more dangerous. Lou didn't want to forget that.

Like a soldier awaiting the verdict of a court martial, Lou stood stolidly in front of the huge mahogany desk that separated him from his boss. In a few sentences, he explained what had happened, then waited for a reaction. Lou had been here many times before, but each time the tension was the same.

"You idiots!"

The spray from the angry words drifted down in a misty cloud. The boss's voice and the violence of his words mirrored his rage. His pudgy fingers were clasped together on the desk in front of him, the knuckles white. He took in a massive breath, inflating his protruding belly even further, like a misplaced beach ball.

"I gave you a simple assignment." The big man's voice was softer now, but the words were acid. "Grab the doctor as he leaves and take care of him." He fixed Lou and Edgar with eyes as cold as a mountain stream. "What part of that didn't you understand?"

"But you told us—"

"I know what I told you. And you made a mess of it." The boss's glare was like a laser beam. After a moment, he leaned back in his oversized, upholstered leather swivel chair and laced his fingers together across his stomach. The movement made the vest of his suit gap slightly.

"What about the other one?"

Lou was on solid ground here. "We got her at her home. Edgar picked the lock. We shoved a pillow over her face until she passed out."

"Go on."

"Edgar shot her in the head. Used the pillow to muffle the shots. We put her in the trunk of the doctor's car, near where we lost him, left it."

"The pillow?"

"A Dumpster on the other side of town."

The boss nodded once, practically a commendation medal coming from him. "Fingerprints?"

"We wore gloves the whole time. The only prints in the car will be the doctor's." Lou grinned. "And his wallet must have fallen out while he was in the trunk. We left it there under her body."

"Where is the doctor now?"

Lou shrugged. "We don't know yet. We're going to go back to the area where we lost him, interview some of the people who work there. If that doesn't work out, I'll make some phone calls."

The big man nodded once. "See that you take care of it. But do nothing that can be traced back to me or to our operation. And, equally as important, nothing that calls the attention of the police to Metropolitan Hospital. We can't afford to have them nosing around there too much."

"No, sir," Lou said. He stood in silence while the boss took a cigar from a leather-covered humidor on the desk and spent a full minute preparing it and getting it properly lit.

The man took a deep puff before he turned back to look Lou in the eye. "Don't mess up again. Understand?"

Lou nodded.

"Well, what are you waiting for? Get out."

Lou turned on his heel and hurried from the room. He didn't look around, but heard Edgar's footsteps behind him. Lou went straight through the waiting room and into the deserted hall outside.

Edgar stopped beside his partner and looked up at him. "So, what's next?"

Lou motioned toward the elevator. "Let's get out of here. I need a drink, maybe two or three."

"Then?"

"Then we find the man we lost."

"And if we find him?"

Lou shrugged his shoulder rig into a more comfortable position. "There's no 'if.' It's 'when.' When we find him, we kill him."

FIVE

Matt's first impression was of colors, like a prism that cut the light into strips and aimed them at his eyes. He turned his head a fraction, but the colors didn't move. He turned a tiny bit in the other direction. The colors didn't change position. Strange. Why didn't they move?

Matt tried to blink. That's when he realized his eyes were closed. The colors were in his mind. Were they real? He tried to open his eyes, but the lids seemed stuck together. He frowned, tried again, and managed to open the left one to a bare slit. Everything was blurred. He appeared to be in a room, but nothing looked familiar. *Try the other eye. Maybe that will help.* Three tries, and the eye wouldn't open. He squinted, trying to sharpen what he was seeing with his one eye, but a gauzy haze clouded his view. And the colors were still there, sort of in the back of his consciousness, not related to what his eye was showing him.

He moved his head a fraction to the right. Something bright was directly above him. Matt tried once more to open his right eye, and this time he succeeded. Would two eyes help? No, all he'd done was transform one fuzzy light into two. *Strange. That's not the way it should be.* He'd have to sleep awhile and think about it.

The next time Matt awakened, he was conscious of sounds. Voices in the far distance spoke words that sounded sort of familiar, like a foreign language long forgotten. A rhythmic beep came from his left. A regular whooshing sound issued from just off his right shoulder. Shuffling steps and an occasional squeak came and went nearby.

Now the colors were gone. Matt willed his eyelids open, and this time they obeyed. He blinked hard and the film over his eyes partially cleared. There were still two lights above him. He concentrated hard and they fused into one. He turned his head slightly right and left. He was alone in a white room, in some sort of bed. Matt tried to move his right hand. It stopped after a few inches. He cut his eyes to the right and saw that his hand was tethered by a padded strap to a metal railing at the side of the bed. Another movement, another glance, confirmed the same situation on his left.

He was tied up somewhere. Why? Was he a prisoner? He knew one thing. He had to get away. Panic spurred his thinking, and foremost in his mind were thoughts of escape.

Matt tried to speak, to cry out, but something was wrong with his voice. He could form the words but, despite his efforts, only a strangled sound emerged. Panic began to build inside him.

Wait! There was something under his right hand. He fingered it, using his sense of touch as a blind man would. A rectangular box, maybe plastic, with several buttons and a couple of dials. A thick cord ran from the end of the box. He started pushing the buttons, all of them. He felt the bed move under him, first up, then down. He heard a sudden noise, and a television set mounted high in the far corner sprang to life. A buzzing sounded outside his room. A figure in white hurried into his field of view.

"Well, my gracious," she said. "Our patient's awake. Let me get the doctor."

———

Ken Gordon entered the room quietly. He satisfied himself that only the dim overhead lights, not the stronger exam lights, were on. Patients recovering from a head injury were sensitive to loud noises and bright lights, and this one didn't need the extra stimulation. Ken put his head near the patient's ear and whispered, "You came through your surgery just fine." Because these patients were typically confused, his next words were meant to help the man on the bed reorient himself. "You're in the Intensive Care Unit."

The man's struggles to speak were thwarted by an endotracheal tube, an airway placed into the patient's windpipe and connected to a ventilator. Ken did a quick scan of the dials and noticed that the man on the bed was "overbreathing" the ventilator, his spontaneous respirations strong and regular enough to no longer require assistance. The chart confirmed he'd been doing this for a while. *Timing's about right for the patient to regain consciousness . . .*

Ken threw a switch and the rhythmic chuffing of the machine stopped. The patient drew in a strong breath, then another.

Ken flipped a mental coin. He didn't want to extubate his patient too early. But he didn't want him struggling either. Sedation wouldn't be good right now. *Take a chance.* "Okay, hang on," Ken said. "I'm going to remove the tube from your throat. Don't struggle."

In a moment, the tube was out. "Take some deep breaths," Ken said.

The man did.

"Now cough."

Again, the man complied. *Good.*

The patient swallowed twice, coughed several more times, and said in a rough voice, "Do I have to be tied up?"

Ken pondered the wisdom of removing the restraints at this point, but finally decided to free his patient's hands. "Okay, now you can move. Just don't pull that IV out of your arm."

"Why . . . why am I here?"

"You had a blow to your head, a bad one. Blood accumulated inside your skull and pressed on your brain. We had to do an emergency operation to relieve the pressure. You did fine, but it's going to take awhile for you to recover." Ken hooked a straight chair with his foot and pulled it to the bedside, then turned it around and sat with his arms resting on the chair back. "We need some information from you so we can let your family know you're here. What's your name?"

"I can tell you that." Ken jerked his head toward the door and saw Hank Truong there, holding out a beeper like a priest presenting a communion wafer. "On their way out of the alley with our John Doe, the EMTs picked this up and threw it in the back of the MICU. They forgot it when they hit the ER, so they dropped it off on their next run, and the clerk gave it to me."

"And this gave you his name how?" Ken asked.

"Simple. I called the number listed on the pager's label and the service told me it belonged to a Dr. Matt Newman." Hank pointed to the bed. "Dr. Gordon, meet the new assistant professor of surgery."

Ken swiveled back to the man lying on the bed. "Is that right? Are you Dr. Newman?"

"I guess . . . I think that's right." The man in the bed ran his tongue over cracked lips. "Can I . . . can I have . . . some water?"

Ken picked up the Styrofoam pitcher of ice chips from the bedside table and spooned a few into the man's mouth. "Suck on these. If you do okay, we'll let you have some water soon."

Hank took up station at the foot of the bed. "Dr. Newman, I'm Hank Truong. We met when Dr. Franklin gave you a tour of the department. I'm afraid there was so much blood on your face when you came in that I didn't recognize you."

Ken leaned toward the man on the bed, the man he now knew was a colleague. "Is there anyone we can call for you?"

A voice from the doorway provided the answer. "You'd probably better start with a lawyer."

The little room seemed a lot smaller with the addition of the latest speaker. Ken pegged him at six-six, maybe two hundred eighty pounds or more. His skin was the color of coal. The scowl on his face and his shaven head added an air of menace. The badly tailored suit he wore couldn't conceal the bulge under his left arm. His shoes were thick-soled and obviously designed more for comfort than style. The man's presence screamed "police" even before he flipped open a leather folder and flashed a gold badge. "Detective Virgil Grimes, Dallas Homicide."

Grimes moved further into the room, followed by a tall, attractive blonde wearing a dark blazer, white tee, and tan slacks. She carried a large purse slung over her right shoulder, and her right hand rested on its open top. The woman pulled aside the blazer to show a badge clipped to her belt, but apparently decided to leave the talking to Grimes.

"Detective," Ken said. "This patient has had surgery for a very serious head injury. He's still recovering. Can you wait outside? I'll be happy to talk with you there about his condition."

Grimes shook his head. "Not good enough. We need to talk to him as soon as he's awake, and it looks like he's awake now."

Matt turned his head toward the detectives. He spoke slowly, apparently searching for words. "I don't . . . remember much. The . . . the men—"

"Wait, before you say anything more, we need to give a little speech." Grimes nodded at his blond companion. "Detective Ames will do the honors."

She pulled a laminated card from her purse but didn't consult it. Her soft Southern accent didn't make the words less chilling. "You have the right to remain silent—"

"Why . . . . are you reading . . . my rights?" Matt asked, after the recitation ended. "I'm . . . the victim—"

Gordon interposed himself between the detectives and Matt. "Stop right there. I'll testify in court that he cannot possibly have understood his Miranda rights. I've already told you that Dr. Newman has suffered a very serious injury to his brain. He's had major surgery, and although I'm happy to see him wake up, there's no way he's in full possession of his faculties. I suggest you come back when I've pronounced him fit to answer your questions. Until then, I'm going to ask you to leave and stop upsetting my patient."

"If you think I'm upsetting him now, he's going to be a lot more upset before we're finished." Grimes shrugged as if trying to settle his shoulder holster a bit more comfortably. "We'll be back tomorrow."

"What's . . . happening?" Matt rasped.

Grimes fixed Matt with a glacial stare. His lip curled a bit, but he remained silent. Then he turned on his heel and stalked from the room, the other detective close behind him.

Hank's face showed his puzzlement. "I'll look in on you later," he told Matt, and followed the detectives out.

Ken looked into the eyes of his patient, eyes that were still a bit glazed. "You're not going to be in any shape to talk for another day or so. I think I can keep that detective away from you until your head clears a bit. But it looks to me like you're going to need a lawyer. If you know one, I suggest you call them."

"I . . . I can . . . call—"

Ken consulted his watch. "It's late. Just rest now. Tomorrow will be soon enough." *I hope.*

"Felony Trial Division, Jennifer Ball."

"It's Matt. I need your help." The voice on the other end of the phone was weak, the words a little slurred.

Jennifer glanced around to make sure none of her coworkers in the DA's office were in earshot. For once, the area around her cubicle was deserted. "Matt, where have you *been?*" She made no effort to hide the anger in her voice.

"I . . . I don't know where to begin. I'm—"

"You didn't show up for our date two days ago. It's not like I'm that hard to reach, and you didn't call me, didn't text, didn't email. I tried to call *you*, but there was no answer. I left messages on your machine and your cell phone, sent you texts and emails, but you never called *back*."

"Jennifer, let me explain."

"It's as though you just dropped off the face of the earth." She squinted her eyes to force back the tears she felt forming. "Listen, I thought—"

"Jennifer, will you let me try to explain?" Matt's voice was still weak, but there was an urgency, a desperation to his tone now. The words were halting at first, then came out faster and faster "I'm in . . . Parkland Hospital . . . in the ICU. I was kidnapped. I . . . I ended up with a head injury. They did a craniotomy . . . Sorry, that's doctor-speak. Uh . . . I had bleeding on the brain. They . . . they did an operation to relieve the pressure. I began to come out of it yesterday, but I'm still sort of fuzzy."

Jennifer tightened her grip on the phone. "Oh, Matt. I'm sorry. What happened? Are you all right? What can I do?" She opened her desk drawer and grabbed her purse. "I'll be right there."

"Wait. Let me tell you the rest of it." She heard him take in a big breath. "I've had a visit from a detective who said he was from homicide. He tried to read me my rights until my surgeon ran him off. I don't know what he wanted, but a homicide detective doesn't hand out parking tickets. This is serious. I need a lawyer."

Jennifer dropped the purse back into the drawer and eased it shut. Her mind churned, looking to escape any possible blowback from this sudden turn of events. She tried to tell herself she was being paranoid, but she knew how the politics of her office worked. Guilt by association was a very real threat to the status she'd achieved, and could put her position in jeopardy.

Jennifer's master plan changed as thoughts of life as a doctor's wife gave way to visions of visiting Matt in prison. The feelings she had five minutes ago were forgotten as new plans evolved. An hour ago, she'd wanted nothing so much as to talk with Matt. Now she wished he'd never called. She wanted all this to go away. No phone call. No Matt in trouble. And definitely no request for help.

"Jennifer, are you there?" Matt's voice held a note of desperation.

"I'm thinking. You know I'm not a lawyer. I'm only a secretary."

"Jennifer, I don't have the strength to argue." He cleared his throat. "You work in the DA's office, and you're bound to know of some lawyers—criminal lawyers. When you come, can you—"

"Matt, listen to me. If you're a suspect in a homicide case, this changes everything. I can't come to visit you. I shouldn't even be talking with you. If things get serious, the detective will bring in an assistant district attorney. It would be one of the ADAs I work with.

This is a clear-cut conflict of interest." *Not to mention what it would do to my future in this office.*

"But I need you—"

Jennifer drew a shuddering breath. "What's your room number? I'll call you when I have a name."

———

Ken Gordon stopped at the door of Matt's room and surveyed his patient. "You're looking better today, a little more bright-eyed."

Matt managed a weak smile. "Bits and pieces are coming back. And I don't feel quite so much like there's a blacksmiths' convention using my head as the anvil."

Gordon eased into the chair at Matt's bedside and stretched out his legs. "What do you remember about what happened?"

"I vaguely recall being called out for an emergency at Metropolitan Hospital. It was probably about two in the morning when I left. In the parking garage, somebody—a couple of guys, I think—jumped me, trussed me up, and tossed me into the trunk of my car. From what I could hear, they planned to take me somewhere to kill me. I managed to escape, hid from them on top of a pile of wooden pallets. I started to climb down after they left, and I must have fallen. That's when the lights went out."

"You have a couple of cracked ribs," Gordon said. "Think you did that falling off your perch?"

"Those are probably from when they jumped me, or maybe when I rolled out of the trunk of the moving car."

Gordon nodded. "You have some cuts and scrapes on your wrists. You're not trying to cover up a suicide attempt, are you?"

Matt started to shake his head, but pain stopped him. "No, they taped my wrists with duct tape. I used the sharp end of a road flare to scrape the tape until it parted. I turned my hands and wrists into mincemeat in the process, but I figured that was better than the sort of ending they had planned for the trip."

Gordon shifted in the chair. "So why did they kidnap you?"

Matt tried to read the neurosurgeon's expression, but it remained a perfect poker face. "Honestly, I have no idea. Just as I have no idea why a homicide detective has such an interest in me."

Gordon levered himself to his feet. "Well, you seem to be doing pretty well after the injury. We'll keep you here in the ICU today. Probably transfer you to a regular room tomorrow. And when that happens, I won't be able to keep detective what's-his-face away from you. So if I were you, I'd get a lawyer as soon as possible."

"I hoped to get a call with a name yesterday." The phone at Matt's bedside rang. "Maybe that's it."

"I'll give you some privacy," Gordon said. "See you later."

Matt gave a feeble wave and lifted the receiver.

"Hello?"

"Matt, I can't talk long." The sounds of traffic in the background told Matt Jennifer wasn't calling from her office.

"I asked you to call me yesterday. What took so long?"

"I shouldn't talk with you at all. This could get me in a lot of trouble."

Matt couldn't believe what she was saying. "Jennifer, we can argue about this later. Right now, I'm in trouble. Did you find me a lawyer? A good one?"

"Write this down."

Matt reached for the pad and pencil he'd asked for in anticipation of this call. "Okay."

"Sandra Murray. Her number is 214-555-7208."

"What can you tell me about her?"

"She's supposed to be the best criminal defense lawyer in the city."

"Anything else?"

There was a brief silence, as though Jennifer was choosing her words carefully. "They say she's not only good . . . she's good looking."

"Don't worry about her looks. I promise I only want to hire her, not date her."

Jennifer refused to take the bait. "Matt, I don't know what kind of trouble you've gotten yourself into, but I don't think we should see each other or even talk until it's cleared up."

Matt heard a *click*. He rattled the receiver back onto its base and lay back, staring at the ceiling. He'd never felt so alone. The girl he thought he might someday marry had effectively washed her hands of him at a time when he most needed her.

Who else did he have? Parents dead. A few friends, none of them close. Just his brother, and he was thousands of miles away. For two years Matt's only communication with Joe had been via email and an occasional phone call.

The emails all had the same central message, "Keep the faith. Have faith. God is in control." Matt wished he could believe that right now, wished he were that strong. But he wasn't. Maybe he should try to contact Joe, although he wasn't sure how he'd do it.

The throbbing in Matt's head intensified. He relaxed back onto the pillow. Too much excitement. He'd try to get in touch with Joe later. Right now, he had to rest.

As sleep began to overtake him, Matt felt like a man trapped in the vortex of a whirlpool, going inexorably down, down, down. As he drifted off, his last thought was that Joe would tell him what to do. He hoped so. Because he didn't have a clue.

SIX

Lou entered the boss's office and stopped at his usual spot in front of the desk. "We tracked him down."

It hadn't been all that hard. When Lou canvassed the area, he learned that a shopkeeper had gone outside to empty trash and seen a man lying in the alley, unconscious, bleeding from a head wound. The shopkeeper called 911, and the EMTs had come and done their thing.

The man was probably still in the hospital. Since Lou had the victim's name and address from the wallet in the trunk of the car, he decided to check out his home first. "Edgar and I went over there late last night. Edgar's pretty good at picking locks—learned about it during his last time at Huntsville. Said his cell mate was a lock man who—"

"Get on with it!" The big man slammed his meaty hand down on the desk.

"Uh, sure. Anyway, we checked out the house. After he goes home from the hospital, we can get to him—easy."

"And how are you going to get into his house again? Depending on Edgar to exercise his talent?"

Lou felt the grin spreading over his face and made no attempt to stifle it. He reached into his pocket and pulled out a key suspended on a small loop of wire. "He had this hanging behind the door in his laundry room. I checked, and it fits the front and back doors. If he's like most folks, he'll never miss it. And if he does, he'll probably decide he misplaced it." He returned the key to his pocket. "We've got a free pass anytime we want it."

The boss nodded. "Very well. Now it's time to rectify your mistake."

Lou nodded. "Yes, sir."

"As soon as the man is back home, I want you to get rid of him. He's a loose end. Do it in such a way that it looks like suicide. Depressed over the murder he committed, and so forth. That way, the whole thing goes away, and no heat comes down on our little enterprise."

"I'm on it." Lou started for the door. He might have failed once, but he'd get this one right. Dr. Matt Newman was as good as dead.

Jennifer dropped her cell phone into her purse and looked through her car windows at the almost-deserted strip shopping center. No familiar faces, no cars she recognized. *Get real, Jennifer. Stop looking for trouble around every corner.* There was no way anyone from her office would come to this area, and if they did, they would have no idea with whom she was talking. True, suddenly finding out she'd been dating an accused murderer might be an excuse for paranoia—but probably not this much.

Jennifer started the car and headed back to her office. This call had used up her lunch hour, but that was okay. Her appetite disappeared when she learned of Matt's predicament yesterday. She drove on automatic pilot as her mind churned with the implications of her situation.

At first she'd figured that going out with Matt had no downside. Jennifer liked him—liked him a lot—maybe even started to love him. His good looks reminded her of Richard Gere, dark, wavy hair and all. He had a stable life, was a professional man who made a comfortable living. After the first few dates, the future that lay ahead of them looked as bright as a Hawaiian sunrise. Jennifer looked on the intrusions of his practice into their time together as a speed bump in their road to happiness, one she could eventually change. But linkage to a man targeted by a homicide investigator was a different thing altogether.

Jennifer shook her head. No, she had to listen to her head, not her heart.

Back at the office, she settled in at her desk and tried to put Matt's predicament out of her mind. She was rummaging in her bottom desk drawer when a voice over her shoulder made her jump.

"Jennifer, are you busy?"

Jennifer swiveled in her chair and saw Frank Everett, one of the assistant DAs, perched with one haunch on her desk. "Uh, I have to finish this project for Mr. Tanner. Why?"

"I wondered if you'd like to have dinner with me tonight."

Wow. She'd never really thought of him that way. But if Matt was on his way out and she wanted to hold on to her position here . . . "I . . . I'm not sure. I'm just out of a relationship, and—"

"It's only dinner. No pressure. But I hate to eat alone, and I'll bet you do too."

Right. It's only dinner—just two colleagues sharing a meal. What was the harm?

"Well . . . I guess that would be okay, Mr. Everett."

He flushed slightly. "Please, it's Frank."

Everyone in the office knew Frank Everett was on the rebound from a particularly messy divorce. He was never going to make *D Magazine*'s list of most eligible bachelors. Everett was a slightly overweight middle-aged man with a receding hairline, stuck in a midlevel job in the DA's office. But as Jennifer worked to rationalize accepting the invitation, she decided that Frank Everett had three outstanding attributes: he was a professional, he appeared interested in her, and he wasn't squarely in the sights of a homicide detective.

Was it terrible to accept this invitation when Matt needed her? On the other hand, how would it help Matt if she sat at home in front of the TV? So why not? "Okay, Frank. I'd love to have dinner with you."

"Pick you up at your place about seven?" Everett asked.

Jennifer did some rapid calculations. Straighten her apartment, in case they ended up back there after dinner. Do her hair. Squeeze into that slinky black dress she'd bought for the dinner with Matt that he'd canceled. If she sneaked out of the office a bit early, she could make it. "Sure. See you then."

"Ms. Murray's office. Can you hold for a moment?"

Matt gave silent thanks that at least the secretary didn't sound perky. He figured that the phone in the office of a criminal defense attorney should be answered the same way as at a mortuary—with somber tones, reflecting an acknowledgment of, and sympathy for, the caller's situation.

He glanced at the yellow legal pad on the rolling table at his bedside. It contained the notes he'd made while he waited for the name of an attorney. Unfortunately, since he had no idea what was going on, only a few lines marred the otherwise pristine surface of the first page. Matt moved the table so it sat across his bed like a writing desk, then picked up his pen, ready for the secretary to return to the line.

"Thank you for waiting. How may I help you?"

Matt took a deep breath and launched into his prepared speech. "My name is Matt Newman. I'm currently a patient in Parkland Hospital's ICU, recovering from surgery after a head injury. When I regained consciousness, a Dallas homicide detective showed up, but my doctor chased him away. He said he'd be back. I have no idea what's going on, but I'm pretty sure I need an attorney."

"And you wish to employ Ms. Murray?"

Did he? He wished to leave the hospital and get on with his life. But under the circumstances . . . "Yes, I do."

"She's in court right now, but I expect to be in contact with her. May I have her call you?"

"Sure." He gave her his room number and the number on his phone. "I'm not going anywhere, but I don't know when they shut off the phones in the ICU rooms."

Nothing seemed to faze this secretary. Matt hoped her boss was as efficient. "Very well. If she can't get through on the phone, Ms. Murray will come to you."

"I don't know about visiting hours. I think they're sort of strict about those in the ICU."

The secretary's tone held a smile when she responded. "Ms. Murray seems to have no problem getting around rules and restrictions. In the meantime, if anyone from the police tries to talk with you, say only this: 'I've contacted my attorney and will have nothing to say until she is here.' Is that clear?"

Matt found that he was writing the words as she dictated them, even though they were easy enough to remember. Just staring at them on the page made him feel calmer. "Got it."

"Good. And if you have any problems in the meantime, call me. I'm Elaine."

Matt cradled the phone and thought back over the conversation. Was he overreacting? Couldn't he simply ask the detective to tell him what was going on? Surely there was no need to engage an attorney. Maybe he'd call Sandra Murray's office back and cancel the request. After all, criminal defense attorneys charged high fees, and his resources were limited.

"Dr. Newman, I told you I'd be back." The black detective—Matt couldn't recall his name—stood in the doorway.

Grimm? No. Grimes? That was it, Grimes. Why was he back? Didn't Dr. Gordon say he was going to keep the police away for another day? Matt found the buzzer and pushed it.

"Do you need something? I'll get it for you," Grimes said.

Matt shook his head, determined to keep silent. Finally a nurse hurried in. "Yes, what do you need?"

Matt was careful to address the nurse directly. "Can you get this man out of here? Call Dr. Gordon."

The detective shook his head. "This is a police matter. If I have to, I can contact the hospital administrator and get all the access I need." He eased his bulk into the chair at Matt's bedside. "But in view of your condition"—he set the word off with air quotes—"I'll keep it short. Why did you kill Cara Mendiola?"

Matt closed his eyes and breathed deeply. This couldn't be happening. His mind whirled while the detective droned on.

The man leaned closer to Matt. "Did you hear me?"

Matt bit his lip but said nothing.

"I asked you a question. What can you tell us about the murder of Cara Mendiola?"

The words hadn't fully registered the first time, but now they hit home. Matt's eyes shot open and he sat forward. The pain in his head brought him up short, and he dropped back onto the pillow. *Cara? Dead?*

Matt's reaction was triggered by surprise rather than any sense of loss. He barely knew the woman. Saw her in the hospital coffee shop, spoke to her as they passed in the halls. He thought back to the last time he'd seen her, and decided it was close to two weeks ago. Now she was dead. And a detective from homicide apparently thought Matt killed her. But why?

Matt pulled the yellow pad closer and read from it. "I've contacted my attorney and will have nothing to say until she is here."

"I can tell you it'll go easier on you if you cooperate. All you need to do is—"

"I've contacted my attorney and will have nothing to say until she is here." Matt parroted the phrase with no inflection.

This went on for a couple of minutes, with Matt as stubborn as the detective. Finally the man snorted. "If that's the way you want to play it." He leaned down and spoke so softly Matt had to strain to hear him. "Don't think you're going anywhere besides jail."

The detective pulled a card from his shirt pocket and tossed it on Matt's bed. "Your lawyer can call me when you're ready to talk."

Matt's dreams were filled with large, menacing men chasing him down a dark corridor while policemen cheered them on. He had just run into an alley that ended in a blank wall when he heard someone call his name.

"Mr. Newman?"

He roused himself with an effort and squinted at the figure just inside the door.

"Mr. Newman?"

"Huh?"

A click, and light flooded the room. When Matt forced his eyes fully open, he saw an attractive woman at his bedside. She pulled up a chair, tossed her head to settle her shoulder-length red hair, and smiled. "Ah, you're awake. Good."

"Who are you?"

"I'm your attorney. Or, at least, I'm the person you called to be your attorney. We'll decide in a minute if that's the way it's going to be."

Matt hitched himself up in his bed and reached for his notepad. He scanned it until he found what he wanted. "So you're Sandra Murray?"

She grinned, and dimples popped up at the corners of her mouth. "Guilty. And that's the last time you'll hear that word come out of my mouth. You're Matt Newman, right?"

"Right. Dr. Matt Newman, if it makes any difference."

A frown flitted across her face but was quickly replaced by a neutral expression. "It may." She reached down and produced a yellow legal pad of her own. "Tell me what I need to know."

"I left the hospital in the early morning . . . What's today?"

"It's a bit after midnight on Thursday morning."

"How did you get in here at this hour?"

"Never mind that. Just tell me your story."

Matt told her what he remembered and then handed over the card the detective left. "The first time he was here, a blonde was with him, but I don't recall her name. I get the impression this guy's in charge, though."

She winced when she read the detective's name. "This is a problem."

Matt was afraid to ask, but he needed to know. "Why?"

"Detective Virgil Grimes works homicides. Are you mixed up in one?"

Matt gave a faint shrug. "Apparently he thinks so. I don't."

The attorney made a note on her legal pad. "The first thing I'll do is call Grimes and find out what kind of a case he has. I just wish it wasn't Grimes."

Matt raised his eyebrows. "Why?"

"He's a pit bull. He generally goes with his gut, and once he gets an idea of who the guilty party is, he doesn't turn loose. Our best chance to get you out of this mess is to convince him he's after the wrong person. That might not be easy . . . even if you're innocent."

"I . . ." He stopped and grabbed his head. "Sorry, when I get upset my head starts pounding." He took a deep breath. "I am innocent. I'm the victim, but no one seems to believe it."

She apparently saw the look on Matt's face, because she made a calming, palms-down gesture. "Don't worry. It's early yet." Murray tapped her pencil against her front teeth. "One thing worries me already though. Why didn't the police believe your story of being kidnapped?"

Matt reached for the water at his bedside and sipped. It was warm, but his throat was so dry he emptied the glass anyway. "I wish I knew why they don't believe me. I wish I knew why they think I killed that woman. I guess I'm going to need a lawyer."

She grinned, and Matt was aware for the first time of a sprinkling of freckles that, combined with dancing green eyes, gave her a surprisingly girlish look, although he judged her to be about his age. "You're going to need a very good lawyer. Fortunately, you contacted one. Let's talk about that."

She named a fee that produced a lump of ice in Matt's stomach. "I don't know how I'll pay that."

Sandra seemed genuinely puzzled. "I thought doctors made lots of money."

"I've been a solo general surgery practitioner for four years," Matt said. "That's just about long enough to establish a patient base. All that time, in addition to rent, salaries, malpractice insurance, and stuff like that, I've been paying back student loans from four years of medical school and five years of specialty training. I'm not exactly swimming in money."

"But once you get out and back into practice, you can earn more. Right?"

Matt shook his head. "I gave up my private practice. I was supposed to take a faculty position here at Southwestern Medical Center." He swept his hand around in a broad gesture. "If things had gone as planned, I'd be staffing residents at this hospital right now. Ironic, isn't it?"

"So you sold your practice," Sandra said. "That should give you a financial cushion."

Matt was getting tired of this, but he had to make sure his attorney understood his situation. "You don't 'sell' a practice anymore. Another doctor paid me a minimal amount for my 'goodwill.' That means he agreed to take over my records and patients, at least the people who wanted to keep seeing him, and I agreed to write a letter introducing him."

The more they talked, the more depressed Matt became. He had resources, but not many, and no real prospects of getting more for a while. Finally he decided that by borrowing from his meager retirement fund, he could meet his lawyer's fees. He thought about the money he'd been putting aside and managed a wry grin. Face it. He wouldn't need a penny of that money if his retirement was spent in prison, or his life was cut short by lethal injection.

After Sandra left, Matt lay in the dark as icy fingers of fear crept up his spine. He felt like he was in pincers, caught between a policeman who appeared convinced Matt was a suspect in a homicide and two men who, either on their own or acting for some nebulous third person, kidnapped him so they could kill him. By all rights his escape from his kidnappers should have brought his night of terror to an end. Instead Matt had the feeling his ordeal was just beginning.

SEVEN

Sandra wasn't sure when the ritual started, but by now it was firmly established. Her first stop each morning was at Starbucks for two coffees. Today one double shot, black Caffè Americano for her, with a mocha latte for Elaine. "I like it because it matches my skin perfectly," her secretary liked to say.

Sandra slid her morning mocha across the desk to Elaine after they'd traded greetings. "Here you are."

"How's your new client?"

"I'll know more when I see the police records, but I think he's in a lot of trouble." Sandra sipped from her own cup and leaned against Elaine's desk. "Why didn't you tell me he was a doctor?"

"Honestly, I don't recall him mentioning it. Does it make a difference? I'd think all that means is that he's more likely able to pay your fees than some of the cases you take on."

Sandra shrugged, finished her coffee, and dropped the cup in Elaine's wastebasket. "It's not that. It's . . ."

"Oh, the thing with Dr. Gordon. Don't tell me that's going to keep you from ever defending a doctor."

"I don't know. I just have this feeling about doctors right now . . ."

Elaine looked over the rim of her coffee cup and fixed Sandra with a meaningful stare. "You mean because Ken Gordon doesn't share your beliefs about God, you're going to assume all doctors think that way?"

"I know it's silly, but Ken was so adamant . . . Oh, never mind." Sandra moved toward the door of her office, turned, and said, "I'm going to return some of these phone calls, then I'll see if I can find out why Virgil Grimes showed up on my client's doorstep—well, actually, at his bedside—and frightened him half to death."

Sandra eased into her office chair and immediately slipped off her shoes. Pumps were professional, but flats were certainly easier on the feet. She picked up a pen and tapped her front teeth. She remembered the words she'd heard from a seasoned criminal defense attorney. *Never ask your client if they're guilty or innocent. They're all innocent, until a jury decides otherwise.* When she'd left Matt Newman's room, she was certain—she couldn't say why—but she was absolutely certain the stakes had been raised in the battle that was ahead, because she thought he was the kind of client an attorney worries most about defending: an innocent man.

Shortly after noon the next day, Sandra strode into Matt's room. She eased into a bedside chair, crossed her legs, and said without preamble, "I spoke with Grimes. You seem to be in pretty big trouble."

Matt pushed the button to raise the head of his bed. "Tell me about it," he said, and tried to focus his hazy thoughts. "I don't know anything that happened after I fell in that alley."

She pulled a notepad from her briefcase and scanned it. "The day after you were found unconscious in the alley, the police got a report of an abandoned vehicle in the area. Cara Mendiola's body was in the trunk. She'd been shot once in the head."

Matt still couldn't get his mind around it. He'd been asking himself why he'd been kidnapped and marked for death. Now he had to add another question: Was it related to Cara's murder? Were her killers the same men who'd kidnapped him? "Why do the police suspect me? I'm a victim here."

"To begin with, she was found in your car."

"That doesn't mean anything," Matt protested. "It was stolen. With me in the trunk. And trust me, I was the only one in there."

Sandra continued as though he hadn't spoken. "When they discovered Mendiola's body, your wallet was under it."

"Obviously it fell out while they had me trussed up in there."

"Grimes thinks it fell out when you put Mendiola's body in the trunk."

Matt's throat felt like a noose was tightening around it. He took a deep breath. "How do they think I killed her when I was lying unconscious in that alley?"

Sandra shrugged. "No one knows how long you were in that alley. Grimes's theory is that you and she drove somewhere, maybe a park, to hash out a lovers' quarrel. You threatened her with a gun. It accidentally discharged and killed her. You panicked. You loaded her in the trunk and went looking for somewhere to dump the body, getting rid of the gun along the way."

"I never—"

She waved Matt to silence. "They say you were in that alley looking for a place to dispose of her body. You climbed up on the stack of wood pallets, lost your balance, and fell, hitting your head."

Matt thought about that a bit. Couldn't forensic evidence show he'd been tied up in the trunk? Fingerprints, hair? No, it was his car. "What about the road flares I used to cut through the tape? They should have been in the trunk. One should have my blood all over it—"

"But they weren't. Just the usual junk, plus Mendiola's body and your wallet."

Matt's mind scrambled to find the key that would prove his innocence. "Did they check the security cameras in the hospital parking garage?"

"One showed you walking out of the hospital. Another showed your car driving away a few minutes later. The area where your car was parked wasn't covered by a camera."

Matt struggled to swallow. "How did they find me here? I was admitted as a John Doe."

"Your white coat, complete with name badge, turned up in the alley where you were found. By that time, the police had discovered your car, and there was a bulletin out to detain you for questioning. Grimes saw the reports about the coat and the injured John Doe, both found in the same alley. He put it together. After that, it was easy."

There it was. Wrapped up in a neat package, tied with a bow. The evidence might not be enough to convict him of murder—Matt hoped Sandra Murray would see to that—but it was certainly enough to ruin his life.

"That's it." Merrilee Ames tossed a thin folder on the desk in front of Detective Virgil Grimes. "Matt Newman's house, his car, his locker at work—clean, no sign of a pistol. He's never had a gun permit. None of his coworkers have ever seen him with one or heard him mention going to a firing range."

Grimes frowned. "There are a hundred ways to get hold of a gun illegally in this town, and another hundred to dispose of it. My guess is that it's in a lake or pond, unless he took a chance and buried it in a Dumpster. Tell them to keep looking."

Ames leaned a hip on Grimes's desk. "Okay. But we've been digging into Newman's relationship with Mendiola, and no one had any inkling they even knew each other. He was a surgeon; she was the head of Internet technology. So far as anyone knew, their only contact was nodding when they passed in the hall or cafeteria." She pursed her lips. "And then there's Newman's story of being kidnapped."

"When you've been at this as long as I have, you learn that people lie—they lie a lot. So I start with the premise that everything a suspect says is false until I can prove otherwise."

A lock of blond hair had fallen across Ames's right eye, and she brushed it back. "That's pretty cynical, Virgil."

"Cynical or not, that's how I operate. And since I'm the lead on this investigation, I guess you're going to have to learn to live with it." He made a shooing motion. "Now get out there and find me some evidence that proves Newman killed Cara Mendiola."

The next day Matt was moved from the ICU to a private room, still fairly close to the nurses' station so they could check on him. He was glad to be recovering but was constantly aware of the murder charge that hung over his head like the sword of Damocles. He expected the burly figure of Detective Grimes to fill the doorway of his room at any moment, a pair of handcuffs in one hand, a warrant for Matt's arrest in the other.

On his second day out of the ICU, Matt, like Ebenezer Scrooge, had three visitors. And, as it did with Scrooge, the news they brought shook Matt. The first was his attorney.

"I need to talk with your doctor," she said from the door. "Let's discuss what happens when he discharges you." She closed the door and dragged the visitor's chair to Matt's bedside.

"I haven't asked Ken . . . er, Dr. Gordon about my discharge," Matt said, "but my guess is that he's going to have to let me go soon."

"Ken Gordon is your doctor?" she asked.

Matt wondered at the surprise in his lawyer's voice but decided to let it go. "Yes, and he should be ready to discharge me soon. I suspect that my chart is on the desk of a utilization nurse right now."

"And that means . . . ?"

"Those are nurses that work for the hospitals or insurance companies. Theoretically, they monitor a patient's care and make sure everything's appropriate. On a practical level, they make sure patients are discharged as soon as it's safe, so somebody else can use the bed and the insurance companies can stop paying for inpatient care." Matt sipped water from the Styrofoam cup at his bedside. "Why do you ask?"

"Because as soon as you're well enough to be discharged, Grimes will want to get a statement and question you."

"Don't I get to appear before a judge and plead not guilty or something?"

She gave Matt a sympathetic glance. "You didn't pay much attention in high school civics class, did you? Never mind. By the time this is over, you'll be an expert on our legal system." She ticked off the points on her fingers. "Point one. Right now you're a suspect. If a reporter were to ask Grimes about you, you're a 'person of interest.' Soon, if he hasn't already done so, Grimes will brief an ADA on the case."

"A what?"

"An assistant district attorney." She touched her second finger. "At some point after your release, probably soon after, Grimes and the

ADA will bring you in for questioning. Don't worry. I'll be there. I don't think they'll arrest you, although they probably will tell you not to leave the city. That's just standard practice."

"No chance of my going anywhere. I don't even have a car. When will I get mine back?"

Sandra waved off the question. "Later. Stay with me. They're moving carefully because of your injury. Grimes will sweat you as much as he thinks he can get away with, but eventually he'll have to turn you loose. However, if the ADA decides there's enough evidence, he'll present your case to a grand jury." She touched a third finger. "And if they indict you, the police will come for you with an arrest warrant."

Matt felt his heart drop to his shoes.

"After you're taken into custody, you're arraigned." Now she had four fingers in the air. "The arraignment is when you appear before a judge. You have the opportunity to hear the charges against you and enter a plea. Most important for now, that's when the judge either sets bail or denies it. The trial comes after that. Often a long time after that."

"But I've been in custody for . . . how long have I been here? Why haven't I been arraigned?"

"Because, despite Detective Grimes's attempt to frighten you, you haven't really been arrested. When you are, believe me, you'll know it."

"Ms. Murray—"

"Please, call me Sandra."

"Okay, and I'm Matt." He grimaced. "I hope that when this is over I still have a name, not a number." He picked up his ever-present legal pad and flipped a couple of pages. "I've been trying to figure out where I'll get the money for bail. How much do you think I'll need?"

Her answer made Matt cringe. "I don't see how I can raise that much."

"Let's talk a little about how bail works," Sandra said. "If you can't put up the money or something worth that much, a bondsman will write the surety for a fee of ten percent of the bail. So we're talking one-tenth of that amount I just mentioned."

She mentioned a figure and he replied, "I guess I can raise that."

A half hour later, when Sandra closed her briefcase and prepared to leave, she asked, "Do you have any other questions?"

"What about my kidnapping? Why don't the police believe me?"

"Apparently because they think your story is a lie, dreamed up to cover the murder of Cara Mendiola. We can use the kidnapping story in our defense if we need to, but our first job is to convince the police you didn't kill her. I'll keep hammering them with the kidnapping, but right now Grimes is pretty convinced it's a fiction." She cocked her head. "Any other questions?"

"No," Matt said. He had no more questions. Unfortunately he had very few answers to the ones already swimming in his head.

The second visitor was Matt's neurosurgeon, Ken Gordon. The gist of the conversation was that Matt was recovering even more rapidly than Gordon hoped. That was the good news. The bad news was that Gordon would have to discharge Matt soon, and both men knew what Matt was facing once he left the hospital.

"Let's make it day after tomorrow. Tell your lawyer about nine o'clock. She'll probably want to be here." He stuck out his hand and Matt shook it. "I hope we'll be having lunch together in the medical center's faculty club real soon."

The third visitor both surprised and angered Matt. Why hadn't Brad Franklin visited before this? After all, the man had hired Matt for a faculty position. Was it too much to expect the chairman of the surgery department to drop by? Sure, he was busy. Matt realized that. But this visit came much too late to suit Matt.

Franklin tapped on the door frame, and Matt motioned him

inside, barely suppressed anger roiling inside him. "Come in, Brad. I've been hoping you'd come by."

On surgery days Franklin wore a clean, crisp, ironed scrub suit he brought from home, shunning the wrinkled garb everyone else wore. He covered the scrubs with a fresh white coat with his name and "Chairman, General Surgery" embroidered over the pocket. Matt had observed this on a previous visit and decided that if the chairman wanted to look better than everyone else, that was his business.

Apparently Franklin wasn't operating today, but his clothes still told everyone he was a cut above average. His unbuttoned lab coat revealed a white-on-white dress shirt set off by a designer tie. Small rubies accented gold cuff links at either wrist. Brad Franklin looked every inch the department chair, and something in his manner today made the hairs on Matt's neck stand at attention. Whatever was coming wasn't good.

Franklin hitched up his trousers to preserve the crease and eased into a chair at Matt's bedside. "How are you doing?" he asked.

"I've been better," Matt said, "but Ken says he'll be turning me loose soon. I guess you know that I have some legal problems to settle, but my attorney tells me the charges the police are bringing probably won't hold up." *Okay, so maybe I'm being too optimistic, but there's no need to tell him how bad things are.* "As soon as I can get that cleared up, I'm looking forward to starting my work here."

Franklin appeared to find something fascinating in the region of his shoes. Still looking down, he said, "Actually, that's what I wanted to talk about."

Matt knew what was coming before the chairman started his next sentence. Sure enough, Franklin said he'd met with the dean, and they'd decided it was in the best interest of the medical center if Matt didn't officially join the staff until after his legal problems were put to rest. "I'm sure you understand," Franklin said.

Matt didn't really understand anything except that the chairman had just pulled the rug out from under him. The prospect of his new salary as an assistant professor of surgery had vanished. He'd already closed his private practice. Other than a few fees dribbling in from final bills and insurance claims, Matt had no real income and no prospects of any. And he was piling up debts faster than he could find a way to pay them.

Matt was already worried sick about getting the money together to pay his attorney. He figured he should be able to scrape up enough assets to cover posting bail. But this was the last straw.

The night before, in desperation, Matt had thumbed through a Bible he found in the drawer of his bedside table looking for comfort. He'd tried to pray. And finally he asked God to give him a sign that things would be all right. Now, as Franklin continued to justify his decision, Matt had one thought foremost in his mind. *If this is Your sign, God, I don't like it.*

EIGHT

Sandra Murray handed Elaine a steaming paper cup bearing the Starbucks logo. "Here you go. Your favorite."

After Sandra settled into the chair across from her secretary's desk, she flipped the lid from her own cup into the wastebasket and inhaled the rich aroma. Today she'd decided to shake things up with a caramel macchiato. Elaine had another mocha latte, and Sandra noticed that it did indeed mirror the woman's skin tones almost exactly. *I hope that when I'm her age, I look that good.*

Sandra sipped, licked a few drops of caramel-flavored foam from her upper lip, and said, "Elaine, how's your pipeline into the DA's office?"

Elaine moved her coffee aside and leaned forward over the desk. "Why? Want me to do a little undercover snooping for you?"

"Haven't developed scruples against that, have you?" Sandra's smile took any sting out of the banter.

"Nope, just want to know what you'd like me to find out. You know me." She fluffed her hair and gave an exaggerated come-hither look. "Always happy to use my feminine wiles to help my boss."

"Still dating Charlie Greaver?" Sandra asked. Charlie, the number two man in the DA's office, was virtually a shoo-in to succeed the current DA, Jack Tanner. If so, he'd be the first African-American in Sandra's memory to hold the position.

"I sometimes accept an invitation to go out with Charlie. After all, I'm a widow who's still in the prime of life, and he's a widower who's . . . well, he's a widower."

"Right now, I'm more interested in his status at the DA's office. I need to know where things stand with my client, Dr. Newman."

"Hmm. You know, Charlie doesn't usually discuss things at the DA's office with me, the same way I don't tell him about stuff at our office."

Sandra grinned. "I'm not asking for anything secret. Just see what you can find out."

"Just to be clear, you want me to take Charlie up on one of his dinner invitations, pump him, and then toss him aside?" Elaine laughed.

"What you do with Charlie after you find out whether Grimes has a case against Newman is your business. You can play catch and release if you want to. If you go further than that, don't tell me."

"Gotcha." Elaine took her first sip of coffee and smiled. "One cup of coffee, and I agree to play spy for you. I've really got to raise my fees."

"Huh," Sandra said. "You can't kid me. You'd do it for nothing. The coffee's just a bonus."

Matt wasn't sure he'd slept at all. Now that he was out of the ICU, the nurses no longer came in every hour or so to check his vital signs. Still, he remained aware of the ceaseless activity all around him: people going in and out of patient rooms, murmured conversations in the hall, the ringing of phones and rattle of charts at the nearby nurses' station. Besides, who could sleep when they knew they might be arrested as soon as they passed through the doors of the hospital into the outside world?

"Knock, knock." A man wearing surgical scrubs paused in the doorway.

"Come on in," Matt said. He sized up his visitor: probably mid-twenties, Asian features, a definite familiarity to his face. Matt had the sense he should know the man, but the name floated outside his reach. His visitor wore scrubs, but that could mean he was anything from a medical student to an OR orderly to a doctor. *See if he introduces himself.*

He did. "Dr. Newman, I'm Hank Truong. I'm the one who brought your pager to you in the ICU. But you were pretty out of it." Hank leaned on the back of the chair at Matt's bedside, but didn't sit down. "Actually I'm the one who saw you when the EMTs brought you to the ER."

It clicked then. "Oh, *right*. Thanks for getting me to the neurosurgeon. You probably saved my life."

"Just doing my job. But I'm glad you made it."

Matt had it figured out by now. "So you're a second-year resident, doing your rotation in the Parkland ER as Pit Boss."

"Yes. I see you've picked up the slang for the resident in charge in the ER. They tell me that duty is pretty much the same as getting a battlefield commission in the service, and I can't disagree. You see a little of everything, and you have to make some tough decisions, often in a hurry."

"Well, I appreciate your coming by," Matt said. "I hope I'll be seeing you again soon."

"I . . . I understand you're about to be discharged," Hank said. "So I wanted to make sure you're doing okay."

Even if the chairman didn't seem to care about his situation, Matt was pleased to find that this resident did. "Medically, I'm fine. Legally? That's another story."

Hank stuck out his hand. "Well, we're all hoping you'll get that straight soon. The residents are looking forward to your joining the faculty and staffing us here."

Matt shook the offered hand. "Thanks."

Halfway to the door, Hank seemed to reach a decision and turned back. "Let me ask you something. This morning I had a patient come in with an infected gash on his lower leg, several days old—maybe a week or so. Of course, it's too late to suture it, so I cleaned it up real well, gave him a tetanus shot, and started him on an antibiotic. But I've read about doing secondary closures on wounds that long after the injury. What's your opinion on that?"

"I haven't tried it, myself," he said. Something clicked in Matt's brain. *Could it be?* A gash on the lower leg, over a week old. "Describe this guy for me."

If Hank was surprised by the request, he didn't show it. Then again, when a staff doctor asked a resident a question, the resident's response was to answer, not wonder why. And Dr. Newman was a staff doctor—sort of. "He had a high-pitched voice," Hank said. "Jittery guy. Short, sort of sharp-faced. Late thirties. Hispanic, I think. I don't recall his name, though."

"I'm betting the name and all the other information he gave was false. And I'd guess he paid cash."

Hank frowned. "Uh, I don't know. Do you want me to check?"

Would it do any good? If nothing else, it might back up his story. "Sure. Please do."

"Where can I call you with the information?" Hank asked.

Good question. Maybe jail? "Tell you what. I'll call you in a day or so. Thanks."

Hank left, undoubtedly to pull the ER record before it could get filed and—if the Parkland system was anything like what Matt had experienced at other hospitals—possibly lost.

"Ready to get out of here?" Ken Gordon stood in the doorway of Matt's room. His rumpled scrubs and unshaven face told Matt the neurosurgeon had been up all night.

"Not sure," Matt replied. "You have a busy night?"

Gordon eased into the chair at Matt's bedside and finger-combed his hair. "Kid—actually, early twenties, but they're all kids to me—riding his motorcycle down North Central Expressway about one a.m. Weaving in and out of traffic, doing about ninety, the police estimate, when he hit a rough spot in the road and lost control. Had on an expensive set of leathers—didn't want to get road rash if he wiped out, I guess—but no helmet."

"Closed head injury, I suppose," said Matt, as much to himself as to Gordon. "Were you able to save him?"

"So far. My part was managing an acute subdural hematoma. He's still in the OR while the general surgeons tend to a ruptured spleen and lacerated liver. The orthopods will have to deal with a fractured arm and crushed pelvis later, if he survives."

"Tough," Matt said. He remembered his own nights on emergency call and wondered if he'd ever get back to practicing medicine. Not if he were convicted of a felony . . . and possibly not even if he were found innocent of the charges Grimes was pursuing. There was such a thing as slinging enough mud until something stuck, and Matt was afraid that the barrage directed against him had just begun.

"Jennifer, I enjoyed dinner the other night."

Jennifer Ball looked up from her computer. Frank Everett was perched in what was becoming his customary position at the edge of her desk. She hated when people did that, but swallowed the words that would move him. "It was fun," she said.

"I have tickets to a show at the State Fair Music Hall next Saturday. Would you like to go?"

Jennifer did a rapid mental run-through of her social calendar and found it distressingly empty. After Matt, Frank was the only person who'd shown any interest in her. She had a twinge of guilt at abandoning Matt so quickly, but she shoved it aside. Besides, Frank could be a valuable asset as things played out. "Sure. That sounds good."

"Great. I've got a meeting with the DA in a few minutes, but why don't I come by here after that? Maybe we can get some coffee."

Was this moving a little fast? Yes, but she feared that if she tried to slow it down, it might stop completely. "Sure. See you then."

Jennifer applied herself to her typing, letting the words flow from her fingertips without making much of an impression on her mind. Only when she finished and hit the Print button on her computer did it register what she'd been transcribing. These were the notes from a meeting between DA Tanner, ADA Greaver, and a detective from the homicide squad. And they concerned potential murder charges against a doctor who was currently recovering from a severe head injury—a doctor named Matt Newman.

She snatched up the five pages of typescript and read it through carefully. The case appeared to be coming together, although much of the evidence was circumstantial. As she turned the last page, she heard someone whistling toward her desk. Jennifer grabbed the papers and shoved them into her top desk drawer just as Frank Everett hove into view.

In addition to the whistling, he was smiling broadly and there was an unusual spring in his step. She didn't have to wait long to find out why, either.

"Forget my offer of coffee. What would you say to dinner tonight? You pick the restaurant—the fancier the better."

Now he was definitely moving too fast. But Jennifer's curiosity got the best of her. Why was Frank back so quickly, and in a mood to celebrate? "I'll check my calendar," Jennifer said. "What's the occasion?"

Everett leaned against her desk, but he must have seen the tiny frown Jennifer let flash across her face. He hooked a vacant chair from the next desk, pulled it toward him, and eased into it. "I'm apparently moving up in the world. I just met with Tanner and Greaver, and they're giving me a plum case. If I get a conviction on this, I'm going to be their fair-haired boy."

Jennifer worked hard to keep her expression neutral. "Will it be a tough one?"

Everett spread his hands in a "no problem" gesture. "I don't think so. I'll know more after I review the evidence and talk to the police, but I'm pretty confident I can nail it." He smiled without mirth. "Yessir, Dr. Matt Newman is going to wish he'd never heard of Assistant DA Frank Everett."

Jennifer's palms were suddenly damp with sweat. She wiped them on her skirt, hiding the gesture by turning her swivel chair toward the clock on the far wall. "That's great, Frank." She struggled to keep her voice level. "Why don't you make reservations at Nana for seven? I'll meet you there."

Everett went whistling on his way, while Jennifer wondered how to keep her new boyfriend from finding out about her old one.

———

Sandra Murray paused in the doorway of Matt's room. "Ready for this?"

She could see the tension in Matt's shoulders, the worry on his face. He tried to smile, but it came out as more of a grimace. "I guess."

"I know you've had visions of police swarming around you, weapons drawn, taking you into custody the moment you pass the front door, but I doubt that's going to happen." Sandra took the visitor's chair and settled a briefcase-sized purse on her lap. "My spies tell me that the DA's office is still building their case. If you were a flight risk, they might bring you in for questioning immediately. But they figure I'd object to the validity of anything they get from you until you're fully cleared by your neurosurgeon, and that's not going to happen until your checkup next week."

"How did you know—"

"I've spoken to your doctor. He wants to help as much as possible." She raised her hand to smooth her hair, but caught herself before she could complete the gesture. "He says he likes you." She paused. "And he . . . we used to go out. But that's over now."

She wondered why she'd added those last words. Why did she feel the need to explain to Matt that she and Ken Gordon were no longer close? Was she developing feelings for Matt? She dismissed the idea as ridiculous. She'd never fall for a client. And especially not for another doctor.

Matt's shoulders slumped. "I hate to confess it, but I sort of dread going out in public looking like this." He pointed to his head.

Sandra nodded. Her client's head had been partially shaved for the surgical procedure. The hair was growing back as diffuse black stubble on that side, and metal staples marked the site of the incision. "Surely you weren't surprised to see that," she said.

"Oh, I knew the technique for the procedure," Matt answered. "But you always figure it's going to happen to somebody else." He touched his skull well away from the staples. "This must make me look like something out of a horror flick."

"Just be glad you're alive," Sandra said. "Now let's get you out of here."

The discharge went as smoothly as any hospital procedure could. That is to say, it moved at the speed of a glacier, but at least it moved forward. Finally Matt was settled in the front seat of Sandra's Volvo SUV. "See?" she said. "No police. No reporters. Nothing."

The scrub suit he'd worn when found in the alley was somewhere in a police evidence locker, so Matt wore a fresh one with Parkland Hospital stenciled on the top and bottom. Ken Gordon had loaned him an extra pair of the clogs favored by surgeons and operating room personnel. Matt had no wallet, no keys, nothing of his own. He'd never felt so helpless.

"I looked up the address of your house," Sandra said. "I presume that's where we're going."

"I don't know how I'll get in. My keys were in the car, and the police impounded it as evidence."

Sandra pulled a shiny key from the pocket of her stylish green pantsuit. "They insisted on keeping the key ring intact, but I finally convinced a sympathetic evidence tech to make a copy of your house key for me."

"You amaze me. How did you manage that?"

"Criminal defense lawyers build up a pretty good network. This guy owed me a favor—and he likes me."

Sandra wondered if she should explain further. *Don't be silly. It doesn't matter to Matt just how much someone likes me, or why.* She decided to let it go.

Guided by her GPS and occasional input from Matt, Sandra soon pulled up outside a modest brick home in a quiet residential neighborhood. Mature oaks dotted the yards all around. There were no tricycles and skateboards lying helter-skelter on sidewalks and porches, no evidence that children lived nearby. Most of the people in these homes were probably the original owners. Their children were long since gone, and the occupants of the houses planned to live out their lives here.

"This is an awfully nice house," Sandra said.

"I bought it when the owner passed away. His children were anxious to sell it, and I made them a decent offer. I'm probably the youngest person in the neighborhood, but that doesn't bother me. I'm never home anyway."

"Well, this is another asset," Sandra said. "You could borrow against it if you need to."

Matt started to shake his head, but stopped and winced with apparent pain. "Afraid not. The bank made me a good deal, let me get the house with a very small down payment. Property values around here have dropped since then, and I'm close to upside-down on the mortgage."

Matt opened the car door and waved away Sandra's offer of help. The twisting involved in his exit brought a grimace of pain, but in a moment he stood resolutely on the sidewalk. "See, I'm fine."

As he shuffled up the walk, his progress was slowed as much by Ken's size 11 clogs on his size 10 feet as his condition. Matt paused at the door, the key in his hand.

"Want me to go in first?" Sandra asked. "Think your potential killers might be in there?" She pulled out her cell phone. "We can call the police and have them check the house if you want."

"No. I can't live the rest of my life in fear." Matt turned the key in the lock, eased the door open, and shuffled inside with faltering steps. In the living room, he dropped onto the sofa. The movement made him screw up his face, but he said nothing. He gestured Sandra to a nearby chair.

"Are you going to be able to make it on your own?" she asked. "Is there a friend or relative we can call to stay with you until you get your strength back?"

Matt waved away the offer. "I'll be fine. Thanks, though."

Sandra made no move to leave. "Why don't I fix some lunch for you? At least let me do that."

Over Matt's protest, Sandra made her way to the kitchen, where she found that Matt's cupboard was about as full as Old Mother Hubbard's. The refrigerator held a quart of milk that was out of date and a few bowls that served as petri dishes for the mold covering their contents. The food in the cabinet would have been sufficient had she wanted to feed Matt dried cereal full of weevils or a can of soup with saltines that had lost their crunch.

She tossed the cereal and crackers into the trash, poured the milk down the sink, and marched back to the living room. "I'm taking you out for lunch. Can you get dressed by yourself, or do you want some help?"

Matt's eyes widened. "I don't need any help, but I'm not sure I'm ready to go out into the world on my own." His hands strayed to his stubble-covered scalp, and he gently fingered the staples closing his incision. "And certainly not like this."

"Don't worry about your appearance. And you're not on your own," she countered. "I'm with you. We're a team. Now find some clothes and change."

After a few more halfhearted attempts to dissuade her, Matt gave in and headed for his bedroom. "And get some shoes that you can walk in," Sandra called after him. "It's time you got used to meeting the public, and I don't like you to shuffle." *It reminds me too much of the way a shackled prisoner shuffles. And that may be coming soon enough.*

NINE

Matt dipped a french fry into ketchup and bit off the end. Although Sandra wanted to take him someplace "nice" for lunch, he'd finally convinced her that a burger was more his speed. They were settled at a back table of a Dairy Queen, the remains of their lunch in front of them.

"I like your new look," Sandra said. Matt had decided that having only half his head shaved made him "look like a freak," as he put it. With her help, he'd used the clipper part of his electric shaver, and now his whole scalp was covered by black stubble. "Sort of a Jake Gyllenhaal effect."

"Now all I have to do is add one of those little beards on my chin to complete the look. More like a young Hector Elizondo." He rubbed his unshaven chin. "Anyway, it looks better than it did. I just hated to ask you to help."

"You're going to need help, so get used to it," Sandra said. She ticked off the points on her fingers. "You don't have transportation. You don't have your credit cards or driver's license. You don't have cash. You don't—"

"No need to remind me. I should have gotten some of this figured out while I was in the hospital, I guess, but I couldn't really get my head around it. It all seemed so unreal. Mainly, when I was awake, I just worried."

Sandra slurped the last drops of her chocolate shake and pushed the cup away. "So it's time to stop worrying and start getting your life back."

"What life?" Matt said. "The police think I'm a suspect in a murder case. My practice is gone, sold to another doctor. My academic position is on indefinite hold. The woman I thought I'd ride off into the sunset with won't talk to me. So I ask again, what life?" He drained his glass of Coke and crunched on a piece of ice. "But you don't want to hear this."

"No, what I want to hear you say is, 'I'm ready to rebuild my life.'"

"How do I go about that?"

"The same way you eat an elephant: one bite at a time. Get new credit cards. You can do that with a few phone calls. Get a replacement driver's license. Borrow a car, or rent one if you're able. Find a job." She crumpled her napkin and shoved it into her empty cup. "And stop feeling sorry for yourself."

Matt shook his head. "Why are you doing this? Taking me home was beyond the call of duty. Now you're treating me like a person, not a client." He spread his hands wide. "I had this mental image of lawyers as cold, calculating creatures that prey on society. But you're actually acting human. Why?"

Sandra didn't answer. She stood and pointed toward Matt's lunch in a "have you finished?" gesture.

Okay, don't answer me. But I'm going to find out. "Sure. Let's go. We might as well get started with the process of putting Matt Newman back together."

Matt thought about opening the curtains in his living room, but decided he didn't want to see the outside world or vice versa. Time to get to work. He settled at his desk, pulled a lined pad toward him, and started a list. As ideas came, he jotted them down, sometimes drawing arrows to move items up or down so they were in the order he'd tackle them. Soon he decided it was time to stop writing and start doing.

Money was first on his list. His wallet was gone, and with it his cards and cash. He could get new credit cards, but he'd need money in the meantime. Go to an ATM machine? Not until he'd replaced his debit card. Cash a check? He wasn't ready to face the world again. Not today, at least. Then he thought of the extra cash he had stashed away.

He started for the bedroom, his thoughts flying ahead of his steps. What if the money wasn't there? The police had searched his house. What if one of them put it in his pocket? Or decided it was evidence and slipped it into a plastic bag like he'd seen on *CSI*.

He opened his sock drawer. There it was, tucked into the corner in an old wallet, his emergency fund. Well, this certainly qualified. Even with the cash in it, the wallet was so flat that, once it was in his hip pocket, Matt reached for it twice to assure himself it was there. He'd feel better when new cards formed a reassuring bulge.

A few phone calls, and Matt was promised a new VISA and American Express card delivered to his home in a day or two. Next, he needed to replace his ATM card. He had a little cash now, so he could wait a bit for the card. He decided to apply online for the replacement.

Transportation came next. He could try to borrow a car, but first he had to get a new driver's license. That meant arranging a ride to the Department of Public Safety office tomorrow. He was about to move on to the next item on the list when it dawned on him: he'd need identification at the DPS office. He scrabbled through the middle drawer of the desk and pulled out his passport. Thank goodness the police hadn't asked him to surrender it . . . yet.

An important purchase crossed his mind, but that would have to wait until he had transportation and a little more money. He scribbled a note in the margin of his pad and circled it. He wouldn't forget that one.

He kept crossing things off his list until eventually he reached the one he'd put at the bottom because he dreaded facing it: *Get a job*. There was no hope of reclaiming his private practice. It was gone, the deal done a few weeks before that fateful trip to the emergency room. Matt told the doctor assuming his practice he'd cover that night for him. *If only . . . No, don't go there. It happened. Move on.*

There was no need to call Brad Franklin at the medical school again. That decision seemed pretty final, and Matt's head understood the logic behind it, although his heart rebelled at the action. What ever happened to innocent until proven guilty?

Maybe one of the surgeons in town needed someone to cover his office while he was gone on vacation, a *locum tenens*. That should be good for a week's income. Then Matt thought back to his own experience. When he was gone on vacation, he'd referred his patients to one of the other doctors with whom he'd shared call. And it hadn't cost him a cent. No, covering for another doctor and getting paid for it was out.

He put his head in his hands. Maybe he should have stayed in the hospital. He might have been able to get a job as an orderly. Or—

An idea struck him. He had been on the staff of Metropolitan Hospital for four years. In that time, he'd made a lot of contacts. Matt decided to call one of them and ask for his help. And he knew just the man to call—a guy who'd been his friend since they were in medical school.

If Matt hadn't tutored him in physiology, Rick would have flunked out his sophomore year. If Matt hadn't pulled a number of all-nighters with Rick, the man couldn't have squeaked through the junior medicine final, the wash-out exam for their med school class. If Matt hadn't introduced them, Rick would never have met his future wife. The years and their career choices might have made their paths cross less frequently, but Matt still considered Rick a friend. He hoped the feeling was mutual.

He reached for the phone and dialed a number he didn't have to look up.

"Emergency Room, this is Judy."

"Judy, this is Dr. Newman. Is Dr. Pearson available?"

"I think he just finished with a patient. Hang on."

Matt could hear snatches of conversation overlaid by the ringing of phones and the strident beep of pagers. Then, "Matt, is that you? Are you out of the hospital? How are you doing? I heard about what happened to you, and I was going to call. How can I help?"

Matt took a deep breath and plunged forward, filling in his old friend. "To top it all," he said, "my job at the medical school sort of fell through. I'm looking for work, Rick."

The silence on the other end of the line made Matt wonder if the connection had been broken. Then Rick said, "Do you have access to the hospital grapevine? I only got word yesterday."

"What word?"

"Hector Rivera, one of my ER docs, quit, and I need to fill his position." Rick paused, apparently considering the implications of what he was about to say. "You know, I'll probably catch some flak for this, but I've known you a long time. Just assure me you didn't murder Cara Mendiola."

"Of course I didn't. What has that got to do with my asking for a job?"

"Don't you think I might get a little heat if I hire you?" Rick cleared his throat. "Never mind, I'll handle it, even though people might think it's too much of a coincidence."

"I'm sorry. I'm not following you. What do you mean?"

"Hector Rivera was Cara Mendiola's fiancé. As soon as the police cleared him, he left to take her body back to her family in Mexico. He's not coming back, and I'm about to hire you to take his place."

"Come on, Charlie. You don't want to come out of this with egg on your face." Sandra Murray swiveled away from her desk and dangled one Enzo Angiolini pump off her toes. "You have nothing to contradict my client's story."

"Sandra, Sandra. I know you're doing what you have to. After all, everyone is entitled to the best possible defense, but come on. That story about being kidnapped, then falling off a stack of crates or something?" Charlie Greaver lowered his voice to a conspiratorial whisper. "You don't really believe that, do you?"

"The question isn't whether I believe it. The question is whether a jury will. And if even one of them believes it, your case goes out the window." Sandra let her shoe slide to the floor, then heeled off the other one. She wiggled her toes. "Don't embarrass yourself and Jack by taking this case to a grand jury."

"Jack and I agree that's exactly where the case should go. And as soon as Frank gets his ducks in a row, that's where it's going."

Interesting. The DA and assistant DA are giving the case to Frank Everett. Nice to know. "Well, you think about it, Charlie, and if you or Jack have second thoughts, give me a call."

Sandra hung up and spun back to her desk, where she made a couple of notes. Everyone at the courthouse knew that Jack Tanner was going to retire soon, and Charlie Greaver wanted to succeed him as district attorney. If she could play on Charlie's need to have a clean record when he ran, she might get Matt off. *Murder trials that end in acquittal are bad PR for a potential DA.* She tapped her pen against her front teeth, then leaned forward and scribbled another note.

Then there was Frank Everett. Frank thought he was an up-and-comer, even though he'd been with the DA's office long enough to know better. She'd gone up against him six times in court—or was it seven? In any event, she'd won every case. If Matt did come to trial, it was nice to know Frank would be prosecuting. But her job right now was to keep that from ever happening.

A dead woman turning up in the trunk of Matt's car, lying on top of his wallet, was pretty compelling evidence against her client. Sandra would need to be at her best to counter that. She already knew the spin she was going to put on the evidence. Matt wasn't a murderer, he was a victim. And there was Matt's story of the kidnapping. Even if the police didn't believe it, she could think of a number of ways it could help her client at trial. What was it she'd said to Matt at their first meeting? *"You're going to need a very good lawyer. Fortunately, you contacted one."* Well, she was a very good lawyer. Now it was time to prove it.

Jennifer Ball sensed, rather than saw, someone approach her desk. She followed the rule formulated long ago by workers in any office: keep your head down, look busy, and maybe they'll leave you alone. She typed faster, her fingers flying, the words hardly registering in her brain. So much of what she did was boilerplate. Use this form. Put this name in at that point. Add the date. Print five copies . . . or six . . . or twelve. Move on to the next one.

"Got a minute?"

She started to swivel her chair, expecting to see Frank Everett standing behind her, her mind already flipping the pages of her mental calendar and finding nothing that couldn't be moved if he wanted some of her time. Frank seemed to be getting serious, and she'd decided that was a good thing. If her past relationship with Matt came out, maybe Frank could protect her from any fallout. At least, she hoped so.

"Sure," she said, barely stopping her tongue from adding, "Frank." It wasn't Frank's voice. Instead, the man standing behind her was Jack Tanner, the DA himself. Jennifer wasn't worried because the boss was at her desk. She'd done lots of work for him, work that was considered so confidential he'd only trust it to either her or one other secretary. It was simply that now the appearance of any authority figure at her desk was enough to make her nervous, afraid her relationship with Matt might come out.

Jennifer summoned up her most innocent smile. "What can I do for you?"

"It's about the Matt Newman case," Tanner said. He was an imposing figure, tall and thin, his full head of silver hair combed straight back. Although most of the men in the office left their coats hanging on the backs of their chairs, Tanner always donned his when he ventured out of his office. Today the suit was a charcoal pinstripe. His blue dress shirt had a white collar, and the knot in his lavender tie was perfect, as always.

"Uh, yes, sir. I know a little." Should she mention hearing about it from Frank? She decided to let it go for now.

"As you may know, Dr. Newman was in private practice, working out of Metropolitan Hospital here in Dallas. His story, which seems sort of thin, is that he was kidnapped from the parking garage there." Tanner shook his head. "Anyway, the police are looking into it, but I have some ideas of my own. I suggested we question some of the doctors who work at that hospital. How well liked was Newman? Did they ever see him with Cara Mendiola, the woman who was killed? And I recall that you used to go out with a doctor who worked at Metropolitan. I'd like to start with him. Thought he might open up a bit, talking about a colleague, if you called him first."

Jennifer could almost feel her synapses clicking as she struggled to find the right answer. "Did someone tell you it was Metropolitan? Oh no. It was Medical City Hospital. That's a whole different part of the city."

"Oh? My family doctor uses Medical City. What's your doctor friend's name?"

Think. Think. She'd seen a name on the board in the professional building when she'd visited her own doctor, a gynecologist. Merchant? Murch? Murchison. That was it. "It was Dr. Murchison, but we broke up, and he was pretty angry about it. I'd rather you didn't bring it up. Your investigator might say something to him and get the phone calls started again."

Tanner frowned. "You know, if he's making harassing calls to you, we can do something about that."

"No, sir. They've stopped. But I'd really appreciate it if you didn't do anything that might stir it up again." *Please, please, please. Let it go.*

"Sure. But if there's any trouble in the future—"

"I'll let you know. And thank you."

Tanner drifted away, and Jennifer felt the pounding in her chest slow. She lifted a half-filled bottle of water from her desktop and drained it in two thirsty swallows, but her throat still felt like a desert.

She couldn't have her name connected with Matt. She wondered how long this would go on. Jennifer turned back to her computer and began taking out her frustration on the keyboard.

"Thanks for the ride. I appreciate it." Matt closed the car door, waved, and headed up the sidewalk to his front door.

It had taken over a dozen phone calls for him to find someone able and willing to take him to the Department of Public Safety office, but now he had a temporary Texas driver's license in his wallet.

Next he had to get a car. Apparently reclaiming his car from the impound lot was impossible, at least until the matter of his innocence of Cara Mendiola's death was established, and maybe not even then. Sandra had made a couple of phone calls, then told him his car was going to remain in custody for a while. He hated to think of the impound bill that was growing day by day. But that was a problem to be dealt with later—maybe even passed on to the company from which Matt was leasing the car. He'd have to ask Sandra.

During his marathon spate of phone calls, he'd broached the subject of borrowing a car several times, but without success. Apparently none of his friends had one to spare, or at least not one they could turn over to a murder suspect. Matt sat at his desk and looked at his list. There were three names below the one who'd finally offered the ride, a doctor with whom he'd gone to medical school. Either Jeff hadn't heard about Matt's trouble, or felt comfortable being alone in a car with a man whose next address might be death row. But it had stopped there. Jeff's wife needed their second car, and Matt got the impression that she didn't even know about Jeff giving Matt this ride.

Three more phone calls, and Matt had officially reached the bottom of the barrel. His replacement credit cards had arrived, and now was the time to put one of them to use. He'd have to try to find a rental car he could afford. At one time, he would have let his fingers do the walking through the yellow pages for the information. Now they could crawl across the keyboard to get the same results. Almost an hour later, he'd discovered that the ads hawking "rental cars for as little as $7.00 a day" were classic bait and switch. The cheapest rental car he could find would run him about a hundred and fifty per week. In the days when he had a steady income, that would have been a bargain. Now, when his income stream was down to a trickle, he wasn't sure.

He'd said he'd take the job in Metropolitan Hospital's ER, but Rick was called away before they could discuss salary. Of course, anything was better than what he had coming in now, which was essentially nothing. In any case, Matt decided he really needed more details.

His call was answered on the second ring. "Emergency Room, this is Pam."

"Pam, this is Dr. Newman." Matt held his breath, but there was no comment forthcoming. So far he'd talked to two ER nurses and detected no censure in their voices. Either they hadn't heard the news, or they elected not to say anything about Matt's situation. *Good in either case.* "Is Dr. Pearson available?"

"Hold on a sec." The clunk when the phone hit the desk almost deafened Matt. "Sorry, I dropped it." This time there was no sound. Pam must have been extra careful.

In a few seconds, Matt heard, "Dr. Pearson."

"Rick, this is Matt."

"Oh, yeah. I meant to get back to you, but it's been a madhouse here. Guess you'll experience that for yourself soon enough, though."

"I can hardly wait." Matt figured anything would be better than sitting at home waiting for the police to knock on his door. "Listen, the police impounded my car as evidence, so I'm trying to find something to drive. You don't happen to know anyone with an extra car sitting around, do you?"

"You know, this is really weird. Hector Rivera left me the keys to his car and told me to sell it for him. Said he'd write to tell me where I could wire the money. It's a Chevy. Low mileage. Pretty decent condition. And he was willing to finance it himself. Maybe we can work something out."

Matt and Rick talked a bit more until the conversation ended much as the previous one had, with Rick saying, "Sorry. Gotta go. I'll call you when this shift ends."

Matt's acquaintance with Hector Rivera had been superficial at best: nods in the hall, an occasional "hello" when they saw each other in the ER. Matt wished he knew more about this man whose job he was taking, whose car he was driving . . . and whose fiancé he was accused of murdering. Right now, it was sort of like wearing a suit belonging to a dead man.

It just didn't feel right.

TEN

After an internal debate that lasted much longer than it should, Matt moved to his desk and picked up the phone. He knew it was probably hopeless, but he had to try one more time. If Jennifer would just listen to his story, maybe he could convince her that this was all a big mistake. Surely his lawyer would get it straightened out quickly.

He'd already tried Jennifer's home number and cell phone. When the calls rolled over to voicemail, he'd left the same message: *"Jennifer, we need to talk. It's important. Please call me."* She hadn't responded, though.

All that remained was calling her at work. She'd told him never to do it, but he felt as though he had no choice. He had half the number dialed when he had a thought. If he dialed her direct line, caller ID would betray him. He hung up and found the main number for the district attorney's office. A woman answered on the second ring, and he asked for Jennifer Ball.

"Who may I say is calling?"

Matt hadn't thought this far ahead. He wasn't very good at improvising, and lying had never been a part of him until now. He took a deep breath and plunged in. "This is her brother. She gave me her direct number, but I've lost it. I'm only in town for a—" He stopped when he realized there was ringing on the line. Either his story had worked or the receptionist hadn't really cared.

Jennifer answered on the second ring. "Felony Trial Division, Jennifer Ball."

"Don't hang up!" Matt hoped the desperation in his voice would keep Jennifer on the line.

"I told you not to call me, especially not at work."

"Jennifer, you've got to listen. I'm innocent. This is all a mistake."

In the silence that followed, Matt could almost see Jennifer thinking, her finger rubbing her chin, her brow furrowed. He'd seen that gesture so many times. It was one of the things he loved about her—or, at least, thought he loved. Now he wasn't so sure.

When Jennifer spoke again, the soft voice had hardened. "Matt, I'm sorry this happened to you. I wish I could help. But if you keep calling, you could get me in trouble . . . big trouble." Was there a catch in her voice? "Good-bye." The last words were almost too faint to understand.

Matt sat for a moment, holding the dead phone, until the strident stutter tone startled him from his reverie. He hung up in the middle of the recorded voice telling him, "If you want to make a call . . ."

He'd never felt so alone in his life. There was one person who might help him think this through—one person who he knew would support him. Although Matt had put it off until now, he really needed to get in touch with Joe, even though his brother was in a remote area of South America. In the past, Joe had always initiated contact when he was within reach of a fellow missionary's satellite phone or if his travels took him to a city large enough to provide a phone or an Internet connection. Matt had an email address for Joe, but there was no telling when the message would get to his brother.

Matt dug through his desk drawer until he came to a set of papers clipped together. They gave Joe's location, which meant nothing to Matt, whose knowledge of geography outside the US was rudimentary at best. Toward the very bottom of the second sheet was a notation that, in case of emergency, Matt could call this number. They'd get in touch with Joe and have him contact Matt.

Matt put the paper aside. He'd make the call in a minute, but right now, he needed some sense of contact, some way for Joe to affirm him. Then he recalled his last email exchange with his brother, a message he'd sent while things still looked good: Matt's relationship with Jennifer, the job at the medical school. Matt opened his email folder labeled "family," found Joe's reply to his message, and read it again.

Little Brother, so glad things are going well. Just remember that bad times will follow good, just as good times will follow bad. The only constant in the world is God. He's in control. Set your sights on Him, and you'll make it fine. Matthew 6:34.

Matt clicked on the utility he sometimes used to call up Bible verses, and read the Scripture Joe had cited. *"So do not worry about tomorrow; for tomorrow will care for itself. Each day has enough trouble of its own."* Matt had to agree. Each of his days recently had presented plenty of trouble. He could only hope there'd be less tomorrow.

He picked up the phone and dialed the number of the Mission Board.

The ring of his phone brought Matt instantly awake, a reaction honed by long experience with being roused by a pager, a phone, or an alarm set for an early case. Surely Joe wasn't calling back this quickly. He eased forward in his recliner, muted the TV, lifted the receiver, and said, "Dr. Newman."

"Matt, did I wake you?"

Matt searched his memory to identify the voice. Then it clicked. Ken Gordon, his neurosurgeon. "I guess I went to sleep in front of the TV." He glanced at his watch—almost eight. "What's up? And why are you still at work?"

"The second question's pretty silly for a doctor to ask. I've just finished my last case of the day," Gordon said. "As for the first, your chart was on my desk when I got back to my office, and that reminded me to check on you. It seems you got away from the hospital without a follow-up appointment."

"I'm afraid I wasn't functioning too well right then. I still had visions of a squad of armed policemen meeting me at the hospital entrance and carting me off to jail."

Gordon laughed. "Well, since you're obviously a free man, let's get you back here. I'll bet you're ready to get those staples out."

Matt stopped with his hand halfway to his head. *Don't rub the incision, don't mess with the staples.* "That would be great. Just say when."

"They've been in for . . . Let's see." Matt could picture Gordon checking his calendar. "Looks like a week, yesterday."

Matt had been counting as well. Surgeons often left staples in place for two weeks to allow for full healing, but the scalp had a rich blood supply and generally healed rapidly, so in that area stitches and staples could come out in ten days, sometimes as little as seven. Maybe Gordon would go for it. "How about tomorrow? Nine days should be long enough. The wound is healed. And I'll be careful—"

"Easy, there. I know you're anxious to get back to your activities, but even after the staples are out, I don't want you doing too much for a few more days. And you shouldn't drive for at least another week."

The argument—well, more like negotiations—went on for another five minutes before Gordon gave in. He would see Matt tomorrow and remove the staples, but his patient had to promise he'd take things easy for another week. Matt carefully avoided further discussion of any restriction on his driving. He'd had no suggestion of a seizure after his injury, and he didn't intend to sit at home for another week. He'd go crazy. It was time to get his life back together. Sandra's words rang in his head. *"What I want to hear you say is, 'I'm ready to rebuild my life.'"*

He was more than ready.

Edgar was playing solitaire, cheating most of the time, when Lou called.

"Be outside your apartment in ten minutes. The big man wants to see us."

"Why?"

Lou's voice got rougher, if that was possible. "I didn't ask him. And if you're smart, you won't either. He says, 'Jump.' We say, 'How high?' Be there in ten."

Edgar raked the cards into a rough stack and shoved them aside. He rose from the card table that did double duty as his lunch counter and the surface where he watched porn on his battered laptop, using a Wi-Fi connection pirated from his neighbor. He stubbed out his cigarette in an empty tuna can that served as an ashtray.

The boss wanted Lou and him. He knew what that meant. Edgar opened the drawer of his bedside table and studied the two pistols there. Both were .38 caliber, which made it convenient when buying ammunition. Both were relatively anonymous, their serial numbers erased with acid. They were belly guns with short barrels, but both packed enough punch to put someone down from close range. And if he had to ditch one, it would be easy enough to replace.

For shooting the woman, he'd used the Smith & Wesson Airweight. Today he'd carry the Chief's Special. Edgar clipped the holster to his belt behind his right hip and covered it with a denim shirt worn unbuttoned over an almost-clean tee.

What else? He patted his pockets. Cigarettes and matches, keys, wallet. He opened the chest of drawers and rummaged beneath his underwear until he found a leather-covered blackjack. He hefted it and slapped it against his palm, feeling the satisfying weight of the lead shot sewn into the end. Edgar shoved the sap into his hip pocket, made sure it was hidden by his shirttail, and headed for the door.

Twenty minutes later, he and Lou walked into the boss's inner office. The big man didn't acknowledge their presence for a moment, busying himself with a stack of important-looking papers on his desk. Finally he looked up.

"When were you planning to take out the doctor?"

Edgar kept his mouth shut. He'd let Lou do the talking. Edgar was content to stay in the background, ready to maim or kill when called upon. He smiled when he thought of what lay ahead. He didn't know the details yet, but he was sure it would be satisfying.

"Tonight," Lou said. "We'll go in about two in the morning. Take him out, make it look like a suicide, the way you said."

The boss was shaking his head before Lou could finish. "Put that aside for a day or two. I need you to convince one of our people to be more cooperative."

Edgar paid little attention to the details, allowing his thoughts to float free. Once he heard the word "convince," he knew his special talents would be put to use. "When" and "where" would be up to the boss and Lou. The "what" and "how" were his.

Matt stood in front of his bathroom mirror and ran his hand over the stubble on his scalp. The staples were out. The incision lines were still pink, but they'd soften and fade and eventually be covered by hair. For now maybe he'd opt for a cap. He had a number of baseball caps in his closet, and this might be the time to make use of them. Then again, the shaved and semi-shaved head look seemed to be popular right now. He was still experimenting with one of those around-the-mouth beards to complement his new look.

Matt made his way to the mailbox and silently rejoiced when he saw the first-class envelope with his bank's return address on it. With his new debit card, Matt could tap the small reserve in his checking account to replenish the cash in his pocket.

The other pleasant surprise of the day was an express delivery of a box with his replacement cell phone. That, at least, had been something he was able to handle over the phone. He inserted the battery in the new phone and put it on the charger—one more step toward getting his life back together.

Back at his desk, Matt pulled his to-do list toward him and was about to make another call when the phone rang. The caller ID showed Southwestern Medical Center. What now?

"Dr. Newman."

"This is Hank Truong. I know you said you'd call me, but I wanted to give you this information before I forgot."

"Sorry I haven't gotten back to you, Hank," Matt said. "I've been sort of busy. What do you have?"

"I checked out that patient I saw with the lacerated leg, and you were right. He used a false ID. The address he gave was a vacant lot in east Dallas, and his insurance information was somebody else's. So I don't know how we might track him down."

Matt hadn't really thought the kidnapper would have been stupid enough to give his real name and address, but it was worth a try. "Thanks anyway, Hank."

"I hope you get better soon. Be sure to let me know if there's anything I can do here."

He guessed it would have been too simple to be able to direct the police to one of the kidnappers. But a patient with wounds matching those of one of his assailants should be some sort of evidence that he didn't just dream up the whole episode. *Oh well.*

Matt still needed transportation, and that meant Hector Rivera's car. After he got it from Rick, assuming he ignored the standard warnings against driving this soon after a head injury, Matt would be mobile again. *At least until the DA . . .* No, he wasn't going to think about that. He had a lawyer, a good one, and he had to trust her. He'd do his job, and hope she did hers.

Matt called the ER but was told that Dr. Pearson wasn't working today. Would Dr. Newman like to leave a message? No, Dr. Newman wanted—make that, *needed* to talk with Rick Pearson today, not tomorrow when he returned to duty. He hung up and was checking Rick's home number in his address book when the doorbell rang.

He wasn't expecting anyone. Maybe his attackers had decided to take the simple approach: ring the bell, shoot him when he opened the door, make a quick escape. He'd even heard of homeowners being shot when they put their eye to the peephole in the door. *Better do it this way.* Matt tiptoed to a window that gave a partial view of the front porch, pulled aside the curtain, and looked out. His whole body relaxed when he saw Rick Pearson standing there whistling.

Matt opened the door. "Rick, come in. I was about to call you."

"I brought you a present," Rick said, and pointed over his shoulder at the gray Chevrolet parked at the curb. "A Malibu, low mileage. Blue book value is something over three thousand dollars, but Hector said he'd take two." He moved inside and headed for the living room.

Matt followed him and pointed toward the room's only comfortable chair. "I could pay five hundred now, maybe spread the rest out over ten or twelve months, if you think Hector would take that." He took a seat at the desk and rummaged for his checkbook. If he ever got his own car back, he could sell this one. In the meantime he had to have transportation.

"Between the two of us, Hector will take whatever I send him." Rick pulled two pieces of paper from his hip pocket. He put the first on the end table beside him. "Here's a note showing you paid two hundred dollars down and will pay the rest monthly over the next year. I only need your signature and a check." He laid the second paper beside it. "And here's the title. Hector signed it before he left. Don't forget to transfer it."

"Rick, are you sure—"

"Listen, Hector was anxious to leave; you need a car. It's win-win." Rick leaned back and crossed his legs. He pointed at the papers on the table. "When you've finished that, I'm going to buy your lunch, then you can drop me at my place. On the way we'll talk about your new job."

Matt found his pen on the floor where he'd dropped it when the doorbell rang. He opened his checkbook and ignored the balance as he wrote the check for the car. One problem solved. Only one, but Matt was willing to take small victories when they came. He had a hunch there were more fights ahead. Lots more. What did that verse say? Something about not worrying about tomorrow, because there will be enough troubles today. *One day at a time.*

The bartender looked up as the door opened. Edgar stood for a moment, letting his eyes adjust. Outside, it was bright and hot and smelled like exhaust. Inside, the bar was dim and cool and smelled of stale beer and staler cigarette smoke. Outside, the noise of traffic was loud. Here the sound came from the jukebox sending forth the nasal tones of Willie Nelson.

Edgar took a stool at the near end of the bar, leaving as much space as possible between him and the other two patrons. Both were bent over their beers, not talking with each other, only occasionally glancing up at the TV set above them.

"Draft beer, whiskey chaser," Edgar said.

The bartender was moving before Edgar finished speaking. He topped off a mug with just the proper amount of foam, poured a generous jigger of cheap whiskey, and put them both on coasters in front of Edgar.

"Run a tab, will you?" Edgar said.

"Can't do that," the bartender replied. "Owner says you owe too much already." He covered the mug in front of Edgar with one hand, the whiskey with the other. "If you can't pay, I gotta take these back."

Edgar reached into his pants pocket and peeled off two bills from a thick roll. "This should take care of it."

The bartender nodded as though hundred-dollar bills passed through his hands all the time. He reached behind the cash register and extracted a slip of paper from a bundle nestled there. It took him a minute to tally up Edgar's tab, but in a moment he opened the cash register, put the two bills inside, and pulled out several others. He slapped them on the bar and said, "We'll play pay as you go until that runs out."

By this time Edgar had tossed back his whiskey and almost finished his beer. He slammed down the mug and said, "Hit me again."

The exchange had caught the attention of the two men at the other end of the bar. "When did you get so rich, Edgar?" one said.

Edgar turned to the questioner. "I do important work for a big man, and he pays me real good." He stopped talking long enough to gulp the second whiskey and down half the next beer. "One more time," he said.

"What big man is that?" the other guy asked.

"You wouldn't know him. He keeps to himself, but he's important, trust me." Edgar smiled. "A really big man."

"What do you do exactly, Edgar?" the first man asked.

Edgar laughed. "I hurt people when they need it. Sometimes I even make them disappear."

The two men shrugged and turned their attention back to the TV. The bartender busied himself cutting lemons. And Edgar continued to drink, silently now. After one more round, he scooped up his change and ambled out without leaving a tip.

The bartender pulled the phone from beneath the bar and tapped out a number. "Lester, this is Solly. Edgar, the little guy who works for Mr. Grande, was just here shooting off his mouth."

He listened for a minute. "Yeah, a little too much. I thought you might want to let Mr. Grande know."

"I appreciate this." Matt scanned the area. No one appeared interested in him or the man sitting beside him outside the zoo's monkey house.

His companion was a short man whose clothes declared, "Salvation Army thrift store." His lifeless brown hair was a week overdue for cutting. When he spoke, his eyes darted everywhere while his lips hardly moved.

Matt pulled a stack of bills, fresh from the ATM machine, out of his pocket and slid them into the man's hand.

"Here you go, Doc." The man handed Matt a brown paper sack as casually as a mother delivering lunch to her fifth grader. "If you hadn't patched me up that time, I wouldn't be here. Glad to do you a favor."

Matt watched the man sidle away. He hated to do this, and not just because the very act put him on the wrong side of the law. But desperate times called for desperate measures, as someone once said. Was it Shakespeare? Or the Bible? He should have read more of both. Then maybe he'd know the answer to that question—actually, to a lot of questions.

His reverie was cut short by a yelling group of preteens, apparently on a field trip to the zoo, herded by teachers en masse to see the primates housed to Matt's left. As they hurried along, one boy said to the friend beside him, "Have you seen the new gorilla? He's huge! I guess he's behind some pretty strong bars."

If Matt had any thought of seeing the exhibit, the boy's words quashed it. *I'm not sure I want to see anything behind bars.* He hefted the sack, which was heavier than he'd expected, and headed for the zoo exit and the parking lot. He had lots to do. *"And miles to go before I sleep."* Another quotation, the source of which eluded him. He thought about that all the way to Hector's Chevy. As he started the engine, Matt promised himself he'd do more reading in the future. He hoped it wouldn't be books taken from the prison library.

Sandra Murray barely noticed the images flickering on the TV in front of her. The sound was low, and she couldn't even remember the name of the program or why she'd tuned in to it. Since she and Ken broke up, her social life was pretty much confined to this: throw some sort of dinner together from the contents of her refrigerator and eat it in front of the TV while reading articles and opinions from a law journal.

The ring of her cell phone roused her. She reached into the pocket of her jeans for it, noticing that her journals had slid to the floor. Try as she might, she couldn't recall what she'd been reading. That was it. No more reading in front of the TV. It was more effective than Sominex in inducing sleep.

Sandra punched the remote to still the set and checked the caller ID on her phone. Ken Gordon's cell. Her mind raced through the possibilities. Had some complication forced Matt back to the hospital, maybe even requiring an emergency re-operation? She wasn't a doctor, but she knew enough about head injuries and bleeding to know that re-bleeds were possible. Was Ken calling her because he knew she was representing Matt? Did she need to— *Oh, get over it. Answer and find out.*

"Ken, what's up?"

"I hope I didn't call at a bad time." Ken's voice was calm, but that didn't mean anything. She'd discovered that the neurosurgeon took everything in stride. Maybe it was a product of dealing daily with life-and-death situations.

"No, no. Just reading some law journals." Her next words tumbled out as uncontrollably as water roaring over rapids after a heavy rain. "Is something wrong with Matt?"

There was a moment of silence while Sandra's heart thundered in her chest. Then Ken replied, "No, not that I know of. And I wonder why that was the first thing you thought of when I called."

Think fast. "I was reading some cases that might apply to his, and

I guess I automatically made the leap." Sandra reached for the bottle of water on the TV tray in front of her, brought it to her lips, and had a healthy swallow. She cleared her throat. "What's up?"

"I've been thinking about us," Ken said. "Maybe we didn't give it enough of a chance. Would you like to have dinner with me sometime and talk about it?"

Sandra's initial inclination was to accept the invitation. After all, she and Ken had parted as friends, and maybe they'd been hasty in their breakup. They'd seemed so right for each other, at least at first. But before she could get the response out, something made her stop— the memory of the first incident that planted a seed of doubt in her mind. Over the next few weeks, the seed had bloomed into full-blown conviction that she and Ken weren't a match.

"I . . . I'm not sure that's a good idea," she said.

"I know why you said that, and I won't try to change your mind right now," Ken said, "but I seem to remember that one of the tenets of that faith you talk about is forgiveness. And that's what I'm asking you to do. Let's put our differences aside and move forward."

The conversation continued for a few more minutes, but it was obvious both of them were uncomfortable thinking back to what had separated them. After she'd ended the call, Sandra closed her eyes and let the film from that episode play out behind her eyelids.

She'd given Ken a copy of a novel she'd enjoyed, thinking since it was medical fiction, he might like it. A couple of weeks passed, and finally she asked him if he'd read it.

"Frankly, I quit about a third of the way in," Ken admitted.

"Didn't like the writing?"

"No, it was well written. I couldn't even find fault with the medical details. But what turned me off was the way the doctor in it always came back to his Christian beliefs. I mean, everything was falling apart for him, but he still prayed and believed God was going to make it come out all right."

Sandra felt a vague uneasiness, but she could no more let the conversation die than she could keep her tongue out of a fresh cavity in a tooth. "And if you'd kept reading, you'd have seen why he felt that way."

"Sorry, but religion has never been a part of my life. Matter of fact, I'm sort of uncomfortable around folks who keep bringing it into the conversation."

"Like me?"

"No, no. I just hate people who are always preaching to me about my relationship with God."

"So you don't believe in God?" Sandra asked.

Ken paused and seemed to gather his thoughts. "I believe in science, in what I can see, what I can prove. I'm not much for that faith stuff."

"And when you operate on a brain, you don't marvel at how a Creator could make such a marvelous operating system for the human body?"

"I don't think much about how we got here. I'm more interested in what I do with what I've been given."

The conversation continued for a while before Ken rather clumsily redirected it to a safer subject. But the warning bells were already going off in Sandra's brain. And a verse kept running through her head, one she'd learned in Sunday school. She hadn't thought much about it at the time, but memorizing it had gotten her brownie points with the teacher. Now she understood it better, or at least she thought she did. *Do not be bound together with unbelievers.* And that's where she appeared to be headed if she didn't steer clear of Ken Gordon.

Sandra placed Elaine's coffee on the center of her desk in their usual morning ritual. "Ken Gordon called me last night."

The secretary looked up sharply. The sudden move made her half-glasses fall off the end of her nose and left them dangling at the end of their chain. "I thought you two weren't seeing each other anymore." She removed the plastic cover and sipped her hot coffee.

Sandra shrugged. "We're not. At first, since Ken's the neurosurgeon who took care of his injury, I thought he was calling to tell me something had happened to Matt . . . to Dr. Newman."

"But I'll bet that wasn't his reason. Am I right?"

"As always. No, he wanted us to have dinner—maybe talk about getting back together."

"And I'm guessing you told him no?"

Sandra bought herself some time by blowing across the surface of her cup. "Right. At one time, I thought I could get past Ken's unbelief, but now I don't think it would work."

Elaine looked up and smiled. "Have you ever considered that maybe God wants to touch Dr. Gordon through you?"

Sandra wasn't sure she had an answer for that. Was she hesitant to try getting back together with Ken because she was developing feelings for Matt? She thought about that for a minute. Then she took a swallow of coffee and turned away. "I'll be in my office if you need me."

As they had several nights before, Lou and Edgar sat in Lou's car, parked about half a block from Matt Newman's house. At midnight, when they'd arrived, one light showed in an upstairs window. In a few minutes, the light went out, leaving the home in darkness. Lou looked at his watch. "We'll give him some time to get to sleep before we go in."

Lou patted the pockets of his black jacket, making sure he had what he needed. His Beretta was tucked into the waistband of his pants, but he didn't plan on using it. If force was necessary, he'd depend on Edgar and the lead-weighted sap he always carried on forays like this. A tap from that on the back of the good doctor's head would put him to sleep faster than the chloroform Lou planned to use. But if they could do this without leaving any evidence of trauma, it would help the police buy the suicide-by-slitting-his-wrists scenario.

Edgar had his cigarettes out and a match in his hand when Lou stopped him. "Put that away. In the dark, this car looks empty. Strike a match, and you might as well light a Roman candle and yell, 'Look at me.'"

Edgar shrugged, but complied. "How much longer?"

Lou consulted his watch. "Give it another half hour."

Finally it was time. Lou checked to make sure the bulb was still gone from the car's interior light. He took the keys from the ignition and placed them behind the sun visor. If they had to leave in a hurry, he didn't want to have to hunt for them.

Both men opened their doors and closed them without engaging the latches. They proceeded on rubber-sole-shod feet across the street, through the shadows, to the rear of Matt's house. Lou extracted thin latex gloves from his pocket and passed a pair to Edgar before pulling on his own. They weren't going to leave any trace of their presence.

Lou eased a can of WD-40 from his hip pocket and sprayed it freely along the edge of the door where the hinges would be. He returned the can to his pocket and exchanged a glance and nod with Edgar. *Showtime.* He produced a key from his jacket, and the lock yielded silently. Once inside he stood in the darkness for a full minute, listening. The only sounds he heard were the hum of the refrigerator and the muted *whoosh* of air moving through the vents.

Lou knew the location of Matt's bedroom from his previous reconnaissance. He nodded toward the stairs, and he and Edgar mounted them single file. At the top they turned left toward an open door. A sliver of light from a distant streetlamp came through the window, casting shadows across Matt's bedroom. Lou reached into the side pocket of his black cargo pants and unscrewed the top of a plastic bottle. He doused a cheesecloth pad and was almost sickened by the sweet smell of the anesthetic. He took a tentative step toward the figure on the bed. A board creaked and Lou froze, holding his breath. Before he could stop him, Edgar moved up beside Lou, producing an even louder creak.

In a single motion, the man in the bed threw the covers aside, grabbed something from the bedside table, and pointed it at the two intruders. "Stop right there. Put your hands up or I'll shoot."

It took only a split second for Lou to take in the situation and react. *When someone already has the drop on you, don't go for your gun. Beat it.* And that's what he did. He dropped what he was holding and made for the door at full speed, almost trampling Edgar, who was a step ahead of him. The unmistakable sound of a shot quickened his feet and the adrenaline dumped into his veins accelerated his heart rate. Both men took the stairs in three quick bounds and bolted out the front door, leaving it wide open in their wake.

Lou had the car moving before Edgar had both feet inside.

ELEVEN

Elaine wasn't at her desk to receive her morning coffee in person, but Sandra didn't think much about it. In her office, she flipped the lid off her own paper cup, shed her shoes, and settled into her swivel chair. She picked up the pile of pink message slips centered on her blotter, but before Sandra could read the first one, her secretary appeared in the doorway. "The top message in the stack is from Matt Newman. Call him right away."

Sandra frowned. Could the police or the DA have contacted her client? She didn't think there'd be any movement from them for a few days. And why was Matt calling her office? Her home phone was unlisted, but she always gave her clients her cell phone number. Why didn't he—? Sandra pulled her phone from her purse, pushed a button, and felt her heart sink when the screen remained dark. She'd neglected to charge the battery last night.

She lifted the phone from her desk, punched in the number, and waited through four rings. Anxiety progressed to apprehension as she pictured Matt being hauled off to jail in the middle of the night, unable to contact her. During the fifth ring, he picked up. "Hello?"

When she heard his voice, Sandra exhaled, then took in what seemed like half the air in the room. "Matt. Sandra Murray. Elaine said your call was urgent. What—"

"I tried to call you when this happened, but you didn't answer. Don't you—"

"Let's not spend the next five minutes on recriminations. I let my cell phone battery die. I'm sorry. Now, what's going on?"

She heard Matt's deep inhalation, a mirror of the breath she'd just taken. "Someone broke into my house during the night and tried to kill me."

Sandra stood and began pacing back and forth behind her desk, tethered by the phone cord. "Are you okay?"

"I'm fine."

"You say they broke in. Did they break the lock, or what?"

"No, they must have had a key."

Sandra found herself going into take-charge mode. "Your keys are in the police evidence room. No telling who has access to them. Call a locksmith as soon as we hang up. I want those locks changed before you leave the house again."

"I can't afford—"

"You can't afford not to do it," Sandra said. "Now tell me the rest of the story."

"They got into the house and were in my bedroom when I scared them off. But this proves I wasn't lying. I really was kidnapped. Someone did try to kill me. And they tried again last night. Now maybe the police will believe me. I'm the victim here."

Sandra leaned forward and pulled a legal pad toward her. "Did you call the police when this happened?"

When he answered, Matt's voice was quieter, more measured. "No. I started to, but then I realized it might cause me some trouble. That's when I tried to call you."

"I sense there's something you haven't told me yet. What is it?"

"I said I scared them off. I didn't tell you how." There was a long pause. "I shot at one of them."

"I didn't know you had a gun," Sandra said.

"Uh, well, that may be part of the problem."

Sandra dropped into her chair, slipped her feet into shoes, and grabbed her purse from the desk drawer. "Stay there. I'm on my way." She started to hang up, but said into the phone before it hit the cradle, "Call a locksmith! And put on some coffee!"

Sandra put her mug on the side table and pulled a legal pad from the briefcase that sat on the floor beside her in Matt's living room. She rummaged in the case for another moment, extracted a ballpoint pen, and said, "Let's hear it. Remember, you're my client. Everything you tell me is protected by privilege."

Matt put his own mug to his lips, found it empty, and set it aside. "I think it would be easier to show you. My bedroom's upstairs." He hesitated. "Honest, this isn't a ploy to—"

"I didn't think it was. Let's go."

Once they were in the bedroom, Matt left Sandra in the doorway while he stood beside his double bed. He looked down at the rumpled covers and started to apologize for the mess, but thought better of it. *Just get on with it, Matt.* "I've been waking up two or three times a night, usually with a nightmare. Last night, I came awake about two a.m. and sensed someone in the room with me. A board creaked. When I opened my eyes, I could see two figures in the shadows over there." He pointed. "I grabbed my pistol from the bedside table—"

"Whoa!" Sandra held her hand up, palm out. "There's that gun again. What gun? The police searched your house, and their reports didn't mention any pistol."

"I know. I was worried that something like this would happen, so I . . . I contacted a former patient, somebody with what you might call connections on the shady side. I bought a revolver."

Sandra grimaced. "We'll deal with that in a minute," she said. "What happened then?"

"I grabbed my gun and yelled for them to stop. Instead they turned and started running. So I fired at them."

"Apparently you missed, or we'd be having this conversation at the police station or the jail."

"No, I didn't hit them. But there's a bullet hole in the wall right beside you."

Sandra looked to her left and nodded.

"And they dropped those." He pointed to a plastic bottle and cloth pad next to the door. "You can't smell it much now, but I can tell you that's chloroform in the bottle. I think they were here to put me to sleep . . . permanently."

"So far I don't see any hard evidence of a crime having been committed," Sandra said.

"What about the chloroform?" Matt asked, his voice rising. "Won't there be fingerprints on the bottle?"

"Maybe, but I'm betting they were wearing gloves. And the bullet hole is simply evidence that you have a gun, one you bought illegally. By the way, if I were you, I'd patch the hole. If the police come back to your house, you don't want them to wonder where that bullet came from and start looking for the gun that put it there." She grimaced. "Sorry, Matt. This doesn't prove your story."

Matt shook his head. "Well, it proves something to me. My kidnapping wasn't something I dreamed up. Two people tied me up, threw me in the trunk of my car, and were going to kill me. And they're still after me. This time they came to my house to finish the job." His voice was almost a whisper as he added, "That's what this means. They know who I am, they know where I live, and they want to kill me."

Matt's breakfast roiled in his stomach, threatening to come back up a lot faster and more violently than he'd been able to choke it down. He shaved carefully, avoiding the beard on his chin. He'd leave it one more day before deciding the goatee question. Matt rubbed lanolin on the incision lines on his scalp, pleased they were less noticeable each day.

He pondered his clothing choice before coming to the conclusion that it didn't matter. ER patients probably wouldn't give his appearance a second glance so long as he could take away their pain, stop their bleeding, set their broken bones, or perform whatever miracle they expected from the physician in the emergency room. Besides, he'd probably be in scrubs, so what he wore to the hospital made no difference.

This afternoon Matt would start his new job as an ER doctor at Metropolitan Hospital. He'd never given much thought to the schedule for emergency room doctors there. There'd always been one or two on duty when he was in the ER, but he had no idea how that was arranged.

"Basically, we have overlapping shifts, but don't concern yourself with that right now," Rick said. "For now, you'll work a straight midshift, three to eleven p.m."

"Thanks," Matt said. He'd try to leave the hospital before midnight. Exiting through those doors much later might bring back memories of the time he'd walked out of them and into a nightmare he was still living. Matt replayed that moment often enough in his tortured memory. He didn't need further triggers.

Try as he might Matt couldn't figure out who could have engineered the kidnapping. Who would want him dead? And why? The more he thought about it, the more his uneasiness increased. And despite Sandra's insistence that he get rid of the gun he'd used last night, he wasn't sure he was ready to give it up.

"Why don't I keep it and apply for a permit?"

"Because there's no way you'd get one," had been her immediate reply. "Not while the police consider you a 'person of interest' in a homicide. But I can turn it in to them without revealing who gave it to me."

Matt still wasn't convinced. He'd feel better with the gun at his bedside, despite its quasi-legal status.

After Sandra left, Matt had talked a locksmith into making a semi-emergency call to change the locks in his house. Whoever had been there the night before apparently had a key, and Sandra convinced Matt that changing the locks just made sense. He paid the man, thanked him, and pocketed two new keys. He'd keep one on his key ring, but wasn't sure who should have the other. He guessed he'd give it to Sandra. Was that stupid? No, right now she was the only person he could trust.

Well, that wasn't true. There was Joe. But Joe was thousands of miles away. While he waited to hear back from him, Matt decided to compose an email and send it. He opened his computer and spent fifteen minutes pouring out his emotions, laying out his fears, venting to his brother. As he hit Send, Matt knew—as though hearing his brother's voice—what advice he'd get in return for the message. "God's in control." Matt tried hard to believe it, but it was difficult.

By noon Matt had worn himself out pacing the house. He wasn't hungry but forced himself to eat half a grilled cheese sandwich, one tiny bite at a time. Fatigue descended on him, but he was smart enough to realize this was more emotional than physical, and no amount of sleep would overcome it. By an hour after lunch Matt couldn't stand another minute at home. Rick had told him he'd need about an hour with the human resources people before starting his tour of duty. If Matt left for the hospital now, he might have some time to kill after meeting with HR, but anything was better than sitting around the house, his mind whirling with what-ifs.

Matt's sticker and gate card that allowed access to the doctors' parking lot were in his own car, somewhere in the police impound lot. Fortunately Hector Rivera had left both these items behind, the former affixed to the back window of the gray Chevrolet, the latter tucked behind the sun visor.

Matt still puzzled over how little anyone could tell him about Hector Rivera. All he'd been able to find out was that Rivera came to work, functioned adequately on his shift in the ER, and went home. And now Matt was about to do those same things, driving to the hospital in Rivera's car, using Rivera's gate card and parking sticker. It still felt weird.

Once inside the hospital, Matt found that, although he knew his way around the clinical areas, he was a comparative stranger to the administrative section. He wandered around reading signs, unwilling to ask for directions, until he found the HR office. Matt entered a large anteroom and took a chair outside the office designated by a nameplate beside the door as that of Sheila Graham, HR Mgr.

Matt sat and stared at the ceiling, unable to get interested in the tattered magazines strewn around the coffee table in the center of the room. Finally an elderly man stalked out of Graham's cubicle. He stopped at Matt's chair long enough to say, "I'm overqualified. Can't pay me what I'm worth. What kind of an excuse is that?" He left, mumbling to himself.

In a few moments an attractive, well-dressed African-American woman emerged from the cubicle and asked, "Did you need to see me?"

"Yes, I'm Dr. Newman. I'm the new ER physician. I believe Dr. Pearson sent through my paperwork." Matt followed her inside and took the chair she indicated.

Ms. Graham flipped through a pile of papers and pulled out a stapled sheaf. "Oh yes. I'll need some information first."

"Excuse me, but I've had surgical privileges here for several years. Don't you have most of what you need?"

Her look was one that adults turned on children to whom they had to explain a particularly simple point. "Doctor, it's not that easy. As a surgeon, you were an independent contractor utilizing this hospital's facilities. Now you're going to be a part of Dr. Pearson's group, one that has a contract with the hospital to run the ER. Different position. So if I could have just a few moments of your time . . ."

Matt thought the process would go on forever. He told her his name, address, date of birth, Social Security number, next of kin, and a dozen other things. He confirmed his malpractice coverage, glad it hadn't lapsed and making a mental note to call the company to give them a change in his status. The questions just kept coming, and Matt thought that if his hair were longer than a fraction of an inch, he'd be pulling it out by now.

He could imagine someone in the information resources department sitting at her computer screaming, "Who processed this new hire, Matt Newman? We don't have his father's middle name. And when was his last tetanus shot? What size shoe does he wear? How are we supposed to run this place without information?"

"May I see your medical license?" Graham asked.

Matt had come prepared. He handed it over. The woman excused herself to make copies of the material she'd collected, leaving Matt to ponder what might lie ahead if he were indicted. He seemed to remember that the application for medical license renewal asked about convictions of a felony, not indictment. Then again, if enough mud was slung, some of it might stick. If it did, he might be forced to find a new city in which to practice.

Ms. Graham bustled back into the cubicle and put Matt's material down in front of him. "I think that does it."

"So, we're done?" Matt asked.

"One more thing, if you don't mind." Graham's tone and facial expression told Matt she was going to proceed whether or not he minded. "Why are you leaving your private practice to come to work as an emergency room physician?"

Matt had already thought this through. It wasn't uncommon for physicians to leave a high-stress practice in favor of a job with regular hours. In the ER, the stress might be high during a tour of duty, the pay might be less than what a doctor could earn in private practice, but when he walked out the door he was through. Finished. Absolved of further responsibility until the next time he came on duty. And that made a much better story than, "I left my practice, but the position I was to take has been put on indefinite hold because I'm accused of murder."

After Matt finished the story he'd rehearsed, Graham looked up from her papers and smiled. "I think that's about it. Do you have any other questions?"

Matt had some, but he'd rather get the answers from Rick. He was ready to get out of here. "No, I'm good." He rose, but stopped when Graham said, "I'm so sorry to see Dr. Rivera go. And wasn't it terrible what happened to his fiancé? I worked rather closely with Cara, since she headed the Internet technology section and was helping us—"

Graham stopped, put her hand to her mouth, and looked at Matt as though seeing him for the first time. "You! I didn't connect the name at first. You're the one they say killed Cara Mendiola. And now you're going to work here in this hospital? How could that happen?" She picked up her phone and stabbed in a number, staring at him all the while. "This is Sheila Graham in HR. I need to see the hospital administrator immediately!"

Matt eased out of his chair and left the room. He knew that Rick had cleared his hiring with both the administrator and chief of staff. He knew that in the American legal system you were innocent until proven guilty. He knew he hadn't killed Cara Mendiola. But despite that knowledge, he had to fight the urge to run. He looked back twice to make sure no one was following him.

Matt strode through the halls with no fixed destination. It didn't matter where he went, so long as it put some distance between him and that last encounter. No matter what came his way today, it couldn't begin to compare with what he'd just experienced. *Bring on the emergencies. I'm ready.*

———

Although it was broad daylight, in the midst of a busy hospital, Matt still found himself looking over his shoulder. One kidnap attempt had gone awry, and two men with guns had failed in an attempt to kill him. But he remembered his mother saying that most things come in threes, and he wanted to take no chances.

Matt decided to hide out in the surgeons' lounge until it was time to start his shift in the ER. By this time of the afternoon, most surgeons had finished their morning cases and were back in their offices, seeing post-op and pre-op patients and probably working their way through a mound of paperwork between appointments. Matt had loved the patient contact, the sense of satisfaction when he made a particularly difficult diagnosis, performed a bit of surgical magic, even saved a life. But the ever-increasing regulations, the morass of forms, the constant battle with insurance companies and the occasional attorney had helped make his decision to leave private practice easier.

He realized there'd be the same problems in academic medicine—the paperwork and hassles wouldn't go away—but he'd hoped there'd be more structure, maybe even more free time as he shared call with his fellow faculty members.

Matt had hoped that the change would please Jennifer as well. But now she'd disappeared from his life, taking with her any chance of a deeper relationship, maybe even marriage. As these thoughts rolled through his mind, the cloud of despair hovering over him since he awoke in that ICU room returned with a vengeance. If there was no Jennifer in his life, why had he—

His cell phone buzzed in his pocket. The caller ID was no help—private name, private number. Matt thumbed the button. "Dr. Newman."

The connection was poor, with static overriding some of the words, but the voice was unmistakable, and Matt felt a smile playing around his lips when he recognized it. "Matt, it's Joe. I heard what happened to you. Are you all right?"

"Where are you?" Matt asked. "I thought you were somewhere in the Amazonian jungle, and as best I recall, there aren't a lot of phones or cell towers there."

"Home base sent word to a nearby missionary via his amateur

radio that my brother had been injured and was in trouble. It's taken me a few days to make it to a phone, but the bonus is that I get to take a hot shower and sleep in a real bed while I'm here."

"Oh, man, is it good to hear your voice," Matt said. "I had a head injury, but I'm recovering. The real bad news is that somehow, the police suspect me of murder, but I have a good lawyer working on that."

"What? What happened?"

Matt filled him in. It helped him organize things in his mind as he related them to his brother.

When Matt finished, Joe said, "I'm glad you're recovering from your injury. I know it must be tough, being unfairly accused. All things considered, how are you holding up?"

Matt took a deep breath. "If you're inquiring about the state of my psyche, I'm hanging on. As for my soul, I'm not sure. I think maybe God's mad because I've been ignoring Him for the past few years."

"God doesn't work that way. Even when you're ignoring Him, He's not ignoring you. And I'm sure He'll be glad you're getting back on speaking terms." Joe's laugh was like a tonic to Matt. His brother had always been able to get him through even the darkest times. Joe managed to hold it together and help Matt do the same when their parents died in a plane crash. "We've still got each other. And we've got God," Joe had said. Matt needed that assurance now.

"Would it help if I came back to the US?" Joe said. "The Mission Board would probably approve an emergency furlough."

Matt had thought about this and reached the hard conclusion that Joe's physical presence couldn't help. "No, there's not really anything you can do if you were here, but I'm glad you called. And there is one thing you can do for me while we're talking."

"Name it, little brother."

Matt looked around to make sure he was still alone in the surgeons' lounge. "Would you pray for me?"

"I've been doing that ever since I got the news," Joe said. "But one more time won't hurt."

Matt bowed his head, closed his eyes, and felt himself relax as he heard his brother's voice, from five thousand miles away, lifting him up and asking for strength, peace, and grace in the midst of trials.

The cell phone was almost lost in the massive hand of Detective Virgil Grimes. "Yes?"

The detective looked around the squad room, but none of the few people there seemed interested in his conversation. He listened intently for a few minutes, then responded, "No, nothing new. What we have is a dead woman in the trunk of Newman's car, with his wallet under her. His story's thin, but there's nothing so far to disprove it."

The response was louder this time, and Grimes was torn between moving the phone away to spare his eardrums and leaving it tight against his ear for privacy. Privacy won. He received his orders silently and without any display of emotion. "Got it. I'll look harder." *And if I have to be a little creative with evidence, I can do that.*

The voice on the other end of the phone spoke a few more words, and Grimes nodded. His response was almost a whisper. "I understand." *You want Matt Newman to go down for murder.*

The detective shoved the phone into his pocket and left the squad room. He had work to do.

TWELVE

Matt was well into his ER shift when a nurse stuck her head through the door. "Dr. Newman, we need you in Trauma One stat!" The words weren't spoken loudly, but there was no mistaking their urgency.

Matt hurriedly covered the area he'd just sutured with a sterile gauze pad. "You'll need to see your doctor in about a week to have the stitches removed from your arm. Call him or us if the wound gets red or starts oozing pus." He turned to the LVN assisting him. "Will you finish putting on the bandage and give Mr. Tomlinson instructions?"

He didn't wait for an answer. Matt strode to the door, stripping off his gloves as he moved rapidly toward trauma room 1. As he went through the door, Matt took in the scene with a practiced glance: two EMTs, a nurse, and an aide surrounded a patient lying on the ambulance stretcher. The unresponsive man's face was streaked with blood from an oozing cut above his eye.

"What have we got?" Matt asked, moving beside the patient.

The lead EMT answered. "Thirty-nine-year-old male ran his car into a concrete abutment on I-35 at high speed. Police think he fell asleep. When we got him, he was shocky, breathing hard. EKG looked sort of funny. Wondered about a heart—"

"Let's have a look," Matt said. He nodded with approval at the two IV lines already in place, the oxygen mask on the patient's face. The monitor displayed low-voltage EKG complexes.

A quick neurologic exam told Matt there was probably no serious brain injury. On the other hand, the heart situation . . .

Matt first noted the fullness of the veins in the young man's neck. The recorded blood pressure was low. Two-thirds of Beck's triad already. He pulled his stethoscope from around his neck and listened to the patient's chest for a moment. Matt held his breath and concentrated. No question. Decreased heart sounds. Three signs out of three. Cardiac tamponade. Bleeding into the fibrous sac that surrounded the heart. A true medical emergency.

Untreated, continued bleeding would press on the heart like a giant hand grasping that life-giving organ, squeezing it to death. Matt had to relieve that pressure, and fast.

First get the blood pressure back up. He spoke to the nurse. "Put a vial of Dobutamine in 250 milliliters of saline and piggyback it to his IV. I'll adjust the dosage in a moment."

Matt turned to the lead EMT. "One question. Was the air bag deployed?"

"Funny thing. No, it wasn't. I wondered about that."

"Some people disconnect them," the second EMT added. "Think they might do more harm than good." He shook his head.

"This patient has cardiac tamponade. We need to get a cardiac surgeon here stat," Matt said. The aide hurried away to make the call. "Meanwhile, let's intubate him."

Matt hadn't put an endotracheal tube into a patient for a while, but was pleased to find that he hadn't lost his touch. The tube slid between the man's vocal cords and into his windpipe on the first attempt. When he had the airway secured, Matt said, "Let's hook him up to the respirator."

"How's his blood pressure?" Matt asked. The EMT turned the monitor slightly so Matt could see it. The pressure had dropped further. "Speed up the Dobutamine drip."

The oxygen saturation, measured by the pulse oximeter on the patient's finger, was low despite the pure oxygen being delivered under pressure. The man was being smothered by his heart's inability to pump blood throughout his body.

The phone in the corner of the room rang, and the nurse moved to answer it. She listened for a moment, hung up, and turned to Matt. "The cardiac team is tied up with another emergency case. It may be half an hour before someone can shake loose."

"That's too long." *Well, I guess it's up to me.* "We'll need to do an emergency pericardiocentesis."

"Don't you want a chest film?" the EMT asked.

"Sure. I want a chest film, an echocardiogram, and a cardiologist standing beside me. But we don't have time for any of that." Matt nodded toward the patient. "This man is dying."

The group went into action, and in a moment Matt looked down at the bared chest of the young man, bronzed by antiseptic, outlined with sterile green draping sheets. There'd been no time to run to the hospital library and check his knowledge of a procedure he'd never performed and only seen two or three times. The ER secretary was trying to locate a thoracic surgeon, a cardiologist, anyone who could help, but right now this was up to Matt. *Welcome to ER medicine.*

After injecting a local anesthetic, Matt used a scalpel to make a small incision under the breastbone. *Careful. Just enough to let the needle slide in easily.* With his gloved hand, he took a large syringe from the instrument tray, attached a long needle, and loaded it with a bit of sterile saline.

"Do we have an electric lead with an alligator clip? I need to put it on the needle and link it to the EKG," Matt said. No one could find one.

Great. Well, there was one more option. Matt turned to the nurse and the EMTs. "Are you familiar enough with EKGs to tell me if the ST segments start getting higher?"

"I am," said the nurse.

"Yes," replied both EMTs.

"That's the only warning I'll have that my needle is touching the heart. If that happens, sing out loud and clear."

Matt paused with the needle tip poised against the man's bare chest. *Please, God. Give me this one.* Slowly he inserted the needle, working to maintain a forty-five-degree angle, aiming at the patient's left shoulder. Every few millimeters, he pushed the plunger and injected a few drops of saline, just enough to keep the lumen of the needle clear. He needed to insert the needle to a depth of about two inches. Wasn't he there yet? It seemed like he should be. *Maybe distance is relative when the target is a beating heart.*

Matt pulled back on the plunger. Nothing. He advanced the needle a bit farther—and blood swirled in the saline remaining in the syringe.

"ST elevation!" Three voices rang out in unison.

Immediately Matt pulled the needle back a bit.

"EKG's back to normal," the nurse said.

"Thanks." Matt advanced the needle again, a millimeter at a time, and with each movement he felt his gut tighten. Once more he pulled back on the plunger of the syringe. Blood, darker than the bright blood of a moment ago, began to flow into the barrel of the syringe. He was in the pericardial sac, and it was filled with blood. *You got the diagnosis right, Matt. Now help the man.*

When the syringe was full, Matt handed it off and attached a fresh one. "What are his vital signs like?"

"Blood pressure is going up," the nurse reported.

Matt repeated the aspiration twice, pulling the needle back once more when the EKG changes showed he was touching the heart again. "Now how's he doing?"

"Vital signs looking better. Oxygen saturation back to almost normal," the nurse said.

"You guys need me down here?"

Matt steadied the needle in place before he looked at the doorway. The speaker was a cardiac surgeon he recognized. "Glad to see you, Lonnie. I've just done my first pericardiocentesis. Let me tell you about it."

"Just the usual this morning?" Elaine asked. "I had dinner last night with Charlie Greaver. That should entitle me to something fancier."

Sandra sipped from her own cup and settled into the visitor's chair across the desk from Elaine. "Maybe tomorrow. Depends on what you learned."

"Mainly I learned that Charlie wanted to talk about Charlie—specifically, about what he's going to do when he's elected DA next year after Jack Tanner retires." Elaine sampled her own coffee, frowned, and blew across the mouth of the cup. "Too hot to drink."

"So let it cool. What about Matt's case?"

"Charlie wants to get things sewed up before moving for an indictment, but Frank Everett is champing at the bit to go with the case. Frank has ideas about moving into Charlie's number two slot when Jack retires and Charlie's the new DA."

Sandra frowned. "So are they ready to move forward?"

"Not yet. But Everett told Charlie he'd have some new evidence soon. And when he's got that, he wants to hotfoot it to the grand jury."

New evidence? Where could they be digging that up? "Is Frank Everett still scheduled to prosecute?"

Elaine tried her coffee, found it to her liking, and drank deeply. "Not sure. Frank's doing the work right now, but depending on how the case looks, Charlie may end up first chair."

Not so good. Charlie is no pushover. Sandra rose and headed for her office. "I have to make a phone call. Buzz me if you need me."

Matt stood in the middle of the emergency room, surrounded by patients hooked up to every imaginable device and monitor. A harsh noise assaulted his ears—one of the devices sending out its electronic warning. He turned in a slow circle, letting his ears search for the source of the noise. Had an electrode from an EKG come loose? Was a patient's oxygen saturation level dropping to dangerous levels? Had an IV being pumped into a patient's system run dry? Or—most dangerous of all—had a patient's heartbeat stilled?

Matt turned this way and that, but everything seemed to be in order. The noise stopped just as he opened his eyes. Then he heard his own voice. *"This is Dr. Matt Newman. I can't take your call, but if you leave a name and number, I'll get back to you as soon as I can."*

"Matt, this is Sandra Murray—"

He snatched the phone off the bedside table and scrambled to turn off his answering machine. "Sandra, I'm here. Just give me a second."

Matt put down the phone and hurried to the bathroom. He was

121

back in a moment, his face still wet from a dousing with cold water. "Sorry. What's up?"

"We need to talk about your case," Sandra said. "Can you come by my office before noon?"

Something about Sandra's tone was different, and it worried Matt. "Is something wrong?"

"Maybe. We'll talk about it when you get here."

They settled on eleven o'clock. Matt hung up the phone, straightened his rumpled covers—what a nightmare that had been—and headed for the shower. He wondered what new development had prompted the call. Whatever it was, apparently his attorney didn't like it.

He tested the water with his hand and adjusted the mix. As he stepped under the spray, he wondered if he was in hot water in more ways than one.

———

Jennifer's fingers glided over the keyboard of her computer like those of a concert pianist, producing an accurate reproduction of the words she heard through her headset while her own thoughts flew in different directions.

The more time she spent with Frank, the more she seemed to think about Matt. All of the good qualities that had drawn her to him—the way he was willing to leave an established practice for a less-stressful position, just to please her—kept whirling through her mind. Why hadn't she just told Jack Tanner from the get-go that Matt was her boyfriend? When had she gotten so career-focused that she was ready to give the first husband material she'd met in a long time, the boot? From what she'd heard, even though Frank Everett and Charlie Greaver seemed ready, even anxious, to pursue an indictment, the case was built on circumstantial evidence. True, the police had found a dead woman in the trunk of Matt's car, but if his kidnapping story held up, he had been the victim, not the perpetrator, and there was nothing of substance to support prosecution.

Then again, if that detective, whatever his name was, found anything more substantial, Matt would undoubtedly be arrested and tried. And she'd been around long enough to know that a not-guilty verdict didn't always wash away the suspicion that surrounded being tried for murder. Did she really want to be the wife of a man who'd been called a murderer, even if he was acquitted? For that matter, could she afford to have her name associated with him and maintain the confidence of the DA and his associates?

Although Jennifer always considered herself levelheaded, making decisions on the basis of practicality instead of emotions, something about her actions continued to bother her. True, she was seeing someone else. But Matt at least deserved a proper good-bye.

Jennifer went back and forth until it seemed her head would explode. She needed to get out of here, take a break.

She grabbed her purse from the bottom drawer of her desk and hurried out of the office. Downstairs, Jennifer took a deep breath and plunged out the door and onto the sidewalk. Dallas might have an anti-smoking ordinance, but every day she and her fellow workers had to run a gauntlet of smokers who obeyed the letter, although not the spirit, of the law by taking up station a measured sixteen feet from the doorway of the Crowley Courts Building to get their nicotine fix.

Jennifer held her breath until she was past them and then paused in the doorway of a clothing store that had gone out of business. She turned her back to the stream of people on the sidewalk and retrieved her phone from her purse. Matt's cell number was still on her speed dial, and she stabbed the number before she could lose her nerve.

Jennifer waited through five rings before she heard a voice that tugged at her heart. *"This is Dr. Matt Newman. I can't take your call, but if you leave a name and number, I'll get back to you as soon as I can."*

It took all her strength not to hang up. She looked over her shoulder to confirm that no one was near, swallowed twice, and said, "Matt, this is Jennifer. I'm sorry I reacted the way I did. We need to talk. When you get this, call my cell." She started to hang up, thought better of it, and added, "I promise I'll answer your call this time."

Sandra gestured to the chair in front of her desk. "Have a seat. Can we get you anything? Coffee? A Coke?"

"I'm fine," Matt said.

She studied her client. There'd definitely been a subtle change in his attitude since she'd first met him. In the beginning, he'd seemed shell-shocked, unable to fully process what was happening to him. She'd had to prod him to start the process of getting his life together. Now he appeared more confident, more at ease. Was it surviving the second attack? Going back to work? Whatever the cause for the change, she was glad to see it. It was easier to defend a client who was emotionally prepared to help in the process and was determined to move on with their chin up. Besides, the difference pleased her from a personal standpoint.

"You're looking better," she said. "Your hair's beginning to grow out."

Matt ran his hand lightly over his scalp, but she noticed he was careful not to touch the surgical scar. "I guess I'm making progress. Now I look like a drill sergeant."

"But you shaved the goatee," she said.

"Couldn't stand the itching," Matt confessed. He looked around him. "I thought you'd have a big, fancy office—part of a large law firm. But you're in solo practice, aren't you?"

Sandra shrugged. "I started out with a big firm. They took me on right out of law school, promised to fast-track me to partner. But I left after a year, opened my own office."

"Why?"

"I'm not just a lawyer. I'm a Christian who happens to practice law. Some of the partners in the firm thought my Christian principles were getting in the way. I disagreed."

Matt leaned forward in his chair. "So they let you go?"

"No, I resigned, then opened my own office so I didn't have to soft-pedal my Christianity to fit in. So far, it's worked." Sandra swiveled slightly in her chair and looked out the window behind her desk for a moment. She waited for him to respond, but there was only silence. Wasn't this the perfect opening to ask Matt about his own relationship to God? She opened her mouth—closed it again. No, it wasn't the time.

When she turned back to face Matt, she said, "I've had some disturbing news today." He reacted with a slight lifting of his eyebrows. "My sources in the DA's office—" Did she detect a flinch? *I'll have to follow up on that.* "My sources tell me they expect some new evidence that will allow them to take your case to a grand jury and ask for an indictment. Do you know what that might be?"

Matt shook his head. "If there's something I haven't told you, it's because I don't know it. I don't know why I was kidnapped. I don't know why someone would kill a woman and leave her body in the trunk of my car. I don't know why someone broke into my house in the dead of night. All I know is that I'm obviously someone's target."

"That leads me to another question," Sandra said. "Are you

ready for me to dispose of that handgun you bought? I can turn it over to the police and claim attorney-client privilege if they ask where I got it."

"Not really. If those guys come back, I don't want to be defenseless."

"Matt, it's possible the police will be back at your house soon with another search warrant. Especially if the DA thinks there's some more evidence to be found. If they find the gun—well, it would be bad."

"Why? We don't have to register guns in Texas. As I read the law, I don't need a license to have a handgun in my home—and probably in my car, so long as it's in the glove compartment."

Sandra had given this some thought. "Two reasons. First, they're going to ask where you got it. A prosecutor could use the fact that you bought it from an unlicensed dealer in some sort of backstreet transaction to paint you as an undesirable character. And we don't want to give them any ammunition, no pun intended."

"I don't know why I'd be worried about being thought an undesirable character. I mean, right now they seem to think I'm a murderer. I'm not sure how much more undesirable you can get."

"Then consider my second argument. How do you know that your 'acquaintance' didn't sell you a gun that's been used in the commission of a felony? Maybe even a murder. All the police have to do is fire a test round and match the ballistics with a prior crime, and you're toast."

"I hadn't thought of that."

"So will you let me get rid of the gun?" Sandra asked.

Matt hated to be unarmed again. Then again, he already had something that would give him protection, and no license was required. "Let me—"

A muted chime interrupted Matt. He drew his cell phone from his pocket, looked at the display, and frowned.

"Do you need to take that?"

Indecision clouded his features for a moment. Then, with a resolute shake of his head, he jammed the phone back into his pocket. "No. It's just someone I used to know. I'll check the message later."

THIRTEEN

The boss's office was cold. The air-conditioning must have been turned to the max, but despite the temperature, Lou was sweating. He was in his usual position, standing in front of the desk to give a report, waiting for the tongue-lashing certain to follow.

This time Lou was alone. Edgar had been dispatched to reason with someone on behalf of the boss—if you could call breaking a man's kneecaps "reasoning."

"He shot at you?" For a moment it seemed that the corners of the big man's mouth turned upward a fraction of an inch. Then his moon-like face settled into its usual countenance, overlaid with the faintest hint of a scowl. "You and Edgar broke in to carry out a plan so simple two teenagers could have executed it, and Newman chased you away with a gun. Do I have that right?"

Lou felt his pulse quicken as he recalled the event. "That's all we could do. Newman was waiting with a pistol. He started shooting, and if Edgar and me hadn't run when we did, you'd be ID'ing our bodies so they could put a toe tag on us."

"Don't be ridiculous," the big man said, with no hint of humor. "You know that if you ever fall into the hands of the law, alive or dead, I'll deny any knowledge of you."

"What I mean—"

"Shut up and let me think!" The upraised hand was the size of a small ham, and the gesture stopped Lou cold. He waited for what would follow.

Behind the desk was a window that looked out onto Jefferson Boulevard, a window that in Lou's memory had always been guarded by a closed blind. Today it was open a fraction, and he was conscious of the movement of cars and occasional pedestrians below. Lou wished he were out there with them.

The boss took a letter opener from his desk and tapped his desk blotter with it. He nodded once, apparently satisfied with his plan, and dropped the opener. "Here's what I want you to do." He folded his hands under his chin and paused as though weighing his words. "Using your key, enter Newman's home when he's not there. Find that pistol and bring it to me."

"Sure. How soon do you need it?"

The big man closed his eyes and appeared to consider the question. He spoke without opening them. "I have some work that will take you a day or so. After that's done, get the gun, with Newman's prints on it, and bring it to me."

"So you want me and Edgar—"

"No. Just you. It may be time to throw Edgar off the sleigh, and I think it's best to keep him in the dark until then."

Lou nodded, although he didn't really understand. *No Edgar on this one. But what's he talking about, that stuff about a sleigh?*

"On the other hand, Edgar's talents are perfect for this little job I have in mind. Here's what you two are to do."

Lou relaxed when he heard the assignment. It was routine stuff, no problem. And there was enough violence involved so Edgar would love it.

"Any questions?" the big man said.

Lou shook his head.

"Then go. I'll expect you back here in a few days, with Newman's pistol. Alone."

"I can't afford a security system for my house," Matt said. "And I don't want to buy a watchdog. With my hours, I'd have to pay someone to look after him and walk him, and I can't afford that either."

Matt felt as though he'd been in Sandra's office all day. They weren't really arguing—more like debating issues. The debate was low-key, and Sandra was winning. She suggested ways Matt could protect himself. He countered with reasons they wouldn't work. She insisted he give her the gun. He finally accepted the validity of her argument.

"I can see why you're successful in the courtroom," Matt said. "You wear everyone down."

"The pistol?"

Matt shrugged. "Yeah, the pistol."

"Will you bring it to me later today?"

Matt consulted his watch. "I've got to go to work soon. It's safely tucked away, and I promise not to shoot anybody with it before tomorrow. How about then?"

"Okay. Call Elaine to let her know when you're coming. I want to be here so I can take it right to the police."

Matt decided he'd had enough talk of guns and police. "So what do we do about this 'new evidence' the DA expects?"

"If you're sure there's nothing you haven't told me, all we can do is wait."

"In case you haven't noticed, I don't do that very well," Matt said. "They say that's what separates surgeons from internists. The internists wait around, adjust medications, order tests, and get their patients well over time. Surgeons want to identify the problem, cut it out or sew it up, and move on."

"Unfortunately you're going to have to take the internist track in this case. But I know how the legal system works, and even though things aren't moving fast enough for you, I'm on top of them. Let me worry about the DA. You get on with rebuilding your life." She chewed her lip, a habit Matt found charming. "And it looks like you're doing a good job of that. Tell me about your new job."

"Metropolitan ER," Matt said. "I'll have to admit it was spooky walking out those doors last night, but I've about decided I can't live my life looking over my shoulder."

"It's about time for lunch. I was wondering—" A muted buzz from the phone on her desk made Sandra stop.

Elaine's voice issued from the speaker. "Horace Allison is on line one, and he sounds pretty upset."

Sandra frowned. "Sorry, I've got to take this."

"No problem," Matt said. "I need to go, anyway. I'll see you tomorrow."

As Matt walked away from Sandra Murray's office building, his last words ran through his mind. *I can't live my life looking over my shoulder.* Actually, that was exactly what he wanted to do, but he resisted the temptation. No question, there was an unfamiliar tingling between his shoulder blades. He'd read in spy novels about people who felt in their guts they were in the crosshairs of an assassin's rifle.

Until now he'd dismissed it as a literary device. No more. He not only accepted it as valid, he knew the feeling all too well.

———

Sandra rummaged through the files on her desk, found the one she wanted, and buzzed her secretary. "Elaine, have we received the discovery material on the Allison case?"

"Just got it. Do you want me to bring it in?"

Horace Allison was a drug dealer, and there was no question in Sandra's mind that his most recent arrest would stand up in court. As part of a plea bargain, one of his middlemen had worn a wire during a drug buy. The resulting audio material was enough to put Allison away for a long time. She wanted to make one final pass through the material provided by the prosecutor, but right now it looked like the best she could do for Allison was see if he had something to trade in return for a lighter sentence. It tore at her guts to be defending someone so obviously guilty, even though—as she kept reminding herself—everyone was entitled to the best possible counsel. Maybe having Matt as a client—

Elaine's voice on the intercom interrupted Sandra's thoughts. "I asked if you wanted the Allison material?"

"Yes, please bring it in. And if you go out for lunch, would you get me a sandwich? Looks like I'll be eating at my desk."

She'd been about to ask Matt to lunch when Horace phoned. Sandra wondered what Matt might have said if there hadn't been an interruption. She knew she couldn't see a client socially while still preparing his defense, but she'd already worked that out in her mind. This would have been a business lunch, an opportunity for her to see him in a more relaxed setting and get more information. The better an attorney knew a client, the better she could defend him.

Sure, you're the queen of rationalization. Admit it. There's an attraction there.

Elaine deposited a large cardboard box, the kind used to store records, on the table beside Sandra's desk. "What kind of sandwich do you want?"

Sandra made a dismissive gesture. "Surprise me." Right now, her appetite was gone. Was it because of the prospect of wading through all that material looking for a flaw in the case against her client, or the fact that she wouldn't be eating with Matt?

Jennifer looked at her watch. Time for lunch, and Matt hadn't returned her call. Should she call him again? In the past he'd always answered her calls except when he was in surgery or with a patient. Even then, he returned them as soon as he could. But that was then, and this was now. This was after she'd rebuffed him when he needed her. She supposed his hurt would be slow to heal—if it ever did.

Jennifer pulled her purse from the desk drawer and stood up. Maybe she'd slip around the corner for a quick bite, and if Matt hadn't called by then, she'd call him again. Everything Jennifer knew about Matt told her that he couldn't have done the things of which he was suspected. On the other hand, his kidnapping story sounded just a bit far-fetched to her. She figured a jury would find it equally hard to believe. And she couldn't afford to be connected to a man charged with—even suspected of—murder, not if she wanted to maintain the trust of the DA.

Jennifer was halfway to the door when she heard a man's voice. "Hey, Jen! Got a minute?"

Frank Everett hurried to where she stood. His dress shirt was wrinkled, his tie askew, and he looked like he'd just stepped out of a sauna. "I've been taking a deposition this morning, and I need a break. How about having lunch with me?"

Decision time. If she went to lunch with Frank, there'd be no opportunity to call Matt, or even answer if he called back. On the other hand, if she turned Frank down, she needed a good excuse, and she couldn't think of one on the spur of the moment. Besides, Frank was her lifeline, maybe her future.

Jennifer had never really understood the expression "a heavy heart" until now. She plastered a smile on her face. "Sure. Where would you like to go?"

"Uh, Dr. Newman. I'm surprised to see you here." The ICU nurse's expression conveyed what her words only suggested. She was surprised he wasn't in jail.

Matt searched his memory bank for her name and came up blank. "I'm working in the ER now. And I decided to check on a patient I had yesterday. Don't recall his name, but he had a traumatic hemopericardium."

The nurse bent over the chart rack, and as she turned, Matt got a better look at the nameplate pinned to her scrub dress. "Candace, what do people around the hospital think of me? Am I going to be treated like a leper everywhere I go?"

She straightened and handed Matt a chart. "Dr. Newman, I try not to pay attention to gossip. But I've worked with you for almost a year, and I don't think you could be guilty of murder. Frankly, when I heard what they were saying, I was shocked."

"Thanks." Matt opened the chart and scanned the progress notes. He kept his head down as he said, "I appreciate your saying that. And, if it makes any difference, I'm totally innocent of all those charges."

"Well, I'll be praying for you." A buzzer sent Candace hurrying off to answer.

Matt tucked the chart under his arm and headed for ICU room 6, where his patient—now Lonnie's patient, he guessed—was located. The blinds were open, and the huge glass picture window gave him a clear view inside. A patient lay on the bed, an endotracheal tube in his throat connected to a respirator that was chuffing at a rate Matt guessed to be about twelve breaths per minute. In addition to two IVs, a tube led from the patient's chest to a drainage setup. A monitor scrolled numbers and patterns across a screen, beeping while displaying information that was incomprehensible to a layperson but critical to medical professionals.

Matt was about to enter when he saw the woman sitting at the bedside, still as a wax figure. Stray strands escaped here and there from her otherwise perfectly coiffed ash-blond hair. She wore a simple navy dress, accented by a single strand of pearls. Her right hand rested on the patient's arm, her left lay in her lap, squeezing a wad of tissue and occasionally using it to dab her eyes.

"Excuse me," Matt said.

The woman rose from her chair, startled. Matt thought he had never seen such sorrow on a face. She blinked back a tear. "Shall I leave?"

Matt had changed into scrubs for his stint in the ER, covering them with a white coat, so there was really no need to explain his presence. Nevertheless, for some reason he felt the need to do exactly that. "No, please stay. I'm Dr. Matt Newman. I'm the doctor who saw Mr. . . ." Matt sneaked a glance at the chart. "I saw Mr. Penland in the emergency room yesterday. I wanted to look in on him, see that he's okay."

"You're the doctor who saved his life," she said. Her tone was as flat as though she were ordering a grilled cheese sandwich.

"I just did what an emergency room physician does," Matt said.

"I diagnosed the problem, then I treated it until I could turn him over to the specialist."

The woman held out her hand. "I'm Roland's mother, Abby Penland. And Dr. Witt told me your quick action saved Roland's life. So thank you."

Being thanked for doing his job always felt wrong to Matt. He murmured, "You're welcome," then busied himself with the read-outs from the monitor until Mrs. Penland took her seat once more.

Lonnie Witt's notes indicated he'd done a thoracotomy—entering Penland's chest—necessitating the chest tube drainage. He'd opened the sac surrounding the heart and sutured a small laceration of the heart muscle. Matt had never done this procedure, but was familiar enough with it to know that Mr. Penland had a period of convalescence ahead of him. On the other hand, without Matt's intervention, the woman sitting at the bedside would be planning a funeral instead of holding her son's hand.

Matt glanced at the clock. "I need to go now. I'm due on duty in the emergency room soon." He started to leave, then turned back. "It was nice meeting you. I hope your son continues to do well."

She rose and took Matt's extended hand in both her own. He noticed that she wore what looked like a platinum engagement and wedding ring set featuring a large emerald-cut diamond, with smaller stones on either side. Although Matt hadn't gone so far as to buy a ring for Jennifer, he'd done some looking and was certain he'd just seen a five-carat diamond.

"Thank you for coming by. And good luck."

Matt started to respond but found that he had nothing to say. Did she mean "good luck" with the patients he was about to see? Or was his predicament such common knowledge that her "good luck" referred to his battle to prove his innocence of murder charges?

As the door closed behind Matt, he decided that looking for motives behind what people said to him was just another unpleasant by-product of the mess he was in. He longed for it all to be over . . . one way or another.

Sandra Murray reached across her desk to still the buzz of the intercom. "Yes?"

"Dr. Newman just called. He's on his way with that package you wanted."

Package? What—*? Oh, the pistol.* "Thanks, Elaine. When he gets here, send him right in."

Sandra pulled Matt's case file from the stack on her desk. It was near the top, the position it had occupied from the beginning. She'd been careful not to short-change her other clients, but Matt's case had been foremost in her mind since that first encounter in his ICU room. That was natural, though, wasn't it, given the charges he faced? And besides that . . . She shook her head and wondered why the man attracted her so.

She'd given up on talking with Charlie Greaver about Matt's case. His standard answer had become, "Talk to Frank Everett." But talking to Frank was like arguing with a stone.

Sandra insisted that the case against her client was purely circumstantial. She repeated Matt's contention that he was the victim, not the perpetrator in this situation. But Frank would only say that one missing piece of evidence was all that stood between Matt and a murder indictment.

What was this mysterious missing piece of evidence? Matt continued to deny any knowledge of such a thing. Was he being straight with her? He—

"Here you are." Matt stood in the door, holding a small brown paper bag. He moved to her desk and deposited the bag there as casually as though he were delivering a half-dozen donuts. "One revolver, unloaded. Five unfired bullets and an empty cartridge case. I didn't get any extra ammunition with it. Guess the guy I bought it from wasn't running a special that week."

Sandra parted the top of the bag just enough to confirm that the contents were as Matt described. "Did you by any chance—"

"There are no fingerprints on the gun. I even wiped down the bullets." Matt sank into the visitor's chair and crossed his legs. "And I've patched the bullet hole."

"Good," Sandra said. "I'm going to tell them that this came into my possession and I wanted to turn it over to them for disposal. To my knowledge it wasn't used in the commission of a crime. Beyond that, I'll claim lawyer-client privilege."

"Won't they infer that it came from me?"

"Let them infer all they want to. There's no way they can tie this to you." She frowned. "Is there anything else they might find in your home or car that could be used as evidence against you?"

"Absolutely not." The response came rapidly, and was accompanied by such an earnest expression, Sandra was sure he was telling the truth.

"Got to head for work," Matt said. "But I wanted to drop this by first. I hope I'm doing the right thing."

"Don't worry," Sandra said. "You are." *At least, I hope you are. Please, God, keep him safe.*

Detective Virgil Grimes left his unmarked car a block away from Matt's house. As he moved along the sidewalk, he wondered when the city would realize that a black Ford Crown Vic with plain steel wheels and basic hubcaps, red and blue strobes faintly visible through the grill, was as clearly a police car as a black-and-white with a light bar on top. But he was entitled to drive a city car, and beggars couldn't be choosers.

Over the years, Grimes had developed the policeman's walk, along with the "I don't want any trouble out of you" stare that marked him as a cop as plainly as flipping open his badge wallet. It was too late to try to disguise it, but if any of the neighbors saw him approaching Newman's house, he figured they wouldn't think it unusual. The man was a suspect in a murder, so a policeman in the area would be as normal as an ice cream truck in a family neighborhood during the summer.

While he was there, Grimes decided he might as well see if he could find a nosy neighbor, some housewife or retired man who spent their day with eyes glued to their window. You never could tell what you might turn up that way. But first he had a little business to take care of.

Grimes rang the front doorbell, not expecting an answer. If Newman had stayed home from work, he'd ask him a dozen or so questions and leave. There'd be another time for what he had in mind today.

The bell went unanswered, so Grimes slid the key he'd liberated from the property room into the lock. At least, he tried to slide it in, but it wouldn't go. He turned the key over and tried again. Still no luck. Maybe it fit the back door. He trudged around behind the house. Same thing.

So Newman had been smart enough to change the locks. If Grimes had a warrant in his pocket, that wouldn't be a problem, but this visit was strictly unofficial. He pulled out a flat leather wallet containing a series of picks and metal strips, possession of which would earn him a nice vacation at state expense if he weren't a policeman.

Richard L. Mabry

Using a talent he'd perfected after a lesson from one of his informants, Grimes had the back door open in less than a minute.

He closed the door behind him and stood silent as a statue, listening to the sounds of the house. Satisfied that he was alone, he moved swiftly up the stairs. Might as well start with the bedroom. That was the logical place.

Grimes had done his share of searches, most of them with a warrant, but one or two without benefit of legal sanction. He knew all the hiding places, knew them better than most criminals, he figured. Once he found the right place, it took him less than a minute to finish the job. He hurried down the stairs, and in another minute he was out the back door, having locked it with even more ease than when he'd entered.

He paused in the backyard and ran through what he'd done, looking for mistakes. Now was the time to correct them. But, no, the house was just as he'd found it—well, almost. And the change wouldn't be evident to Newman or anyone else until Grimes wanted it to be.

FOURTEEN

"I'm going to take a break," Matt said. "It looks like everything's under control."

Someone unfamiliar with an emergency room might have taken exception to Matt's characterization, but in truth, things really were under control. Patients waited with varying degrees of tolerance for reports of lab work or X-rays. A nurse prepped the hand of a teenage boy for suture of a laceration as soon as the nerve block Matt had done took effect. And an orderly wheeled a woman in labor off to the delivery room, where her obstetrician waited. Things were busy, but they were under control.

In the break room, Matt pulled a Coke from the fridge, held it briefly to his forehead, then popped the tab and took several swallows. He opened his locker and checked the display on his cell phone. It still registered "One missed call" and "One new message." He'd recognized Jennifer's cell phone number when she phoned earlier, and chosen to ignore the call. Maybe he was angry about her earlier rejection of his pleas for help, her eventual refusal to even talk with him. It might be that he wasn't sure he wanted to try rekindling a romance that appeared to have flamed out. But whatever the reason, pure perversity or hesitation at what might follow, he hadn't dialed her number—hadn't even listened to her message.

"Dr. Newman, I think the boy in two is ready for you to suture his laceration."

"Thanks," Matt called to the nurse's retreating back. He recognized how lucky he was to have Carol as the head nurse on this shift. A doctor might be important, but the nurses were what kept the ER running. For that matter, the same could be said of any unit in the hospital. Matt made a mental note to thank Carol and the rest of the staff.

He looked at his watch and decided he had time to listen to Jennifer's message. He probably owed her that much. He had come to the end of the message and was about ready to hit the delete button when he heard Jennifer's tentative addendum to her message. "I promise I'll answer your call this time."

He decided that if Jennifer was trying to shame him into returning her call, she was close to succeeding. More than anyone, Matt recognized what it cost her to leave that message. Of all the people he knew, Jennifer Ball was the least likely to admit she'd made a mistake. Shouldn't he at least give her credit for trying?

Before he could change his mind, Matt pushed the speed-dial button for Jennifer's cell phone. It had rung once when Carol hurried in. "We need you right now! Cardiac arrest!"

Matt ended the call, barely conscious of the sound of Jennifer's tentative "Hello?" as he broke the connection.

In Trauma Room 1, two EMTs labored over a thin elderly man, still on the ambulance stretcher. One performed chest compressions while the other squeezed an Ambu bag to force oxygen through a tube in the patient's windpipe. Carol was injecting something into the IV line taped to the patient's wrist. *Probably Cordarone. Might help, wouldn't hurt.*

Matt picked up the EKG tracing that still hung from the machine. There were a few squiggles, but nothing to suggest organized cardiac activity.

"Was he like this when you found him?" Matt asked the EMT doing chest compressions.

"Yeah. His daughter called him for supper, and when he didn't answer, she went to his room. Found him on the floor, like this."

"We shocked him, but no response," the other EMT added. "Shoved a backboard under him and I did chest compressions all the way to the ER."

Matt motioned the men to stand aside. "Give me a second." Matt lifted the old man's eyelids, revealing large pupils that didn't shrink when he shone his penlight into them. He put his stethoscope on the cold, ashen skin of the patient's chest. He held his breath and listened but, as he expected, heard nothing. What now? Inject adrenaline directly into the heart? Try another electrical shock to restart the heart? No, it was too late for all that. It was probably too late when the daughter found her father. "He's gone." Matt pulled the sheet over the old man's face and stepped back. He looked at the clock on the wall and gave the nurse the official time of death.

Matt knew what he had to do next, and he dreaded it, the same way he'd dreaded all the other occasions like it. Sometimes the practice of medicine was the most gratifying thing in the world. And sometimes, when you had to deliver bad news, it was the worst possible job a person could have.

He paused at the door leading to the waiting room and glanced at the name on the sheet of paper Carol had handed him. *God, please give me the words to say.* Matt wondered how he could continue to pray for guidance at times like these, even though his current prayers for deliverance seemed to go unanswered. Was it nothing more than a ritual? If that was all there was to it, he truly was a man without hope. And right now, hope was all he had.

———

Sandra was deep in thought about a complex legal point when the intercom buzzer sounded.

"Detective Grimes is on line one. He's calling about the Newman case."

"Thanks, Elaine. I'll take it." Sandra picked up the receiver and said, "Detective Grimes, this is Sandra Murray. How can I help you?"

Grimes's voice, when filtered through the phone, seemed even more menacing than it did in person. "We need to ask the doctor a few more questions. Can he come in this morning?"

Sandra checked her watch. Ten a.m. Matt should be awake by now. "Let me call him and see. I'll get back to you."

Matt sounded a bit sleepy but didn't seem to mind Sandra's call. "Maybe we'll learn why Grimes is so unwilling to believe my story," he said. "Do you want me to go directly to the police station?"

"No, come to my office. We can take my car, and I'll bring you back here for yours after lunch." Sandra wondered why she'd added the lunch date. But then, it wasn't really a date. It was a professional meeting. She hoped that once their session with Grimes was over, she and Matt would still have an appetite.

After she ended the call with Matt, Sandra buzzed Elaine. "Call Detective Grimes and tell him Dr. Newman and I will be at his office in an hour." As though she'd just thought of it, she added, "And I'm going to have lunch after that. Am I free until two?"

Elaine's smirk showed in her voice. "I'll make sure you are. You and the doctor enjoy your lunch."

———

Matt followed Sandra into the squad room, thankful for her presence, and totally unsure of what was going to happen.

Grimes rose from his desk. "Doctor, Counselor. Thanks for coming." There was no sign of the blond detective. Matt couldn't understand that. Didn't they always work in pairs? Since Sandra didn't seem concerned, he decided to keep quiet and wait for developments.

Matt wasn't sure what he expected. Maybe sitting in a hard chair with a bright light shining in his face. Maybe two detectives playing "good cop, bad cop" as they volleyed questions at him like tennis balls out of a machine. *You've watched too many detective shows.*

Grimes ushered Matt and Sandra into what Matt decided was an interview room. The only furniture was a table with two chairs on either side. Grimes pointed them to the side of the table farthest from the door. Matt eased into his chair and decided that, although it wasn't upholstered, he'd certainly sat on less comfortable furniture.

The wall to Matt's right featured a large mirror. Matt figured it was one-way glass, allowing his actions to be monitored from the next room. Probably wired, as well. Sandra sat to his left, a calming presence.

"I guess—" Grimes stopped when the door opened and the tall blond detective entered and took the chair next to him. "Dr. Newman, I believe you've met Detective Merrilee Ames. She'll be sitting in with us today." He pointed at Sandra. "This is Dr. Newman's attorney, Ms. Murray."

The two women nodded at each other, and Matt felt the temperature drop ten degrees. Was there a natural rivalry between police and attorney? Or was this tension because two beautiful women were in the same room? Matt noticed that Ames wore a wedding ring, and wondered if being married made it easier or harder for Sandra to accept her.

Grimes went through what Matt figured was a routine for interviews of this type: the tape recorder, the Miranda warning. Sandra had warned him, and he took this in stride.

"Now, Doctor, tell me one more time what happened to you when you left the emergency room on the night of . . ." Grimes consulted the notepad in front of him and added the date.

Matt went through it all. Grimes and Ames listened without comment, the woman occasionally jotting a note, Grimes displaying no emotion and very little apparent interest in Matt's narrative. "I tried to climb down from my perch, my foot slipped, and that's all I remember until I woke up in the ICU."

"Your story initially was that you had no recollection of some of these events," Grimes said. "Did you invent these details later?"

Ames frowned. She'd been silent so far, and Matt wondered if this was her cue to intervene as the good cop.

Matt opened his mouth, then felt Sandra's hand touch his arm lightly, a reminder not to give in to his temper. They'd covered that in detail on the ride over. He took a calming breath. "No, trauma to the head, especially a severe injury such as I experienced, typically results in what we call retrograde amnesia. The patient has no memory of events leading up to the injury. In my case, as often occurs, those memories returned later. What I've told you are the facts."

The interview went on in that vein for a while, until Grimes said, "What would you say if we told you we had evidence that you and the deceased, Cara Mendiola, were involved in procuring and selling controlled substances. That she threatened to go to the authorities with her knowledge, and that you killed her to shut her up." He delivered this with the attitude of a magician producing, if not a rabbit from a hat, at least a card that an audience member had chosen.

"I'd say—" This time Sandra's grip on his arm was almost painful. Matt stopped.

Sandra's stare was like an icicle launched at Grimes. "Detective, if you have such evidence, trot it out. If not, I believe this interview is over."

Up to this point, Ames had done a credible imitation of a sphinx. She spoke for the first time. "Counselor, I believe you should advise your client—"

"I'll take care of the advice, Detective." Sandra managed to make the title an invective.

Grimes's expression never changed. "You'll see our evidence soon enough. In the meantime, Doctor, please stay where we can reach you at short notice."

"If you want me," Matt said, "you'll probably find me in the emergency room, trying to save lives. Not ruin them, as you seem to enjoy doing."

Sandra picked at her chef's salad and decided she wasn't hungry. She noticed Matt hadn't eaten much either. "I guess that meeting with Grimes killed your appetite too," she said.

"I suppose that's it." Matt crumpled his napkin and dropped it on his plate, covering the remains of his tuna sandwich.

For a moment the silence between them was interrupted only by the sounds of traffic and an occasional burst from a jackhammer as crews worked on the street outside. Sandra had picked this small downtown sandwich shop because it was near police headquarters. She hadn't counted on the noise, but right now it seemed like it wasn't going to hinder their conversation. Matt sat silent as a statue, staring through the plate glass window but obviously taking no note of what was beyond it.

"Anything you'd like to share?" Sandra asked.

"Where do I start?" He ticked off the points on his fingers. "I'm still a suspect in a murder case. The police say they have evidence that I've been involved in a narcotics ring. Someone kidnapped me with murder in mind, although I haven't the foggiest notion why, and it appears they're not going to rest until they succeed. My girlfriend . . . make that ex-girlfriend, blew me off when I needed her." He started to touch his thumb to emphasize the fifth point, then dropped his hands to his lap. "I guess that's enough."

Sandra filed away the "ex-girlfriend" remark. She'd get back to that later. "You're not a suspect, you're a person of interest," Sandra said. "And Grimes was yanking your chain with that evidence thing. If they had something, we'd know about it."

"Great. So I don't have to worry about the police coming for me in the middle of the night. All I have to worry about is that someone will eventually succeed in knocking me off." He dug a potato chip out of the mess on his plate and bit into it fiercely, chewed, and swallowed. "I'm still not sure I did the right thing, giving up that pistol. If I didn't have—never mind."

"If you didn't have what?" Sandra asked. "Do you have any other illegal weapons I don't know about? If so, you need to let me have them. Now!"

"Nothing illegal," Matt said. "Let's just leave it at that for now."

They exchanged glances that communicated as effectively as though she'd asked if he was finished and he'd answered in the affirmative. Both pushed back their chairs and made their way out into the downtown heat and noise.

Sandra started to ask Matt again if he had another weapon of some sort, but decided a busy sidewalk wasn't the place for that conversation. *Change the subject. Bring it up later.* "I'll drive you back to my office to get your car," she said.

They stopped at the curb as the pedestrian signal across from them changed from Walk to Don't Walk.

"Sorry I snapped at you," Matt said.

"I've had worse. Don't hold back. Snap if it helps."

When the signal once again showed Walk, Matt moved out ahead of her, apparently in his own world, oblivious of what was going on. To their left, an engine roared. Sandra turned that way and saw a car speeding through the intersection toward Matt. She opened her mouth to scream, but the sound was drowned out by a loud *thump*.

Reflexes carried her backward into the arms of a stranger. "Are you all right?" the man asked.

"I'm fine, but the man I was with—" The words died in Sandra's throat when she saw Matt lying in the gutter at her feet and heard a car speed off with a screech of rubber on the pavement.

FIFTEEN

The police had come and gone, promising to search for the hit-and-run driver. They as much as said the odds of finding him were slim, and Matt couldn't disagree with their assessment. As it was, he felt lucky to be alive and relatively uninjured. Now if he could just convince the EMTs of it.

The Mobile Intensive Care Unit, or MICU, idled at the curb while the two emergency medical technicians alternately argued with and tried to cajole Matt, who perched on the edge of a stretcher in the back of the vehicle. "Doctor, just lie down so we can strap you in. We need to take you to the hospital and get you checked."

"I'm okay," Matt said. "I was stunned but didn't hit my head. I got knocked down and my hip is sore. That's it." He shrugged. "I've had worse bumps than that playing flag football."

Matt knew the words were a lie when they left his mouth, but he was pretty sure all he had were some bad bruises, and he wasn't about to spend the next two or three hours in an ER. He'd been on the other side of that scenario too many times.

"But, Doc—" the lead EMT began.

"No, you look," Matt cut in. "I'm a doctor. I think I'd know if I was hurt badly enough to go to the ER." He looked at his watch. "Matter of fact, I need to head for an emergency room right now to see patients myself. In my *own* car."

"Doc, you know that when we're called to the scene of a traffic accident, we're supposed to take the victim to the nearest ER." The paramedic looked at his partner for confirmation and received a vigorous head nod in return.

"Actually," Matt said, feeling firmer footing beneath his argument, "you're required to do that unless, in your professional opinion, the person is not seriously injured—"

"We aren't sure of that without some X-rays. Not after you—"

"Let me finish. A competent person—that's me—can refuse to be transported. And I refuse." Matt eased off the stretcher and stepped down from the back of the MICU. "I'll give you thirty seconds to decide if I'm mentally competent and let me exercise that right. Then I'm going to ask my attorney over here to drive me back to my car so I can get on with my day."

Sandra touched Matt's arm. "Don't be so stubborn. If you're not concerned with your own health, at least do this for me."

"So you can sue someone for injuring me?" Matt knew the words stung, and regretted them immediately.

Sandra didn't take the bait. "If the driver of that car was actually trying to hit you, we'll need proof of your injuries."

Matt took a deep breath, grateful that there was no pain to indicate cracked ribs this time. He still had occasional twinges from his last episode. "Tell you what." He turned to Sandra. "How about if I ride with *you* to the ER? And let's go to Metropolitan. It's as close as any other hospital, and as soon as the doctor on duty clears me, I can go right to work."

The lead EMT nodded assent. "Just let me get a couple of signatures from you, Doc." He looked at Sandra. "Thanks, ma'am."

In Sandra's car, Matt said, "Wait! This isn't going to work. My car is at your office. How am I going to get home when my shift ends?"

"I've already thought of that. Call me a half hour before you're due to leave, and I'll pick you up."

"That will be almost midnight. I can't—"

"Yes, you can, and you will. No arguments."

"Shall I call your cell?" Matt asked.

Sandra reached into her purse, pulled out her cell, and appeared to scan the display. "Yes. And the battery's charged, so I'll get the call."

It wasn't a long drive, and when they were near the hospital, Matt said, "Follow the Emergency Room signs. You can double park long enough to let me out. And when you come for me tonight, that's where you'll wait."

"Fine, but don't think I'm going to drop you off and drive away. I'm going in with you. I want to make sure you register just like a patient, and when you fill out the HIPAA forms, I want to be listed as able to receive medical information about you."

Matt wondered if she'd been reading his mind. He'd intended to check in with the doctor he was relieving, ask him for a once-over-lightly exam, then start his shift. "You don't miss a trick, do you?"

"No, and don't forget it." She parked in a slot for emergency patients and opened her door. "And stop trying not to limp when you walk. I've already noticed it, and I intend to ask the doctor who examines you to get some X-rays."

Matt threw up his hands. "You know, ER doctors hate pushy family members. And pushy lawyers are even lower on the scale."

A smile flitted across Sandra's lips. "You may think I'm pushy now, but before this is all over, you're going to love me."

Matt let her precede him through the automatic doors. *I wonder what she meant by that.*

Why did I say that? It just popped out, but what did I mean? Sandra hoped that by the time they were through the automatic glass doors she'd think of a way to salvage the situation. The best she could muster sounded lame to her, though. "You're going to love me when I make the threats of prosecution go away. Together we might even be able to find who's trying to kill you, and get the police to put them away instead of you."

Halfway down the hall, Matt stopped and turned to Sandra. "I appreciate what you've done, and I know you'll do more. But right now I need to go relieve the doctor on duty, who happens to be my boss. This job is about all I have to hang on to right now, and I'd hate to lose it in the first week."

Matt turned down a hallway marked "Staff Only." Sandra was on his heels as he charged into the ER. "You have to register," she said, as loudly as she dared. "You promised me—"

Matt headed straight for a man dressed in gray-green scrubs covered by a wrinkled white lab coat. His sandy hair was tousled, and behind wire-rimmed glasses his gray eyes looked tired. He swung those eyes up from the chart in his hands and said, "I was beginning to think I'd have to call the jail to see if the police had you in custody." He grinned, but it looked to Sandra as though he was half-serious.

"Rick, I'm sorry," Matt said. "The police had me in for an interview. While I was downtown, a car hit me as I crossed the street."

"Are you okay?" The worry in Rick's voice and on his face seemed genuine.

"A few bumps and bruises, mainly the left hip and thigh where the fender clipped me. But my attorney here—" Matt nodded toward Sandra. "She insists I get checked before I can go to work."

Sandra stuck out her hand. "Sandra Murray. I'm sorry to barge in here—"

"Rick Pearson." His handshake was firm but gentle. "No problem." He clapped Matt on the shoulder. "You walked in here, so I'm guessing you don't have a fractured hip or broken leg." He motioned to a room. "Let me have a look at you. Then we can get some X-rays."

"I'll be in the waiting room," Sandra said. "Shall I get him checked in at reception?"

Rick thought about that. "I'm not sure Matt's insurance coverage as an employee has kicked in yet. Let's make this an unofficial visit for now. If there's anything serious, we can start a chart."

"But I need something to document his injuries," Sandra said. "I intend to follow up with the police and make sure they do everything possible to track down that hit-and-run driver."

Rick offered to dictate a note summarizing his findings, and Sandra accepted that. When Matt turned away to follow Rick into the exam room, she touched his sleeve. "Let me know. I'll be in the waiting room."

"No need to wait around," Matt said. "I can call your cell."

"No, I want you to look me in the eye and tell me you're okay. Better yet, I want Dr. Pearson to tell me."

She found a seat in the waiting room, as far as possible from the TV set suspended overhead, and started to pick up a *People* magazine from goodness-knows how long ago. She stopped with her fingers inches from the cover. How many hundreds of hands had held that same magazine, hands belonging to people waiting for word that their loved one's illness or injury was serious or minor, praying while they waited, powerless for a life or death verdict? She didn't know how Matt and Rick did it.

When an attorney heard a verdict, the client either went free or was escorted from the courtroom in handcuffs, while the lawyer stuffed papers into a briefcase and left. She wondered if a doctor who delivered bad news to a patient or a family was able to turn off their emotions and move on to the next case with no thought of the consequences. Or did they have feelings for the people involved—feelings like the ones she was developing for her client?

"I'm sorry, Counselor. That's all the information I have right now."

Sandra murmured her thanks and returned her cell phone to her purse. She'd slipped out of the waiting room to move her car, thinking she might be here at the hospital for a while. While she was there, she'd taken advantage of the privacy of her auto to call the police for an update on Matt's accident. Unfortunately, by the time the police arrived on the scene, many of the witnesses had left the area. She couldn't really blame them.

She'd given her story to the patrolman who responded to the call, but got the impression that her answers were pretty much like everyone else's. License plate? *Just got a glance at it. Texas plate, I think.* Make and model of the car? *No idea. Sedan, not an SUV, but most of them look alike to me. Dark color—black, dark blue, maybe dark green. It happened so fast.* What did the driver look like? *Not sure. Only got a glimpse through the tinted side windows.* Did he slow down, try to stop? *Absolutely not.* The usual bulletin would go out to body shops in the city: report any dark sedans with damage to the right front fender or bumper. Likelihood of catching up with the offender? Close to zero.

"There you are." Dr. Pearson waved at Sandra as she walked in the door. "You said you wanted me to give you my report. Matt told me it was okay, so I'm not going to get in trouble for violating the

HIPAA regulations." He looked around. "Let's find someplace a bit more private."

In a few moments, they were seated on a sofa upholstered with cracked brown Naugahyde. "This is our break room," Rick said. "Not fancy, but it serves the purpose."

"What about Matt?" Sandra asked.

"No serious injuries. A bruise about the size of a dinner plate along his hip and thigh, probably where the car fender brushed him. A couple of abrasions on his knees and palms from the pavement. No fractures."

"So where is he?"

"He insisted on going right to work. I offered to do a double shift so he could go home and rest, but he was having none of it."

That sounded a lot like the Matt she was coming to know. "Will he be okay?"

Rick rubbed his chin. "You know, doctors hate to hear that question. We can make an educated guess, but there are no guarantees."

"I mean—"

"I know what you mean, and yes, I'm pretty sure he'll be fine. Just in case, I'll ask the charge nurse to keep an eye on him and call me if there's any problem."

Sandra shook Rick's hand. "Thanks for checking him. I guess you want to get home to your family now."

Rick looked down, seemingly surprised at the wedding ring on his hand. "Oh, you noticed that? Probably should take it off, but hope springs eternal." He twisted the ring. "My wife and I are separated right now. She and my daughter are with her folks in Arizona."

"I'm sorry." She knew she should let it lie, but before she could stop them, the words tumbled out. "It must be hard being married to a doctor."

"That's one of the reasons for this rough patch—not the only one, but we don't need to go into that." Rick frowned. "I thought maybe things would get better when I went into emergency medicine. The stress is unbelievable at times, but the hours are regular. I don't make as much as some specialists, but . . . You don't want to hear all this. Sorry."

No, she didn't want to hear about how hard it was to live with a doctor. She'd had to confront that once and thought it was a dead issue, but things were changing. Why had she taken on Matt as a project? Why was she coming back for him after his shift, instead of letting him take a taxi? "I hope you work it out," Sandra said. *And maybe that goes for me too.*

Lou swallowed hard, then cleared his throat a couple of times. "We've got a little problem."

Once more he stood in front of the big man's desk. When he looked at the rug he almost expected to see a bare spot from his shuffling feet. The throw rug on which he stood probably cost more than all the suits in Lou's closet, and there was a rumor that it concealed bloodstains on the floor beneath it, blood from a man who tried to pull a double cross. Lou wasn't certain of the truth behind that story, and he wasn't about to find out.

"We've got a problem?" the boss echoed. "*We've* got a problem?" The sneer in his voice was mirrored on his face. "Since when do your problems become mine?"

"Sorry. I guess *I've* got a problem." Lou made a conscious effort to keep his expression neutral. "I visited the doctor's house last night while he was at work. He's changed the locks, but that didn't keep me out." He paused, waiting for praise, but got none. He steeled himself before delivering the news. "I searched the whole place, looking for a pistol, but it wasn't there."

"But you're sure he had one?"

"I know he had it when Edgar and I were there. I saw it. He shot at us with it. He—"

"I asked you a simple question." The boss's voice was quiet, but his tone was unmistakable.

"Yessir. I didn't find a pistol."

The big man was silent for a few moments. The blinds were closed today. It added to the trapped sensation Lou always felt in this office—trapped with an unpredictable man who might at any time dispatch Lou with no thought other than how to replace a bloody throw rug afterward.

After what seemed like forever, the boss swiveled back. "Can you get an untraceable handgun?"

Lou didn't even have to think about that one. He knew a dozen places where he could get a Saturday night special. If nothing else, he could get one of Edgar's. "Sure."

The man opened his center desk drawer. His hand disappeared for a moment, and Lou shifted his weight to the balls of his feet, ready to dodge whatever was coming. But the hand emerged holding two hundred-dollar bills. "Get one and come back here tomorrow."

Lou pocketed the money. "Alone?" Again, no Edgar. Maybe it was that sleigh thing the boss talked about. *Well, better him than me.*

"Alone." The boss leaned back. "Do you see where this is going?"

Lou nodded. The big man turned his attention to a pile of papers on his desk, and Lou took his cue to leave. He only relaxed when he closed the office door behind him. Lou had a lot to do, but he was still alive to do it. And if he understood the man correctly, in the near future that might not be true for at least one of the other players in this scenario. He had to make sure that person wasn't him.

In his car Lou dialed Edgar's number.

"I need an untraceable handgun," Lou said when his partner answered.

"Why?"

"You don't need to know. Just get one and bring it with you when I tell you."

There was a moment's hesitation. "That's gonna cost. How much you willing to spend?"

Lou felt the two bills in his pocket. Might as well make a profit while he was at it. "A hundred bucks."

"You got it."

Lou ended the call. *No, Edgar. You got it. Or at least, you're gonna get it.*

Jennifer hit Print, leaned back in her secretarial chair, and stretched. Although some typists might suffer from carpal tunnel syndrome, her primary problem at the end of the day was a set of neck muscles that were tense as violin strings. She needed a massage, but her budget didn't run to such an extravagance.

She shoved the papers on her desk into a drawer and locked it. Closed down her computer and turned it off. Time to get out of here. She'd pick up the letter she'd just printed out, put it in Mr. Tanner's inbox, and be through the door before one of the assistant DAs could catch her and try to guilt her into doing "just one more thing."

She had taken only a few steps when she heard, "Jennifer, got a minute?"

She recognized the speaker's voice even before she could turn around to confirm his identity. "Sure, Frank. What's up?"

He stood right behind her, suit coat over one arm, holding his briefcase with the other hand. "Relax. I'm not going to ask you to stay late and work. Matter of fact, I wanted to ask if you'd like to have dinner, then maybe hit one of the clubs—have a few drinks, dance, let our hair down."

I have a lot more hair to let down than you do. "Um, I'd need to go home and change. Freshen up a bit. Would that work?"

Everett consulted a wristwatch that appeared to be a Rolex. She'd seen it up close and knew it was a knockoff. *So like Frank Everett—all about appearances. Do I really want to hook up with somebody like that?*

"Why don't I pick you up about seven?" he asked.

Jennifer did a quick inventory of her options, but they all seemed to begin and end with Frank. Matt had called, but must've lost his nerve when he heard her voice. If that was the best he could do . . . "Sure, Frank. About seven?"

"Perfect," Frank beamed.

They shared an elevator, then went their separate ways. As Jennifer climbed into her car, she tried to ignore the faint gnawing of her conscience. Why had she said yes to Frank? He was nice enough, but . . . Thoughts of Matt crowded into her head. Should she try once more to call him? No. When she left the voicemail on his cell, it sort of put the ball in his court. She pushed thoughts of Matt aside and headed home to get ready to meet Frank. After all, a bird in the hand . . .

SIXTEEN

Sandra was parked in Metropolitan Hospital's ER lot by eleven thirty p.m. Nurses and other employees emerged, some in groups, some singly, all hurrying to their cars. She watched a couple of ambulances roll in and discharge their cargo. Still no Matt. Should she call his cell? No, he must be busy—probably too busy to take her call.

It was half past midnight when Matt walked through the automatic doors, looking at his watch and shaking his head. By that time the area was almost deserted again.

"Sorry." Matt dropped into the passenger seat and buckled in. "I should have warned you that sometimes it's a struggle for a doctor to break away."

Sandra eased out of the parking lot and set a course for her office, where Matt had left his car. "I understand." She started to say more, but closed her lips firmly to stop the words from coming out. *No need to go into my past history with Ken. Not now, at least.*

"I really appreciate this, Sandra. I hate it that I've kept you up so late."

"No worries. Now how did your shift go? Any problems after the accident this afternoon?"

Matt shifted in the seat and rubbed his hip. "About what you'd expect. Nothing major."

They rode in silence for a while, absorbed in their own thoughts. Sandra was grateful not to have to hold up her end of a conversation while she tried to sort out her emotions. Despite her assurances to the contrary, Grimes's statement about new evidence against Matt worried her. Even more worrisome was the knowledge that someone was trying to kill her client, someone whose identity and reason were a total mystery both to her and to Matt. And tucked into one small corner of her brain, surfacing from time to time, were her feelings about the man sitting next to her. Attorneys fought to avoid emotional involvement with a client. And she'd vowed never to have another relationship with a doctor. Now here she was, digging in her heels as she felt herself dragged toward both.

"Penny for your thoughts." Matt's voice from the darkness beside her brought Sandra back to reality with a start.

"Just thinking about your case," she said.

"Which part? My problems with the police or the likelihood that there's someone out there aiming at the bull's-eye on my back?"

"Actually, both," Susan said. "I think Grimes is bluffing, but just in case there's something there, I plan to tap into my resources at the DA's office to see if I can find out more."

Matt's laugh had no humor in it. "Interesting. I used to have a source at the DA's office, but she pretty much abandoned me as soon as she heard I was in trouble." He dug his cell phone from his pocket and scanned the display. "No missed calls, so I guess she's—"

Matt fell silent, and Sandra wondered where his thoughts had taken him.

After about fifteen seconds, he took up where he'd left off. "I guess she's decided not to try getting back together with me."

Sandra flicked a glance sideways at Matt. The poor guy had lost his future job, lost his girlfriend, and someone had tried to kill him—was still trying. He had every reason to be deep in thought.

Matt shook his head like a football player who'd had his bell rung. This was the second time it had occurred—a momentary lapse, a few seconds when it seemed someone had hit the Pause button on his ability to speak, or move, or think. He couldn't ignore it anymore. When he got home, he'd find an all-night pharmacy and fill a prescription. If he was right, medication should take care of the problem, at least control it. He couldn't afford to go through a full workup and all that entailed. *Not right now.*

He turned to his left and summoned a smile, although he wasn't sure Sandra could see it in the darkness. "Sorry about that. I guess I got lost in my thoughts."

Her laugh carried relief. "No problem. Been there myself." She slowed the car and turned into the parking garage by her office building. "Are you sure you're okay to drive?"

Matt held up both hands in surrender. "Please, Mom. I'm a big boy. That car didn't hurt me that badly, I seem to be recovering pretty well from my head injury, and I can find my way home just fine."

There were only three cars left on that level of the garage. Either the drivers of the other two encountered mechanical problems that made them abandon their vehicles or, on a happier note, they'd ridden with friends to a dinner or a party or . . . whatever. Matt climbed out of Sandra's car, then leaned back in through the open window.

"Thanks for picking me up—and for caring about me. I'll talk with you tomorrow."

"No, you'll talk with me tonight," Sandra said. "Or rather, this morning, since it's well after midnight. Call my cell when you get home. And I'm going to sit here until I'm sure your car will start."

Matt decided not to argue. It was nice that someone cared. And that began a stream of thoughts he'd been trying for several days to suppress. It seemed to him his attorney cared for him more than legal obligations dictated. That was okay with him, since he'd found himself drawn to Sandra, wondering what might have happened if he'd met her under better circumstances. Would she have abandoned him in his time of need, as Jennifer apparently had?

Matt's car started on the first try. He waved to Sandra, backed out of the parking space, and headed down the ramp and toward home, navigating on autopilot while he thought. He had some things to figure out, and the first was how to make sure he stayed alive.

Matt kicked off his shoes, stretched, and booted up his computer. A cup of coffee sat on the desk to his right, a safe distance away from the keyboard. He'd learned that lesson the hard way. The clock on his desk showed it was a quarter to two, but he wasn't sleepy. Chances were that once he had a hot shower and hit the bed, he'd sleep like a rock, but this was more important than sleep.

He had the site for the National Library of Medicine bookmarked. A couple of clicks, entry of a search term, and he was looking at a confirmation of his self-diagnosis. Petit mal seizure, sometimes known as "absence seizures," was characterized by brief bouts such as stopping in the middle of a sentence or freezing without movement for fifteen seconds or more. Caused by lots of things, one of which was a head injury. It was sometimes associated with a number of other signs and symptoms, all thankfully absent in his case.

The implications were numerous, all too bad to contemplate. What if he had a petit mal seizure while caring for a patient? If one happened while he was driving down Central Expressway, would he crash and kill himself and innocent bystanders? Or what if his mysterious kidnappers returned, and he had a seizure, an absence spell, while trying to fight them off? As a physician, he knew he should seek medical help. And he would . . . eventually. For now, he was prepared to undertake one of the worst things a doctor could do—self-medicate.

He scrolled down the page, then checked a couple of other sites and wrote down the name and dosage of the drug he wanted. He leaned back until he was staring at the ceiling and, with his eyes still open, uttered a prayer that was no less fervent for its simplicity: *Please, God, let the medicine work.*

Twenty minutes later he was in a 24-hour Walgreen's, presenting the pharmacist with a prescription written on a pad from his now-defunct private practice. Matt knew it was perfectly legal for him to self-prescribe, especially since this was neither a narcotic nor a habit-forming drug. And if the script had been written on a sheet torn from a Big Chief tablet, it would still be valid. But he didn't want to have to go through a long explanation.

Matt had his hand on his wallet, ready to pull out his proof of Texas licensure, but the pharmacist, an older man with nicotine-stained fingers, simply glanced at the prescription and said, "Hang on. Won't take a minute to get this ready."

Apparently the man was glad of the company, because he talked incessantly during the time it took him to fill the prescription. "What'd you do, run out of medicine? Lose the bottle? I get that a lot. People come in here late at night, wanting a pill or two just to tide them over until their doctor's office opens. Handy to be a doctor yourself, isn't it?"

Matt opened his mouth, but the pharmacist's questions appeared to be rhetorical. He prattled on, and soon Matt was letting the words roll past him without really considering their meaning. In a moment, the pharmacist plunked a white plastic bottle onto the counter in front of Matt. "Ethosuximide, 250 milligram caps. One BID. Right?"

"That's right. I appreciate your getting right to it." Matt slid a credit card across the counter and signed for the transaction.

"Don't guess I need to give you instructions on how to take it, side effects, things like that." The pharmacist stuck out his hand. "Thanks for coming in. Hope you'll send your patients to us, especially when they need something in the middle of the night. That's why we're here. I've been divorced for ten years, and the other pharmacist I share this duty with is a widower. No reason to be home, so we might as well be working."

The man was still talking as Matt eased away from the counter and hurried to the front of the store. He stopped there long enough to buy a cold can of Coke. In his car, he used it to wash down one of the red capsules. He was tempted to take a second dose, but he'd encountered too many patients who'd fallen prey to that misconception. *If one's good, two's better, and maybe I'd better take three just to be sure.* Overdoses were a common occurrence in the emergency room. He'd already encountered two cases in the short time he'd been working there. No, he'd stick to the normal dose—one capsule twice a day. And pray they worked.

Matt lay in bed and stared at the ceiling. He'd expected to fall asleep immediately, but it was as though his eyelids were spring-loaded, designed to pop open the minute he closed them. Nothing helped. Not the hot shower. Not the warm milk. Not the half a chapter of the boring novel from his bedside table. Nothing.

Finally he rolled out of bed and slid his feet into slippers. He'd cranked the thermostat down, hoping the cold air would help him sleep. Matt slipped on a robe and padded to the living room. He flipped on the TV and surfed through the channels. As he did, an old Bruce Springsteen song ran through his head. Nowadays he could get a lot more than fifty-seven channels, but there was still nothing on. He punched a button on the remote and watched a muscled pitchman with six-pack abs fade away in midsentence, still extolling the virtues of his exercise device.

There was a Bible on the coffee table in his living room, left behind by his brother. "This is too big for me to carry around on the mission field," Joe had said. "Hang on to it for me until I get back. You might even read some of it. I've marked a few of my favorite passages."

Matt hefted the thick, leather-covered book and felt a wave of shame because he hadn't opened it since Joe left. He paid no more attention to it than the magazines that occupied the space beside it. No, that wasn't true. He changed out the magazines every month. But he could see the place where the Bible sat, outlined by the dust that had gathered around it since he put it there.

He held the Bible on his lap and tugged at the thin purple ribbon that hung from the binding. On the page that opened, sure enough, Matt saw a passage marked in yellow highlighter. "God is our refuge and strength, a very present help in trouble. Therefore we will not fear, though the earth should change, and though the mountains slip into the heart of the sea."

Matt could identify with those sentiments. Sometimes he felt as though the earth were crumbling beneath his feet and there was nothing left for him to hold on to. *I'm hanging on to a new job by a thread, the police suspect I'm a murderer, someone—I have no idea who—kidnapped me and still wants to kill me, my girlfriend's gone, and I'm pretty sure I've developed a neurologic complication from a head injury. What do You say to that?*

Matt sat for a moment with his head bowed. He didn't know what he expected—perhaps some thunderous voice from heaven, some kind of a sign in reply. But there was only silence. *Maybe this is all nonsense* . . . But as he read through those words a second and yet a third time, peace stole across Matt's heart. He hadn't taken a tranquilizer, but he felt as though one were circulating through his veins. He wouldn't fear, even if things seemed to be crumbling around him.

He nodded slowly. *Okay, God. I get it. I'll take You at Your word.*

The summons to the boss's office had included the admonition to come without Edgar, so Lou stood alone before the big man.

"We need to make Dr. Newman's protestations of innocence totally unbelievable and let the justice system neutralize him." The smile that spread slowly across the boss's face held no mirth. "And to do that, we're going to throw Edgar off the sleigh."

Lou shook his head. "Throw him off . . . ?"

"I'll explain in a minute. Now, here are your instructions."

The plan was simplicity itself, although it rocked Lou back on his heels. He started to ask the boss if he was sure, but clamped his lips shut instead. The boss was always sure. And if not, it didn't make any difference. He was the boss. Instead, Lou said, "I can do that."

"Then do it, the sooner the better."

"Okay. I'll do it tomorrow night. But can we talk about one more thing?" Lou took a deep breath. He wanted to sit down, but there were no chairs in front of the desk—probably on purpose. "Money."

The big man raised one eyebrow. "Money?"

Lou swallowed hard. Too late to turn back now. "I've worked for you for a couple of years. You pay me well enough, but this stuff lately is a lot more risky. And now you want me to . . . Well, I wonder if I don't deserve more money. Sort of like combat pay."

The big man's hand moved toward the center drawer of his desk, and Lou smiled as he recalled the crisp $100 bills that source had previously yielded. But instead, the pudgy hand emerged holding a pistol. Almost automatically, Lou catalogued it: Ruger, semi-automatic, long barrel, probably a .22 caliber. Not just a pistol for close work such as the one Edgar carried, but the tool of a serious marksman.

"Hey," Lou said, raising his hands. "No need for that."

"I didn't get where I am now by sitting behind this desk. I've done what you're doing and a lot worse. And I can do it again." The big man rested his hand, still holding the gun, on the desk. "To put your mind at rest, my current enterprises are growing rapidly—and profitably. In addition, I have a couple of other ventures that are almost ready to go into operation. When that happens, your share of the money will more than satisfy you. And, of course, you'll be getting a larger share once we toss Edgar to the wolves."

Glad for a chance to change the subject, Lou asked, "I don't understand this talk about sleighs and wolves."

The big man seemed to have forgotten the pistol, but it remained centered on the desk, the barrel pointing at Lou. "It's an old Russian tale. A rich man and his wife are riding across the snow in a sleigh with their driver and a servant. They're pursued by a pack of wolves. The rich man orders the driver to throw the servant out of the sleigh, and while the wolves devour him, they make their escape."

"So you're saying we might need to give up Edgar to take attention away from ourselves? But if the police get hold of him, he'll spill his guts inside of ten minutes."

"No one said that the person who's thrown to the wolves has to be alive."

Lou felt a grin starting, but that expression was wiped off his face when the boss raised the gun and gestured with it. "If I were you, I'd stop pushing for money. Because no one said that the person who gets thrown off the sleigh has to be Edgar either."

Lou's stomach churned as though he were on an elevator in a free fall. "Er . . . I didn't . . . I wasn't trying to . . . to push. I just meant . . ."

"I know what you meant. But now that we're clear about where we stand, I don't anticipate any further problems. If there are, though, remember one thing. The sleigh."

SEVENTEEN

Matt was at his kitchen table, reading the paper and working on his second cup of coffee of the morning, when the ring of his cell phone interrupted his perusal of the sports page.

"Good morning, Sandra."

"I take it caller ID gave me away?"

Matt didn't want to tell her he'd already assigned her number a special ring tone, the theme from *Law and Order*. "Uh, yeah, sort of. What's up?"

Although Matt's short night had left him feeling groggy, Sandra sounded positively chipper this morning. "I wanted to see how you're feeling this morning. In case you've forgotten, you were hit by a car less than twenty-four hours ago."

Matt moved in his chair, trying without success to find a more comfortable position. He felt as though he'd just finished two-a-day workouts with the Dallas Cowboys. "I'm a little sore, but nothing I can't get through." He went for the quick change of subject. "Anything new from the DA's office?"

"Haven't tapped my sources yet this morning, but I doubt it. For now, don't worry."

Words jumped to Matt's tongue. Words like, "Easy for you to say," and "You're not the one facing a life sentence . . . or execution." But he choked them back. He truly believed Sandra was totally on his side, and he had to trust her judgment. Instead he said, "I'll try not to."

"Are you working tonight?"

"Yes. Same shift as yesterday," Matt said. "Do we need to get together sometime? I could meet you for lunch."

She hesitated, and he wondered if he'd crossed a line. Then he heard pages turning. She was checking her appointment calendar.

"Sorry. I have court appearances later this morning, a luncheon meeting with another lawyer, and clients all afternoon."

"Oh, right. Maybe another time." Matt tried to keep the disappointment out of his voice. *Get over it. You're not her only client. And your interest in lunch wasn't really professional either.* "So, I guess we'll talk if either of us learns something about the case."

He ended the conversation but didn't return immediately to the story he'd been reading. Regardless of the season, the sports news didn't change much—some teams won, some teams lost, and somebody wanted more money. Come to think of it, life was sort of like that. And right now, he felt as though he was losing—big time.

Matt spent the morning at his desk, surfing the web about petit mal seizures. He'd had no more "absence spells" since starting the medicine, but he knew that two doses probably wouldn't be effective this quickly. Maybe his spells had been isolated instances. On the other hand, he couldn't ignore the possibility that perhaps his head trauma and the surgery afterward had left him with brain damage that would cause long-term symptoms.

Matt had a definite advantage over a lay Internet user—he knew to restrict his search to authoritative sites, such as those from medical institutions. The worldwide web was filled with posts from people with a personal or economic ax to grind. "Follow this diet . . ." "Take this naturopathic medication . . ." "Let our specialists evaluate your need for counseling and therapy." No, he skimmed past those in a hurry.

He looked at the textbooks filling the bookcase in the corner of his living room. They contained a great deal of information about general surgery: situations where surgery was indicated, the techniques of the various procedures, critical aspects of follow-up care. On top of the bookcase was an uneven pile of medical journals, some with dog-eared pages and yellow sticky notes marking papers Matt wanted to study further. But since his accident, his focus had shifted to neurology, a subject sorely lacking in his medical education and surgical training.

An hour after he started, Matt leaned back and rubbed his eyes. It was time to come face-to-face with reality. Either his "absence spells" represented petit mal seizures caused by permanent damage to his brain, or they were transient late consequences of what was called "minimal brain injury" or MBI syndrome, although "minimal" was hardly appropriate in his case. He was hoping for the latter, because that problem might be a temporary one. The proper diagnosis would hinge on an EEG—what a layman would call a "brain wave" test. Presence of an abnormal focus in the brain would confirm petit mal seizures. If that happened, Matt would need to be on medication for an indefinite period. He would be restricted from driving. He'd have to alter his practice of medicine significantly—perhaps retrain in something like radiology or pathology, where a spell wouldn't pose a risk to patients.

Matt knew he ought to call Ken Gordon and report what was happening, but he knew where that would lead. Ken would order tests—an EEG, probably some others. That would settle the matter, but might also change Matt's life forever. He reached for the phone but stopped with his hand in midair. He'd only had two spells. He was on the right kind of medicine to prevent further episodes. And he didn't want to compromise the plan that had taken shape in his mind over the past few days.

He felt sure that the people who framed him for the murder of Cara Mendiola were the ones responsible for his kidnapping and the home invasion that followed. Matt had no doubt they'd try again. He could never feel safe until his attackers were behind bars. And, since the police didn't seem interested in taking his story seriously, Matt figured it was up to him. If they came after him—and, perversely, he hoped they would—he'd be ready.

Was this the result of watching too many John Wayne movies? Matt hoped not. But deep down he knew there'd be something very satisfying in bringing these men to justice while clearing his own name. His decision made, he logged off his computer and moved to the kitchen, where his medicine stood on the counter. Matt half-filled a glass with water and swallowed one of the capsules. *God, if You'll keep me healthy until I can do this, I'll have the EEG and accept the consequences.* He wasn't sure God would be particularly pleased with the bargain he was trying to make, but it was the best Matt could do.

If the way to catch the men who wanted to kill him involved his being bait in a trap, so be it. But this time he was going to be prepared when that trap sprang. Back in the living room, he picked up a gym bag he'd pulled from the attic and started packing it with things necessary to put his scheme into action.

The best place to catch him would be after work, in the dark parking garage. His schedule put him in that location on a regular basis. They'd tried once to get him there. He found himself hoping they'd try again.

He'd be vulnerable to a bullet during the walk to his car. It had been surprisingly easy to buy a Kevlar vest at a supply store near police headquarters. It would be hot and uncomfortable, it wouldn't protect against a head shot, and Matt realized he'd be tempted to stop wearing it after a few times. But he hated to leave any loopholes for a would-be attacker. He shoved the vest into the bag.

Matt intended to be careful, to not let anyone sneak up on him again, but if they did, the pepper spray from this small cylinder could reach up to ten feet and immobilize an attacker long enough for Matt to subdue him. For that he had plastic handcuffs, the type used by police when making mass arrests. They didn't clink like metal cuffs, took up very little room in his pocket, but would secure a man for as long as necessary.

If the attacker got the upper hand and Matt was bound with duct tape, he was ready to free himself this time. To the contents of the bag, he added a disposable scalpel, the blade protected by a plastic shield. Not only would the scalpel cut through tape, the surgical knife would be an effective weapon in close quarters. He'd tape it to his ankle each night.

Finally Matt planned to wear cargo pants, buttoning his cell phone into one of the outer pockets so he couldn't lose it.

There it all was, the equipment Matt hoped to use to catch his attacker. It reminded him of that passage in the Bible that talked about putting on the armor of God. Well, he planned to be armed— armed and dangerous. Now all he had to do was wait for his attacker to take the bait.

The little deli on Commerce Street was packed. It was a favorite place for lawyers and staff from the nearby court building to snatch a quick lunch. Patrons were crowded in like a New York subway car during rush hour, but the roar of a hundred voices was as effective as white noise, providing privacy for conversations like the one Sandra was concluding with another lawyer.

"So it's settled. We'll see if the DA will try both cases jointly," Sandra said.

"And you'll take the lead."

Sandra dabbed at the corner of her mouth with a paper napkin. "Make sure it's okay with your client."

Larry Vanover smiled at her from across the table. "It'll be okay. I don't mind being second chair when both our clients are facing twenty to life. Not if the best defense attorney in the state is working with me." He reached for the check. "Guess this is an expense I can bill to my client . . . unless you have one you'd rather charge for it."

That sent Sandra's mind scanning over the case files currently on her desk. Certainly, the most important one was Matt's. She hoped Elaine would have some news for her tonight about the DA's plan to take the case to the grand jury.

"Uh, earth to Sandra," Larry said. "You just went somewhere. Want to share the journey?"

Sandra shook her head. "Sorry. I was thinking about a particular case."

"Want to bounce anything off me? You know I'd keep the information in confidence, sort of a lawyer-to-lawyer consultation. I wouldn't even bill for it, if you'll have dinner with me."

"Sorry, Larry. I can't discuss it. And thanks for the invitation, but I'm going to pass."

Larry dabbed at his lips with a napkin, then tucked it under the edge of his plate. "Okay, but I'm going to keep asking."

This was probably the third time Larry Vanover had asked her out. The first time, she'd been seriously involved with Ken Gordon. The second invitation had come shortly after her breakup with Ken, and at that point she wasn't ready to date again. But why didn't she accept this bid? Larry was a successful attorney, handsome, witty, and unmarried. He was obviously interested in her. What kept her from going out with him?

Matt.

They rose from the table, which was occupied by two more lawyers before the busboy could finish cleaning it. Sandra thanked Larry for lunch, assured him she'd call soon, and headed back to her office, navigating the six blocks on automatic pilot as she tried to sort out her feelings for her client.

Lou leaned against the wall in Edgar's little hole-in-the-wall apartment, preferring not to risk his bulk on the room's one spindly chair. "We'll do it tonight. I'll come by for you at ten."

"What's up?" Edgar asked.

"We're gonna pay a visit to our old friend Dr. Newman."

"We tried that once," Edgar half-whined. "Lucky to get away. Why are we going in there again?"

"Because the boss said so." Seeing Edgar's expression, Lou decided some reassurance was in order. "It's different this time. Here's the deal. We park a couple of blocks away. We do our thing to get us past his locks. When he comes home we're waiting for him. He opens the door, we're ready, he's not."

Edgar nodded and licked his lips. "Yeah, and odds are he won't have a gun in his hand this time."

"But I will," Lou said. "I'll put a couple of bullets into him. Stuff some hundreds in his pocket, break open a baggie of something and spill it near him. Then we split and let the police take it from there." He smiled and spread his palms. "The police write it off as a drug deal gone bad. He's dead, so they hang Mendiola's murder on him and close the case. No more heat around Metropolitan Hospital, and everything's back to normal."

Edgar chewed on that for a minute. "Sounds perfect. Real genius."

"That's why he's the boss," Lou said. "Do you have that handgun lined up? Revolver, automatic—doesn't matter."

"Uh. Sure."

Lou handed him a hundred. He was betting Edgar would bring one of his own guns and pocket the money. Even better. "Bring it tonight. We'll put it by Newman's hand, make it look like he was going to shoot." Lou handed Edgar more bills. "I need you to pick up a bag of crank and one of H. We'll use those tonight."

"Why me?"

"Because I said so," Lou said, effectively ending the conversation. "I'll see you at ten."

"Dr. Newman, this is Randy Harrison. He's a second-year medical student. He'd like to shadow you on your shift tonight, if that's okay."

The nurse apparently took Matt's nod as confirmation. She turned away, her white Reeboks squeaking on the polished floor.

The young man wore a hospital scrub suit partially covered by a short white coat of the style favored by pharmacists and students in some medical schools. "I appreciate this," he said. "I'll know more after

I get into my clinical years, but I'm interested in emergency medicine as a career. And I figured I'd like to get a taste of it now."

Matt looked him up and down. Light brown hair, cut short and neatly combed. Metal-rimmed glasses, functional rather than some of the designer frames that were so popular. *Squared-away* was the phrase that came to Matt's mind. "Okay, here are the rules. I'll tell patients you're a med student, observing unless they have an objection. They almost never do. Then—"

"I know. Keep my eyes open, my mouth shut, and we'll talk later."

Maybe this wouldn't be as much trouble as Matt feared. "Exactly. Let's get started."

After a bit Matt and Randy had seen a representative sample of patients for a Friday late evening in a large city emergency room: injuries from sprains and bruises to broken bones, belly pains caused by everything from indigestion to appendicitis, and all manner of respiratory infections. So far there'd been no motor vehicle accidents, and only one heart attack victim, an elderly man obviously dead on arrival.

"Learn anything?" Matt asked as they grabbed a cup of coffee in the break room.

Randy made a face. "Well, I know that the coffee in this ER is as bad as what we get back at Parkland Hospital. Other than that, it's been good to see—"

"Dr. Newman." The nurse stuck her head through the doorway. "Young male with severe flank and groin pain. Says he's had kidney stones before and thinks he's having an attack now."

Matt pulled aside the curtain to the cubicle where the patient lay still and was greeted with moans, curses, and imprecations. "I'm Dr. Newman." He nodded toward Randy. "He's a medical student who's—"

"I don't need your life histories!" the man almost screamed, now writhing on the gurney so hard that Matt thought he might fall off despite the safety rails. "I need something for this pain! I've had it before. I can probably recognize renal colic better than either of you. Just give me some Demerol. Please, something for the pain!"

Matt leaned closer so he could keep his voice low. "Mr.—" He consulted the clipboard the nurse had handed him. "Mr. Glover, we need to find out what's going on. The sooner we make the diagnosis, the sooner we can give you something to help. We'll start an IV to give you some fluids, and then they'll take you around the corner to radiology for a special X-ray called a CAT scan. If you have a kidney stone, we'll see it there."

By now the nurse was standing behind Matt. He turned to her. "Start an IV with Ringer's, and get him to radiology for a CT of the abdomen. Rule out kidney stone."

Matt didn't wait for an acknowledgment, but snapped the curtain shut as he left. He could see the question in Randy's eyes, so he addressed it as they walked to the work area shared by the nurses and ER physicians. "So why didn't I give him something for pain? Right?"

"The man was obviously hurting," Randy said.

"You could call me cynical, although I prefer to think of it as being experienced," Matt said. "One of the most common ploys of a drug addict hurting for a fix is to fake either severe back pain or a kidney stone. It's become common enough that we have to confirm their story objectively first. Otherwise we'd become a Demerol- and morphine-dispensing station."

"Why not get a urinalysis? Simple enough. Microscopic hematuria would confirm a stone."

Matt shook his head. "These guys are smarter than that. Sometimes they prick their finger with a pin and seed their specimen with a couple of drops of blood. And there are other ways to get blood into their urine, ways that would make most people cringe. Addicts will do anything when they're hurting for a fix."

Matt finished scribbling a few notes. He handed the chart to the ER secretary and said, "He's going for a CT. Let me know when it's done." Then he led Randy off to examine more patients.

Almost an hour later, Matt jerked a thumb toward the back of the ER and said, "Let's get some more of that terrible coffee, Randy."

In the break room, the first words out of Randy's mouth were, "How did you know that patient didn't have a kidney stone?"

"Someone with a kidney stone can't get comfortable. They're in constant motion, looking for a position that relieves the pain, but there isn't one. This guy was totally still when I walked in, and he was already settling down when I left."

"Why did he go ahead with the CT?"

"There's always a chance that some ER doc will over-read an X-ray and call a spot somewhere a renal calculus. And as long as there's a possibility of a fix, these patients will do anything." Matt sniffed at his coffee and tossed the nearly full cup in the wastebasket. "Even hold still for a CT."

"I saw him after you talked to him to give him the X-ray results. He'd ripped out his IV and was hurrying toward the door, dripping blood from his wrist."

"He'll staunch the bleeding, wait a bit, and try another emergency room."

Randy sipped from his cup, made a wry face, and, like Matt, tossed his Styrofoam cup into the trash. "I guess I have a lot to learn if I want to do emergency medicine."

"You'll do fine, especially if you take a residency in the specialty."

"You didn't?"

Matt finished his coffee. "My training and practice were in general surgery. I sort of got pushed into emergency medicine by circum-stances." He stood and started back to the ER. "But you know, even though I've had to do some learning on the fly, it's been pretty good." *Of course, I might be hauled off to jail tomorrow, but right now I'm enjoy-ing the experience.*

Lou and Edgar crouched motionless in the darkness of Matt Newman's kitchen. All Lou could hear were the sounds of an empty house: the refrigerator cycling on and off, an occasional creak common to older homes, a muted *whoosh* as the air conditioner delivered cool air. He pointed a gloved finger toward the stairway, then put his mouth next to Edgar's ear. "Check upstairs. I'll look around down here. Make sure no one's home."

Three minutes later, they reassembled at the foot of the staircase. "No one around," Edgar said. "Where do you want to wait for him? The living room?"

Lou drew a penlight from his pocket and checked his watch. Ten thirty. Newman would be home in about an hour. The timing seemed right. "Yeah, let's move in there."

Once in the living room, Lou checked to make sure the drapes were drawn before turning on a table lamp. He let out an involuntary sigh as light erased the shadows in the room. Two men poised in the dark made him think of a scene from a horror movie. In this case, though, Lou knew how it was going to play out.

"I'll get behind the door. You stand there in the center of the room with your gun in your hand." Lou pointed. "I'll kill the light before he gets here, and when he turns it on you'll be the first one he sees. He'll probably turn around to run. That's when I step out from behind the door and shoot him."

Edgar edged back until Lou said, "That's perfect."

"There's a chair here. Why don't I sit down until we hear him outside?" Edgar said.

"Okay, but first, let me have that extra gun I asked for."

Edgar pulled a revolver from his pocket and handed it over, butt-first. Lou took the revolver, pulled a dirty handkerchief from his hip pocket, and wiped the piece carefully.

"Good idea," Edgar said. "We can press his hand on it after he's dead so it'll have his fingerprints."

"Oh, I've got a better idea," Lou said. He pointed the revolver at Edgar and shot him five times in the chest.

The little man slumped to the floor with a soft sigh like air escaping from a balloon. The smell of cordite and death hung in the room.

Lou pocketed the pistol and rummaged in Edgar's pockets with gloved hands until he found two plastic baggies. He opened one, wet his finger and tasted a tiny bit of the contents, then dropped that bag into his pocket. He spilled white powder from the other on the floor and dropped the partially opened container near his former partner's outstretched left arm.

Edgar's own gun already lay next to the corpse's right hand. Perfect. Lou took a moment to survey the scene. Had he forgotten anything? The money! He pulled a wad of bills from his pocket and shoved them into Edgar's. Shame to leave that money behind, but it was necessary.

One last glance, then Lou turned off the light and let himself out the front door.

As he walked quickly to his car, Lou had no second thoughts about what he'd done.

No, if somebody had to be thrown off the sleigh, better Edgar than him.

EIGHTEEN

As he walked to his car, Matt felt a familiar tingle between his shoulder blades. He'd left off the Kevlar vest tonight—too bulky, too hot, too much trouble. He kicked himself for doing it, and quickened his pace as he navigated through the shadowy spaces of the parking garage. Matt unlocked the car, opened the driver's side door, and swept his gaze over the backseat and floor space to make sure he was alone. Only when he was certain did he hurry inside and push the door lock button.

Matt leaned back and took a deep breath. He'd been too busy all evening to break for food, making do with coffee and sodas snatched between patients. A burger and fries sounded good. After all, there was no reason to hurry home.

He drove to his favorite drive-through fast food restaurant, only to discover it was closed for renovations. *I saw the sign last week and completely forgot.* It took Matt another fifteen minutes to find something that was still open. He ordered a cheeseburger, fries, and large Coke. The cook seemed to be in no hurry to get the order ready. Matt hoped that would mean fries fresh from the deep fryer, instead of a batch that had sat under a heat lamp for half an hour. When a hand delivered the food through the window, Matt breathed in the rich aroma of grilled meat and hot grease and decided to pull around into the parking lot to eat before the food got cold.

By the time he turned into the street leading to his house, Matt was yawning. But what he saw ahead brought him fully awake. Police cars and emergency vehicles were parked helter-skelter in the street, their red and blue strobes painting a surreal picture over the area. Yellow tape cordoned the front of his house.

He eased his car past a police cruiser and an ambulance before a patrolman stopped him. "Crime scene, sir. No one allowed in here."

"Uh . . . it's my house," Matt managed to say. "What's going on?"

"You're the person who lives here?"

"Yes," Matt said. "Can you—"

"Sir, please step out of the car. Keep your hands where I can see them at all times." The policeman's voice was firm, and suddenly there was a pistol in his hand.

Matt complied. "What's—"

"Sir, please lean against the car with both arms out. Spread your legs."

Matt had seen this on TV but never imagined it could happen to him.

The policeman's tone told Matt he meant business. "Stay in that position, please." Then he yelled, "Murphy, Rogers. Get over here. This is our man."

Scuffling feet approached, then another voice said, "Just stay as you are. No sudden moves."

Matt thought he'd been subjected to indignity at the hands of TSA screeners at the airport, but that was a breeze compared with what followed. Brisk hands frisked him, ripping away the tape that held a scalpel to Matt's ankle. The policeman gave a low whistle when he found the pepper spray in Matt's pocket. "You're ready for anything, aren't you?"

"I can explain," Matt said.

"Save it. Now step back and turn around. Put your hands up and keep them where I can see them." Matt did so and saw that the first policeman, his gun still trained on him, had been joined by two others, a man and a woman. The newcomers hadn't drawn their guns, but their hands hovered near their weapons, and the retaining straps of the holsters were unsnapped.

The man had sergeant's stripes on his sleeves, and he took charge. "With your thumb and forefinger remove your wallet from your pocket. Take out your driver's license and show it to us."

Matt complied.

"Okay, you can put it back." He spoke into a microphone clipped to the epaulet of his dark blue uniform, his voice too low for Matt to understand the words.

"Can I put my hands down?" Matt asked.

"Not yet," the sergeant said.

Matt bowed his head, not so much in prayer as in defeat. He'd been through so much, and now apparently there was going to be more piled on him. He closed his eyes. *Lord, I don't understand. I can't stand much more—*

"Well, well, just the man we wanted to see."

Matt recognized the voice and his heart sank. He looked up to see Detective Virgil Grimes, his grin like a death's head on Halloween.

"Is he clean?" Grimes asked.

"He had what looked like a surgical knife taped to his ankle, and a canister of pepper spray in his pocket. No gun."

Matt swallowed three times before he could get the words out. "What's going on?"

"That's what we hoped you could tell us," Grimes said. He jerked his head toward one of the cars. "Take him to the station. We'll question him there."

"Wait," Matt said. "Why won't you tell me what happened? Why can't I go into my house?"

"Because it's a crime scene," Grimes said. "We're searching it right now, and I'll bet what we find is going to put you away for a long time."

———

Sandra heard the noise but couldn't process it. Not her alarm clock—that was a buzz guaranteed to have her feet on the floor and her hand slapping the off button in a matter of seconds. Not the telephone. Not the smoke alarm. But something was most definitely assaulting her eardrums and interrupting her sleep.

Cell phone. That was it. She turned on the bedside lamp, snatched up her phone, and answered, hoping it was something important. She'd been awakened occasionally by wrong numbers, usually from drunks unable to navigate the keyboard of their phones. If that's what this was, she'd give the caller an earful, guaranteed to sober him up. "Sandra—" she croaked. She cleared her throat and tried again. "Sandra Murray."

"Sandra, this is Matt. I was about to give up on you, and I think I only get one phone call."

"Matt? Where are you?"

"I'm at police headquarters. They say someone was killed in my house while I was at work tonight—last night, I guess it is now—and they suspect me."

Sandra swung around and slid her feet into slippers. Automatically, she checked her bedside clock. A little after one a.m. She shrugged a robe over her shoulders. "Are you under arrest?"

"I don't know. They didn't say I was, didn't handcuff me. Just brought me here in the back of a police car. They said they wanted me to answer some questions."

"Who's 'they'?"

"Detective Grimes and his partner."

"Tell him you have nothing to say until your attorney is present. I'll be there in half an hour."

By this time Sandra was in the kitchen. She flipped the switch on her coffeemaker, glad she'd followed her usual routine of having it ready to brew when she awoke. She had a hunch she had a long night ahead of her. While the coffee bubbled into the carafe, she pulled a suit and blouse out of the closet and headed for the shower. When Sandra strode into the police station, she wanted to appear in charge—even if she didn't much feel like it right now.

As soon as Sandra entered the interview room, she saw a disheveled and beaten-down Matt Newman. She caught his eye and shook her head. "Don't say a word."

Detective Grimes turned from his seat across the table from Matt and smirked. "He hasn't, Counselor. But that doesn't mean he can't listen, and I've been giving him an earful. Want to hear what I have to say?"

"I need some time with my client. Please wait outside."

Grimes shrugged and jerked his head toward the door. Detective Ames eased away from her position against the wall and followed Grimes out of the room, closing the door softly behind her.

Sandra took the chair beside Matt. She opened her briefcase and pulled out a legal pad. "Have they advised you of your rights?" she asked.

"Yes. I got the Miranda warning when they put me in the squad car for the ride here. I wanted to ask if I was under arrest, but I didn't say anything until we got here. That's when I said I wanted a lawyer."

"Good. But did they talk with you in the car?"

"Yeah. I think they were hoping I'd react to what they were saying, but I kept my mouth shut."

"What did they say?"

Matt dry-washed his face, then let his hands fall limply on the table. "They got a 911 call about gunshots at my house. The responding officers found my front door unlocked and a man inside, shot to death. He had a gun beside one hand, an open baggie of white powder in the other."

"And they think you're responsible?"

"Apparently."

"Obviously you weren't there when this happened. Did you come directly home from the ER?"

"No. I stopped for a cheeseburger after I got off. Drove home and found the place crawling with cops."

Sandra tapped her fingernail against her front teeth. "Okay. Let's get Grimes and Ames back in here and see what they've got. Let them ask their questions. Look at me before you answer. If I nod, then give them the shortest answer possible. Don't volunteer anything. And if I raise my hand, shut up, even if you're in the middle of a word. Clear?"

"Clear."

———

Matt had heard stories that, in some police stations, chairs on this side of the table had the front legs shortened slightly so suspects were always pushed forward and had to reposition themselves. Whatever the cause, he found himself constantly squirming, trying and failing to find a comfortable position.

Grimes did it by the book. He asked permission to record the interview, repeated the Miranda warning, had Matt sign a statement that he'd been advised of his rights. After a few questions about who Matt was and what he did, the hard part started.

"Dr. Newman, can you account for your whereabouts this past evening?"

Sandra answered before Matt could open his mouth. "During what time frame?"

Grimes frowned at the interruption of his questioning. "From ten p.m. to the time you arrived at your house."

Matt looked at Sandra, who nodded. "I was in the emergency room at Metropolitan Hospital working until eleven, maybe closer to eleven thirty. I was hungry, so I decided to eat before going home." He went on to explain his search for an open fast food restaurant. "After I finally got my food, I sat in the parking lot and ate. Then I drove home."

"So you have no alibi for the time from eleven thirty to twelve thirty?"

"Not really."

"How about at the fast food place?"

"I used the drive-through. I doubt that anyone would recognize me, though. I handed them my money, they handed me my food, I left."

"Did you use a credit card? Did you save the receipt for your food?"

When Sandra didn't put up the stop sign, Matt said, "No, I paid cash. And when I finished my meal, I threw the wrappers and sack in the trash, along with my receipt." *That's what I get for not littering, I guess.*

"Detective," Sandra said. "Why is my client implicated in all this?

Do you have any evidence that he was involved in this, rather than just being an innocent victim whose house was the scene of a break-in that ended in a fight between the perpetrators?"

"I guess you want to cut to the chase," Grimes said. "We don't think this was a break-in. It doesn't appear that any door locks were forced. We think the doctor here let the dead man in to sell him drugs. It went bad, and your client shot him."

"So where's the gun he used?" Sandra asked.

Matt remembered how hard he'd fought when Sandra asked him to give her his pistol. Now he was glad he had. Otherwise one of the intruders might have found it and used it to shoot the other one.

"We didn't find a handgun, but there was a rifle in the house. Ballistics is working on that now."

"That's—" Sandra's glare cut Matt off.

"I need to consult with my client," she said.

When the detectives were gone, Sandra asked, "I thought we'd been through this. No guns in the house, right?"

"The rifle belongs to my brother, Joe. He asked me to keep it for him when he left home. It was on a shelf in my closet. It's unloaded, hasn't been fired in years. I intended to get some ammunition for it. Just haven't got around to it yet."

"So that was the 'perfectly legal' protection you had in mind," Sandra muttered.

Matt gave a sheepish nod.

Sandra tapped on the door and Grimes returned, followed by Ames. When they were back in place, Sandra told them about the rifle's owner. "Joe is on the mission field, and it would be difficult to contact him. But the simplest thing is for you to do the ballistics. I'm sure that will clear my client."

"I don't think we need to worry about that right now. The rifle was unloaded and hadn't been fired since who knows when." Grimes shrugged. "But that won't clear him. We sort of figure the doc used a handgun. Easier to hide later."

"Did you find one?" Sandra asked.

"Not in the house," Grimes said. "We think that when he drove up tonight he'd already gotten rid of it—but we'll find it."

"So far all you have is a crime committed in my client's house. That's no reason for you to hold him."

Grimes shrugged. "We've identified the victim as Edgar Lopez. Small-time criminal, several arrests, no convictions. How do you know him?"

"I have no idea who you're talking about."

Grimes reached into a thin folder on the table in front of him, extracted an eight-by-ten photo, and shoved it toward Matt. "Maybe you knew him by another name. Recognize him?"

The picture showed a small, thin man sprawled on his back, sightless eyes staring into eternity, his countenance asking a question that would never be answered.

"Never saw him before in my life," Matt said.

Grimes plunged ahead as though Matt hadn't responded. "Lopez had a baggie of heroin beside his hand and a roll of bills in his pocket. We think this was a drug deal gone bad. And you were right in the middle of it."

Sandra glared at Grimes. "Why do you think Dr. Newman would have anything to do with drugs? His prescribing practices have never been questioned."

"All that means is that he hasn't been caught," Grimes said. "But I don't necessarily mean prescription drugs. If you look at the neighborhood around the hospital where your client practiced, you can find a drug dealer on most corners."

"That's thin, Detective. We both know that you can find drugs, and for that matter, prostitution, in several areas of any large city. But it doesn't mean—"

There was a tap at the door. A uniformed officer entered and whispered in Grimes's ear. The detective nodded once and addressed Matt. "I was about to suggest that we do a nitrate test on your hands to see if you've fired a gun recently."

"Great." Matt held out his hands. "The sooner the better."

"How about right now. And while we're at it, we'll check your shirt. Sometimes we get blowback from the gun, and it leaves residue."

Matt started to unbutton his shirt. "Take it. I'll just need something to wear."

"We'll give you something," Grimes said. "Matter of fact, we're going to give you some really nice coveralls to wear." An unspoken message appeared to pass between Grimes and the uniformed policeman who'd remained in the room after delivering his message.

The cop stepped around to Matt's side of the table and gestured for him to stand up. "Matt Newman, you're under arrest. Please put your hands behind your back." He pulled a set of handcuffs from a pouch on his belt and Matt felt cold metal bite into his wrists. Matt received the Miranda warning for the third time that night. When he'd heard the words on TV, they'd been part of the drama. Tonight they were very real.

Sandra was on her feet, eyes blazing. "What's the charge? Surely you're not planning to accuse my client of this murder. You have no credible evidence."

Grimes smiled without mirth. "Oh, we'll have some soon enough. We have officers scouring the area for the gun he used. But in the meantime, the crime scene techs found something in his house that will support our holding him."

Matt forgot about Sandra's admonition to keep silent. "On what charge?" he blurted.

"Possession of narcotics with intent to sell. The team just found a large bag of white powder taped to the back of your nightstand drawer. Their field test suggests it's heroin. And I'll bet when our lab analyzes it, it'll match the stuff spilled next to the corpse in your living room."

When Elaine unlocked the office door, lights were on and she heard movement in the back room. This was definitely not what she expected at eight a.m. on a Saturday. Elaine pulled her cell phone from her purse, punched in 911, and kept her finger on the Send button as she crept through the waiting room and peeked around the other door where light showed—Sandra's office.

Sandra was behind her desk, her hair mussed, her eyes red-rimmed. Elaine imagined this was the way her boss looked after pulling an all-nighter in law school.

"What are you doing here?" Sandra asked.

"I might ask you the same thing," Elaine replied. "I came in to finish up some typing. How about you?"

Sandra yawned, ran her fingers through her hair, and said, "It began when I got a call after midnight. Matt Newman was at the police station being questioned."

Elaine cleared the numbers from her cell phone. Then she eased into a client chair and listened intently as Sandra related the events of the past several hours. "So he's in custody now on a drug charge?"

"Right. The murder's a gray area, and they don't really have anything to let them pin it on Matt. But a kilo of heroin is going to be hard to explain."

Elaine shook her head. "Don't tell me you haven't already thought of this. Planted evidence! Who was in the house before the heroin was found?" She ticked off the possibilities on her fingers. "The man who was shot. The man who shot him. And, of course, there's another possibility."

"Yeah, I was thinking the same thing. The police. How hard would it be for someone to swipe a bag of H from the property room? They have evidence in there that probably dates back twenty years, and it would never be missed."

"So who planted it?"

"Start with the patrolmen who responded to the original call. I'll bet one of them stayed with the body and called it in while the other searched the house." Sandra shook her head. "Or the crime scene crew, although they generally work as a team, with two people at a time in any room."

"And you don't think one of them could do this while the other one was across the room?"

"I don't know." Sandra pressed her hands to her temples. "I've got a headache. The Starbucks downstairs should be open. Would you do the coffee run this morning? Double espresso for me. I've got some work to do."

Elaine rose but didn't make a move to leave. "I almost forgot. I had dinner last night with Charlie Greaver. Frank Everett's still saying he expects new evidence to turn up soon."

They shared a long look. "Like a baggie of heroin?" Sandra asked.

Elaine shrugged. "Maybe."

Sandra picked up a pen and started doodling on a legal pad. Elaine recognized the caricature of a gallows from a children's game she used to play. Hangman.

"If the analysis on that bag of heroin gives him what he needs,

Frank'll have his secretary typing up a true bill for the grand jury in a heartbeat," Sandra said. "Someone's trying to railroad my client into prison." She completed the drawing of a hanged man and added X's for eyes. "And it's my job to keep it from happening."

———

Matt looked around the cell. He'd seen a number like it in movies and TV programs, and apparently the people responsible for those sets had visited this jail for a model. The walls were bare. A metal toilet occupied one corner with a washbasin on the wall beside it. A metal cot held a mattress covered by a single blanket. It was a one-person cell. Maybe all the holding cells were. Or maybe they thought the isolation would loosen him up. But he couldn't confess to something he hadn't done.

He slumped on the cot, his head in his hands, and tried to think. Things had gone pretty much the way he'd figured, although his knowledge came mainly from watching episodes of *Law and Order* and *The Closer*. The police had fingerprinted him and taken photos— mug shots, he guessed they called them. They'd swabbed his hands for what they told him was a nitrate test, to see if he'd fired a gun recently. He knew the results would be negative, but the policeman who administered the procedure remained stone-faced about them.

After that, Matt was given jail garb, depositing his clothes in a plastic sack to be taken to the police lab where they'd look for blood splatter or evidence of blowback from a revolver. And finally the cell door slammed behind him with a sound that sent his heart into his slipper-clad feet.

One thing Matt hadn't been prepared for was the noise. He'd somehow envisioned jail as a place where prisoners brooded in solitary silence. Instead, he was treated to a cacophony of slamming cell doors, yelling inmates, and various other sounds.

Matt hadn't slept at all. There was the noise, of course. Then the thin mattress atop the metal shelf that passed for a bed made sleep difficult, and the working of his mind made it impossible. How many more days would he be in here? What was going to happen next?

He hoped Sandra was hard at work, arranging to get him out. It was Saturday, and that might slow things down. When would he have a bail hearing? And how could he come up with whatever amount the judge set? He was scraping the bottom of his financial barrel, struggling to meet his obligations. If his salary at the hospital stopped, he'd be sunk.

In the books his brother, Joe, had left behind was one about Dr. Gordon Seagrave, the missionary some called "the Burma Surgeon." Matt had picked it up one day, interested because it was about a doctor, and once into it, he'd read the whole book. Although Seagrave devoted his life to serving the medical and humanitarian needs of the Burmese people, after a change in government, he was charged with treason and arrested. Despite suffering many indignities, Seagrave never lost hope and his faith never wavered. Matt recalled Seagrave's words: "Everyone should be in prison for at least four months, on suspicion, and sick half the time. Only then can they treasure freedom."

Matt had been jailed on suspicion. He wasn't sick, except in his heart, and the expression "heartsick" had new meaning for him. He hoped he wouldn't be here four days, much less four months. But when that cell door opened for him, like Seagrave he'd treasure his freedom.

NINETEEN

"Double espresso." Elaine handed Sandra a steaming paper cup wrapped in a Starbucks sleeve. She laid a small white sack on her boss's desk. "And you need some food, so I brought you one of the cranberry-orange scones you like."

"Low fat?"

"Of course."

Sandra looked up from the law book on her desk, but held her place with her finger. "Thanks."

Elaine dropped into a chair and turned back the flap on the lid of her coffee. "I know you. You'll get engrossed in your search for just the right point of law, and ignore your coffee and the scone. Take a break, will you?"

Sandra used a yellow Post-It note to mark her place, closed the book, and shoved it aside. She pulled the scone from the sack and broke it in half. "You want some?"

"Had one. It didn't survive the elevator ride. Thanks, though."

Sandra blew across the surface of her cup, took a sip of coffee, and felt the caffeine begin working. Probably all in her head, but she'd take it anyway. She nibbled the scone and washed it down with more coffee. "I should have asked you to bring back a newspaper."

"Thought of that," Elaine said. "But you say all this took place around twelve or one. That's about the time the paper gets printed. If there's anything in the news right now, it will be on radio, TV, or the Internet."

The clock on Sandra's desk showed 7:15 a.m. Maybe she could catch the tail end of a local TV newscast. She fished the remote out of her desk drawer and turned on the small set almost hidden among the law books on the shelves behind her. She swiveled around in time to see the picture replaced on the screen by what appeared to be a booking photo of Matt, overlaid by a banner that said "Breaking News." Sandra turned up the volume.

"This just in to the Channel Four newsroom. Local doctor Matthew Newman is in police custody after an overnight shooting at his home. Sources tell us that the episode may represent a narcotics deal gone awry. Dr. Newman was also involved, but never charged, in the death of Ms. Cara Mendiola, with whom he worked at Metropolitan Hospital. Police are still working that case, and sources tell us that Newman remains a person of interest."

The anchor moved to another story, and Sandra turned off the set. "How did they get that?" she said, as much to herself as to Elaine.

Elaine finished her coffee and handed the cup to Sandra, who deposited it in the wastebasket under her desk. "Shouldn't be hard to figure that out," Elaine said. "Who had the information?"

Sandra chewed and swallowed the last bite of scone. "My best guess is someone at the police station. My money's on Grimes, but that could be anyone from another detective to the patrolmen to a janitor cleaning in the area."

"Could be," Elaine said. "And there's another group to consider."

Sandra lifted her coffee cup to her lips, found it was empty, and discarded it. "Yes, the DA's office would be involved by now. It could have come from there."

"I'd be surprised if Jack Tanner let it leak at this stage," Elaine said. "Or Charlie Greaver."

"On the other hand, I wouldn't put it past Frank Everett," Sandra said. "He's been salivating to get this case, and he's just the kind of guy who'd like to start trying it in the media before Matt is even arraigned."

Elaine stood. "Well, I'll leave you to your work. I guess with the cat out of the bag, it doesn't really matter who untied the drawstring."

Sandra thought about that. True, it didn't matter who leaked the story, but it might help to know who was responsible. If there was someone with a vendetta against Matt, it might be a good idea to keep an eye on them. And wasn't Matt's old girlfriend a secretary in the DA's office? Jennifer something or other; she'd get the name from Matt. Meanwhile, Sandra added that name to what was becoming a long list: people who could be out to get her client.

Matt, in his orange jumpsuit, sat slumped on the side of his bunk and stared at the floor. He had no idea what time it was. The cell had no windows, and the low-wattage lamp behind a wire cage above his head had burned constantly since his arrival. They'd taken his watch along with his clothes and personal possessions.

How long since his last dose of medicine? He hadn't had any more petit mal seizures . . . or had he? During his absence spells he had no real sense of time passing. It was only afterward that he looked back and realized he'd had another seizure. If he was going to be here very long, should he ask for medication? That would mean seeing a jail doctor, admitting his problem, letting it become a matter of record. No, for now he'd keep quiet and hope for the best.

Apparently Matt wasn't going to be mixed with the jail population at mealtime. Earlier someone had slid a tray of what passed for breakfast through the slot in his cell door. Lukewarm coffee, a stale roll, everything tasting like it had been soaked in rancid dishwater before it was brought to him. Nevertheless, Matt had cleaned his plate. Now he was hungry again. When would they feed him lunch? Were the isolation and hunger designed to soften him up? If so, it was working.

"On your feet. You've got a visitor." A female guard stood outside his cell, a huge ring of keys clipped to her belt. She wasn't wearing a gun, but she rested one hand on a mean-looking baton hanging in a loop on her pant leg.

He shuffled to the door. "What do you mean? Who?"

She shook her head. "Turn around. Put your hands behind you."

He complied without question, and in a moment he heard the cell door open, felt cold steel clamp around his wrists. She laid a heavy hand on his shoulder and turned him. "That way. And don't even think of giving me any trouble. I'm right behind you."

Matt wanted to respond, maybe with a smart remark, but he bit his tongue. No need to antagonize her. She was just doing her job. Job! He'd forgotten about his own job. He needed to get word to Rick that he wouldn't be able to work his shift this evening. Matter of fact, he had no idea when he'd be able to return to his work at the hospital—if ever.

"Can I use the phone?" he asked his escort.

"What for? To call your lawyer? She's the one waiting to see you."

Her tone didn't invite dialogue, so Matt remained silent. In a few minutes, he was back in a room that looked very much like the one in which he'd faced Detective Grimes a few short hours ago. Sandra Murray sat in a chair on one side of the table, and she gestured toward the empty one opposite her.

The guard unlocked the handcuffs and chained Matt's right hand to the chair in which he sat, a chair that he'd already noted was bolted to the floor. She fixed Sandra with a glance that had seen it all and didn't believe most of it. "I'll be right outside, Counselor. Knock when you're through." As the guard closed the door, Matt noticed that there was no knob on the inside.

Sandra pulled out what Matt decided was the most important implement in any lawyer's armamentarium—a yellow legal pad.

"What's—" Matt started to ask.

Sandra hushed him with an upraised hand. "We don't have much time, so let me talk first. Then you can ask questions."

What Matt heard drove him deeper into despair. He already knew about the 911 call and what the police found when they responded. Sometime after daybreak, the police discovered a pistol in a nearby storm sewer. They believed it to be the murder weapon, but ballistics results were still pending. The gun had been wiped clean of fingerprints, and the police figured the shooter had worn the latex gloves they found along with the gun.

"So what? They found what's probably the murder weapon and the gloves the killer wore. But none of that ties to me," Matt said.

"No, but they can use the drug possession charge to hold you while they work on connecting you to the murder."

Matt took a long breath in through his nose and let it out slowly through pursed lips. "Okay. What's next?"

"They'll probably question you later today," Sandra said. "They'd love to get a confession, of course. Depending on what kind of case they can put together, they can at least charge you with the drug possession. If they do that, there'll be a bond hearing, probably on Monday, and the amount of the bail will depend on the charges."

"Doesn't matter. I doubt that I could make bail of any amount. I'm pretty much at the limit of my resources."

"Let's don't worry about that right now," Sandra said. "God will provide."

As they had with increasing frequency lately, words from his brother, Joe, echoed in Matt's mind. *"Remember, little brother. We may not see it, but God's got it under control."* Matt certainly hoped so. Maybe there was a ray of sunshine in there somewhere, but right now all he could see in his life were storms.

Lou knew he should feel a little more relaxed today when he stood before the mahogany desk. After all, killing Edgar at the direct command of this man should have forged some sort of bond between them. On the other hand, a few days ago the boss had leveled a pistol at him, making him fear for his life. No, there might be a bond, but deep down, Lou knew the man on the other side of that desk would always be in charge, willing to kill anyone who got in his way—even Lou.

"I take it that Edgar is no longer in the land of the living," the big man said.

Lou thought he'd done it right, but that didn't mean the boss would. He shifted his weight from side to side. He clenched and unclenched his fists. "Yeah. And from what I hear, the police fell for the setup. Newman's in custody while they look for the gun I used."

"Wiped clean of fingerprints?"

"No prints on it, and I used latex gloves—the kind they wear in surgery."

The boss made the leap immediately. "And Newman's a surgeon. He probably had a few pair lying around for when he painted or did something else that would get his hands dirty."

"On the nose. I found them when I was in his house the first time, most of them still in the paper wrapper. I pocketed a couple of pair in case I needed them. Turns out I did."

"Are you sure the police will find the gloves?"

"I dropped both the pistol and the gloves into the first storm drain I came to. That's generally where the police start looking, and since we're in the worst drought in years, nothing's going to wash the evidence away before they find it." Lou felt his heart rate slowing. "I wouldn't be surprised if the police have them already."

"And the drugs?"

"I had Edgar buy some and give them to me. His fingerprints are all over the bag of heroin I dropped by his hand after I spilled some of it on the floor."

"You said 'give them.'" The boss narrowed his eyes. "Was there more than the heroin?"

Whoops. Lou hadn't intended to mention the crank Edgar bought. That was a little bonus Lou planned to keep for himself, considering the price of methamphetamines. "Slip of the tongue. Just the H. That's all."

There was a period of silence during which Lou felt his heart creep up into his throat. Finally the boss opened his desk drawer, and Lou tensed, ready to drop to the floor, wondering if he could draw his gun before the first bullet hit him. Instead, the big man reached in and withdrew a roll of bills. He peeled off ten that bore the image of Benjamin Franklin. "Good work. Now lay low. I'll be in touch when I need you again."

Lunch for prisoners was a bologna sandwich on limp white bread, accompanied by something that might have represented pasta salad, a few chunks of fruit swimming in sugary syrup, with watery orange Kool-Aid to wash it down. Matt gobbled it as though it were a T-bone from Bob's Steak and Chop House.

An older man in an orange jumpsuit like Matt's delivered the lunch tray. Before the man rolled the cart away, Matt called, "When's the evening meal?"

The man, probably a trustee, didn't pause or turn, just spoke over his shoulder. "About five."

"What'll it be?"

The cart was out of sight now, but Matt heard the reply from down the hall. "Look at what's on your tray. That's what you'll get, lunch and supper most days. Get used to it."

How long was this going to go on? If they charged him and moved him to the general population, would he eat in the mess hall? Surely the food couldn't be any worse there. Or could it? Besides, Matt remembered all the stories he'd heard of how dangerous prison life could be. Inmates getting stabbed with "shanks" made from toothbrushes or spoons stolen from the mess hall, their handles sharpened into weapons. And what went on in the communal shower didn't bear thinking about.

Matt slumped onto the edge of his bed, buried his head in his hands, and wondered again how this was all going to play out. Without particular conscious thought, he began to pray silently.

God, I could pray for deliverance, but it's either going to happen or it isn't, and whichever way it goes, You've already planned it out. So what I really need is patience to get through, and wisdom to do the right thing.

I guess I should just pray the way You taught us. 'Our Father, which art in heaven . . .'

Matt continued on to the end of the prayer, although the words "Thy will be done" stuck in his throat.

What had Sandra said? They had to charge him pretty soon, although she'd been vague on the exact time limit. Before that they'd question him some more. He wished he had a watch, or a clock, or even a window so he could keep track of time by the progress of the sun. But he had none of that.

He passed the afternoon pacing his cell, his mind darting back and forth like a trapped animal, looking for a way out of the mess he was in. Every time there was a noise in the corridor, his heart leaped. Maybe Sandra was waiting to see him. He'd even take more questioning by Grimes and Ames. Anything to escape the confinement of these bars.

The familiar rattle of the food cart brought him to the cell door. He took the tray, grateful for the break in his routine, although not particularly pleased to see that the trustee who brought him his lunch hadn't lied. Another bologna sandwich, a mound of mushy green peas, more fruit chunks, and a paper cup of Kool-Aid, grape this time.

If supper was being served, that meant it was about five o'clock. No word from Sandra. No summons to meet with the detectives. So Matt would spend another night in the cell. He didn't know if he could stand it.

More important, he'd been without his medicine for a day now. What if he had a seizure? What if the next one wasn't just an absence spell, but a full-blown convulsion? Would he get medical help? And if so, how would that affect his life after he got out of jail, assuming he got out of jail at all?

He ate as he thought, chewing and swallowing without really

tasting, knowing he had to stoke the fires, keep up his energy. Matt wasn't sure how much he could take. Only God knew. That brought a wry smile to his face. Sure, God knew, but He wasn't saying. The best Matt could do was take one minute at a time. He stretched out on his bunk and tried not to think about what might lie ahead.

TWENTY

Sandra stabbed the numbers into her cell phone as though she were punching Detective Grimes in the eye. She didn't know what type of vendetta the detective had against Matt, but she couldn't imagine a simple thirst for justice driving a man this hard. Surely there was something in his background—maybe a grudge against doctors—that made Grimes act the way he did.

She steered her car out of the parking garage, her mind working a mile a minute. It was Monday, and she'd received a phone call less than an hour before that Matt was going to be arraigned at eleven a.m. on the drug charge. Sandra was worried about the matter of bail. Her hope had been that the police would drop that charge, or if not, that she could cast enough doubt on their findings for the judge to throw out the case. Judging from what Frank Everett had told her when he called, he'd managed to get the case on the docket of a judge who owed him a few favors. It was beginning to look like her client would continue to spend time in jail unless she could work a miracle.

"Dr. Pearson."

Sandra almost dropped her cell phone when her call was answered. "Rick, this is Sandra Murray. I'm Matt's attorney."

"Yeah, I remember," Rick said. "What's up?"

"Can you be at the courthouse at eleven o'clock? Sorry for such short notice, but Matt's being arraigned, and I need a character witness to testify that he has ties to the community, a steady job, and such."

There was silence on the line for so long Sandra wondered if the call had been dropped. She was about to check her signal strength when Rick said, "Sure. I'll be there. Do you think he's going to be in jail long? I mean, I don't mind working a double shift occasionally, and some of the other docs would probably do it once or twice, but . . ."

"That's the second thing I wanted to mention. I'm going to do my best to get him released on bail, and it would help if you made it clear that he has a steady job."

Rick's forced exhalation was like a north wind in her ear. "Sandra, I've stuck my neck out for Matt so far that I look like a giraffe. The hospital administration has gone along with me to this point, but this arrest might be the last straw."

"He's being framed, and I think we have a pretty good chance of proving it. But it's going to take time, and I'm trying to keep him a free man while I do it." She wondered what else she could say to convince Rick. She settled for, "Just do what you can for him today, will you? We'll figure out tomorrow when it comes."

"On your feet."

The voice of the guard startled Matt. This one was a burly African-American, his shaved head glinting in the pale light of the corridor. If Matt had been tempted to try to overpower his earlier escort, no such thoughts crossed his mind now. This man looked like an offensive tackle who'd just been released by the Pittsburgh Steelers and was angry about the experience.

Matt backed up to the cell door and held his hands behind him. "Where to this morning? Does Detective Grimes want to talk to me again? Is it my attorney?"

"Nope, you're headed to court."

"Am I going to be tried? Already?"

The guard shook his head, apparently amused at how little this jailbird knew. "You must be new at this. This is your arraignment. They tell you what you're charged with. You enter a plea. They talk about bail. I'm betting I'll see you back here before my shift ends."

Matt stumbled through the routine of transport to the courts. There he exchanged a few words with Sandra before he was herded into the courtroom and seated in the front row along with a number of other men and women in prison garb.

He'd told her that if the judge set bail at anything over a few hundred dollars, he wasn't going to be able to meet it. As he waited, he ran through the problem once more. Was there someone he could call? Thinking about that depressed him even further. His parents were dead. His brother was a missionary whose life exemplified the phrase "poor as a church mouse." Friends or colleagues? Aside from Rick, no one he'd ask to put up bail. And Rick had already done too much for him.

When Matt first entered the courtroom, he didn't see Sandra, and he felt panic building in his chest. Had she been called away? Was something wrong? Did this mean he was going to be sent back to jail and brought back tomorrow? He wasn't sure he could tolerate another night in that cell. More bologna sandwiches. Hours of trying to sleep despite the noise all around, intensified at times by someone beating on the bars of his cell or yelling incoherently. *"Get used to it,"* the trustee had said when Matt asked about jail food. He wasn't sure he could get used to any of it.

When Sandra slipped in through a side door, stowing her cell phone in a large purse, Matt relaxed. He tried to anchor his emotions to the smile she gave him, but couldn't do it. Sandra would try, but he knew things were hopeless.

Matt listened to other prisoners being arraigned, but kept losing his concentration. He heard a door close at the rear of the room, and turned in time to see Rick ease into one of the back seats in the court-room. His colleague flashed him a tentative thumbs-up and winked, but it was obvious to Matt that Rick's heart wasn't in it.

When Matt's name was called, the bailiff tapped him on the shoulder and motioned him to step forward and stand by his attorney before the bench. The judge asked questions in a bored monotone, and Sandra answered as though she'd said the words hundreds of times—which, come to think of it, she probably had.

"Do you understand the charges?"

It took Matt a moment to realize the question was addressed to him. He looked at Sandra, who gave him an almost imperceptible nod. "Yes, sir."

"How do you plead?"

This time Sandra answered for him. "My client pleads not guilty, Your Honor."

"We'll set the date for trial. Do you have a motion for bail?"

"We ask that my client be released on his own recognizance. He has a spotless record, has roots in the community, and I have a witness in the courtroom who is prepared to testify that my client is of good character and holds a responsible position with a major hospital here."

A middle-aged man in an ill-fitting gray pinstripe suit rose from his seat at the table behind Matt. "Your Honor, the prosecution opposes bail. This man is a person of interest in two murders. The victims were found in his car and his home respectively. It would be a travesty—"

The judge rapped his gavel twice. "Your objection is noted, Mr. Everett. However, I believe the matter before us is possession of narcotics, not suspicion of murder."

The prosecutor eased back into his chair, but not before casting a look at Matt that would have melted ice.

"Your Honor—" Sandra began.

The judge steamrolled right past Sandra, who clamped her lips shut. "I believe I've heard enough, Counselor. I will grant bail in the amount of—" He paused and stared off into the middle distance, as though the sum were written on the far wall of the courtroom. "One hundred thousand dollars."

Matt's heart sank. He could handle one hundred dollars, even a thousand. But a bail bondsman charged 10 percent of the amount of bail, and ten thousand dollars was out of the question.

The next words out of Sandra's mouth caught Matt's attention like a cold towel to the face. "Your Honor, we're prepared to meet that. Shall I make arrangements with the clerk?"

She took Matt by the elbow and herded him to a small desk at the side of the courtroom. He opened his mouth, but she silenced him with a look.

Sandra bent over the desk and whispered to the man there as she pulled her cell phone from her purse. "We're prepared to put up surety in the amount of one hundred thousand dollars. I'll need to make one phone call, and I can let you speak with a banker who will provide that guaranty."

In an hour, Matt—now dressed in his own clothes, including a new shirt Sandra had purchased and brought him—walked beside her toward her car. "Okay, now tell me. How did you manage that?"

"Hang on." Once they were inside the car, she turned so she was half-facing him. "As I was about to enter the courtroom, I got a call on my cell phone. I didn't recognize the number, but the caller ID said Hargrave and Banks. That's one of the most prestigious law firms in the city—maybe in the whole Southwest—so I decided to take the call."

She started to put her key in the ignition, but Matt stopped her. "Hold on. If this has to do with why I'm free instead of eating a bologna sandwich and listening to the guy three cells down rattle the door to his cell, I want to hear it all."

"Well, it gets better from here," Sandra said. "It was Ernest Banks himself calling—Hargrave is long deceased, by the way—asking if I represented you. When I told him I did and explained you were about to be arraigned, he said, and I quote, 'My client is prepared to guarantee his bail, and if we can offer any assistance to you as you prepare his defense, simply call me.'

"I was stunned, but had the presence of mind to ask how high they'd go on your bail. You're not going to believe what he said."

"I'm not believing any of this," Matt said.

"He said, 'Up to a million dollars. If it's higher than that, call me, and we can probably arrange it.'"

Matt's brain was doing loop-the-loops. "Who would do this for me?"

Sandra smiled at him. "Let me test your memory. Do you remember a patient that came into the ER with blood in the sac surrounding his heart? You did an emergency procedure to decompress it—probably saved his life."

"Sure. I was scared to death at the time because I'd never done a pericardiocentesis, but there was no other option."

"Well, whatever that long word means, you clearly saved the man's life. But the clincher is that you showed you cared about him. You visited him in the hospital the next day. You talked with his mother, answered her questions, tried to comfort her."

"You mean—"

"Apparently news of your arrest reached Mrs. Penland. She picked up her phone, called her lawyer, and told him to find out who was representing you and offer assistance, including getting you bailed out."

Matt didn't know what to say. This was truly an answer to prayer— a prayer that he'd offered not totally believing God had any interest in hearing him. "I still can't believe she'd go to such lengths . . ."

"Again quoting my new best friend, Mr. Banks—who now insists I call him Ernie—Mrs. Penland said you weren't the kind of person the police said you are, and you didn't belong in jail. She thought you should be in the ER, saving lives."

TWENTY-ONE

Matt had assured Sandra there was no need for her to drive him home. When the taxi pulled up at the curb, he saw shreds and balls of yellow crime scene tape scattered about the lawn, but there were no cars and no people around. He let himself in the front door, and his eyes were immediately drawn to the area rug in his living room, where a rough body-shaped chalk outline circumscribed an irregular blot of dried blood. As Matt skirted around the spot, he wondered if he could ever get his home restored to normal. And even though his lawyer said he could start the cleanup process, he worried that anything he might do would cause problems for him later with the police.

Matt half-expected to find drawers left open, clothes and books on the floor, but other than dust left behind by fingerprint technicians, the remainder of the house looked pretty normal. He vaguely recalled that there were companies that specialized in cleaning up crime scenes. Not that he could afford it. For now, all he wanted to do was wash away the scent of jail that clung to him like a blanket. The house would come later.

But first he had to get back on his medication. He hadn't had any more petit mal seizures, even though he'd missed several doses, but he couldn't take any chances. He'd left his pill bottle tucked away behind glasses in his kitchen cabinet between bottles of Tylenol and Motrin. But when he looked, all of them were gone. Had the police taken them for analysis? With the drug charges against him, it made sense, he guessed.

Since Matt was a physician, it wasn't an insoluble problem to replace the Ethosuximide, although it was a definite inconvenience. He made a trip to a drugstore, gave the pharmacist a prescription, waited impatiently for his medication, and drove home, all the while expecting to wake up finding that he'd suffered another absence spell.

In the kitchen, Matt spilled one of the red capsules into his palm and washed it down with a few sips of tap water. *Please let the medicine keep working.*

Matt took a long, hot shower, lathering and rinsing several times. The clothes he'd worn went into the laundry hamper. He liked the new shirt Sandra purchased for him. It was something he might have picked out for himself, and he'd definitely keep it. He made a mental note to pay her for it.

He hadn't slept well in jail, so he decided to stretch out for a nap. When he woke, he looked through the window of his bedroom and saw lights going on in the deepening twilight.

He dressed in a clean golf shirt and jeans, and padded in his bare feet into the living room, giving a wide berth to the reminder of the murder that had taken place there less than two days ago.

He lifted the phone and heard the stutter dial tone that told him he had voicemail. The first two messages were hang-ups. Then he heard a familiar voice. "Matt, this is Rick. I'm assuming you won't be able to work your ER shift tonight. I'll cover it, but I'm worried. I've caught some flak already about hiring someone who's under suspicion of murder. The whole time I was in the courtroom this morning I hoped I wasn't going to have to get on the stand, because I didn't know what I'd say. We need to talk. Call me."

He erased the messages and looked at his watch. There were almost five hours to go before the shift Rick was working for Matt ended. Matt wanted desperately to crawl back into bed, pull the covers over his head, and try to forget the ordeal he'd just gone through. But Rick was a friend, and Matt wanted—no, he needed to make things right with him.

Half an hour later, Matt walked into the ER and looked around. As he figured, the place was abuzz with activity. He finally spotted Rick coming out of a cubicle, flipping off his gloves and reaching for a clipboard held out by a nurse. Behind the curtain, adult voices were bickering.

"Rick, can we talk for a minute?"

Matt couldn't interpret Rick's expression. "I'm sort of busy."

"I know. I'm back, and I'll take the rest of this shift if you'd like to leave."

Rick scribbled on the clipboard and handed it back to the nurse. "Make sure she's up to date on her tetanus shot. Follow-up appointment with the plastic surgeon on call." He jerked his head toward the break room. "And I'm going to take five minutes."

Once inside the room, Rick closed the door and leaned against it. "Ten-year-old girl with facial lacerations. Fell off her brand-new bike."

"How's she doing?"

"She was a real trooper. Held still for the anesthetic shot, didn't move while I sutured the lacerations. Now she's sniffling because her parents are bickering. Dad wants to let her back on the bike, Mom wants to throw it in the Dumpster."

Matt knew he didn't have much time, so he jumped into the explanation he'd prepared. "Rick, I appreciate your filling in for me. When I came home Friday night . . . well, Saturday morning, I . . ."

Rick listened quietly as Matt went through the whole scenario: finding the body, being taken into custody by the police, his release on bail. He even shared what he and Sandra had discussed about the likelihood the narcotics had been planted in his bedroom.

"So someone is trying to frame you," Rick said.

"You bet—for the Mendiola murder, for this murder, for a narcotics violation. I've got a real enemy out there somewhere. Fortunately, I have a good lawyer on my side, and I keep telling myself that God's in control—He'll take care of me. But right now I need to convince you that I'm innocent."

Rick moved away from the door, drew a cup of coffee from the urn, and drained the cup in three quick swallows, grimacing after each one. "Okay. I can take the heat from the front office, but you need to keep me posted of new developments. If I get blindsided by something like this in the future, I'm going to have no choice but to cut you loose."

Matt held out a tentative hand. Rick hesitated a moment before shaking it.

"Now, can I finish the shift for you?" Matt asked.

"I don't have anyone at home to hurry to," Rick said. "But it's really busy right now. Want to hang around and work until things slow down?"

"Sure," Matt said. "Let's get to it."

It was time to do something he'd learned early in his medical training: compartmentalize. For the next three hours, Matt put his problems aside and concentrated on one thing—the practice of medicine. The variety of patients flowing through Metropolitan Hospital's emergency room that night was enough to test him, and he found himself searching his memory banks for the answer to a particular diagnostic or therapeutic dilemma. But each time, he was up to the task. And not once did he think of the charges hanging over him.

"It's an ear infection," Matt counseled a young mother who bounced her almost-two-year-old daughter in her arms. "I'll have the nurse give you a sample of the antibiotic, and you can get the prescription filled tomorrow." He rummaged through a cabinet until he found an instruction sheet. "This tells you how to handle fever and pain. She should be better in a day or so, but if you have any problems, call your pediatrician."

A nurse stuck her head through the opening in the curtains surrounding the cubicle. "Excuse me. When you're through, Dr. Pearson asked me to tell you that it's slowing down, and you can head home."

Matt nodded and turned back to make sure the mother had no other questions. As he left, he grasped the cuffs of his blue exam gloves and flipped them into a trash can in a gesture he'd repeated countless times. That action triggered a thought, but it danced just outside Matt's consciousness, harder to grasp than a drop of quicksilver. *Oh well*. It would come to him.

Sandra looked up from the law books and files on her desk when she heard her secretary's voice on the intercom. "Dr. Gordon on line one."

She punched the button. "Ken?"

"Hi, Sandra, I, uhh . . . ," he said. He paused awkwardly, as if he didn't know how to proceed. "Listen, I was calling because you're representing Matt Newman."

"That's right. Why?"

"He missed an appointment recently, and that worries me a bit."

Did doctors get that concerned when patients failed to follow up? Maybe this was a special case, since the patient was also a colleague. "There are lots of reasons why he could have missed the appointment." Like being held by the police. "I'll see him soon, and I'll ask him to call and reschedule."

There was silence on the other end of the line, long enough for Sandra to wonder if the call had been disconnected. Finally she said, "Is that all?"

Ken cleared his throat. Sandra had learned this meant he was about to embark on a subject that made him uncomfortable. "I guess I should come clean about the real reason I'm calling."

"That might be good," Sandra said. "I'm no expert on the way doctors run their practices, but I figured you have secretaries to make calls like this."

"You always could see right through me," Ken said. "It's true that Matt missed an appointment. However, when I last saw him he was doing pretty well. I'd like to see him one more time, but this gave me an excuse to talk with you."

There it was. Sandra thought there'd been a clean break, but this was Ken's second attempt to re-establish their relationship since that dinner at Reunion Tower. Gently but firmly, she told him that wasn't going to happen.

Ken's voice was tinged with hurt. "Didn't Jesus say something about forgiving? What was it? Seventy times seven?"

"Don't try to quote the Bible to me," Sandra said. "As I recall, you pooh-poohed my dependence on faith. Seems you told me you only believed in things you could prove scientifically."

"Maybe you could convince me otherwise. I think we should get together and talk about it."

A cramp made Sandra realize she was holding the phone in a

death grip. She switched hands and took a deep breath. "Ken, I'm not ready to have this conversation. Not today. Not right now, with one of my clients—and one of your patients, I might add—facing murder charges." She grabbed a pen and scribbled a note. "I'll mention the follow-up appointment to Matt. Thanks for calling."

So there it was. She thought the breakup was behind her. She was trying to move on, and had hoped Ken would do the same. At the time he seemed to accept the fact that her faith and his lack of it was reason enough for them to split. Obviously he was having second thoughts. Was she? She wished she knew.

Deep in her heart she realized she was developing feelings for Matt. Matt was a doctor like Ken. Did that mean he only believed in things he could see and feel and prove? Actually she had no idea about his relationship with God. Was she setting herself up for another fall? She'd have to cross that bridge soon.

Sandra reached for the Bible she kept in her office. It had belonged to her grandparents, both of whom were now dead, and she'd vowed that if she ever attained a public office, she'd be sworn in with her hand on that Bible. For now, though, she needed a word of direction. And what better place to find it?

She was still looking when Elaine tapped on her open door. "Your client Mr. Johnson is here. Shall I send him in?"

"Give me five minutes, please." Sandra reluctantly put the Bible away, shuffled through the files on her desk, and pulled out the one she needed, breathing a quick prayer for guidance—not only in her professional life, but in her private life as well.

After he awoke the next morning, Matt took a circuitous route through his living room, avoiding the spot where the murder victim's body had been. When he came in last night from the ER, he was too energized to sleep, so he'd decided to take back his home. The area rug stained with the man's blood was in a Dumpster now. The bloodstains on the hardwood floor yielded to vigorous scrubbing with cold water and hydrogen peroxide. Fingerprint powder had been wiped away. All traces of the crime and the police presence that followed were gone from his house. Still, the memories lingered.

He hadn't actually seen the body—just the bloodstains and the chalk outline—but there was no question that this room would never be quite the same for him. Matt wondered if he should consider moving. He was turning over the economics of selling this place and buying another versus renting something smaller, maybe even an apartment, when it hit him. He couldn't afford to commit to the purchase of another house. Besides, it was foolish for him to make any long-term plans. There were still people out there who obviously wanted to kill him, or failing that, to put him out of circulation for a long time. *Why consider where you're going to live when the State of Texas might be providing your room and board for the foreseeable future?*

He checked the time: five minutes until noon. Last night, Rick's parting comment to Matt was, "Call me about noon tomorrow. There are some other things I want to talk about—but this isn't the time or place."

Had Rick changed his mind while they were both working? Was he going to fire Matt after all? If that happened, what else could Matt do? He could try some of the other emergency rooms in town. Maybe catch on at a walk-in clinic, the ones he and his colleagues jokingly referred to as "Doc in the Box."

Matt was well aware that his legal fees were piling up. His income from ER work was barely enough to meet his expenses, but eventually there'd be a day of reckoning. And if he was arrested again, there was the question of bail. Would Mrs. Penland feel the same way if he were charged with murder? Would she guarantee his bail a second time?

One problem at a time. Matt sat at his desk, reached for the phone, and punched the number for Rick Pearson's home. At the fourth ring, about the time Matt figured the call was going to voicemail, he heard a husky voice. "Dr. Pearson."

"Rick, it's Matt. Did I wake you?"

"No, I just haven't talked since I went to bed last night." He cleared his throat. "Let me turn on the coffee." After a few moments, Rick came back on the line, sounding more normal. "Thanks for calling."

Matt felt his own coffee moving back up into his throat, and he swallowed hard to keep it down. "You wanted to talk?"

"Yeah, but it would probably be better face-to-face. Can I come over? Or maybe we could meet somewhere for lunch."

They settled on a place and agreed to meet there in half an hour. As Matt shaved and dressed, he imagined all sorts of scenarios, none of them good.

Virgil Grimes sat hunched over his desk and read through the notes scribbled on the pad in front of him. Around him, the squad room was relatively quiet today. He hoped it would help him concentrate better. The information he had wasn't all he wanted, but it was a step in the right direction.

First there was the gun: a snub-nosed .38 caliber Smith & Wesson Airweight revolver found in a storm drain two blocks from Newman's house. Ballistics tests were still pending, but Grimes was willing to bet this was the weapon involved in the murder at Newman's house.

No fingerprints on it, of course. Serial number erased with acid. The lab geeks could work on bringing it out so the gun could be traced, but dollars to donuts it would prove to be a dead end.

Then there were the gloves found lying with the gun in the same storm drain. Of course, there was gunshot residue on the gloves. That was to be expected. But more important, the gloves matched the size 8 latex surgeon's gloves found in Newman's garage, still in their paper wrapper.

Grimes tapped the pages, grinned, and said, "Newman, you're going down."

The detective pushed back from his desk, grabbed his coat, and hurried out onto the street. He walked a quick block away and ducked into a coffee shop, where he paid for a cup and took it to a booth in the back. He looked around and made sure there was no one he recognized around him before pulling out his cell phone and punching in a number.

"It's me. We're getting close to having something that will tie Newman to the killing at his house."

"Keep me informed."

"I will." He ended the call and blew across the surface of his cup. *Might as well enjoy the coffee before heading back to the squad room.* As he sipped, he hoped this latest turn of events would ease some of the pressure on him. Of course, it was increasing on Newman, but that wasn't his worry. Right now Grimes's major concern was himself. *Look out for number one.* And the only way number one could get out of trouble was to make sure Newman was in it—deep.

TWENTY-TWO

Matt scanned the little café and saw no sign that Rick had arrived before him. He checked his watch, discovered he was a couple of minutes early, and took a table that promised a degree of privacy.

A waitress hurried over. She placed a glass of ice water and a napkin-wrapped set of silverware in front of Matt. "Menus are over there." She pointed to a stack of laminated cards, book-ended on one side by salt and pepper shakers and on the other by bottles of ketchup and hot sauce. "Something to drink?"

"I'll have a Coke." Before she could turn away, Matt told her he was expecting someone to join him shortly. She nodded absently and scooted away, returning in less than a minute with Matt's drink as well as another set of silverware.

While he waited for Rick, Matt freed a menu from the stack and considered his lunch selection. Maybe a ham and cheese, although the tuna melt sounded good too. As Matt thought about it, his mind kept going back to a glass of Kool-Aid and a cold bologna sandwich on soggy white bread. He heard again the trustee's words, *"That's what you'll get, lunch and supper most days. Get used to it."*

No, he had to put that out of his mind. He was out of jail. He was innocent of any charge the police might bring against him. He had a good lawyer on his side. *Don't make plans about going back to jail. Make plans to live your life to the fullest after you've been cleared.* Memories of Gordon Seagrave's captivity and words about freedom flooded Matt's mind.

Matt turned his attention back to the menu, but looked up when Rick took the seat opposite him. "Sorry, I'm a little late."

"No problem," Matt said.

After they ordered, Matt took a deep breath and jumped right into it. "I guess you want to talk about the legal problems I have. Are you under pressure to fire me?"

Rick shrugged. "Some, but until a jury says you're guilty, I say you've got a job."

Matt took a deep breath, and somehow felt that it contained more oxygen than before. "Thanks. I won't let you down." He sipped his Coke. "But if this isn't about work, what's the occasion for the meeting?"

Rick seemed to be looking everywhere but into Matt's eyes. "I guess you know that Judy and I are separated."

"I'm sorry to hear that," Matt said. "I'd heard rumors but didn't pay any attention to them."

"Part of the problem was my hours. That's why I switched over to emergency medicine. I make a little less money, but the hours are predictable."

"I was headed in the same direction myself. But I take it that wasn't enough for Judy," Matt said.

"It helped, but she said the real sticking point was my refusal to discuss religion. She's pretty staunch in her faith, and I'm—well, I'm lukewarm at best. Not an atheist, mind you. I realize there's a God out there somewhere. I just don't know how He fits into my plans . . . or I into His, for that matter."

Uh-oh. Matt shifted in his seat and stretched his neck. If Joe were here now, he'd be able to jump in with Scripture, quoting chapter and verse from memory. He'd know what to say, how to respond to where Rick was leading. Matt, on the other hand, felt at a loss.

"I . . . I'm not sure what I can do to help," Matt finally said.

"I've paid attention to things you say," Rick said. "Even last night you said something about God being in control. And with your brother being a missionary and all . . . Anyway, I figured you'd know more about religion than I do." He spread his hands. "When I was growing up, the only time you'd hear the word 'God' around our house was when my father was cussing. Right now I'd like to believe that I can put my problems in His hands, but frankly, I don't know how."

"I'm not sure I'm the best authority for you," Matt said.

"I was hoping you could at least tell me about it. This whole faith thing—what it means to be a Christian."

The years rolled back and Matt was once again a teenager, sitting on the edge of his bed while his brother explained the same thing Rick was asking. Some of it didn't make a lot of sense to him, but Joe kept coming back to one central truth—freedom from the consequences of our sins was a free gift, purchased by Christ, and available to everyone. It seemed too easy simply repeating what Joe called "the sinner's prayer."

"I prayed that sinner's prayer with my brother, and honestly, I didn't feel much different. But he said it was okay. That I'd grow and mature in time." Matt shrugged. "He said we never reach perfection, but we don't have to sweat it. Because Christ is. Perfection, I mean."

Matt pulled into the parking lot at Metropolitan Hospital, still turning over in his mind his time with Rick. He'd already thought of a dozen things he could have said better, a number of Scriptures he could have quoted if he'd had a Bible or, better still, had memorized them. But what was done was done, and he thought the end result was good. At least, he hoped it was.

He killed the engine, unbuckled his seat belt, and was about to open the car door when his cell phone buzzed against his thigh. He dug into his pocket and looked at the display. The call was from Jennifer.

The continued buzz of his phone was a counterpoint to the rapid beat of Matt's heart. Why was Jennifer calling? Hadn't she made it clear she wanted nothing more to do with him once he'd come under suspicion by the police? Then again, he'd tried to return her last call and hung up without talking with her. Surely she deserved better than that. Besides, was there still a spark of feeling in the relationship? Maybe she wanted to apologize. Maybe she'd changed. Maybe.

What if that were the case? Did Matt want the relationship back? Or was he past her? And could that be because of his feelings toward Sandra?

Answer the call, Matt. Get it over with. Before the call could roll over to voicemail, he answered. "Hello, Jennifer."

Her voice—carefully neutral—gave him no clue about her reason for calling. "Matt, I'm glad I finally caught you."

"I have a few moments now," Matt said, striving to be equally noncommittal. "What's on your mind?"

She took a deep breath and let it out in Matt's ear. "Matt, we had some great times together. I really thought we were going to . . ."

What? Get married? Ride off into the sunset together? Matt

wished she'd get on with it, but he was determined not to help her. He kept silent.

"I don't know how to put this," she said.

She wants to get back together. I can feel it. Now the wrestling match started again. Part of Matt wanted to say, "Yes, yes. Let's recapture what we had." But another part, a quieter voice, but one that spoke with the weight of reason behind it, whispered, "Does she really love you? Can you depend on her? Would the two of you really be happy?"

As it turned out, Jennifer's next words rendered Matt's internal debate fruitless. "I've been seeing someone else. It's only been a few weeks, but it's getting serious in a hurry. He's even hinted there might be a ring in my future. If he asks, I'm going to say yes." She paused. "I thought you ought to hear it from me," she said.

Matt was stunned. There were so many things he wanted to say— *You're rebounding into this relationship . . . Give me one more chance . . . We can make things work out.* But as each thought crossed his mind, he dismissed it. The truth of the matter was that Jennifer wasn't the woman God had for him. He thought he knew who it was, but it was too soon to pursue her.

"Thanks for letting me know, Jennifer," Matt managed to say. "I wish you all the best."

He had the phone a foot away from his ear, his finger poised to end the call, when he realized Jennifer was still talking. "Sorry. Say that again, please."

"I shouldn't be telling you this, but I think I owe it to you. I hear things here at the DA's office. You should stay in close touch with your lawyer, especially tomorrow."

There was a sharp *click*. Jennifer was gone—in more ways than one.

Matt pondered her words, and a chill ran up his spine as he thought about what might be going on now. Was he about to be arrested again?

Should he call Sandra? No, not yet. He was supposed to have a working lunch with her tomorrow. They could discuss it then. For now, it was time to go to work.

There were people in the ER waiting for him to help them, people who were sick, or injured, or in some cases, hovering on the brink of death. If this was to be his last night practicing medicine, he could at least leave behind a legacy of healing.

He stepped out of his car and strode purposefully toward the glass doors into a world where what he did counted.

The infant screamed. The mother sobbed. Matt, with medical student Randy Harrison behind him, worked to project an air of calm in the midst of the sea of emotion that roiled in the small cubicle.

"Tell me again what happened," Matt said. The noise and activity of the emergency room waxed and waned outside the cubicle's curtains, but never fully ceased. Matt struggled to keep his voice level, his words reasonable. *Never let parents see you flinch. They're depending on you.*

"I was changing her diaper when she . . . she had a fit." The harried mother swept her hair away from her face with the back of one hand and tightened her grip on the crying baby. "Her eyes rolled back in her head. She shook all over. She tinkled and . . . and then she went limp."

A faint beep was almost lost in the noise. The ER nurse, tonight a motherly African-American named Ruth, put down the electronic thermometer and said, "Forty-point-five Celsius." Matt made the automatic conversion to the more conventional Fahrenheit number: one-oh-five.

"Thank you," Matt said. He turned his attention back to the

mother. "Why don't you hold Kaylee while I examine her? What you're describing is what we call a febrile convulsion. I need to find out why she has such a high fever so I can treat the cause."

"She had a fit. Aren't you going to give Kaylee something before it happens again?"

As Ruth moved gently to the mother's side to help hold the struggling infant, Matt rubbed the end of his stethoscope against his palm to warm it, then placed it on the child's chest. He listened carefully before he replied. "Febrile seizures are a sign, not a disease. Kaylee's unlikely to have another one, and if she does, we'll handle it. The main thing now is to see what kind of infection is causing the fever and get her started on treatment for that."

He flexed the child's head forward and allowed himself to relax a bit when he felt no resistance, saw no drawing up of the legs. *Good, not likely to be meningitis.* A few more minutes and Matt was certain of the diagnosis. "Kaylee has a pretty severe ear and throat infection. Has she had a cold recently? Been around any other sick children? Maybe in day care?"

"I have to work—single mom—and I can't really afford day care. So she stays with my sister, and her kids have bad sore throats. Why? Did they cause this? Is it my fault?"

Matt made a palms down gesture. "No, just gathering information to help me decide what kind of antibiotic would work best." He glanced down at the ER record. "She's not allergic to any medicine?"

The mother tossed her head and blew to reposition a strand of hair, apparently no longer willing to take even one hand off her crying child. "She's never had much. She has had all her shots, though."

Matt looked at the birth date and did a rapid calculation. The child would be almost two years of age. "But no shots recently?"

"No. Is that wrong?"

"Not at all. But I need to make sure there's nothing else that might contribute to the fever." He unclipped a pen from his pocket and wrote on the ER form. "I'm going to start her on an antibiotic. She should get better within a day or two. Ruth will talk with you about things you can do and medicines you can give Kaylee to keep her fever down. If she's not better in three days, she needs to be seen again. Ruth will give you the names of two pediatricians you can call."

"I . . . I can't afford . . ."

Matt could almost feel the cold stares of the bean counters who hated the way uninsured patients used the ER as their family doctor. *But what can I do?* "Or you can bring her back here. We'll be happy to look at her again."

Matt went on to assure the mother that the odds of Kaylee having another seizure were small, and there was no need to start anticonvulsants at this point. As he spoke, Matt thought through his treatment decisions to make sure he hadn't missed anything along the way.

"Do you have any questions?" Matt asked.

When the mother shook her head, Ruth said, "Wait here. We'll give Kaylee the first dose of her antibiotic, and something to help bring her fever down." Matt's last vision of the scene was a far cry from what had greeted him when he first parted the curtains. The mother seemed calmer, and Kaylee now rested quietly in her arms.

As they walked away, Randy, in a short white coat over hospital scrubs, turned to Matt. "You handled that really smoothly."

"Thanks. I haven't taken care of a child with a febrile seizure in years, but this crash course as an ER doc brings it all back. With the right training, you could do the same." Matt studied the face of the medical student. "Think that might be what you want to do?"

"I thought so. But my 'almost father-in-law' is a plastic surgeon in town. He has pretty much a high-end practice, and he and my girlfriend are pressing me to go into that specialty, maybe even join his practice. They think I'm crazy to even consider emergency medicine."

Matt could see the scenario as clearly as though someone had diagrammed it for him. A prospective father-in-law wanted to be sure his daughter enjoyed the prestige of a doctor husband, along with the comforts provided by a good income. He guessed that wasn't unlike what Jennifer had pushed for—a comfortable life. She wanted Matt to be successful and make a lot of money, yet always be available for her. Matt had been unable to convince her that she couldn't have it both ways. He hoped Randy would be smart enough to make his own decision.

"What antibiotic did you choose?" Randy asked. "And why did you give an antibiotic anyway? Aren't a lot of those infections viral? Why didn't you wait to see if the child got better on her own?"

Matt was ready for that one. He'd heard it before, usually from physicians in academia. "Yes, I chose to give her an antibiotic: amoxicillin," he said. "And in case you're wondering, I read the journals and attend the lectures. I know about the argument you have in mind, but I don't practice in an ivory tower. To my mind, the studies are inconclusive."

"But—" Randy said.

Matt plunged on. "Even though there's a school of thought that antibiotics aren't needed for otitis media, I defy those doctors to defend their position while standing in an ER late at night with a crying child and a distraught mother who's just seen her baby convulse."

Ruth stopped beside them. "Got her settled." She turned to Randy. "I almost forgot you were there, you were so quiet."

Randy grinned. "I remember what I was told on my first night in the ER—keep my eyes open and my mouth shut."

Ruth handed Matt a chart but addressed Randy with a matching smile. "You'll never get in trouble that way."

Matt glanced up at the clock on the wall. He'd stopped wearing a watch because it continually snagged on the exam gloves he pulled on and off dozens of times a night. "Ruth, how's it look out there?"

"About average. It'll quiet down later, though." She turned to Randy. "Here's something you may not know. There's nothing in the books about this, but you can mark it down. Four a.m. will be when things hit bottom. The ER is slower. The staff is sagging. But the patients that come in are either really sick—heart attacks, traffic accidents, that kind of thing—or suicides." She grimaced.

"And I'll bet the docs love it when they get awakened at that time," Randy said.

"Absolutely right," Matt said. "I've been on both sides of those phone calls. Even if the doctor can handle the problem over the phone, most of the time they can't get back to sleep, but it's too early to get up."

Randy shrugged. "Leslie's dad says that's another reason to go into plastic surgery. He keeps telling me that for a while I may have to take care of the drunks who come in with lacerations, but pretty soon I can slough those off to a general surgeon or an ER doctor and plan on sleeping through the night."

"What do you think about that?" Matt said.

"I don't really know. Dr. Stokes thinks he's got my life planned out for me . . . Maybe I should be grateful for it."

"Or maybe you should make your own decisions instead of letting someone else make them for you," Ruth said in a quiet voice.

Matt wondered if he hadn't been guilty of the same thing, giving in to Jennifer's subtle pressure. He surprised himself with the next words out of his mouth. "Just pray about it, Randy. Turn the decision over to God." *I wish I'd learned that lesson a little earlier myself.*

TWENTY-THREE

"I've got a lunch appointment with Matt Newman." Sandra put Elaine's morning coffee on her desk. "Remind me about a quarter to twelve."

Elaine waved her boss to a chair. "I had dinner last night with Charlie Greaver."

Sandra didn't expect a long conversation. She ignored the chair. Instead she leaned a hip on Elaine's desk and sipped her coffee. "And what did you find out?"

"About Dr. Newman? Not really anything. But it was an interesting evening."

"Are you going to tell me about it or just sit there and keep me guessing?" Sandra asked.

"Charlie and I have had occasional dates for the past couple of years. You know—lonely widower, eligible widow. It was mainly a case of having someone to talk to, a companion for the theater or a party. I probably went out with him once for every two or three times he asked me. But since I've begun accepting all his invitations, I think he's getting more serious."

"I'm sorry if I've put you in a bad position."

Elaine toyed with her coffee cup. "Actually, you haven't. I've always enjoyed Charlie in an offhand sort of way, but since we're seeing each other more often, I've gotten to know him better, and I have to say, I like what I see."

"That's great," Sandra said.

"Um, sort of. You see, because both Charlie and I are getting more serious, I worry about trying to pump him for information about your client."

Sandra noticed the subtle shift. Previously, Matt had been "our client." Now he was Sandra's. "So what I hear you saying is that you don't want me using you as a pipeline into the DA's office."

Elaine suddenly seemed to find the top of her desk terribly interesting. Without looking up, she said, "If there's a bombshell, I'd probably pass it on to you. But otherwise, I'd like to concentrate on my relationship with Charlie. I don't want to be a spy, and that's what I feel like now." She met Sandra's gaze. "I hope that's okay with you."

Okay? Sandra wasn't sure. She'd counted on information from Charlie Greaver via Elaine as sort of an early warning system. On the other hand, she had to admit that the ethics of the situation had bothered her a bit. She made up her mind. "Elaine, I'm happy for you. You've been alone long enough."

———————

Matt looked around the coffee shop. If any of the eating places along Elm Street downtown deserved the title "hole in the wall," this one did. But Sandra said the sandwiches they served were delicious, and it was conveniently near her office, so Matt had agreed to meet her here at noon.

The clock on the wall behind the lunch counter said five minutes to twelve. The place was full already, but as Matt was about to give up he spotted a couple vacating a small table in the back corner. He hurried over and hovered while a sweating busboy dumped the dirty dishes into a plastic tub and took a few pro forma swipes at the table-top with a moist rag.

Matt plopped into the chair that faced the door and placed the folder he was carrying in the seat opposite it. A waitress hurried over, spotted the folder, and asked, "You meeting someone?"

"She'll be here in a moment," Matt said. "One Coke and one Diet Coke. And leave the menus. We'll be ready to order in a minute."

She huffed away, obviously aware that the quicker patrons ordered, the quicker they were served, paid, and vacated the table, leaving tips in their wake. Matt decided to make sure his tip reflected the waitress's patience—or lack thereof.

He was staring at the front door for what seemed like the hun-dredth time when Sandra breezed through it. Matt felt a strange sensation in his chest when Sandra eased into the chair opposite him, and wondered for a second if he'd developed a heart murmur. But he knew what it really represented: a heart problem, just not one that demanded an electrocardiogram or stress test.

Sandra placed Matt's folder on the edge of the table and covered it with her purse. "Sorry. I think I'm a few minutes late."

Matt took a long drink of his Coke. "No problem. Just glad we could get together."

"Before I forget, your neurosurgeon, Dr. Gordon, called me. He said you'd missed a post-op appointment. He wants you to be certain to reschedule."

Matt looked at his cell phone and punched a couple of buttons. "No record that he called me or sent a text. Why did he call you about it?"

Sandra twisted in her chair. "I guess because . . ." She took a deep breath and started again. "Ken and I used to go out—were pretty close, in fact. I think he used that call as an excuse to talk with me."

Somehow, in his struggle to understand his feelings for her and cope with the drama in his life, Matt had managed to ignore the possibility that Sandra could be in a relationship. Should he try to find out if she still had an interest in Ken Gordon? It was none of Matt's business, but picturing her dating another man was hard to take—which told him his own feelings were probably genuine, not just rebound or transference. He wanted to ask questions—a lot of them—but decided to keep silent. Right now Sandra was his attorney, and that's all she could be until the shadow hanging over him was gone.

Matt had a couple of hours to kill before going on shift. He decided to go back home and sneak in a short nap. Things had been busier in the ER recently, and he had a hunch he'd need the rest.

It seemed he'd no more than stretched out on the couch and closed his eyes than his cell phone buzzed in his pocket. He checked his watch and discovered he'd been asleep for a half hour—just long enough to get into sound sleep. That was the life of a doctor. *Sleep when you can, and expect to be awakened before you're ready.*

"Hello?"

"Matt, this is Rick. Do you have a minute?"

Matt stretched and yawned. "Sure. What's up?"

"I appreciate the time you spent with me yesterday."

"No problem. Have you talked with your wife?"

"Yeah, I called her after I left your place. She says she's happy I've taken that step of faith, but I want to show her I'm serious. I figured that getting involved in a church would be a good way to do that."

Matt rubbed his hand over his head, noting that the stubble was now turning into longer hair. "That's a good idea, Rick. But you've already taken the only step that's necessary. Attending church is definitely a way we can grow in the faith, but it's not a requirement for being a Christian."

As he spoke, Matt realized he was a card-carrying, genuine hypocrite. He'd let his own church attendance, as well as anything else that would help *him* grow in the faith, slide, using the excuse of time pressure due to his profession. First it was because he was too busy in med school, then in his residency training, and most recently in his practice. Why hadn't he made the time and exerted the effort? Other doctors did. And now Rick was looking to him, and he was ashamed of his example.

Matt snapped out of his self-recrimination long enough to catch the tail end of what Rick was saying. "So I was wondering if I could go to church with you this Sunday. I think I'd feel better if I went with someone I know."

"Um, Rick, I have to confess that I haven't been going regularly myself lately." *Lately? Try not for several years.* "But I'll tell you what. I'll ask around and get a recommendation. And I promise, we'll go to church together soon."

"Great. I'll probably see you at the hospital, but if we don't connect, give me a call."

Matt signed off and returned the phone to his pocket, wondering what he'd gotten himself into. He thought he'd done his good deed for the decade by sharing with Rick about Christianity. Was he going to have to help the man every step of the way as he grew spiritually? Sort of like the Chinese philosophy that if you save a man's life, you're responsible for him from then on?

Lord, I'm not sure why this is happening. I'm pretty sure I have enough on my plate right now. What would Joe do in a situation like this? Matt had no doubt on that account. Joe would say, "I can hardly wait to see what God has in mind."

———

The pain got Matt's attention. He looked down and saw coffee cascading over the side of the cup he held, bathing his hand before forming a dark brown puddle on his kitchen table. He set both coffeepot and cup aside, then snatched a mass of paper towels from the roll on the countertop and dropped them on the coffee lake.

Matt grabbed a bag of frozen peas from the freezer and held them to his throbbing hand. He was alone in his kitchen, which was both good and bad. Good, because no one had witnessed what might have been a petit mal seizure. Bad, since he had no way of knowing whether this was simply an instance of daydreaming or another absence spell.

He remembered something his mother had told him about treating burns, a remedy his medical mind rejected as having no scientific basis. But he'd seen it work when Joe came home from the pool one day with sunburn. The burn on Matt's hand was probably first degree, which was the same thing. *Might as well give it a try.*

Matt opened his refrigerator and dug around until he found a half-full container of half-and-half. His mother had used cream, but this was the closest thing he had. Feeling foolish, Matt poured some of the liquid over his burned hand, then soaked a dishrag with more and wrapped it around the burn.

He finished cleaning up the mess on his table, and was surprised to find that by the time he was done, the pain in his hand was almost gone. Maybe it was all in his mind, but then again, there were lots of things in life he didn't understand but that still worked. He just took them on faith.

Should he call Ken Gordon and set up an appointment for an EEG? Was he taking too big a chance by self-diagnosis and self-treatment? Maybe the episode was just a bit of daydreaming, easily cured by drinking some of that coffee he'd been pouring. *Then again . . . No, don't think about the alternative. Continue the medication and hope for the best.*

He looked at his watch. Time to get ready for his shift in the ER. But first he retrieved the amber pill bottle from its hiding place behind the spices in his kitchen cabinet. Matt had put his medicine in an inconspicuous place after replacing the bottle the police took. He doubted that anyone would be looking through his kitchen cabinets, but he wanted to keep his problem secret if he could.

Matt tried to swallow the pill dry, but it stuck. The sensation of a lump in his throat was a familiar one to him, and it hadn't always followed a pill lodging there. More often than not it came when the stress became too great. This time it cleared when he drank a glass of water. He wished he could get rid of the unpleasant feeling as easily at other times.

With his eyes open, standing in the middle of his kitchen, Matt tried to summon the right words to pray about his seizures. As he'd come to do more and more often recently, he wished Joe were here. He'd know what to say, how to phrase it. Joe probably wouldn't approve of trying to bargain with God, but that's what Matt did. "Lord, if there's another spell, I'll go see Ken. I promise. But please give me one more chance. Please."

Sandra pushed back from her desk and stretched her arms above her head. The morning had promised to be full of drudgery, slogging through a sea of legal opinions as she prepared to defend Matt

Newman against the charge of possession of narcotics with intent to sell. But the phone call she'd just received changed all that.

She needed to share her news with Matt, and the sooner the better. Sandra consulted her watch: nine thirty a.m. If Matt was still working the mid-shift and getting home after midnight, he might be asleep. On the other hand, if she were in his shoes, she'd want to hear this news, even if it meant cutting sleep short.

She dialed a number she was coming to know by heart. Matt answered after four rings, and his voice confirmed that she'd roused him from sleep. "Hello?"

"Matt, this is Sandra Murray. I'm sorry to wake you, but I think you're going to want to hear this."

"Hang on." She heard his footsteps thumping away, then the sounds of water running. He was back in a moment. "Okay, I've splashed some water on my face, and I think I'm almost awake. What's the big news?"

Sandra had rehearsed this in her mind but still wasn't sure how to put it. She decided to plunge right in. "The police have dropped the narcotics charge."

"What . . . How . . . Why did they do that?"

"Remember that Grimes told you about the packet of white powder found in your bedroom? His exact words were that their field tests 'suggested' heroin. As it turns out, they field-tested it three times onsite, and only one was faintly positive for heroin. That was enough for Grimes. He wanted to hold you and he did."

"I sense there's more to the story."

"Absolutely," Sandra said. "The police lab did a full analysis on the sample. And can you guess what they found?"

"Apparently not heroin," Matt said.

"Bingo. It was almost pure lactose. There were a few faint traces of heroin on the inside of the plastic bag. My guess is that it once contained heroin, but someone removed it and replaced it with lactose, figuring no one would ever know the difference."

There was a moment of silence on the other end of the line. She figured Matt was processing the information. When he spoke again, it was obvious he had reached the same conclusion she had. "Someone wanted to incriminate me by planting heroin in my bedroom. But they fouled up. How do you think it happened?"

"Remember I've mentioned about the police property room, where things are filed and forgotten? It's not out of the question that someone who needed some cash might get access to a bag of heroin from an old case, pour the drug into a new bag, and substitute a similar amount of lactose for it. And no one would ever know, unless that particular bag was later lifted from the property room and planted so it would be found in a search."

"So someone with access to the property room planted what they thought was heroin." Matt cleared his throat. "Who do you think did it?"

"Right now, there's no way to know. The police would have access, of course. It's not far-fetched to think a person from the DA's office could get in there. But when you think about it, almost anyone could get it done if there was enough money involved."

"The police could have planted it while they searched my house," Matt said.

"True, but you're gone for long stretches of time, and you'd be surprised at how easily some people can get past a locked door. The bag could have been put there anytime, waiting for the right time to phone in an anonymous tip to the police." She frowned. "Honestly, we still don't know who's out to get you. But someone certainly is."

TWENTY-FOUR

The elderly man lay on a gurney, his head elevated to make it easier for him to breathe. A middle-aged woman hovered beside him, fiddling with the two-pronged plastic tube feeding oxygen into his nostrils.

Matt gave them what he hoped was an encouraging look. "Mr. Alexander, I'm pretty sure you have bronchitis, but we'll do a chest X-ray and some lab work to be certain it's nothing more serious. The nurse will arrange for those, and I'll be back as soon as I've seen the results."

The woman followed him through the drawn curtains that marked off the cubicle. "Doctor . . ."

"Mrs. . . ." Matt looked at the ER sheet and noted the next-of-kin name and relationship. "Mrs. Berry, I think your father is going to be fine. His oxygen saturation is good, his temperature is only slightly elevated, and he doesn't seem to be in any distress. I'm going to check to make sure I didn't miss an early pneumonia when I listened to his lungs. We'll do a white blood count and a microscopic exam of his sputum. If it looks like he has a bacterial infection, I'll get him on an antibiotic."

"Why not give him one anyway?" she said.

"We need to know what we're treating. If this is due to a virus, antibiotics won't help. We have to give the right medicine." He made a patting gesture. "Rest assured, we'll take good care of your father."

After giving his orders to the nurse, Matt started away. As he passed a trash container, he inserted the first two fingers of his right hand under the cuff of his left glove and flipped it into the receptacle. He repeated the procedure with his other hand. As the gloves hit the trash can, the thought that had been tickling at the edge of Matt's consciousness for days flashed into his mind as clearly as though it were projected on a screen. "I've got to make a quick phone call," he said over his shoulder, and strode off toward the break room.

In a moment Matt heard Sandra's voice, heavy with sleep. "Don't tell me the police have you in custody."

"No, and I'm sorry to call so late, but this has been rattling around in my brain just beyond my reach, and I had to act on it before it got away again."

Her sigh was audible. "Okay, what's so important?"

"Do you have any influence with the police lab? Can you get information about their tests?"

"Probably. I have a few people over there that owe me favors. What do you want to know?"

Matt hoped this didn't sound silly once he voiced the words. "The police were going to test the gloves they found for gunshot residue. They may do this anyway, but make sure they turn the gloves inside out and look for fingerprints on the inside. I read somewhere that if the person isn't sweating too much, it's sometimes possible to get fingerprints off the inside of latex gloves."

He heard a drawer open and close, then the click of a ballpoint pen. "Okay, that's usually pretty standard, but I'll check to make sure they did it. Anything else?"

Matt didn't speak. There was another vision tickling his consciousness. The dark alley. Two figures intent on finding him, the largest of the two with one arm extended in front of him, a pistol in the other. The sound of the other man stumbling over a trash can, crying out in pain. And Hank Truong's story of a man with a laceration on his shin.

"Matt, are you there?"

"Yeah. See if you can find out which glove had the gunshot residue on it. And check the autopsy report on the guy who was shot in my house. See if he had a recent injury to his leg. His right leg."

Sandra wiggled her stocking-covered toes under her desk. She longed to be back in law school, when the uniform of the day included sweats and oh-so-comfortable Reeboks. The shoes she wore these days were a lot more stylish, but by the end of the day, her feet screamed for relief.

The silence on the other end of this phone call was stretching out much too long for comfort. "Jerry, are you there?" No answer.

Matt's phone call had kept her up most of the rest of the night pondering the ramifications of his requests. She was pretty sure the police lab would already have done the tests he wanted. The results might point to Matt as the shooter. If so, Grimes would undoubtedly charge Matt with murder. But suppose the tests favored Matt's innocence. Maybe she could turn Detective Grimes away from her client before they brought such a charge. To this point, Grimes certainly seemed single-minded in his determination to put Matt behind bars. And he stubbornly refused to even consider Matt's kidnapping story, investigating it in the most cursory of ways. She felt as though she were hitting her head against a wall.

Jerry's voice brought her back to the present. "Are you still there?"

"I'm here," Sandra said. "Can you tell me what you found?"

"Uh, yeah. I was thinking . . . I'm not sure I ought to do that," Jerry Klipstein said. "You know the procedure is for me to send these to the detective in charge of the case. He gives them to the DA, and eventually you get the information."

"Jerry, I've known you since you were a kid. I used to babysit you and your little sister. I'd think that by now you'd trust me. You know I'll get those results anyway. Why not let me have an advance peek at them?"

"Well . . ."

Sandra knew she was going to win this one. She just had to be patient now. "Tell you what. I'll ask you a few simple questions. Just answer them. No paper trail. No one but us will ever know."

The silence stretched out, but eventually Jerry said, "Okay. Ask me. But just a few."

"Did you find fingerprints inside the gloves?"

"We looked at the tips of the fingers, but it's almost impossible to lift usable prints from inside latex gloves."

Maybe it was her legal training, programming her to look at how answers were phrased. Whatever the cause, Sandra's next question was, "Did you find fingerprints anywhere else on the gloves?"

"Good one," Jerry said. "Yes. People tend to take rubber gloves off by pulling on the cuff. They use their dominant hand first, and since it is still gloved, there won't be prints on the non-dominant glove. But a right-handed person will then use their bare left hand to peel off the right glove."

"And did you find prints on the cuff of one glove?"

"Yes. We found an identifiable print of the thumb and first two fingers on the cuff of one glove."

"You're really making me work for this. Which glove?"

"The left glove . . . the same one the gunshot residue was on."

Virgil Grimes sat at his desk and fumed. He felt the acid move from his stomach into his throat. He took a sip of the cold coffee in his cup, but that just made it worse. The heroin should have been enough to let them hold Newman until they gathered evidence to convict him of Edgar's murder. But an envelope full of lactose wasn't going to do it. If he'd just—

"Virgil?"

The single word, spoken in a soft Southern drawl, was enough to tell Virgil Grimes that Merrilee Ames was standing across the desk from him. He signaled his annoyance at the interruption with a frown, then counted to five before looking up from his computer monitor. "What?"

She held up a large manila envelope like a quarterback brandishing a Super Bowl trophy. "The reports on the Edgar Lopez shooting are back. And I think you're going to want to see them."

Grimes took the envelope and unwound the red string, looped around two cardboard buttons, holding it closed. Inside were a dozen sheets of computer-printed material.

"Is it going to help me more than the negative tests for gunshot residue on Newman's clothes?" he asked. He'd had to scramble to find an expert who'd swear that it was possible to fire a handgun and not have blowback residue on one's clothes. But he was tired of trying to pull figurative rabbits out of a hat.

"Check the ballistics report first," Ames said.

Grimes knew he should wave her to a chair, but chose to keep her standing. Since Ames had been paired with him, he'd chafed at having to partner with a woman who'd only earned her gold badge a month earlier. His previous partner and he were both veteran officers, old school, hardened by dealing with criminals, and savvy in the ways of the world—that is, the underworld. Neither had flinched if they had to bend a few rules to put away the bad guys. But Norm had retired to Florida and probably spent his time playing shuffleboard and eating the early bird special at Denny's. Now instead of a partner who would look the other way when it was necessary, Grimes had Ames, an eager beaver who watched his every move.

He pulled a pair of reading glasses from his shirt pocket and slipped them on. He tried not to wear them around other people, and he hated for Ames to see them now, but Grimes didn't want to miss anything. He shuffled through the sheets to find the ballistics report. The gun found in the storm drain near Newman's house was described as a .38 caliber revolver, Smith & Wesson Airweight. Someone had made an attempt to remove the serial numbers with acid. Although the lab could probably bring them up by some of their newfangled methods, it didn't matter. Dollars to donuts, the weapon was stolen.

When found, the pistol's chambers contained five empty shells. He skipped the technical stuff about lands and grooves, but his eyes lit up when he read the conclusion. Test bullets fired from this gun were a match for the slugs removed from the body of Edgar Lopez.

Ames had moved, uninvited, to his side of the desk and was reading over Grimes's shoulder. "Keep reading," she said. "Check out the next page."

Grimes frowned. The only thing he hated more than being told what to do was being told what to do by a woman. He gritted his teeth but didn't say anything. But after he flipped to the next page, his anger dissolved. When an investigation provided bullets fired from an unidentified gun, the techs entered the characteristics of the slug into a database. Now, through the magic of computerization, those unidentified bullets could be compared with those test-fired by other guns sent to the lab. And in this case, the computer had yielded a hit. The .38 special Airweight that murdered Edgar Lopez was also the gun that killed Cara Mendiola.

Lopez had been offed in Newman's house. Mendiola's body was found in the trunk of Newman's car. Newman was linked to both crimes. Grimes could practically taste victory, but he was careful not to voice his thoughts. It wouldn't do for Ames to hear him say it. But he certainly thought it. *Newman, you're going down.*

Matt's finger hovered over the doorbell. He looked around him and wondered, for about the hundredth time, what he was doing here.

It had been surprisingly easy to find the address, and at the time, he thought this trip was the right thing. But the further into this area of Highland Park he ventured, the more out of place Matt felt. Around him were homes that belonged on the pages of *Architectural Digest*, houses that would sell for a million dollars or more, provided the owners decided to part with them. Circular driveways served as parking places for Lexus and Mercedes sedans and SUVs, with an occasional BMW or Porsche thrown in for variety.

Matt's choice of gray slacks and an open-necked white shirt under a blue blazer was certainly appropriate for most occasions. But now that he was here, he felt as out of place as his nondescript Chevy parked at the curb in sight of all those high-priced autos.

This is the right thing to do. Get on with it. He pressed the bell and soft tones inside the house announced his presence. In a moment, he heard footsteps approach. The peephole darkened, then the door opened. Matt expected to be greeted by a maid or even a butler. Instead, the woman who opened the door was the one he'd come to see. There was a moment's hesitation as she scanned his face before recognition lit her eyes with genuine pleasure.

"Dr. Newman. How nice to see you," Abby Penland said. "Please come in."

Matt followed her inside, taking in the beautifully furnished and decorated rooms as she led him toward the back of the house. The far wall of the room they entered was composed of glass panels. Two sliding glass doors in the center led to a covered porch where several chairs were grouped around an umbrella-shaded table.

"You . . . you have a lovely home," Matt said.

"Thank you. Would you like to sit out on the porch? It's quite comfortable."

"That would be nice." Matt's throat suddenly felt as though he'd been gargling with sandpaper. He tried unsuccessfully to clear it.

"Let me get us something to drink. How about fresh lemonade?"

Matt nodded and was surprised once more. He expected Mrs. Penland to ring for a servant. Instead, she excused herself and told him to have a seat outside. She returned in a few moments with a tray bearing a frosty pitcher and two glasses of ice. After pouring for both of them, she settled herself in the chair next to Matt. "I must say, this visit is a surprise. But I'm glad you've come."

"I thought I should thank you in person. It was totally unexpected and very gracious of you to put up my bail. You need to know that I won't do anything to disappoint you."

"You mean you don't plan to skip out on your bail and catch a plane for Mexico?" The words were accompanied by a twinkle in her eye and a smile flitting across her lips.

"No, I have no intention of doing any such thing. Besides that, and I'm sure your attorney has told you this, the charges have been dropped. Someone tried to set me up to look like a narcotics dealer, but they got tripped up. So your money is safe."

"I know. Mr. Banks called me with the good news. Not that your innocence surprised me. I'm a good judge of people, and the way you made the effort to check on my son, to assure me, told me a lot."

"How is Roland?" Matt asked.

"Doing well, thank you. His brush with death has done a great deal to improve his driving habits. Much more than any admonitions from his mother, certainly."

"I'm glad to hear that. Please give him my regards."

Mrs. Penland said, "Roland is my only son, so what you did is very special to me. Only a few doctors would have taken the risk you did to save his life. Even fewer would have cared enough to follow up."

Matt tipped the glass to drain the last of his lemonade, and Mrs. Penland immediately poured more for him. He nodded his thanks. "I think you give me more credit than I deserve, but thank you." He drank deeply, then set the glass on the table. "I've taken enough of your time."

She touched his arm lightly. "Before you go, there are a couple of other things."

Matt sat back in his chair. When in doubt, say nothing, and that's exactly what he did.

Mrs. Penland gave him a smile that would have done the Mona Lisa proud. "Just because I live in a nice house in Highland Park doesn't mean I'm unaware of some of the uglier things going on in Dallas. For instance, I know about the murder at your house. And my attorney, who has sources in the district attorney's office, tells me the police still consider you a suspect in that murder."

Matt could only nod and wonder what was coming next. He didn't have to wait long.

"Dr. Newman, are you a murderer?"

It took Matt a moment to process the question. This lady certainly didn't pull punches. He took a deep breath. "No, ma'am. I'm not."

"I thought as much, but I prefer to hear it directly from you." She finished her lemonade and set the glass aside. "Should the police arrest you for murder or for any other crime, real or fabricated, you should have your attorney contact Mr. Banks. My initial offer still stands. I'll provide surety for your bail up to a million dollars."

"I . . . I don't know what to say."

"A simple thank you is sufficient."

"Thank you," Matt said. "I'm touched." He pushed himself up from his chair. "I guess I really should be going."

Mrs. Penland made a hand gesture for him to remain seated. "I said there were a couple of things on our agenda. Don't you want to know what the second one is?"

"Um, certainly."

She reached out and placed her hand lightly on his. "If you'll let me, before you go I'd like to pray with you." Then she amended her statement. "Pray with you—and for you."

Matt was overwhelmed. He'd come here to thank a woman for going the second mile for him, and he was leaving with her assurance that she was confident of his innocence, her pledge to back him even further, and the support of her prayers. How could he possibly fail? As she began to pray, Matt flashed back on another Scripture he'd heard Joe quote. *"Those who are with us are greater than those who are with them."* Right now Matt wanted badly to believe that.

"Aren't you going to read the whole report?" Merrilee Ames asked.

"Yeah, yeah. I'll read it when you're not hanging over my shoulder,"

Grimes grumbled. "But I've seen enough. I need you to put together a warrant for the arrest of Dr. Matt Newman. The charge is two counts of murder: Cara Mendiola and Edgar Lopez. Bring it to me when you've got it ready. I want to be sure it goes to a judge who owes me a few favors."

Ames glared at him and stalked away. Grimes was already fantasizing about knocking on Newman's door at four a.m. and taking him into custody. He knew a couple of people at the local TV stations who'd love to be tipped off. If they just happened to have reporters and cameramen at the police station when Grimes brought in Newman, the doctor's perp walk would be all over the morning news. Too bad it wouldn't make the early edition of the papers, but you couldn't have everything.

Grimes polished his reading glasses with the end of his tie and slipped them back on. The next page of the report was mainly fingerprint data. There were no prints on the gun—nothing unexpected there. There were, however, fingerprints on the empty shell casings in the revolver's chambers. Crooks so often forgot that, and Newman obviously had fallen into that trap.

The next sentence caused Grimes to slow down a bit. The prints on the cartridges weren't Newman's. They matched those of the deceased, Edgar Lopez. That still worked for Grimes. Matter of fact, it meant that it wasn't so important to trace the ownership of the weapon. Newman had shot Lopez with his own gun.

Grimes turned the page. This was about the gloves. There was gunshot residue present on them, which jibed nicely with the absence of fingerprints on the gun. No surprise there. Was the lab able to lift any prints from inside the gloves? No. Grimes shrugged. Despite what people who watched *CSI* and shows like that expected, usable prints inside latex gloves were about as common as flying pigs.

He started to lay the reports aside when the last paragraph on the final page caught his eye. Through some of their magic—Grimes didn't care how they did it—the techs lifted identifiable prints of a thumb and first two fingers from the cuff of the left glove. This should seal it.

He read the name. Rubbed his eyes, squinted, read it again. Slowly, carefully, he squeezed the paper, sheet by sheet, crumpling each into a wad the size of a golf ball. Then he slammed them into the wastebasket as though chucking rocks at a rat. With a kick that sent a painful shock into his foot, he made the basket careen across the squad room. Then, muttering words he hadn't learned in Sunday school, Grimes moved off to find Ames before she finished that warrant.

TWENTY-FIVE

Matt wondered what new development might be the cause for this visit to Sandra's office. She'd called him that morning to see if he could come by sometime before noon. When he asked for details, she'd put him off, saying she'd rather discuss it in person.

It seemed to Matt that every time there might be a ray of hope in his case, something new had come up to dash his hopes. He wondered what new problem loomed on the horizon. Oh well. He was about to find out.

Sandra asked him to close the door before taking a chair. A meeting with his attorney behind closed doors wasn't unusual, but in the past it had generally signaled something bad. Matt sat down with a sigh, resigning himself to yet another blow, another hurdle to clear. He crossed his legs, leaned forward slightly, and said, "What's the news this time?"

Sandra smiled, which seemed a bit out of character for meetings like this. Was the smile because she was about to earn even more fees? At what point would Matt have to admit that he was at the end of his resources? When would he be forced to give up the fight?

"First, let me warn you that this isn't official. I got this information through a back channel into the police lab, probably even before Grimes and Ames heard it. So, for now, this has to stay between us."

"Fair enough. What did you find out? Does this have something to do with the questions I gave you during our late night phone call?"

Sandra touched the tip of her nose. "Bingo. And I don't know how you got onto that track, but you were right. Some of that information appears to clear you, and not just from the Lopez killing."

Matt listened intently as she explained the police lab findings. It was impressive how Sandra could fit the building blocks of evidence together. He could see how she'd do well laying out a case to a jury.

When she was finished, she asked, "Any questions?"

"Lots, but first let me see if I have the high points correct. The gun the police found was not only the one that killed that hood—Edgar something or other—but also the one that shot Cara Mendiola. Edgar's prints were on the shell cases, so it was his weapon. There was gunshot residue on the left glove and fingerprints on the cuff of the right glove, so the person who shot Edgar was left-handed."

"Correct," Sandra said.

"I'm right-handed, and can get affidavits from a dozen people to that effect, so that makes me less of a suspect for Edgar's murder." Matt scratched his chin. "Do the prints on the cuff of the glove tell us who shot him?"

"You bet. They belong to a small-time crook named Lou Hecht. He's been arrested a couple of times for felony theft, but the charges never stuck. When the computer ran his known associates, number one on the list was Edgar Lopez."

"So Edgar shot Cara Mendiola. And Hecht shot Edgar. But why were they in my house?"

"We can only guess. But here's another question for you," Sandra said. "You asked if the dead man had evidence of an injury to his right shin? As it turns out, he had a fairly new scar there. Now it's your turn to tell me what that means."

Matt had to resist the temptation to jump in the air, pump his fist, and shout, "Yes!"

"From the expression on your face, I take it this is welcome news."

"It ties things up in a neat little package," Matt said. "Remember the story of my kidnapping? One of the guys, the smaller one, tripped over a garbage can and cut his leg—his right one. That was Lopez. I'm betting that when you check out Hecht you'll find he's a big man with a voice like a cement mixer, and that he's left-handed. Those are the two guys who kidnapped me. And they're still out to get me—or, at least, the one who's still alive is. I don't know the reason, but maybe now someone will believe me."

"I'm happy for you," Sandra said, "but I have to warn you. The police and the DA haven't seen this evidence yet. Until they do—and until they buy into it—you're still a person of interest in two murders."

"But what do you think?" Matt held his breath until Sandra smiled.

"I think you're in the clear. Barring some totally weird development, I think you're not going to need a lawyer anymore."

Was this the time? Matt worked up his courage, cleared his throat twice, and said, "Since it appears we're no longer attorney and client, I have a question I want to ask you."

It was midafternoon and midweek. Lunches were over—whether a hurried sandwich at Subway or a two-martini version at The

Palm—and the tiny bar on a side street in downtown Dallas was essentially deserted.

The contrast from the sunshine outside to the gloom inside the room made Grimes squint. He paused in the doorway for a moment to let his eyes adjust. The bar was at the back—six stools, only one occupied. Booths stood along the right wall, all of them empty. Grimes took a seat in the first booth, facing the door. A waitress sidled up and slapped a coaster in front of him. He ordered a beer. He didn't plan to drink it, but he needed something on the table to keep the waitress at bay. This was a business meeting, and as soon as his business was concluded, he'd be out of there. Meanwhile, he didn't want to do or say anything that would make her remember him or the man he was meeting.

He didn't have to wait long. In a moment, a man took the seat opposite him, as furtive as someone sneaking into an X-rated movie. He waved the waitress away before she could get to the booth, and hunched as though by making himself smaller he could avoid being noticed. Grimes almost expected him to turn up the collar of his suit coat and burrow his head down into it.

"Relax," Grimes said. "You're acting like a spy selling government secrets. Nobody you know is going to come in. Let's get this meeting over, then you can get back to being a respectable—"

"Never mind that. Just confirm it for me. I want to hear it from your own lips."

"Yeah, the murder case against Newman is up in smoke. None of the evidence I thought we could use is going to hold up. Matter of fact, it probably supports his original story about—"

"Hold on!" The words were whispered, but the venom showed through.

The waitress returned and put a Miller Lite in front of Grimes.

He nodded his thanks and waved her away. He centered the bottle on the coaster and focused on the drops of condensation that worked their way slowly downward.

Once the waitress was out of earshot, the man said, "So now there's no case against Newman for drug possession or either of the two murders that involved him. There'll be no arrest, no trial. Right?"

Grimes nodded.

"Okay, then here are your new orders. Eliminate him, and make him look dirty when you do it."

Grimes held up both hands in a "stop" gesture. "Whoa. I was willing to bend some rules to arrest the man. But if I'm hearing you right, you don't want a policeman anymore. You want a hit man. I don't do that."

The man took a thick envelope from his inside coat pocket and waved it. "You'll do it if you don't want this mailed. It's already stamped and addressed." He turned it so Grimes could see.

Grimes removed a rumpled handkerchief from his hip pocket and wiped his forehead. "Can you promise me that if I get rid of Newman, the stuff in that envelope will never see the light of day?"

"If you eliminate the good doctor, this will end up in your mailbox. Then you can burn it, shred it, or read it on cold winter evenings. Whatever."

Grimes shoved the handkerchief back into his pocket. He moved his bottle off the coaster and began to make wet interlocking rings on the table. His eyes downcast, he said, "How long do I have?"

"A week. After that—"

"All right. I'll do it. Now get out of here."

He watched the man slip out the door. Then Grimes lifted the beer to his lips and drained the bottle in several swallows, regretting that he hadn't ordered a double shot of bourbon instead.

The big man sat in his oversized leather swivel chair, an unlit cigar in his fingers. Lou was in his usual position in front of the desk, his eyes keeping careful watch on the man's right hand. The boss could almost read Lou's mind—*If the hand goes into the desk drawer, will it come out with a roll of bills or a gun?* The thought made him smile.

"I think it's time to clean up this mess," the boss said. "All I've wanted since you and Edgar botched the kidnapping was to make sure Newman didn't point a finger at either of you and send the police looking for me. Now I guess this is the best way to do it."

He eased the middle drawer of his desk open. Lou shifted nervously, flexing his fingers a bit like an old-time gunslinger about to slap leather. Ever so slowly, the big man moved his left hand into the open drawer. He smiled. "I think you'll like this," he said, and extracted a wad of cash. He laid it on the desk and waited for Lou's reaction.

Lou relaxed visibly and let out the deep breath he'd been holding. "What do I have to do to earn that?"

Like a snake, the boss's right hand darted into the desk drawer and emerged with a pistol. "Just die." He pulled the trigger and felt the gun jump in his hand. It pleased him that the hole in Lou's forehead was perfectly centered over the bridge of his nose. It was good to know he hadn't gone soft or lost his touch despite all the years behind the desk.

Lou crumpled to the floor like a marionette after its strings were cut. Blood from the bullet hole soaked slowly into the area rug beneath him.

The sound of the shot still reverberated off the walls as the door to the boss's left opened and a tall, powerful black man emerged. He wore a perfectly fitted dark suit and white shirt, accented by a conservative tie. His hair was short, his small Van Dyke beard neatly trimmed. He moved with the grace of a ballet dancer, but about him was an aura of barely contained strength, and his eyes signaled the heart of a stone killer.

The dark man didn't look at Lou, but instead fixed a neutral expression on the man behind the desk. "Is this why you wanted me here?"

"Yes, Lester. Your job has two parts," the boss said. He shoved the roll of bills forward. "First, roll him up in that rug and get rid of the body. Weight him down and toss him in a lake, dump him at a construction site and cover him with cement . . . I don't care what you do. I just don't want him to be found—ever."

Lester pocketed the money without counting it. "Sure. What's the other part?"

The boss drew two sheets of paper from an inside pocket and handed them to Lester. "Find this man, kill him, and make him disappear the same way."

"Consider it done." With no more apparent effort than a man shouldering a sleeping bag, Lester rolled Lou into the area rug and slung him over his shoulder. He exited via the same door he'd entered.

The boss leaned forward and touched a button on his phone. When his secretary answered, he said, "Get another rug for in front of my desk." He didn't wait for a reply.

TWENTY-SIX

Matt had worked so many nights in a row that he couldn't believe he was somewhere other than the hospital at this time of day. Rick had readily agreed to switch shifts with him to free up his evening. Now Matt sat in one of the nicest restaurants in Dallas with a beautiful redhead whose good looks drew admiring glances from every man in the room.

Matt tried not to flinch when he saw the prices on the menu. He figured his credit card was good for the cost of the evening, and that was all that counted right now.

He was certain he could eventually dig himself out of his current financial hole, now that he didn't have to plan for more legal fees. And there would be a steady income stream so long as he worked as an ER doctor. That train of thought reminded him—he'd have to talk with Brad Franklin at the medical center about the faculty position again.

"What are you thinking?" Sandra's voice cut into Matt's reflections.

He looked up at her over the menu. "Sorry. I guess my mind was wandering."

"If you're worried about paying these outrageous prices, we can go somewhere else. Or we can split the check."

Matt knew that what his parents called "going Dutch" was common in the modern dating world, but somehow he couldn't accept it. Even before he was old enough to date, Matt's grandmother gave him some advice: *"Show your respect for a woman by opening doors for her, pulling out her chair, and paying the check."* His mother repeated the admonitions when Matt reached his late teens. Matt knew those rules were hopelessly old-fashioned now, but the tapes still played in his head, and he couldn't ignore them.

"We're fine," he said. "Order anything you like. We're celebrating."

"For good reason," Sandra said. "But I have to tell you, Matt . . . I was surprised when you asked me to dinner. I figured that when my legal services were no longer required, seeing me would just remind you of painful times."

"Are you kidding? I don't think I'd be sitting here as a free man without your help." Matt wondered how open he could be, and decided to spill it all. "Sandra, I don't think what we have is just a lawyer-client relationship anymore. Sure, I'm grateful for all you've done, but I'm feeling a lot more than just gratitude. What I feel is . . ." He hesitated, searching for the right word. "I like you, Sandra. A lot. And I'd like to build on our relationship, to get to know you better, now that things are returning to normal for me. How about you?"

The silence that followed was long enough for Matt to consider digging a hole and climbing in. Had he misspoken? Was this a major gaffe?

Sandra took in a lot of air, then breathed out slowly. "Matt, I almost didn't agree to take you on as a client. When you called from the ICU and asked me to defend you, I'd just come off a tough breakup . . . with a doctor, Ken Gordon. Frankly, I never wanted to have anything to do with doctors again, except maybe to sue them."

The words came out before Matt could stop them. "Why did you break up with Ken?"

"Not because of his hours—I mean, in my profession there are times that emergencies come up. And not because of any acrimony between lawyers and doctors, all the old jokes notwithstanding." She gave him a half-smile, then drank from her glass of water. "Ken told me again and again that he was a scientist. He believed in what he could see, feel, prove. And that didn't include God. I got the impression from him that most doctors were that way."

"I'm—"

"I know. I shouldn't make that generalization. Not all doctors feel the way he does. But a lot of them do, and God's important to me. I could never consider spending the rest of my life with someone who doesn't share my beliefs."

Matt tried to organize his thoughts. He could tell her about his background: a brother who was a missionary, the devout Christianity of his late parents, a childhood of attending—well, sometimes being dragged to—church. But he realized that wasn't what was needed here. This wasn't about them, it was about him, and he had to admit he fell short in that department.

"I guess you could say I'm a nominal Christian. I said all the right things once, but after that I never moved very far up the ladder in my faith . . . at least, until recently. When all this came down—the kidnapping, the attempts on my life, being in jail—that gave me the shove I needed. As hard as all this has been, it's taught me to lean on God."

"You're not one of those people who suddenly believes in God because it's your only way out, are you?"

"No, I realize that God doesn't play that game. What I've learned is that He's in control, even when things seem darkest. I have to trust Him. I can't fix everything single-handedly, much as the surgeon in me wants to try." He cast her a rueful smile.

Sandra didn't say anything, but she moved her hand across the table and covered Matt's. "Thanks for being so honest."

This seemed a good time to get something else off his mind. Matt shared a bit of Rick's story with Sandra. "He wants me to attend church with him on Sunday, and I don't have a clue where we could go. Do you have a suggestion?"

As it turned out, she did. She told him about the Bible church she attended. "I think you and Rick would like it, and you'd certainly be welcome. Would you like to meet me there?"

"Very much." Matt fiddled with his silverware. "But I haven't heard you answer my original question. I've told you how I feel about you. What do you think about me?"

She squeezed his hand. "Yes, I feel the attraction too. But . . ."

Matt felt his heart stop. "I was afraid there was a 'but' coming."

Sandra ignored the comment. "But up to this point, neither of us has had the chance to look beyond getting you free from your legal problems. Since that's out of the way, I think we should take our relationship forward a step at a time, see where it leads us." Her smile told Matt there were more feelings there, feelings he hoped she'd express as time went along.

"Sure," he said. *Well, at least she didn't say no.*

"Looks like it's going to be a light evening." Nurse Rita Jaynes passed Matt a clipboard with the information for the next patient. "This is a three-year-old girl with a sore throat and fever. Probably another case of strep throat. We're seeing a lot of it, especially out of that particular preschool."

"I don't know why we don't let you treat these patients, Rita, instead of just triaging them. Let's have a look."

In about ten minutes, Matt had done a history and physical exam and confirmed Rita's impression. He explained to the mother, ordered a strep rapid test, and was about to go on to the next patient when Rita tapped him on the shoulder. "Ambulance just brought in a man you probably need to see stat. I put him in treatment room 1."

Matt recognized the EMT who met him at the door. Stan Ullom was more than an EMT. He'd completed full paramedic training, and Matt trusted his judgment. "Tell me about it."

"Fifty-nine-year-old white male, developed severe abdominal pain about an hour ago. He told his wife it was just indigestion, but after it got worse despite antacids, she called us. Blood pressure's down and pulse up a bit. He's sweaty and pale, sort of shocky. I wonder about a perforated ulcer."

"Meds? History?"

"Mild hypertension in the past, controlled with diuretics. High cholesterol, on Lipitor, but no history of heart disease. No GI problems in the past. Heavy smoker. Moderate alcohol intake, the wife says."

Matt sensed, more than heard, someone behind him. He turned and saw Randy Harrison. "Okay if I watch?" the medical student asked.

"Sure." Matt covered the distance to the gurney in three long steps and looked down at the patient, ignoring the beeps of monitors, the network of tubing already in place, seeing only the man under the thin sheet.

Stan had taken up station across from Matt. "His name is John Ferguson. His wife stopped at the desk to give them his information. I can get her when you're ready to talk with her."

Matt processed the words, but his attention was already on the patient. He was as Stan had described him—pale skin beaded with perspiration, rapid breathing, teeth gritted in obvious pain.

"Mr. Ferguson," Matt said, bending down near the patient's head, "Tell me about it. Where do you hurt?"

The man's hand moved. Matt turned back the sheet to see the patient's index finger pointing to the center of his abdomen. Diagnoses raced through Matt's mind, most of them discarded as unlikely, some already helping him form his differential diagnosis.

"Acute abdomen of some kind?" Randy whispered behind him. "Appendix? Gall bladder? Perforated ulcer?"

Matt shook his head. "Not sure yet." He touched his fingers to Ferguson's abdomen and felt a slight pulsation despite the rigid muscles. Carefully, Matt probed a bit deeper, and frowned at what he felt. He applied his stethoscope to the belly, closed his eyes, and tried to block out the ambient noise of the emergency room. Then he heard it. Not the tinkling bowel sounds and rushes of intestinal obstruction. Not the deadly quiet of a ruptured appendix or perforated ulcer. The sound he heard was an intermittent *whoosh*. He touched two fingers to Ferguson's wrist and confirmed that the noise was synchronous with the man's pulse.

"I need to talk with his wife," Matt said to Stan. As the paramedic exited the room, Matt turned to Rita, who had moved into position beside him, and said, "Get the vascular surgeon on call here stat. Cross-match for ten units of whole blood, and have them send down two unmatched pints of O negative right now. Call the OR and alert them to set up for an exploratory laparotomy and probable repair of a leaking abdominal aneurysm."

"What about a CAT scan to confirm the diagnosis?" Randy whispered. "Maybe an ultrasound?"

Richard L. Mabry

"It would help to have a CT, even an MRI, but if that leak turns into a frank rupture, he could bleed out in a minute or two right there in radiology." Matt shook his head. "I don't think we should gamble. He needs to go directly to the OR."

Rita returned with a woman in tow. She looked younger than her husband, although it was hard to tell. With some makeup and attention to her hair, she would probably have been beautiful. Right now she looked a wreck. "What is it, Doctor?" she asked.

Matt turned from the patient to the wife and back again. "Mr. Ferguson, you have an enlargement of the major blood vessel running through your body—the aorta. It's bulging like the wall of a balloon, and the pressure of your pulse against it can eventually cause it to burst. We need to repair it before that happens." He went on to explain the procedure and answer questions. "I need your permission for the surgery. We've called a specialist, and he'll be here shortly." He turned to Rita and said, "Who did you get?"

"Dr. Rawlings."

"Excellent," Matt said. "He'd be my first choice. Good surgeon, well trained."

"What if he doesn't get here in time?" Mrs. Ferguson asked.

"I'm a general surgeon. I'm going up to the operating room with your husband. If something happens before Dr. Rawlings gets here, I'll step in."

In a moment, with questions answered, forms signed, and two units of O negative blood in a container under the gurney, Matt and Rita wheeled Ferguson into the elevator, trailed by Randy, who insisted on coming along to help.

"Is the anesthesiologist in the OR?" Matt asked.

"He should be there by the time we get to the holding area," Rita said. She checked Ferguson's blood pressure and frowned.

270

"Dropping?" Matt asked.

"A little. And the pulse has gone up. I'd say he's leaking a little more."

The elevator was cool, but Matt felt sweat trickling down his spine. He'd assisted in repairs of aortic aneurysms during his training, but had never been the primary surgeon on one. What if this one broke before Rawlings arrived? If the big blood vessel blew, it would mean Matt had to quickly open the abdomen, clamp off the aorta, sew a graft into place, and do it rapidly enough that there was no damage to organs deprived of blood circulation. It was tricky under the best of circumstances. Matt wondered if he was up to the challenge.

"Check the vitals again, would you?" Matt asked.

Rita complied. "No change."

Please, God. Keep him stable until Rawlings gets here. And if I have to do the surgery, help me do it right.

The elevator doors slid open. A nurse and Dr. Ellen Komitsky, an anesthesiologist, were waiting. "I've got it, Matt," Ellen said. "You might want to get into a clean scrub suit."

It wasn't necessary for her to explain. She and Matt were on the same page. He might end up doing the case, and she wanted him ready. He motioned to Randy. "Come on. You need to change too."

Five minutes later, Matt stuck his head in the OR. "I'll scrub up so I can help prep and drape." No one voiced the thought that was in everyone's mind: Matt might have to do more than that. He grabbed a cap and mask, made sure Randy knew how to work the sink controls, and began the scrubbing routine he'd done so many times in the past.

Soon Matt bumped the swinging doors with his hip and backed into the OR, his dripping arms in front of him, elbows bent, hands high. He dried his hands with the towel the scrub nurse handed him, slid his arms into the sterile gown and turned so the circulating nurse could tie it, and shoved his hands, first one and then the other, into sterile gloves held open for him.

The anesthesiologist said, "His pressure's dropping. I think the leak's increasing."

Matt noted that the O negative blood was already running in via two IVs. "Any word from Rawlings?"

"Nothing," the circulating nurse said.

Matt took a deep breath. "Let's go, then."

Ferguson looked pale and vulnerable, lying naked beneath the bright glare of the overhead light. The orange color of the antiseptic on his abdominal skin added a surreal touch to the picture. Matt and the scrub nurse draped sterile green sheets over the patient, leaving only the abdomen exposed through a central opening.

Matt took his position at the patient's right. He looked at Ellen, sitting at the head of the table. "Ready?"

She nodded.

"Randy, stand opposite me. I'll tell you what to do." Matt held out his hand toward the scrub nurse. "Number ten blade."

Matt sensed the vulnerability of the patient, the awesome responsibility on his own shoulders, as he felt the scalpel slap into his palm. He breathed a prayer and, with a single stroke, made a vertical incision from just below the patient's breastbone to the bottom of his abdomen. Matt dropped the scalpel on the instrument table and held out his hand. The nurse slapped a clamp into his palm.

"Randy, you get a clamp too. Just get the major bleeders. We'll deal with them later."

In a moment, Matt held out his hand again. "Deep knife." Then he heard a soft voice behind him.

"Want some help?"

Matt relaxed like a coiled spring with its tension released. "You don't know how good it is to see you, Clint." He stepped back, and Dr. Rawlings took his place.

"I understand we have an aortic aneurysm that's leaking, so while I continue the surgery, why don't you fill me in on the details?" Rawlings took the scalpel from the instrument tray. "And would you like to assist me?"

Matt took Randy's place across the table from Rawlings and gave him a rundown on the patient's situation. "I didn't think it was safe to take the time for a CT. And, frankly, I don't know enough about the endovascular procedure to try one. I thought it was safer to go in this way."

"And you were right," Rawlings said. After a few moments, the surgeon pointed with a suction tip at the pulsating aneurysm of Ferguson's abdominal aorta and the pool of blood accumulating around it. "If you hadn't brought him right to the OR, he'd probably have ruptured this little beauty and died while he was downstairs."

Behind him, Matt heard the phone buzz. The circulating nurse answered and a murmured conversation followed. Then she said, "Dr. Newman, that was the ER. Dr. McGee is here early, and he's going to cover the rest of your shift. You're clear to stay here as long as you're needed."

Matt couldn't recall ever being more tired . . . and yet feeling more alive. He was proud of the diagnostic pickup he'd made. Clint Rawlings had complimented Matt's skills as an assistant. And despite dismal survival statistics had his aneurysm actually burst, John Ferguson would most likely pull through. Matt was exhausted, but he felt good about the evening's work.

After the surgery, when the patient was safely in the recovery room, Matt and Rawlings talked with Ferguson's wife and their son, who'd joined her. Then Matt dragged himself to the ER locker room and changed out of his scrub suit. *I am so ready for this night to end.*

Matt rolled his shoulders to ease the tension as he walked to the parking garage. His watch told him it was almost two in the morning. His body said it was even later than that. All he wanted was a quick, hot shower followed by eight or maybe ten hours' sleep.

He unlocked his car, wondering, now that his legal problems were over, if he could afford to get the nonfunctional remote keyless feature repaired. Oh well, he'd worry about that later. Matt climbed in and started the car. He put it in reverse but kept his foot on the brake as he leaned his head against the steering wheel. He felt as though he could go to sleep right then and there. But the next thing he heard woke him like a bucket of ice water.

"I was beginning to think you weren't coming." The voice was unfamiliar, the tone menacing. Something cold and hard pressed against the back of Matt's neck. "Keep both hands on the wheel where I can see them. We're going for a little ride." The sound that followed might have been a chuckle, but Matt saw no humor in the situation—especially after the next words. "But only one of us will be coming back."

TWENTY-SEVEN

Matt drove without conscious thought, his mind frozen. He navigated the streets according to the directions from his captor. When he finally began to think, he wasted a minute or two mentally kicking himself for letting his fatigue make him vulnerable to the trap.

Because he'd been tired and preoccupied when he left the hospital, Matt's pepper spray was still on the top shelf of his locker, along with the handcuffs and scalpel. He did have his cell phone in his pocket, mainly because grabbing it was an automatic reaction. Matt only hoped he'd have a chance to use it.

And who was this man? In the rearview mirror, Matt got glimpses of a tall, broad-shouldered black man. His clothing, what Matt could see, continued the monochromatic theme of deepest black. The voice certainly wasn't the gravelly one he'd come to identify with Lou Hecht. It was deep but smooth, with a faint Caribbean lilt.

"Who are you?" Without thinking, Matt added, "Where's Lou?"

"Lou's the same place you're going. Now shut up."

When they reached a darkened industrial area, his captor said,

"Pull over here." Warehouses were butted together, walls touching, their loading docks empty. Matt wheeled into a parking lot that by day undoubtedly was home to a number of eighteen-wheelers. Now his was the only vehicle in sight.

Matt tensed his neck and shoulder muscles, waiting for the shot that would end his life. Could he wheel around, grab the gun, and overpower the man? Maybe on his best day it would be worth a try, but not now.

The only sound in the car was the ticking of the cooling motor. Matt was ready to say, "So shoot. Don't keep me waiting any longer," when his captor said, "Get out of the car."

Matt opened the door and stepped out, happy to smell fresh air one last time. The moon was a bare sliver. One streetlight half a block away, together with the faint security lights over the nearest loading dock, gave barely enough illumination for him to see his attacker as he exited the backseat. It confirmed Matt's first impression: a black man with the build of a linebacker, a calm expression and dead eyes. The gun in his fist had the squared-off appearance of a semi-automatic. *Too bad*. Matt had read somewhere that it was sometimes possible to grab the cylinder of a revolver and hold it tightly enough to keep it from revolving and firing. Then again, after three hours holding retractors, he probably didn't have the strength in his hands to do that anyway.

"Who are you?" Matt asked again.

"Guess it won't make any difference if you know the name of the man who kills you. You can call me Lester," the smooth voice answered. "Now turn around, lean over the hood of the car, hands behind you."

Matt felt cold metal against his wrists, then the familiar click and bite of handcuffs. His scalpel, had he brought it, would be useless anyway. What he needed now were bolt cutters.

Lester reached into Matt's pocket and removed his cell phone.

"I don't think you'll be needing this." Lester leaned into the car and pushed a button. The trunk lid sprang open, and Matt knew where he was going next. Maybe he had a chance. After all, he'd done it once before.

"I've heard about your last escape act. Don't bother looking for the emergency release." Lester lifted a T-shaped piece of plastic from the floor of the trunk and waved it in front of Matt before tossing it away.

There had to be a way out—unless Lester planned to shoot him here, then take his body somewhere and dump it. Matt didn't have to wait long for the answer.

"Climb in. Make yourself comfortable. We've got a long ride. You can use that time to make your peace with God . . . if you believe in God."

Matt climbed in and watched the few stars visible through the opening disappear as Lester slammed the lid. Once more, Matt was in what amounted to a coffin. How many times could he escape death? Surely this was it. *God, I need help. Please.*

In one sense, Matt was glad of the darkness. He recalled that moving lights could sometimes trigger seizures in people with such disorders. That would be the last thing he needed.

The car started and began to move, slowly at first, then more rapidly. Matt bounced around in the trunk with every pothole and sharp turn, his mind darting about like a rat caught in a maze.

He struggled vainly against the handcuffs, then remembered the maneuver he'd tried with his first kidnapping. It hadn't worked because the duct tape bonds were too tight. But Houdini had done it with cuffs, and this time Matt thought he could as well, given the few inches of slack the handcuff chain afforded him.

He ignored the pain in his muscles as he drew his legs up under him and worked his hands down behind him, straining with everything he could muster to pass the handcuff chain beneath his feet. Matt had almost completed the maneuver when a cramp in his shoulders made him relax. He tried again, and once more had to stop. One final effort, and this time he was determined to ignore the pain, to move on despite it. Finally the chain caught on the heel of his athletic shoe. He took a deep breath and shoved his hands forward while pulling his legs as far upward and backward as he could. He sawed the chain of his handcuffs farther and farther forward, until he felt his hands come free in front of him.

Matt lay back and breathed deeply, wanting to get as much oxygen to his tortured muscles as possible. In a moment he explored the area above him and confirmed that his captor had indeed removed the emergency trunk release. He took a mental inventory of the material in his trunk, and found it woefully wanting. The jack handle and jack were stowed under the spare tire. No road flares with spiked ends. No battery jumper cables to be used as a noose. No flashlight to shine in his attacker's eyes or use as a club. Nothing.

God, You helped David slay Goliath, but You equipped David with a slingshot and some rocks. All I have are my bare hands and my wits. Please let those be enough.

Matt had no idea how long Lester had been driving. He was pretty sure they were out of the city and onto a highway of some sort. Potholes and sharp corners had been replaced by long stretches of straight driving. An occasional *whooshing* sound accompanied by the car's swaying suggested the passing of a large truck. Then the driver turned sharply once more, and Matt sensed the roughness of an unpaved road and heard the occasional ping of gravel against the car's undercarriage.

The car rolled to a stop. Matt had decided on his last-ditch strategy, and in preparation he rolled himself into a crouch, his back hard against the trunk, his feet beneath him ready to spring as soon as the trunk lid was opened. Lester would be expecting him to be on his side, his hands shackled behind him. The relative freedom of having his hands in front of him, coupled with the element of surprise, might be enough. And if it wasn't . . . well, a bullet was coming sooner or later.

The trunk lid clicked and opened a couple of inches. Lester must have used the latch release inside the car before he exited himself, expecting his captive to be immobilized by his hands cuffed behind him. Matt made an instant decision. He pushed the trunk lid upward, clambered out, eased the lid almost closed, and scurried around to hide behind the rear fender on the passenger side. He scanned the area. They appeared to be at the end of a gravel service road, the headlights illuminating a rocky ridge with infinite blackness beyond it. Matt thought he could make out several piles of chalky rocks off to either side. Weren't there some abandoned quarries in this part of North Texas? And as he recalled, most of them were filled with water. Matt had an idea of what Lester was planning, and it made him shiver, despite a temperate night.

Hadn't he said that Matt was going where Lou was? Did that mean Lou was in that watery grave? The thought gave him no joy, since it was obvious Lester had the same destination in mind for Matt.

There was no traffic on the road, no buildings around—the perfect spot for an execution. Lester probably planned to shoot Matt where he lay in the trunk, roll down the windows, and shove the vehicle into the water. If the quarry was deep, Matt would just disappear beneath the surface.

The driver's door opened. In a moment, Matt heard a splash somewhere past the built-up verge. His captor must have thrown Matt's cell phone into the water. Footsteps on the gravel announced Lester's progress toward the rear of the car. Matt crouched lower as the man approached the trunk. The footsteps stopped, and Matt risked a peep. Lester had his gun in his right hand. He stood for a moment with his left hand on the trunk lid, then flung it upward. "Okay. Time to take a little swim."

Matt was pretty sure what Lester's next move would be, and he planned his own actions accordingly. He crept toward the gunman, staying low and moving slowly, and when Lester bent over to look into the empty trunk, Matt struck. He bumped the back of Lester's knees with his own, and Lester responded by throwing up his hands to keep his balance. Matt reached up to drop his handcuffed arms over Lester's head, centered the chain on the gunman's Adam's apple, and pulled for all he was worth. He put his knee in Lester's back to bend him backward and keep him off balance, making it harder for the stronger man to fight.

Lester brought his gun up over his left shoulder, but Matt saw it coming and ducked to the right. The man was gasping already. He fired. Once. Twice. Three times. The third shot grazed the back of Matt's left shoulder, and he felt blood start to flow. The pain hadn't started yet—he knew it would soon—but when it did, he had to ignore it and maintain his pressure.

Lester's struggles grew weaker. He waved his gun, but apparently his oxygen-starved brain couldn't send the signal to his trigger finger. Then the gun dropped to the ground, and the man slumped forward. Matt resisted the impulse to let up the pressure on Lester's neck. He might be playing possum, and this was a game with mortal consequences. What if Matt went too far, choked Lester to death? Was it justifiable? But if he let up too soon, Lester might turn on him again.

Matt eased the pressure slightly and managed to get his thumb over Lester's carotid artery. At first he thought he'd killed the man, then he felt the pulse—very faint and very slow. The pressure had not only cut off the blood supply to Lester's brain, it had stimulated the receptors in his carotid artery and slowed his heart rate to dangerous levels. Nothing to be done about it. Matt had to act before his captor woke up from the choke hold.

Matt kicked the gun away and freed his arms from around Lester's neck. The gunman slumped over the sill of the trunk. Matt's left arm was almost useless. He used his right hand to paw through Lester's pockets until he found the handcuff key. Blood from his shoulder wound ran down his left arm onto his hand, making it difficult to unlock the cuffs, but he finally managed. He cuffed Lester's arms behind him. With one arm out of commission, there was no way Matt could lift the much larger man, but he eventually got his right shoulder under Lester and tipped him over the rim of the trunk, then slammed the lid.

Matt picked up the gun and shoved it under his belt. He reached back to feel the gunshot wound in his left shoulder. The bleeding was a slow ooze—nothing arterial. There was no good way to put a pressure dressing on it, though. He needed to get help before he passed out. Did Lester have a cell phone? He should have looked, but was afraid to open the trunk and risk being attacked.

Matt slid into the car and had a moment of panic. Were the keys still in Lester's pocket? Matt had heard of people hot-wiring cars, but he'd never figured out how that worked. In the books, the hero just removed the collar from the steering column, ripped some wires loose and crossed two of them, and the car started. He wished he'd acquired that knowledge, but he had no clue.

He held his breath as he fumbled along the dash with his good hand. There they were! The keys were in the ignition. The lights were still on, but seemed dim. Did the battery have enough strength remaining to start the car? Matt was willing to bet that Hector Rivera hadn't spent a penny more on the car than was absolutely necessary, and odds were that the battery wasn't new.

Matt turned the key in the ignition. The car growled a few times and Matt's heart sank. He tried it again, with the same result. Should he stop, in the hope the battery would recover? No time, he had to get help. He turned the key and the engine caught at last. *Thank You, God.*

Matt shifted into reverse—wouldn't do to run into that pond and finish what Lou started—and turned the car around. He heard a thump and a muffled shout from the trunk. Lester was waking up. Matt only hoped the handcuffs would hold him until he could get to help. He squinted, as though by doing so he could see beyond the dim headlight beams, and started off into the darkness.

"Mister? Are you okay?"

Matt roused himself from the fog that enveloped him. He was in a car, his head resting on the steering wheel. His left arm and shoulder were throbbing with pain. And a terrible noise issued from the rear of the car.

The boy leaning in the driver's side window looked to be about eighteen. His streaked blond hair was two weeks overdue for cutting. His faded yellow T-shirt bore the words "Alvord Bulldogs" in faint black script. Matt turned his head to look through the car windshield and saw he was parked in front of some sort of convenience store. Although the events of the night were coming back to him, he couldn't recall pulling in here.

"Are you okay?" the boy asked. "I'm the only one here tonight, but I can call for help. It looks like you're hurt." He paused as the banging from the car's trunk increased. "And we need to get whoever's in the trunk out."

"No!" Matt said. "Yes, call the police. I need help. But don't let that man out of the trunk. He tried to . . ." And then darkness closed over him.

TWENTY-EIGHT

"You're mighty lucky to get away like you did," the deputy said.

Matt had to agree. The little town of Alvord had no police department, so the boy had called the Wise County Sheriff. The responding deputy removed Lester from the car trunk and took him into custody. An ambulance took Matt to the nearest hospital. Now he was in an open jail cell in Decatur, the county seat, his left arm in a sling and a heavy bandage covering his shoulder on that side, talking with a deputy and trying to figure out what came next.

"After you told me your story," the deputy said, "I called the Dallas police department, since that's where all this started. I told them that the guy in the trunk had kidnapped you, apparently wanted to kill you. They said they'd send a couple of officers to get him—give you a lift back too. Should be here in about an hour."

Matt read the nameplate on the deputy's uniform. "Look, Deputy Combes, if one of those policemen is a detective named Grimes, I don't want anything to do with him. He's out to get me. I'm not sure who I'm more afraid of, Grimes or this guy." He gestured to the next cell, where Lester lay stretched out on his cot.

Lester frowned at Matt through the bars, but said nothing.

"Suit yourself," Combes said. "But you're going to have to give the police a statement sometime. They're coming here to get that guy. If you want to ride back with them, you don't have to say anything all the way to Dallas. And your attorney can meet you at the station there."

Matt thought about that. Surprisingly enough, his watch was still running, and it showed the time to be about four in the morning. He could call Sandra. She'd probably come to get him, but what Combes said made sense. He didn't have to answer any of Grimes's questions. He'd call Sandra from police headquarters and refuse to say anything until she was present.

"I guess that would be okay." He lay back on the cot. "I think I'm going to rest until they get here."

A hand shaking his good shoulder roused Matt from a troubled sleep. "Newman, wake up. We need to talk."

Matt opened his eyes and saw the dark, scowling face of Detective Virgil Grimes. He started to push himself upright, but stopped when little men with hammers started beating on the muscles of his left shoulder. He dropped back onto the bunk. "I have nothing to say until I see my lawyer."

Grimes's grin had no mirth in it. "Somehow I thought you'd say that. Do you want to ride with us back to the police station in Dallas? You can call your lawyer from there."

Matt had decided it was probably his best option. He agreed, and in a few minutes was following Grimes and Lester, his hands cuffed in front of him, shackles on his legs, out of the little jail toward a dirty, black Crown Victoria. Grimes shoved Lester into the backseat, buckled the seat belt around him, and slammed the door.

He turned to Matt. "You ride up here with me."

Matt stopped with the passenger door half-open. "I thought they were sending two policemen. Why a detective? Why you? And since you're here, where's Detective Ames?"

"Guess there were no officers free to send. I was up for the next detective call, so here I am. As for Ames, I don't know." Grimes shrugged. "I called her, but she didn't answer. But don't worry. I can handle this guy." He jerked his head toward the backseat, then patted the bulge under the left arm of his wrinkled suit coat.

Matt wasn't sure what to do. He hated to get into the car with these two men, one who'd just tried to kill him, another who seemed determined to put him behind bars or on the path to death row.

"Get in. I'm not going to ask you any questions," Grimes said. "And if you wait here for a ride, you'll be half a day getting home. We'll finish our business at the station in forty-five minutes or less. Then you can rest."

Matt still had misgivings, but he climbed in. Grimes had the car moving before Matt could get his seat belt fastened. When they turned onto the highway, Matt saw a sign that told him Dallas was sixty-five miles away. There was still at least an hour before sunup, maybe more, so he leaned back and closed his eyes.

He awoke as the car slowed and Grimes steered it to the right. Matt looked around him. This was a rest area, but a very basic one, with only a tiny restroom building fronted by a water fountain. The area was dimly lit. There were no other cars or trucks in view. Grimes pulled to the back side of the complex and guided the car over grass into a stand of trees that almost hid it from any passersby.

He stopped the car, killed the motor, and turned to face Matt. "Here's how it's going to go down." He hooked a thumb at Lester, who was yawning in the backseat. "He's going to be shot while attempting to escape."

"Man, I'm going back to Dallas. My lawyer will have me out on bail in no time. I'm not going to try to escape."

"Oh, but you are. And you're going to use this." Grimes pulled a small pistol from his coat pocket and tossed it over the backseat to Lester. "It's a Beretta Tomcat. It's small, and the sheriff must have missed it when he searched you."

Lester didn't take long to process the information. He pointed the gun at Grimes's head and pulled the trigger. Matt ducked, but all he heard was a sharp click.

"Oh, sorry. It's not loaded. I'll add some bullets after you're dead, before I drop the pistol by your hand."

"That's murder," Matt said. "Why would you do that?"

"Simple. The idea behind this whole thing is to kill you. But I can't leave a witness behind, can I? This guy will try to escape, and you'll help him. You'll both get shot. I'll probably get a commendation. And you'll go down as an accessory."

Matt was stunned. "Why? Since the time you came into my ICU room, you've acted like it was your purpose in life to get me. *Why?*"

"Let's just say I have my orders."

"Wait a minute," Lester said. "We may be getting our orders from the same guy. You can go ahead and take care of him, and I'll tell any story you want. We're probably both working for the big man."

"You know, under other circumstances I'd probably be interested in knowing more about this big man, but I've got just one job to do, and sitting here talking isn't getting it done." Grimes pushed a button to unlock the car doors. "This is your chance. Open the doors and start running. I'm going to give you a head start." He pulled a mean-looking semi-automatic from his shoulder holster. "I'll count to three. Then I open fire."

"Wait!" Matt said.

Grimes got out and walked around the car to open Lester's door. "Almost forgot that door doesn't open from the inside. Have to let you out so you can try to escape." He pointed with his gun toward the woods. Grimes looked first at Matt, then at Lester. "Better run. I'm going to start counting."

Matt gathered his feet under him, pushed open the door with his good hand, and sprinted toward the nearest trees. He heard Lester's footsteps right behind him, his strides shortened by his shackles, his legs churning to cover ground. Matt hunched his shoulders in the automatic reflex of people who expect to feel a bullet in the back any second. Beside him, Lester began dodging right and left, his harsh breathing and clanking chains an accompaniment to the *thump-thump* of his strides.

"One." Grimes's voice was clear on the early morning air. "Two."

"Hold it right there." A pair of headlights blinded Matt. He recognized the voice of Detective Merrilee Ames, whose Southern lilt had given way to no-nonsense tones. "Drop the weapon, Grimes. You don't have a chance."

Another pair of headlights blazed from the other direction, accompanied by a harsh baritone. "State Troopers. Hands behind your head. You're covered."

Matt flung himself to the ground. When there was no gunfire, he risked a glance around. Two Dallas police officers dragged Lester to his feet and shoved him back the way he'd come. Two men in the distinctive pewter-colored uniforms and western-style hats of the Texas Department of Public Safety, the State Troopers, were handcuffing Grimes.

Ames's voice carried to Matt, and it was music to his ears. "Virgil Grimes, you're under arrest. You have the right to remain silent . . ."

Matt sighed and lowered his face to the dew-laden grass. Maybe his ordeal was over at last.

———

"Thanks, guys. I'll talk with your supervisor later today." Ames waved to the two State Troopers, who touched the brims of their hats and drove away. Five minutes later, the two-car convoy was moving through the predawn light toward Dallas. The two Dallas policemen, with Grimes and Lester handcuffed in the back, led the way. Ames and Matt followed in the car Grimes had driven.

Matt felt the letdown as his adrenaline overload dissipated. He leaned back in the seat and closed his eyes. In a moment, his curiosity overcame the need for sleep. He opened his eyes and turned to Ames. "How come Grimes was the one who came for me?"

"Probably left word with the police dispatcher to call his cell if anything came in about you. That's what I would have done." She shrugged. "It's a reasonable request. After all, you were still a 'person of interest.'"

Matt shook his head. "I don't understand any of this. Don't get me wrong. I appreciate your saving my life. But . . ."

Ames took her eyes off the road long enough to glance toward Matt. "But you'd like to know what's going on."

"That would be nice."

"I was assigned to partner with Grimes to keep an eye on him. The brass heard whispers that Grimes had run up some gambling debts. Soon he was taking bribes and extorting money to keep the collectors at bay. It wasn't long before we found out someone had actually paid off his debts, but now they owned him—and they intended to manipulate him for their own end."

"Do you know who? And what they wanted?"

"We think we know. Once we get Grimes in an interview room, I'm pretty sure we can get the information. He's not going to take this fall himself when he can give up the person behind it. Policemen like to play 'let's make a deal' just as well as criminals do."

"What about Lester?"

"Unless I miss my guess, that's Lester Hardaway—a hired gun and a good one. We don't know the person who was running him, but we'll find out. If he's got any useful information, he'll try to bargain his way out of the charges."

"Think they're serious enough to make him talk?"

"Kidnapping and attempted murder? He'd sell his grandmother to cut a deal."

Matt rubbed the places on his knees he'd skinned when he hit the ground. "In the car he talked about the big man. Does that name mean anything?"

"Doesn't ring a bell."

"How did you know to follow Grimes tonight? And why weren't you with him in the first place?"

"I wasn't with him because he didn't call me. We got lucky, though. The deputy back in Wise County called the wrong number. Instead of the police dispatcher, he dialed the Detective Bureau, and my sergeant answered. He recognized your name and called Grimes at home, but he also alerted me about what was going down. I figured Grimes might use the chance to get rid of you. So I got a couple of policemen and an unmarked car and took off."

"Did you follow him?"

"Actually we've had a GPS and a hidden microphone in his car from the time this whole investigation started."

"Why did you bring in the State Troopers?" Matt asked.

"Jurisdiction. I didn't know where Grimes would make his move. He'd be driving through two or three counties, and I couldn't coordinate with that many sheriffs. So I arranged for a car with a couple of DPS troopers to meet us near the jail where Grimes planned to pick you up."

"So you were back there all the time."

"We followed you from the time you left the jail. I could hear every word said in that car—and we were recording it too."

"So you've got him for attempted murder."

"For that, for kidnapping, for extortion and taking bribes. The DA's going to have a long list to choose from."

"Thanks doesn't seem enough," Matt said. "You saved my life."

"It's my job," Ames said. "Besides, you saved my brother's life, so I guess we're even."

Matt frowned, trying to recall a patient named Ames. "I don't understand."

"My married name is Ames," she said. "My maiden name is Penland. Roland Penland is my brother."

Matt would have given anything for an old-fashioned back-scratcher. The colleague who examined him in the emergency room had confirmed that the injury to his left shoulder was only a flesh wound. The doctor redressed the wound, replacing the bulky pressure dressing with a lighter bandage, and told Matt he could stop using the sling. The pain wasn't so bad now, but the itching under the dressing was about to drive him crazy.

It hadn't been easy to complete the knot in his tie with one arm functioning poorly, but Matt managed. He wanted to look his best for this appointment. Now, dressed in his best suit, Matt sat with Sandra outside the office of the Dallas County District Attorney. Matt looked forward to getting back to work tomorrow. Today, however, he had an appointment to keep.

"The district attorney will see you now," the secretary said. She ushered them into a corner office where a man sat behind a moderate-sized, very cluttered desk. File folders and law books had been pushed aside to make a central work space, which at the present time held two thin manila folders. Certificates, awards, and photos of famous people, most of them shaking hands with Matt's host, were displayed on two of the office walls. The other walls bore shelves filled with books.

The man behind the desk looked to be in his early sixties. He wore a striped dress shirt and conservative tie. A suit coat hung on the back of his office door. Reading glasses rode on the tip of his nose, partially hiding sad gray eyes. His silver hair was full and combed straight back. Matt thought he looked as though he bore burdens no one else could see.

The man rose and extended his hand to Matt. "A pleasure to meet you, Dr. Newman," he said. "I'm Jack Tanner."

Tanner turned to Sandra and smiled as they exchanged hand-shakes. "Ms. Murray, you're more lovely every time I see you. Are you sure I can't coax you away from private practice to work here? I can offer you less money and a cramped office."

"Jack, I appreciate the offer, but I guess I'd better stick to defending the innocent."

Tanner motioned them to chairs and turned toward the man standing beside him. His appearance and bearing said "lawyer" long before Tanner introduced him. "This is Charlie Greaver, my second in command, so to speak. Charlie's in line to succeed me when I retire, if the voters of Dallas County agree. I hope you don't mind if he sits in."

Greaver wore a beautifully tailored tan suit that contrasted with his chocolate-colored skin. A gleaming white shirt and striped brown, gold, and red tie completed the ensemble. Matt couldn't see his feet, but he'd bet the assistant DA was wearing well-shined brown wingtips.

Greaver nodded at everyone and took a chair at the side of Tanner's desk.

There was a light tap at the door, which opened to admit Detective Ames. She strode to a spot in front of the desk, gave Greaver a nod, and addressed Tanner. "You wanted to see me, sir?"

"Please, have a seat."

Ames smiled at Matt and Sandra and took the chair to their right.

Tanner opened the two folders on his desk, glanced at them briefly, then closed them. "Detective, I'd appreciate it if you'd tell Dr. Newman and Ms. Murray what you've discovered since the arrest of Detective Grimes and the man who tried to kidnap the doctor."

"Certainly." Ames half-turned toward Matt and Sandra. "I'm presuming, Ms. Murray, that your client shared the gist of the conversation we had in the car as we returned to Dallas."

Sandra nodded.

"We subsequently interrogated both Lester—whose full name is Lester Hardaway—and Detective Grimes. I'll start with Hardaway. He was hired by someone generally called 'the big man.' His real name is Bernardo Ignacio Grande. Grande's a disbarred lawyer, working from an office in Oak Cliff where he provides documentation, green cards, insurance papers, drivers' licenses, and just about anything else you could wish for illegals living here in the region. He has quite a nice operation, and it's expanding rapidly."

She paused, apparently awaiting questions. When there were none, she went on. "Grande had a working arrangement with two people at Metropolitan Hospital: Dr. Hector Rivera and Cara Mendiola. He started with Dr. Rivera. Rivera was an illegal alien for whom Grande provided forged papers allowing him to practice medicine in the US. Soon he persuaded Rivera to work for him, gathering information—birthdays, Social Security numbers, anything he could get—about patients as they came through the ER, especially those who died there. Dead persons make excellent shadow identities for false papers.

"Rivera fell in love with Mendiola, who headed the Internet Technology section at Metropolitan. Eventually Rivera told her what he was doing. Rather than being shocked, she found ways to use her position in IT to steal even more personal information. Since there were now two of them working for Grande, Mendiola thought they deserved more money—at least twice as much, perhaps more. She pushed Rivera into presenting their demands. Grande decided he could get along without the two troublemakers, so he sent Hecht and Edgar Lopez to dispose of them. The men were to kidnap Rivera as he left the hospital after a late shift, take Mendiola from her home, and kill them both in such a way that would divert any suspicion away from the hospital."

That was what Matt needed to connect the dots. He'd thought repeatedly that he was figuratively walking in Rivera's shoes: taking the job he'd left, driving his car. Now it made sense. This was yet another instance in which Matt had substituted for Hector Rivera. "They got me by mistake," Matt said.

"Right. Rivera was ill that night and didn't go to work. The description Hecht had was sketchy. You were a dark-haired doctor, coming out of the ER after midnight, headed for a gray Chevrolet. So they took you. When you got away, Hecht decided to go ahead and get rid of Mendiola, leaving her body in your car to make it look as though you had killed her."

"And the attempts after that?"

"At first Grande wanted to divert attention from Metropolitan Hospital, where you were kidnapped, so he tried to put you under suspicion so no one would believe your kidnapping story. When that didn't work, he tried to frame you for murder, sacrificing Lopez to do it. And after that failed, Grande killed the other kidnapper and hired Hardaway to get rid of you. He wanted nothing that would lead back to him."

Matt looked at Sandra, who had been scribbling notes. She asked Ames, "Have you picked up Grande?"

"I headed a team that went to his office with an arrest warrant earlier today. We confronted him, and he immediately reached into his middle desk drawer. One of the men with me saw a gun in the drawer, and when Grande's hand started to come out with something in it, the detective shot him. Grande's now at Parkland Hospital in critical condition."

"Did he have the gun in his hand?" Sandra asked.

Ames shook her head. "No. He was holding a roll of bills."

Tanner made a face. "So he thought he could buy his way out of trouble, but all he did was buy even more."

"Jack, I appreciate your having Detective Ames give us the rest of the story," Sandra said. "What about Grimes?"

Matt could barely see the nod Tanner gave Ames. Now maybe he could find out why Grimes had been after him, and who was behind it all.

Ames crossed her ankles and leaned forward in her chair. "As I told Dr. Newman, we discovered that Detective Grimes had accrued gambling debts he couldn't pay. To pay the vigorish—the interest on the debts—he had to scramble, and eventually he was so far over his head that there seemed no way out. That was about the time Dr. Newman turned up in the Parkland ICU with a head injury and a not-very-believable story, and Mendiola was discovered dead in the trunk of Newman's car. That's when Grimes was contacted and told in no uncertain terms that Newman was to be arrested and go to trial for murder."

"Who would do that? And why?" Matt asked.

"You'll see," Ames replied. "Someone, we can call him Mr. X, discovered that Grimes was in the pocket of some shady people. Mr. X contacted them, paid off Grimes's debt—probably for a fraction of what it was worth—and let Grimes know that from now on he was working for him. Mr. X wanted one thing from the detective. He wanted Matt Newman charged with the death of Cara Mendiola."

"I repeat, why?"

"At first because he saw prosecuting your case as his ticket to advancement in the DA's office, maybe even the stepping-stone to becoming the district attorney when Mr. Tanner here retires. To make things even more interesting, as things progressed, he became infatuated with your former girlfriend. Even though she tried to keep that prior relationship secret, somehow the man found out. At that point, he decided it would be good to get you, Dr. Newman, out of the picture so there'd be no chance of a reconciliation."

Matt raised his hand slightly like a fifth-grader asking permission to speak. Tanner and Greaver exchanged looks. Apparently they knew the answer to the question Matt was about to ask, and weren't happy about it. But he asked it anyway. "Who is this Mr. X?"

Ames said, "You can see for yourself. The arrest should have taken place just a few minutes ago."

She opened the office door, and two policemen brought in a middle-aged man in handcuffs. He wore a wrinkled business suit. His pale blond hair was receding in front to meet an advancing bald spot. Rimless spectacles couldn't hide eyes that darted right and left.

"I don't know what this is about," the man said. "What's happening?"

Tanner stood and fixed the handcuffed man with a gaze that would pierce armor plate. "Dr. Newman, in case you don't recognize him from your court appearance, this is Assistant DA Frank Everett. Or, I should say, former assistant DA." To the police, he said, "Get him out of here."

As the police marched Everett through the doorway, Matt caught a glimpse of the office beyond, where an attractive woman with blond hair sat wide-eyed, her mouth a perfect O, her cheeks redder than any cosmetic could produce. *Oh, Jen. Was he the one?* Matt felt a twinge of compassion. Then the door closed.

———

"So what's the verdict?" Outside the exam room, phones rang, bits of conversation floated by, and the business of the neurosurgery clinic went on as usual. Matt blocked all that out and focused his attention on Ken Gordon.

At first Gordon's expression betrayed nothing. He glanced at the chart in his hand but didn't open it. Then he looked at Matt and smiled. "It's all good."

Matt took a deep breath for what seemed like the first time in a week. "My EEG is okay?"

Gordon took the rolling stool opposite where Matt sat on the edge of the exam table. "Your EEG is fine. My guess is that you don't have any residuals of your traumatic brain injury. The couple of spells you describe might have been an aberration—the brain's a funny thing— or they might have been a case of emotional overload causing you to drift off." He shrugged. "We may never know. What we do know right now is that you have no evidence of an abnormal EEG focus. You don't have petit mal seizures. You're cleared for full activity."

They talked a bit about getting Matt off his meds, and then Gordon hitched his stool closer. "Matt, I need to ask you something."

Matt's antenna tingled. He knew Gordon and Sandra had been an item at one time. Was the neurosurgeon going to make another try? Was he about to ask Matt to step aside?

"You may know that Sandra and I dated for a while."

Here it comes. Matt nodded, afraid to say more.

"We broke up mostly because she has a deep faith in God, and I'm too pragmatic to believe in something without scientific evidence to back it up." Gordon's frown seemed genuine. "You've been through an absolute nightmare, but from what Sandra tells me, not only has your faith held up, it actually got stronger through all this. I can't understand that. You're a man of science, the same as me. How do you explain your continued belief in God?"

Matt was confused. Did Gordon want to effect an outward change so he could make another try at Sandra? Or was he genuinely interested? On the one hand, Matt knew this was a great opportunity to witness—to share how his faith had been metaphorically tested by fire and forged into something stronger. But if he did, was he also giving Gordon ammunition he could use to get back together with Sandra?

No, this was important. If Matt could help Gordon get closer to God, he had to do it. If Matt and Sandra were supposed to be together, it would happen, and if not . . . well, God was in control. *I couldn't have said that a month ago, could I?*

The past few days Matt had actually been reading his Bible, finding long-forgotten passages jumping out at him. One of them came to mind now, an encounter when Jesus ran up against the same kind of "I can only believe it if I see it" doubt.

"Ken, are you saying that you only believe in things that are rational? Maybe only things you can see?"

"Right. I guess I find it hard to believe in something I can't see or understand."

"Ken, there are lots of things you can't see, but you still believe they exist," Matt said. "I can't see God, but I can see the results of His working all around me. He's sort of like the wind. We can't see it, but we know it's there . . ."

Matt had two phone messages. The first was from the medical student, Randy Harrison. "Dr. Newman, I appreciate your letting me watch and help with that aortic aneurysm. Spending time in the emergency room with you has really opened my eyes. Sure, some of the stuff you do is routine, and some of it's frustrating, but you actually get the chance to save lives. I've already told my girlfriend I'm not going to try for a plastic surgery residency. I think she's about to break it off with me, but that's okay. Better to find out now instead of later. I hope I'll see you back in the ER soon."

Matt put his feet up on the coffee table in his living room and thought about the time he'd spent as an ER doctor. He'd worried that he wouldn't be equal to the task, that his training wouldn't be sufficient. There were a few areas he had to brush up on, but by and large he found that his surgeon's mentality—make the diagnosis, treat, move on—fit well in the ER setting.

The next message was from Brad Franklin. "Matt, we need to talk about your faculty position. Give me a call." He'd left his office number, and Matt dialed it now.

"Dr. Franklin's office, this is Peggy."

"Peggy, this is Dr. Newman. I'm returning Dr. Franklin's call."

"Oh, it's good to hear your voice. Are you doing all right?"

Matt spent a couple of minutes assuring Brad's administrative assistant that, although things had been tough for a while, they were looking up now. Finally she said, "He just got off another call. Let me put you through."

Matt spent a bit of the silent time wondering what Brad was going to say. He hadn't really come off all warm and fuzzy when Matt was lying in the ICU without a friend. Then again, Matt could see Brad's point. Hiring a faculty member who was a primary suspect in a murder case might not sit too well with the Board of Regents.

"Matt, sorry to keep you waiting. How are you?"

"Doing better, thanks." Matt started to give Brad a recap of the latest events, but the chairman didn't really give him a chance.

"The reason I called is that we had to go ahead and fill that faculty vacancy. I mean, the fiscal year has started, and we needed someone to see those patients and staff the resident clinics. Of course, if you want to apply for next year—"

"That's okay, Brad. I understand. Thanks anyway."

Matt ended the conversation and wondered why he hadn't told Brad up front that he was no longer interested in the position at the medical school. No matter. Rick had given assurances that Matt's position in the ER was his as long as he wanted it, and it was looking like that would be quite awhile.

***

"Dr. Newman, so good to see you." Elaine came out from behind her desk and enveloped Matt in a warm hug.

Matt noticed the ring on Elaine's left hand, the white gold band in stark contrast with her caramel skin, the sparkle of the diamond matched by the sparkle in the woman's eyes. "I see that congratulations are in order. Do I know the lucky man?"

"I believe you met him yesterday. It's Charlie Greaver, the assistant DA."

"Wonderful. Let me wish you both the best."

Elaine leaned close and whispered in Matt's ear. "It's lonely without someone to share your life. Remember that."

He whispered back, "Funny you should say so. That's the reason I'm here today."

Elaine's smile vanished, replaced by a look best described as dead serious. "I guess Sandra Murray's the closest thing I have to a daughter," she said, "so I hope you'll forgive me for asking this. But she's been hurt before, and I don't want that to happen. What are your intentions?"

Matt considered the question for a moment. "I want to get to know Sandra better. Let her get acquainted with me—not as a client, not as a doctor, but as a person. Like you said, she's been hurt before. I don't want to add to that. But I think we both need someone in our lives. Doesn't the Bible say something about it not being good to be alone? I want to fix that—for her and for me."

"You know, you may be just the right man for the job." Elaine smiled and gestured toward Sandra's office. "Go right in."

Matt hadn't been this nervous since his junior year in medical school, just before the internal medicine exam. He stopped in the doorway to watch Sandra at her desk, bent over an open law book, her finger tracing the line she was reading.

A curl of red hair kept dropping forward into her eyes, and rather than stopping to push it into place, Sandra puffed out her lower lip and blew the strands away. She repeated this a second and third time before she looked up and saw Matt.

"If there's something that bothers you that much, you really should take care of it," Matt said.

Sandra got up and moved around the desk. "Sounds like a good rule." She reached up and repositioned her hair clip. "Is that better?"

Matt took a step toward her. "I think so." His eyes moved from her red hair to sparkling green eyes to full lips shaded by just a touch of lipstick. His gaze lingered there for a moment before he went on. "There's something else that needs fixing—your lips."

Sandra edged closer to him. "What's wrong with them?"

"Let me show you." He closed the distance between them and reached out toward her.

She held up her hand. "You'd better do one thing first."

Matt frowned. "What's that?"

"Close the door."

He turned away and said over his shoulder, "You'll stay right here, Counselor?"

"Doctor, you couldn't move me."

In a moment they embraced and their lips met. After a few seconds, she leaned back, looked in Matt's eyes, and said, "Yes, I think that's what's been missing."

For the first time in weeks, Matt allowed himself to relax. "Thank you."

"Did you say something?" Sandra asked.

"Yes . . . but not to you."

READING GROUP GUIDE

1. What was Matt's relationship to the Lord at the start of the novel? At the end? What factors affected the change? Were there outward signs that signaled it?

2. Although we never meet Matt's brother, Joe, face to face, we see him reflected in e-mails and things he's said before to Matt. What's your impression of Joe? Why do you say that?

3. Sandra justifies her refusal to be engaged to Ken Gordon using the Scripture that counsels avoiding being linked with unbelievers. How do you interpret that Scripture? Does it apply to marriage? Friendship? Business relations? Do you think God can use a Christian, linked in some way to an unbeliever, to change that person's relationship with God?

4. Sandra freely admits that she left a promising position to strike out on her own in order not to stifle her Christian witness. Does this resonate with you? Have you or someone you know ever done, or even contemplated doing, something like this? Does it always work out well?

5. We have no direct information about Elaine, Sandra's secretary, so far as whether she is or is not a Christian. What do you think is her status in that regard? Why? Short of asking a direct question, what might help you determine someone's relationship with God?

6. When Rick tells Matt he wants to become active in church to show his commitment to his new faith, Matt ponders the meaning of such an action. Do you think church membership is the badge of a true Christian? What actions and attitudes mark a Christian? How are they demonstrated?

7. What was your impression of Mrs. Penland, the mother of the man whose life Matt saved? Have there been instances in your life when a prior action, taken with no thought of reward, paid off for you?

8. Do you think the Christian element of the novel detracted from or added to its value to readers?

ACKNOWLEDGMENTS

The average reader may picture an author sitting alone at a computer, tapping out prose that goes directly to the printer, but that's not the case. It requires a cooperative effort among many people to take a story from inspiration to publication,

It started with my wonderful agent, Rachelle Gardner, who believed in me when it seemed that few did. She's been with me every step of the journey and remains a great advocate, a trusted sounding board, and a true friend.

My close friend, golf partner, and attorney (in that order), Jerry Gilmore, read the first draft of this work and made a few suggestions. It's evolved since then, and if there are legal errors, they're mine, not his, but I appreciate Jerry's participation.

Stress Test went through a number of edits, and I want to thank Lisa Bergren for exercising her talents to assist me with them.

From there, the manuscript goes to the publisher. I'm fortunate enough to work with one of the best teams around, the folks at the Thomas Nelson imprint of Harper Collins Christian Fiction, under the very capable direction of Daisy Hutton. My editor, Amanda Bostic, deserves and gets my undying gratitude for all her work. Managing editor Becky Monds and her colleagues did a great job shepherding the work from galleys to printed book, following which the creative and energetic Katie Bond and her team made sure others heard about it. To everyone involved, my sincere thanks.

As I sought to master the craft of writing, so many authors have become not just colleagues and mentors, but true friends. You know who you are, and I appreciate it more than you can know.

I'm grateful for the support of my family, and especially want to thank my granddaughters, Cassie and Kate, for letting me occasionally turn off the videos of Little Bear they were watching on my computer so I could get back to writing.

My wife, Kay, remains my partner in story development, my first reader, my most demanding critic, and my biggest fan. Most important of all, she taught me how to smile again. Thanks, dear.

I spent ten years as a professor at Southwestern Medical Center in Dallas, where I was privileged to work with faculty, residents, medical students, and staff. For twenty-six years before that, I engaged in the private practice of medicine. Some settings in this book are real, others are fictionalized, but none of the characters represent real people. But to all my colleagues and friends in the medical field, thanks for thirty-six great years.

My loyal readers merit a special thanks. Without your interest, my novels would still be rattling around in my head.

Last, but certainly not least, let me echo the words of Bach and Handel who signed their works thusly: *Soli Deo gloria*—to God alone be glory. That is indeed my earnest desire.

—Richard Mabry

AN EXCERPT FROM *HEART FAILURE*

AVAILABLE OCTOBER 2013

Adam Davidson and Dr. Carrie Markham strolled out the doors of the Starplex Cinema into the warm darkness of the springtime evening. As they made their way through the few cars left on the parking lot, Adam's right hand found Carrie's left. She took it and squeezed, and his heart seemed to skip a beat. His fingers explored until they felt the outline of the diamond ring he'd placed there just a week ago.

She leaned in to briefly rest her head on his shoulder. "I never thought I could be this happy."

"Me either." And if he had his way, this is how it would be for the rest of their lives. Two people in love, enjoying their small town lives, their only worry what movie to see on their regular Saturday night date.

A loud noise in the distance made them both stop. Then Adam saw a shower of color on the horizon, about where the ballpark would be. "Fireworks show. The Titans must have won." *Get a grip, Adam. Stop jumping at every noise. You're safe.*

When Adam first met Carrie eight months ago, she was fragile and hurting, as skittish as a baby deer, obviously still bearing the scars from the death of her husband almost two years earlier. Her only interest seemed to be her medical practice. Otherwise, she went through life without apparent enjoyment or direction. But, little by little, he'd seen her start to smile, to laugh, and eventually to love.

Carrie had restored the smile to Adam's life as well. He still had his own problems, even though he hadn't revealed them to her (and hoped he never had to), but having her in his life made him certain that the life he now lived, so long as he lived it with her, would be all he ever wanted.

These things were supposed to take time, but in just a few short months each of them had decided that the other was the person needed to fill the hole in their life. The culmination had come with Adam's proposal and Carrie's acceptance last week. They hadn't set a wedding date yet, but for now Adam was content to watch Carrie plan and bask in the glow of their shared happiness.

The couple reached Adam's car and climbed in, but had not yet fastened their seat belts. Carrie was talking about where to go for ice cream when Adam saw the dark SUV approach from his right, moving at a snail's pace. When the vehicle was directly in front of Adam's Subaru, its side window came down to reveal the glint of light on metal as the driver's hand extended outward.

Adam's next action was reflexive. If he was wrong, he could apologize. But if he was right—He was already moving when he heard the shots.

<hr />

"I think a chocolate . . . no, make that a hot fudge sundae." Carrie leaned back in the passenger seat of Adam's Forester. "That would—."

The impact of Adam's arm across her shoulder pushed her down until her head was below the level of the car's dashboard. Then Carrie heard it—a flat crack, followed by two more in rapid succession. Muffled thuds sounded above her, and she pictured bullets boring into the headrests at the place where her head and Adam's had rested just seconds ago. Carrie cringed against an expected shower of glass, but only a few tiny pieces sprinkled down on her.

The faint ringing in her ears after the shots didn't mask the screech of tires and roar of an engine. When the noise subsided, all that remained was the rapid thud of her heartbeat echoing in her ears.

Carrie huddled with her head down, her breath cut off as much by fear as the pressure of Adam's body atop hers, a human shield. She felt his soft breath in her ear as he whispered, "Are you all right?"

"I . . . I think so. How about you?"

"I'm okay." The pressure holding her down lessened. "Stay down until I tell you it's safe." Carrie turned her head to catch a glimpse of Adam peering cautiously over the dashboard.

Her heart threatened to jump out of her chest while her mind wrestled with what just happened. After a seeming eternity, Adam bent down and said in hushed tones, "I think they've gone. You can sit up."

Carrie raised her head just enough to peer through the damaged windshield. When nothing moved in her field of vision, she eased upward to perch on the edge of her seat. A few cars were still on the lot of the theatre after the last Saturday night show, probably the vehicles of employees closing down for the night. There hadn't been many people in the last showing, and judging from the parking lot, most had left before Carrie and Adam.

"Are you sure you're not hurt?" Adam's voice, full of concern, brought Carrie back to the moment. He brushed a bit of glass from her seat, then tossed the handkerchief he'd used onto the floor of the car.

Carrie unfolded from her crouch and eased onto the seat. "Just scared is all," she said. "You?"

"Not a scratch."

He reached across to hug her, and she turned to find shelter in his arms. They stayed that way for a long moment, and the trembling inside her slowly eased. "What . . . what was that about?"

"Nothing for you to worry about." Adam's voice and manner were calm, and Carrie felt comforted by his very presence. Then, as suddenly as the turn of a page, he released her and swung around to face forward in the driver's seat. His next words were terse, clipped. "We have to get out of here." He reached for the ignition, key in hand.

"Wait a minute!" Carrie pulled her cell phone from her purse and held it out to him. "We can't leave. We need to call 911."

Adam took her arm, perhaps a bit more firmly than necessary, and pushed the phone away. He shook his head. "No!"

She flinched at his response, at the tone as much as the word. "Why? Someone shot at us. We should call the police."

"Look, I don't have time to explain. Now can we go?" Adam's voice was low, but the way he said them made the words an order, not a request.

What's the matter with him? She took a deep breath, and let it out slowly. Twice she started to speak. Twice she stopped.

Adam turned the key and reached for the gearshift lever.

Carrie saw his jaw clench. She was terrified, but Adam wasn't so much scared as—she searched for the right word—he was cold and determined. The change frightened her. "If this was a drive-by, we need to report it. Maybe the police can catch them before they kill someone."

Although Adam's voice was low, there was intensity to his words that Carrie had never heard before. "You have to trust me. There are things you don't know, things that make dangerous for me to deal with the police right now." He pointed to her seat belt. "Buckle up and let's leave. I'll explain soon."

Carrie wanted to argue further, but she could see it was no use. She put away her phone and fastened her seat belt.

The lights on the theatre marquee went out. In the distance, a siren sounded, faint at first but growing louder. " We're out of here," Adam said. He put the car in gear and eased out of the parking lot, peering through the starred windshield to navigate the dark streets.

Carrie studied Adam as he drove. Most men would be shaking after such a close encounter with death. He wasn't. Maybe she didn't know Adam as well as she thought. Maybe she didn't know him at all. And that scared her even more than what they'd just experienced.

They rode in silence for a few moments, and during that time, Carrie recreated the shooting in her mind. Then something clicked—something strange. She turned to Adam. "You pushed me down before the shots were fired. You didn't react to the shots. You knew they were coming."

Adam glanced at her but didn't respond.

Carrie thought about it once more. "I'm sure of it. First you shoved me below the dashboard. After that I heard three shots. How did you know what was about to happen?"

He continued to peer into the night. "I was backed into the parking space, so I had a good view of the cars moving down the aisle in front of us. A black SUV pulled even with us, and the barrel of a pistol came out the driver's side window. That's when I pushed you down."

"Lucky you saw it."

Adam shook his head. "Luck had nothing to do with it. I'm always watching."

His response made her shiver. She hugged herself and sat silent for the balance of the trip.

When they slowed for the turn into Carrie's driveway, Adam said, "Is there room in your garage for my car?"

"I suppose so. It's a two-car garage, and one side is empty. Why?"

"I don't want to leave my car where someone can see it. Open the garage, and let me pull in. We'll talk once we're safely in your house."

Carrie found the garage remote on her key ring and raised the door. When they were inside the house with the garage door closed, she took a seat on the living room sofa. She watched and listened with increasing puzzlement as Adam went through the small house drawing drapes, closing blinds, and making sure all the doors were locked.

Finally, Adam returned to where Carrie waited. He started to sit beside her on the sofa, apparently thought better of it, and sank into a chair. "I've wrestled with this all the way home. I thought I was finally safe, but maybe I'm not. I know what I'm going to tell you may change things between us, but you deserve an explanation."

That was the understatement of the year. Thirty minutes ago, she and Adam were a newly engaged couple, winding down a enjoyable evening. She figured that by now they'd be feeding each other ice cream like two lovebirds, talking seriously and making plans about their future together. But instead . . . "Yes, you owe me an explanation, a big one. So explain."

"Let me say this first. What I'm about to tell you started long before I met you. My life has changed in the past eight months. I'm different, and it's because of you. I'm . . ." Adam leaned toward her. He clenched and unclenched his fists. "To begin with, Adam Davidson isn't my real name."

ABOUT THE AUTHOR

Photo by Jodie Westfall

A retired physician, Dr. Richard Mabry is the author of four critically acclaimed novels of medical suspense. His previous works have been finalists for the Carol Award and Romantic Times Reader's Choice Award, and have won the Selah Award. He is a past Vice President of American Christian Fiction Writers and a member of the International Thriller Writers. He and his wife live in North Texas.